MOSAIC

MOSAIC

SUSAN MOODY

Delacorte Press

Published by
Delacorte Press
Bantam Doubleday Dell Publishing Group, Inc.
666 Fifth Avenue
New York, New York 10103

The trademark Delacorte Press® is registered in the U.S. Patent
and Trademark Office.

Manufactured in the United States of America

BOOK DESIGN BY DIANE STEVENSON ■ SNAP-HAUS GRAPHICS

FOR TONI SAUNDERSON

MOSAIC

-- PART - ONE --

ISTANBUL

• 1 •

If she had never gone to Istanbul . . .

If she had not met Nicholas . . .

If—even—Anna had been less beautiful, less given to careless love and casual acquaintance . . .

. . . what then?

Would none of it have happened? Or would she simply have reached the same crossroads by another route?

Who knows? Certainly not Fran. Afterward, long afterward, she was to tell herself that she couldn't possibly have foreseen any of it. Not Istanbul, not violent death and numbing terror. Not love. And certainly not Daniel, so pure yet so dangerously flawed that in the end. . . .

But better to begin at the beginning.

■■

Istanbul. Spires and minarets. Curved white sails in the harbor. The harsh call of the muezzin. Smells of kerosene and drains, fish grilling over charcoal, hot sugar. Half-glimpsed filmic faces. Wailing music and the slow click of the backgammon counters from cafés and shops no wider than a doorway. And always the bustle and flow, the constant beating of the wave of the East against the rock of the West, two cultures existing side by side: high heels and short hemlines alongside ankle-length skirts of faded black cotton, stretch limos caught impatiently behind plodding donkeys loaded with kindling, wooden cottages nestled against looming concrete blocks, modern agnosticism amid the ancient faith which bound together the People of the Book.

Istanbul was so unlike anything Frances had previously known that it might have belonged to another planet. Yet as soon as she stepped off the plane, she was aware of fitting in. Like a hare, she had found her form. Istanbul might be alien, but it gathered around her with the comfort of an old sweater. Other Europeans she was to meet would moan about the lack of water, the dirt, the state of the sidewalks or the telephones. For the most part, she hardly noticed them, though occasionally the backed-up loos, the wildlife emerging from the taps, the polite circumlocutions of even the most trivial conversational exchange, would irritate her to the screaming point. Never for long. Whenever she thought she could no longer stand it, this city full of whispers caught her up and held her to its heart.

She loved it. All of it. But best of all was the Topkapi Arayi. Istanbul was centered for her in the Seraglio of the former sultans of the Ottoman Empire—not in the Blue Mosque or the bazaars or on the two-tiered Galata Bridge, but here where the women of the Harem used to walk. Although she visited the museum to marvel at the collections of precious artifacts, she preferred to wander around the gardens, through the great courts where, in the heyday of the Grand Turk, it was forbidden to speak above a whisper. As always with places where history seems to have crystallized—the Forum in Rome, the Pyramids—the essence of those who had gone before was strong, the air rank with the distillation of long-ago loves, angers, frustrations, desires.

Especially was she aware of the women who had once trodden these paved walks or gazed from the hooded windows. She fancied that their oval-eyed ghosts still lurked, urgent behind the screens of fretted stone, deprived of ordinary female expectations, doomed to be pale moons to the sultan's distant planet. The tensions and intrigues which must have flourished as potent as belladonna behind the Harem walls sometimes seemed still to be almost tangible.

■■

In the summer, she discovered, the gardens were always crowded. It was autumn now, the tourist season over. Usually Fran had the courts and kiosks to herself, though one afternoon she saw Mr. Kalkan walking beside the reflecting pool. He held the hand of a small boy in white shorts and shiny black shoes. Behind him was a woman, fashionably dressed, heavily made up, her glossy hair brushed into a pleated roll at the back of her head. With her were two little girls. Fran turned away. Mr. Kalkan would not wish to meet her here, would dislike introducing her or saying who she was. Such an overlap of his personal and his business life would be distasteful. No doubt the wife knew of the English lessons he was taking. To meet the young woman who supplied them would give unnecessary substance to an abstract that she was probably happy to keep vague. Besides, in spite of Sultan Mahmud and his westernizing reforms, in spite of Kemal Atatürk, this was still an oriental city. Islam lay less than the skin's thickness below the surface of the 1990s. However easily the modern businessman might assimilate the idea of one-on-one meetings with an unchaperoned unmarried girl, even for the innocent purpose of dissecting the English language, the family man would still find it uncomfortable. Next time he appeared for his lesson, she did not mention having seen him. Courteous and friendly though the Turks were, they preferred to keep private what lay beneath their smiles.

Because she, too, kept most of herself hidden, she felt at home here. Never for a moment did she regret having given up her job as an editor on a national daily—subeditor, if she was honest—in order to come here in search of—what? Adventure? Excitement? Color? All three, perhaps. In London she had been in a rut, her mind gone stale. Here, every day glittered with a multiplicity of possibilities. Yet, when she first found the message on her desk—Ring Anna back with a telephone number she did not recognize—she forgot to do so.

Was it meant? Who can say? The newspaperwomen she worked with all seemed to have developed a skin of toughness that she had no wish to find covering her own sensibilities. Tough for tough's sake: she knew she would not like herself if it happened to her. Looking back, it seemed remarkable that Anna's first call came just as she had begun to register and define a growing dissatisfaction with the way her life was developing.

They had been friends at Oxford, sharing a house on Walton Street during their final year with three other women. Anna Fairchild, red-haired and cream-skinned, was irresistible to men—and found men irresistible. It came down to much the same thing. Like dogs around a bitch, they bayed and shuffled at the door all through the spring and summer, sometimes making do with one of the other girls in the house, drinking mugs of instant coffee, disguising lust under the fragile web of love. Anna, who hid a shrewd brain beneath her Sloane Rangerish protective cover, worked toward a good degree while keeping six or seven of them dangling at once. She and Fran had subsequently remained close friends, even though sometimes as much as a year went by without their meeting.

After university, Anna went to visit relatives in Sydney and there, in typical Anna fashion, found herself hosting a local radio arts program, which was a huge success. Fran, meanwhile, had gone to Toronto to work on a newspaper. She loved the dramatic Canadian winters, the outdoor summers, the watery wilderness only hours north of the city. When a chance came to move to Vancouver, however, she took it delightedly. The big beautiful city on the bay at first seemed exciting, but after a while began to pall. She drifted southward for a while, taking casual jobs where she could find them. Waitressing, secretarial work, housecleaning, researching for a temperamental writer of hospital romances: she told herself it was all experience that would come in useful one day, if only as memories when there was no present left. She stayed in San Francisco for several months before taking a train across the States to Philadelphia, where her grandparents still lived. They seemed to have aged more years than they should since the last time she had seen them: her father's unexpected death had stripped them of their defenses against time and age. She watched her grandmother's hand shake as she lifted the heavy black skillets from the stove and saw, for the first time, how important were the accepted patterns of birth and death. It was wrong for a child to die before its parents. In a way, she, his daughter, had perhaps found his loss easier to bear because, at some deep level, she *expected* to outlive him, whereas for them, to live on when their only son was dead set the world out of joint. When she left them, she kissed them good-bye, and seeing the tears in their eyes, felt infinitely old.

■■

Anna was persistent. She called again. And again, leaving more messages. Fran, as though she hoped to escape, kept forgetting to respond to them. Until eventually karma, fate, kismet—call it what you will—decided enough was enough. Next time Anna called, Frances was at her desk.

"Thank goodness I got you, darling," Anna cried. "I was about to give up and ask someone else."

"Ask them what?" Fran said. Anna always assumed you knew what she was talking about.

"To come with me."

"Where to?"

"Oh sorry. I forgot you didn't know. Guess what."

"What?"

"I've been offered the loan of a flat for six months in—guess where."

"Belfast? Siberia?"

"Don't be silly. It's this man I used to—um, you know . . . be in love with. The one from Christ Church who used to give those fearfully erotic lectures on Gerard Manley Hopkins. Andrew something."

"Watson, do you mean?"

"That's right."

Fran tried not to think moralistic thoughts about people who slept with other people and afterward could not even remember their names. "What about him?" she said.

"He's got this cousin who's got a friend, and the friend's got this flat . . . only next month he's off to California for six months and he wants someone to house-sit for him over the winter. We wouldn't even have to pay any rent. Six months, Fran! Doesn't that sound absolutely marvelous?"

"Riveting, so far," began Fran. "But wh—"

"Do say you'll come," begged Anna.

"Before I give in my notice," Fran said, "where exactly are we headed?"

"Oh," Anna said, "didn't I say?"

"No."

"Sorry."

"You still haven't."

"Istanbul, actually."

"Istanbul." Frances paused. For a brilliant moment, she saw plumes, scimitars, turbans, white towers topped with golden crescents, sultans obese upon silken cushions, naked houris beside a marble pool. Half-forgotten fragments of the *Arabian Nights,* scraps of Ali Baba and Suleiman the Magnificent, the fall of Constantinople, the topless towers of Ilium, compressed themselves together in her mind like an old car crushed into a cube, the whole sprinkled with the magic dust of danger. She knew she would be a fool to turn the opportunity down. Before she could say so, Anna spoke again.

"Well," she demanded. "Yes or no?"

"Yes," said Fran. "Definitely yes."

■■

Before they left, she went over to Paris for a week. Twenty-seven, with a flat in London and a life of her own, yet the comfortable old house on the edge of the little village of Précy-St.-Léger, nine miles northwest of Paris, was still home. Emilie, her mother, smiled, not looking up from the watercolor she was working on. "Istanbul, darling? Sounds marvelously exciting." In spite of fifteen years in the United States and ten in England, her English was still strongly accented.

"I hope it will be," Fran said. On the paper under her mother's paintbrush, freesias on fragile green stems drooped ethereally from a yellow porcelain vase.

"Janissaries," said Emilie. "Didn't one of the sultans herd them all down into the sewers and set fire to the lot? I suppose it's one way to get rid of a dissident army." She shaded flower petals in palest lilac and rose. "They died like rats, I read somewhere."

"Those were violent days," Fran said.

"It's a blood-soaked city. I hope you will be safe, *ma petite.*"

"It's not like that now."

"Perhaps." Laying down her brush, Emilie offered an aperitif in glasses that had once belonged to her grandmother. "My mother always told me that if I was captured by a Turk, I must kill myself."

"Did she say how?"

"No."

"Or why?"

"According to her, the Turks all had flashing gold teeth and did the most unspeakable things to women."

"Lucky there weren't too many of them hanging round Neuilly when you were a girl," said Fran.

"Ah, but the possibility made my childhood infinitely exciting," said Emilie, smiling. "Were you aware that one of the sultans drowned all his concubines in the Bosphorus?"

"Mother, you know the oddest things."

"It's a fact. There was a French ship in the harbor at the time which sent a diver down to look at a leak or something. He saw them all there, two hundred and fifty silken sacks standing upright at the bottom of the harbor, swaying like streamers of seaweed among the fish and the anchor chains."

"It must have given him a shock," Fran said.

"Nothing like the one those poor women got, tied up in a sack and dropped over the side of a boat," said her mother. She looked over her glasses at her daughter. "Will you write to me while you're away, Françoise?"

"I expect so. I usually do, don't I?"

"A lot can happen in six months."

Fran looked through the French windows at her mother's garden. The clocks had not yet gone back but it was already darkening out there among the beds full of late roses and chrysanthemums. Shabby petunias spilled from tubs and pots; the lawn needed cutting. Blotched yellow leaves from the pear tree lay damply on the grass. Soon Emilie would be out restoring order to late summer's untidy growth: pruning, clipping, making everything neat.

"Maybe," she said. "But not to you."

"What else is there to happen to me, now that your father is gone?" Emilie picked up her brush again and washed pale yellow around the delicate edge of a bud. "I miss him ferociously, you know."

"I know." Fran did not add that she did too.

■■

There were more good-byes to make. Max Blum was her adopted godfather, self-proposed on discovering that godparents were something Tom and Emilie Brett had failed to supply their daughter with. Fran, aged thirteen and beginning to feel the need for an adult who was not also a parent, had enthusiastically agreed. Over the years, she had come to look on his house in one of the streets off Haverstock Hill as a second home. Although it was obvious only when he opened his mouth, Max was American. A bachelor, large, comfortable, and tolerant, after thirty years based in London he was practically indistinguishable from an Englishman. When Tom Brett was sent from the United States on his first foreign assignment, Max was already well established in the field. Working on the same projects, over the years the two men had become close friends. It was Max who originally pushed Tom into applying for secondment to Europe.

A year or two ago, Max had retired. He had been enthusiastic about it, claiming that at last he would have time to complete his memoirs—a project he had been engaged in for as long as Fran could remember—and to tidy his files. They were comprehensive and indiscriminate; among his colleagues he was known as Magpie Max. Fran suspected that neither files nor memoirs had so far been touched, that Max was much too busy enjoying the absence of the tension which had hallmarked his long working life.

"I'm off to Istanbul for six months," she said, settling into a shabby armchair with a whisky. The room was hot: Max had never come to terms with British drafts and relied on three or four plug-in heaters to back up the central heating and the fire burning in the grate.

"And you've come for some godfatherly advice, I'll bet."

"No."

"I'll give you some, anyway. . . ." He paused. Then, his voice serious, he said, "Take care."

"That's it?"

"You want more? Then step soft."

"Are you being Istanbul-specific here, or would you give me the same advice if I were heading for Manchester?"

"There's a lot of stuff going down out there right now that you want to steer clear of. So don't get involved. I know what you're like. Just remember you're a tourist."

"Thanks, Max." Fran looked around the shabbily elegant room which extended from the front to the back of the house. It had once been two rooms; now only a pair of faded velvet curtains divided drawing room from workplace. "How's the book going?"

"Fine. Just fine." Max jerked his chin at his paper-piled desk set against a wall in the other half of the long room. "A lot of research needed, though."

"I thought you'd done it all."

"Well, yes, I had. But i'm looking at another project right now."

"You mean you've given up on your memoirs?"

"Not exactly given up. This is something that came out of them. I was writing about one of the first domestic stories I covered: the Farlow suicide. I was sitting here trying to figure out why he did it, and I started wondering why any of them do it, all those rich successful guys who suddenly decide to slit their own throats or point a gun at their heads."

"Didn't Alvarez already write something on those lines?"

"He wrote about suicide, yeah. But he approached it from a different angle. I thought some specific case histories, the events leading up to them, could be kind of interesting." He shrugged, pulling a pipe from the pocket of his battered cardigan. "There've been a spate of them recently. I thought it might make a good story."

"Isn't it usually the same old thing: Money doesn't buy happiness?"

"Not necessarily." He laughed, digging dirty fingers into his tobacco pouch. "It'll be best-seller stuff. You want my advice, better order your copy now."

"I'll be sure to do that."

"And keep in touch."

"I promise."

■■

Andrew Watson's cousin's friend's flat in Istanbul occupied the whole upper floor of one of the old-style wooden houses in the conservation area of the city. Most of them had either been neglected for years or torn down and replaced with ugly concrete buildings. Now they were being renovated and sold for inflated sums. This one had not yet been touched, however. The paint was peeling. Tufts of coarse grass and chickweed sprouted between the curling tiles of the roof. A rotting outside staircase led to the first floor, though Frances later discovered that the flat could also be reached via a flight of chipped marble stairs leading up from a sandalwood-scented hall on the ground floor.

But once past the pitted wooden door, the place was sumptuous, more lush, more richly colorful than the most sybaritic of pashas could have dreamed. Its owner appeared to have embraced orientalism with the same fervor as Lawrence of Arabia, then added a tendency to excess. The flat sprawled through three or four reception rooms and five bedrooms, all of them crammed full of possessions: multicolored cushions with tassels at the corners, ewers of jade or copper, swinging brass lanterns, low tables inlaid with marble or mother-of-pearl or both.

The big cushions proved to be an alternative to the furniture, most of which was fragile and inlaid. Some of it collapsed at a touch; the rest looked as if it might do. Everywhere there was color, curves, decoration, painted flowers.

Openmouthed, the two girls stared around them. "My God," breathed Anna. "It's like a palace."

"Pure *Arabian Nights*," said Fran.

They walked through the rooms, marveling at the intricately carved and inlaid screens which gave onto balconies or small pools containing golden carp. The walls were hidden by fabulous carpets, arabesqued and blossomed, that shone silkily when the lamps were lit. Glowing miniatures and illuminated calligraphic exhortations from the Koran decorated what wall space was left.

The bedrooms were furnished with carved chests that Fran would later come to recognize as Koran boxes, and swathed in embroidered hangings. They smelled of stale perfume and staler sex. Anna sat on the edge of one of the elaborate postered beds. "Can you imagine making love in this?" she said.

"Easily," said Fran. She wondered whom she might meet in the coming weeks, and whether they would sigh and kiss together under the painted flowers. Probably not. Men you could like were plentiful. Men you could fall in love with—bear go to bed with—were pretty thin on the ground.

"I mean, that would really be an experience," Anna said. Already she had the predatory look of a female coming into heat. "The whole thing's a terrific turn-on, don't you think?"

"You ought to carry a warning sign," said Fran, laughing. "This woman could endanger your health."

"Well, really," Anna said, pouting at herself in a brass-inlaid mirror. "I hope you're not suggesting I'm diseased."

"Not diseased. Just overpowering," said Fran. She touched a curved dagger which hung from a brass hook. Real turquoises, real gold. "At least we won't have to waste time visiting the museums. There's more than enough to look at here. The man who owns the place must know an awful lot about Islamic art."

"And be extremely trusting. For all he knows, we could be a couple of sneak thieves," Anna said, languidly lifting the tumbling red hair on her neck with one hand as she lay back on the embroidered pillows. "I say, darling. You aren't going to start poking around in the poor chap's possessions, are you?"

"Poor, the chap definitely is not," Frances said. "You don't pick up stuff like this in the local Oxfam shop."

"Wherever it came from, it's his, not yours," Anna said firmly. "You know what you're like: always prying into other people's things. Nosy as hell."

"It's called the reporter's instinct," Frances said.

"It's called nosy as hell."

Frances sighed. "I do try. Really I do. It's a hideous compulsion I have. Soon as I see something I know I shouldn't look at, I just have to."

"Good thing you went into journalism, really," said Anna. She grinned at her friend. "You've got all the necessary vices: gross insensitivity, lack of morality, imperviousness to the feelings of others. Not to mention an ability to lie your way into the most sensitive places and a total disregard for—"

"Don't go on," Frances said. "Please. Otherwise I may have to slit my wrists."

"Just remember who'll be held responsible, will you? I don't want some raging homosexual—"

"Anna, please. Where's your basic compassion, your tolerance of those who are different from you?"

"Well, he must be, mustn't he? Look at the place. But whatever, I don't want to find him beating down my door and demanding to know why there are sticky fingermarks all over his stuff. So just watch it."

■■

Frances and Anna spent those first weeks in Istanbul as tourists. As they learned their way about, they drank the city in, snuggling into it until it became theirs. They made contact with other Europeans living there, and because, however cheap the living was, money did not stretch indefinitely, they found themselves jobs. In London, Anna had been working for a monthly glossy magazine. Here, she had no trouble in getting herself a job with one of the American-based companies on Istiklal Caddesi.

"It was that letter of introduction that Martin Scott gave me. You remember him, one of the law tutors at Magdalen," she said when she came back from the interview.

"Sure it was," said Fran, who was standing at the window looking down on the Golden Horn, which glittered below in the curves of the embracing hills. "And nothing at all to do with the neck of that dress you're wearing."

"You're just jealous because I got a job straight off."

"Not at all. I'd hate to be at the beck and call of some man who's more interested in my body than my typing speed. I like to be independent," said Fran.

Which was why she took a job as a part-time teacher of English at a secretarial college. She also advertised for private pupils and soon had as many as she wanted. The two jobs still left her time to walk the small cobbled streets of the Old City, to marvel at the ravishing sapphire richness of the Blue Mosque, to sip tea in the pavement cafés, to take the bus up one of the steep hillsides on which Istanbul was built and walk back down into the heart of the busy, changeless city, watching the movement of the clouds above the Asian shore, the ferries chugging across Marmara, the spires against the waters of the Golden Horn.

■■

Topkapi, with its ghosts, remained the place she preferred. Of all the women who crowded, unseen and unheard, among the delicate kiosks and the reflecting pools, one in particular caught her imagination. Aimée Dubucq, the one they called the French Sultana. She had been a gently bred convent girl from Nantes, forced by the vagaries of wind and tide into the path of an Algerian corsair and from then on, with no more control over her fate than a dried leaf, to the Harem of the Turkish sultan. How had she come to terms with the unquestioned assumptions of that alien court, as she was taught the subtle ways of concubinage in the Harem school? What must she have felt, that virgin daughter of a Catholic civilization, as they drilled her in the techniques of seduction and arousal, the sexual nuances of touch and position? And how did she endure being forced into the bed of a man three times her age, whom, despite his wealth and position, she can have regarded as no more than a barbaric heathen?

At least she had taken her revenge. It was perhaps the only

revenge available to a woman in her cloistered position. She reared her son with a European outlook. Along with an excessive taste for French champagne, she gave him a conviction that the French were the most civilized people on earth. When he became the Sultan Mahmud II, known as the Reformer, he had deliberately set about dismantling the institutions of his own empire, westernizing it to such an extent that the Ottoman rule eventually crumbled. Fran liked to wonder whether Aimée laughed at the thought of it, locked away in her gilded cage. And whether her laughter in any way compensated for her tears.

■■

Anna went down to Bodrum for a weekend with some of the people from her office. It was Fran's first chance to poke around and find out more about their unseen host. Was Anna right? *Was* she impervious to the feelings of others? She didn't think so. She preferred to think she was genuinely interested in learning about her fellow humans, and a person's possessions said more about him than hours of conversation.

In thirty minutes or so she had gained quite a bit of knowledge about the fellow human who owned their temporary lodging place. Andrew Watson's cousin's friend dabbled, for instance, in recreational substances. More than dabbled, she realized a little later. Was *big* in them, she concluded later still, shutting down the ebony-and-ivory-veneered lid of one of the Koran boxes on a cache of plastic bags full of white powder. She had never seen heroin or cocaine, but nobody had to tell her that this was not sugar she was looking at. She suppressed the feelings of unease the discovery roused in her. She told herself it had nothing to do with her how the guy earned a living. Nor what he was. Which was some kind of a minor pervert, judging by the explicit magazines she found in other boxes, plus items of rubber whose function she could not even guess at, and the photographs.

For the most part, the photographs were softly pornographic. They came in albums, the velvet covers of which were richly encrusted with semiprecious stones and silver thread. Generally they featured boys with eyes that might have witnessed the demise of the dinosaurs. One or two faces stood out, corruptly beautiful. Frances didn't linger over them, flicking through them then shutting the book away. Knowledge is power. It could also make you feel slightly sick.

She opened the doors of the closets in the room where Anna

slept. Racks of handmade shoes stood next to a box of flat leather slippers. Above them, brocaded and embroidered caftans hung next to conservative wool suits. She turned the jacket of one and read the label. Savile Row, W1. Hmmm. From a shelf she lifted down a square jade box, decorated with rubies mounted in gold to resemble tiny flowers, which stood on dragon-headed feet of gold. For a moment she held it, her hands careful. The jade was cool under her fingers. It was fanciful to imagine that across the centuries she could feel a tremor of the energy that had gone into its making—or was it? Why shouldn't a residue of that creative impulse have remained like a sheen of oil on a lovingly crafted object like this? She thumbed back the sliding lid. Inside, a pouch of green satin velvet, heavily embroidered with half-moons of silver, lay folded round some heavy object. Carefully she removed it and unwrapped the contents. In a house like this, it could have been anything from a silver ingot to a bracelet of pigeon's-blood rubies.

It was a gun.

For a moment Fran could not take in the fact. The thing lay there among the silver crescents, blunt and dangerous, the light dull on its steel-black surface, ugly as a cobra.

A gun. Guns killed people. She would have said that very little shocked her, yet she was irrationally shaken. Gangster movies and TV cop shows had made guns like this as familiar as teabags. It was just that teabags were not designed to kill. Could it be that the unknown cousin's friend had actually used it? Had pumped lead into a living body and watched it die? The weapon she was holding announced the physical possibility of death more explicitly than anything Fran had previously come across.

Remembering how she had visualized the Istanbul trip as spiced with a kind of sinister piquancy, she went over to the shuttered window. Istanbul always seemed full of it, whether real or imagined. But when did sinister become dangerous? She had wanted excitement, hadn't she? Expected it, even. So why act so dismayed when she found it?

About to push open the shutter, she stopped suddenly and drew back. Down below, in the cobbled street, a man stood staring up at the windows. A European. He wore a hat, something smart and trilbyish which cast shadows over the top half of his face. Although she could not see his features clearly, she was pretty sure he was the same man she had noticed a couple of days ago. He had not been staring then, just walking rapidly up the hill, away from the house. She would probably not have paid any attention to him then except for an indefinable impression she had received, as she turned the corner, that he had just run down the wooden staircase from their door.

Standing slightly away from the window, she watched him through the slats. His head was angled back under his hat brim, hiding his eyes. It was impossible to see his full expression. Yet something threatening about him—the breadth of his shoulders, perhaps, or the set of his mouth—warned her to keep herself hidden.

She was still holding the gun. For a brief moment, a crazy thought flashed through her mind: how much trouble it would save if she lifted it and fired through the half-open windows at the man below. The thought was so alien that she could scarcely believe her brain had formulated it. She was appalled. Deliberately shoot a complete stranger, for no reason? Save *trouble*? What did she think she meant?

She turned away from the window and pushed the gun back into its pouch. She closed the lid of the jade box and returned it to the shelf. It was inevitable there would be one hidden in this apartment. Drugs were big money. If you were dealing, you would naturally possess the means to protect your investment. As for the man outside, he could be anything. A friend of their host. Part of the same drug ring. One of his customers, unaware that the owner was away for several months. The police, keeping an eye on them. Or perhaps nothing more than a passing stranger.

The Call to Prayer began beyond the windows, floating from the nearest mosque like a ribbon of sound above the rooftops. When she next peered through the shutters, the man in the trilby had gone.

••

Anna came back pleased with her weekend. Although it was winter, she had managed to sunbathe. There had been a couple of new men in the group, both of whom had succumbed to her creamy charm.

"Nothing's as good for the skin as admiration," she said. "Except sex, of course." She stuffed *taramasalata* and sliced cucumber into fresh pieces of pouch bread and examined her face in the round mirror on the kitchen wall. "Oh, lovely. You've got some of those delicious little goodies."

Fran did not mention the gun. Nor the drugs. The two girls lounged among the cushions, eating puff pastry filled with spinach and goat cheese, which Fran had bought from the bakery around the corner.

"There was someone watching the house yesterday," she said.

"What, that man in the hat?" Anna said.

"How did you know?"

"I've seen him before. As a matter of fact, he followed me to work one day. Right to the door."

"Were you worried?"

"Not in the least. They're always following you in Istanbul. He's probably one of our landlord's discarded lovers or the security police checking up that we aren't spies or something." Anna licked her fingers. "Mmm. Aren't these things absolutely delicious?"

"If we're not paying rent, can he be our landlord?" Fran said.

"Probably not. Actually there was someone down at Bodrum this weekend who'd met him. She said he's absolutely gorgeous. Madly compelling eyes, she said. And definitely gay, like I thought."

"How did she figure that out?"

"She said she absolutely threw herself at him at a party somewhere and he wasn't the least bit interested. Just smiled coldly and moved away before she could so much as ask his name."

"Perhaps he just doesn't like pushy women."

"Don't be so censorious, darling."

"How did she know he lived here?"

"Pure chance." Reaching forward, Anna took another pastry from the dish. "She just happened to be going by one time in a taxi when she saw him coming down the steps."

"When was this?"

"I don't know. A couple of weeks ago, I think."

"What? After we got here, you mean?"

"I suppose so. Or maybe it was further back, before we got here. I'm a bit vague about the details."

"I wonder what he was doing," Fran said. There was something unnerving about the idea of the man whose house they were occupying still being in the city when they had supposed him to be abroad.

"Naturally, this girl didn't stop to ask. Especially not after the brush-off he gave her at the party. She said he had this really frigid expression on his face."

"Plus madly compelling eyes? He sounds like Ivan the Terrible in that Eisenstein film."

"Except for the right-angled beard."

Fran made a grab for the last little pastry before Anna could get it. "Yum. Why don't you dash down and get some more of these?"

"Why don't you?" Anna said lazily.

"I got the last lot."

"Oh, all right."

■■

Fran did not see the man watching their house again. After a while she forgot about him.

2

"HE'S ENGLISH," ANNA SAID.

"Who is?" Frances looked up from her book.

"Peter. This man who's asked us to a party next Friday. His father's something high up in the War Office." Anna put both her hands at the back of her head and cushioned the weight of her thick red hair. "I don't like him much."

Frances laughed. "What's the point in going, then?"

"He's rich, darling. Just as well, really. When you've got no chin to speak of, you need some compensation. Also, he's got this rather dishy brother."

"Earmarked for your personal attention, I suppose."

"You bet."

Ostentatiously, Fran turned a page. "I'll look forward to hearing all about it when you get back."

"You've got to come, Fran. Peter will be terribly disappointed if you don't."

"How can he be? I've never met him."

Anna's white skin turned faintly pink. "Well," she began. "*Actually* . . ."

Fran slapped her book shut. "Procuring again, Anna?" she said coldly.

"Darling, so crude."

"You don't want the Chinless Wonder yourself so you've fobbed him off with promises of your gorgeous pouty-mouthed friend—i.e., me."

"How did you know?"

"Because you used to do it all the time at Oxford. And while I'm stuck in a corner being chatted up by some wimp, you're off having a marvelous time with Prince Charming. I bet this Peter's got damp hands and something disgusting stuck in his teeth."

"Just tell him you're engaged. That's what I do. Anyway, it's time you met some of the other English people here."

"Who says?"

"I do. It will broaden your outlook. And besides, it could lead to some more pupils."

"If they're English, they're hardly likely to want lessons on how to speak the language."

"But they may know people who do. Also," said Anna, transparently improvising, "there'll probably be some Turks there too."

"Oh great," said Frances sarcastically. "Do you want me to appear in mortarboard and academic gown, or should I just carry a placard advertising English lessons at giveaway prices?"

"Might not be a bad idea."

"Unfortunately, I can't come."

"You don't know what date it is."

"Whenever it is, I'm already convinced I've got a pressing previous engagement that night. Two, in fact."

"Why two?"

"In case the first one falls through."

"Rubbish, darling. You're being very stupid. It could be very useful for you. Anyway, you know you always enjoy parties when you get there."

■■

Anna was right. In the end, though she felt curiously reluctant to go, Frances allowed herself to be persuaded. The triumph of hope over experience, she told herself as they waited for a lift in the foyer of the modern apartment building where Peter and his brother were living. Despite years of experience, there was always the hope that *this* party, however much it resembled every other party she had ever been to, would be different.

It was.

Unlike all other parties she had ever been to, Nicholas Marquend was also there.

She was standing on the flat's small balcony, watching the lights reflected in the harbor below and taking a breather from Peter, whose teeth were okay but whose damp hands wandered. She had talked to perhaps half of the people there, danced a couple of times, taken an address from a girl who worked at the University of Istanbul, accepted an invitation to another party the following weekend. This one was in full swing by now, voices loud, cigarette smoke thick as pillows against the ceiling.

A man carrying two full glasses pushed between the curtains and joined her.

"Here," he said. "You looked as if you could do with this."

Frances turned. He handed her one of the glasses and she raised it to her mouth before replying, taking him in. English. Taller than she was by a couple of inches. Good mouth. Dark hair worn slightly long. Military shoulders. She had noticed him earlier, almost hidden by a curtained door. He had been watching her, his eyes half closed. In the way that women always know, she had felt the beginnings of excitement at the base of her stomach, the knowledge that this could be the start of something. She had been sure he would eventually seek her out.

It was not yet fully dark. Below them, a Russian freighter slowly negotiated one of the bridges between Europe and Asia, its lights casting a romantic glow over the rusting foredeck and dirty funnels. White-sailed caïques drifted behind in its wake, pale as the wings of moths. The dome of Aya Sofya hung in the floodlights, and near it, the roofs of the Blue Mosque. So beautiful. And so . . .

"Peaceful," he said. "It never fails to lift the heart." His voice was deep and strong.

"That's the intention," she said. "That's what they're for, all these places. St. Paul's Cathedral. Notre Dame."

"The mosque in Córdoba."

"Yes. To inspire one with the littleness of self."

"And the grandeur of God," he said. "Or Allah. Or whatever you call the entity you believe in."

She looked out again at the lights. "Have you been inside the Blue Mosque?"

"Many times. Why?"

"It always makes me believe more in the entity of Man than in anything else."

"Perhaps." He tasted his own drink, watching her over the edge of the glass. "I'm Nicholas Marquend, by the way. Usually known as Nick. And you?"

She did not want to tell him. Letting go of her name, passing it over into his keeping, she had the feeling that she might not get it back, or if she did, that it would no longer be the same. She hesitated. Then: "Frances Brett," she said. "Often known as Fran."

■■

Afterward, when he had gone from Istanbul, she was to wonder what it was that she had found so attractive about him. He was not especially good-looking. Not especially wise, or witty, or warm. He made no particular bid to attract her. He did not make her laugh, though, until then, she would have said that was a prerequisite in any relationship she had with a man. Perhaps it was the purpose she sensed in him that she liked, though she was not to understand what that purpose was until months later. Or perhaps it was his closedness. The challenge he represented. The determination she felt to make his bleak eyes light up with something—anything. Or perhaps it was simply the recognition—immediate though imperfectly understood—of some bond between them that would last beyond the grave.

In the first instance, it was something teasingly familiar about him that caught Fran's attention. She felt sure she had seen him before, though she could not imagine where. He told her that he came from the West Country, had gone to Sandhurst straight from school— she was right about the shoulders—had served his stint with the British Army and was now working for a firm of French winegrowers.

"Why are you in Istanbul?" she asked. "Holidaying?"

He dropped his eyes for a moment before looking directly at her. "We're hoping to open up new markets for the kind of fine champagne that's produced by Pierrey et fils—they're the people I'm with. We think it's the right time to get ahead, look eastward before our rivals have the same idea. Turkey is an obvious point at which to start."

"A Muslim country?" Perhaps it was the very steadiness of his gaze, but for some reason Frances felt he was telling her something that was a certain distance from the truth.

"Perhaps," Nick said easily. "But also the strategic gateway to Russia."

"Big wine drinkers, the Russians, are they?"

"Not yet. But the Russian economy is going to burst wide open any minute now. Since *perestroika,* their purchasing power has increased but the goods still aren't there to be bought. They'll *have* to look westward."

"And when they do, here you'll be."

"Precisely. Meanwhile, there are other reasons to be in Istanbul. It's a capital city, an international center, full of sophisticated, glamorous people. Like yourself." He half smiled, so that she was not sure whether he was being serious. His teeth were very white and even.

"And how much success in selling wine to them have you had so far?"

"A fair amount."

"That's interesting." Frances could already see a newspaper article in it. "New Trends in Marketing" . . . "Old Wine in New Bottles" . . . something like that. Wine was always a glamor subject. "Which section of this cosmopolitan society are your customers going to come from? Or can't you generalize?"

"I could generalize all evening. Even particularize," he said. "However, to do so would mean talking shop. That's something I dislike in others, and loathe in myself." Effortlessly, he changed the subject. "Tell me what you're doing here."

Frances did so. She hoped she did not sound too much like the cliché of an angst-ridden journalist, tortured by the ephemerality, the essential meaninglessness of her profession, fleeing from the rat race to Find Herself.

"Why journalism?" he asked.

"It runs in the family."

"Father? Mother?"

"Father," she said briefly. She did not particularly wish to discuss her father with someone she barely knew. Partly because she was not always certain she could control the tears that thinking of him could still bring.

"You wouldn't—you aren't by any chance related to Tom Brett, are you?" he said.

When she nodded, he said enthusiastically, "My God. I've always been a tremendous admirer of his work. Some of his dispatches from Vietnam—and Israel, during the Six Day War—were absolutely brilliant."

"Yes," she said. She wished he would stop.

"It was appalling, when he was killed. And so"—he looked at her more closely, head slightly on one side—"so odd that he should have been in that particular quarter of Beirut. I suppose reporters of his caliber put themselves in such danger all the time that it's amazing more of them aren't injured. There was a cameraman with him, wasn't there?"

"Yes," said Fran. "François Vacherot. He was a nice man."

For a moment his hand touched her shoulder. "It's probably of no comfort whatsoever, but your father must be missed more than most men."

She looked up at him. "Actually, that *is* a comfort. I was very proud of him. It's why I do what I do."

"Why did you come to Istanbul to do it?"

"Basically, because it was a chance to get away from London for a while. Although I live there at the moment, I don't really feel I belong there."

"That's not surprising, really," he said. "With an American father and a French mother."

"How do you know that?"

"It was . . . mentioned," he said.

She assumed some delicacy stopped him from saying where. Probably in the obituaries, after Pulitzer prize–winner Tom McFarlane Brett had been caught in cross fire while reporting on the unrest in Lebanon.

"Ever thought of writing something more substantial than reportage?" he asked.

"No. You need a Message, and I haven't got anything more than an overdeveloped bump of curiosity."

"That's a shame," he said. She guessed him to be in his early thirties. His glance moved syrup-slow over her face and hair and came back to her eyes. His own, she noted, were the kind of gray that reminded people of winter streams, until you looked at them closely. Then you saw that the bleakness was no more than camouflage, behind which passion lurked, hotblooded, tender-fleshed, like a pike hiding behind a screen of waterweed in a slow-moving river. "I should imagine any message you sent would be a fascinating one."

"You sound horribly patronizing."

Without smiling, he said: "You're right. I really didn't mean to."

Very lightly, he put the tips of his fingers on her elbow. "Why don't you let me take you out to dinner sometime, to show you forgive me?"

Standard stuff, Frances thought: the stock lines of party flirtation, with responses so familiar she could have spoken them in her sleep. Except not quite. Perhaps the fact that he was not smiling added significance to what he had said—gave it extra weight. Perhaps it was the way the touch of his hand set up tremors in other parts of her body. Perhaps it was the feral way his slow gaze had, without pausing, gathered in all the information about her that he would require. *I sing the body electric,* she thought. Only in her case, the body was singing all over, needing no voice for its song.

"I'd like that," she said.

"When?"

Carefully, she looked away from him. "The weekend?"

"Better still." He looked quickly at his watch. "I've got the day off tomorrow. There's probably lots of things you haven't seen yet. Let's do something together."

"Let's," she said.

■■

It was not until he walked out on her that she realized how little time they had actually been together during the following weeks. While it was happening, it seemed as though they spent every spare minute in each other's company. Nick filled her days to such an extent that his actual physical presence was only a small part of the whole blazing takeover of her life. What had she done before she met him? What had she thought about, dreamed of? She was occupied by him, the way a small defenseless country is occupied by a larger, more aggressive neighbor. She was sunk in him, submerged, waterlogged. Yet, surveying those weeks from the future, when it had become the present, she was able to see how manipulated she had been by love. The hours they were together were so intense that they overflowed into the hours when they were apart. Nick's work seemed to take him away from the city a lot, often without warning. Sometimes she would find a bunch of roses laid against the door at the top of the wooden steps with a message canceling a meeting. Sometimes the phone would ring and a strange voice would pass on the information that Mr.

Marquend had unexpectedly been called away. Whether he was with her or not, he occupied her mind.

■■

The following day, they bought pistachios and dried apricots in the Spice Market across the bridge and ate them on the ferry which took them up the Bosphorus to the Black Sea. Together they leaned on the boat's rail, watching the astonishing skyline float past. Domes and minarets, roofs of mosques, copper-green or gold, waterside restaurants set on long wooden stilts; Europe on the one hand, Asia on the other. Their arms lay side by side, touching, reverberating like the beat of a war drum. At Anadolu Hisar they climbed up to the ruined fortress from where, more than five hundred years before, Mehmet the Conqueror had set off to vanquish the combined armies of the Holy Roman Empire and take Constantinople for himself.

"Extraordinary," Nick said.

Frances watched a sand-colored bird which hung in the bowl of space enclosed by the hills, floating motionless on the air currents beneath the sun.

"What is?"

"To think that the leadership of the Ottoman Empire was left to such chance. I mean, the sultans didn't make dynastic marriages, or choose wives for their breeding potential. It was all so haphazard. The eldest male heir inherited and that was that, whatever the quality of the blood that flowed in his veins."

"It's ironic that in spite of being among the most powerful and despotic rulers ever known, all the sultans were the sons of slaves."

"Applied democracy," said Nick. "Anyone, whatever his background, was able to rise to the very top. You could be the son of an Anatolian goatherd, and still end up ruling Egypt. Lovely."

"If you were male."

"The women did all right."

"A few of them. A handful."

"A woman was always the most powerful person in the empire," he said. "The sultan's mother." He shook his head. "God, the strength of maternal ambition. It moves a lot more mountains than faith ever could."

He fell silent. Abruptly he swept the binoculars hanging around his neck up to his eyes. She watched him focus on a fishing boat chugging across from one shore to the other, his mouth thin and tight. Even without the glasses she could make out the figures of two men, one with his hand on the tiller, the other sitting at the prow.

The bird—a falcon? a kite?—dropped suddenly toward the ground, almost too swiftly to follow with the eye.

■■

The following week, he took her across the Bosphorus to Usküdar. They walked around the huge barracks built by Selim III where Florence Nightingale earned fame as the Lady with the Lamp. The place was heavy with significance: the Crimean War . . . the bleeding remnants of the Light Brigade . . . the mouth of death and the jaws of hell. The hospital where Miss Nightingale had once done her rounds had returned to its original function as a military installation, but her rooms had been preserved as a museum. The guide's voice was bored, his eyes hidden by dark glasses. Tourist stuff. There was even a period lamp on what they said had been her desk.

"I hate this place," Nick said. He held Fran's arm tightly.

"We can go back now, if you want."

"Not just yet."

"We didn't have to come."

He did not answer.

They walked toward the British Crimean cemetery to look at the English gravestones. Ahead of them, a man came out of an arched door set flush in the wall. He stared up and down the street, his head turning with the quick defensive movements of a bird. Through sunglasses, his eyes caught hers for a short moment, then he walked away in the opposite direction. Because Nick had stopped to tie his shoelace, Fran had time to register the remarkable beauty of the man's face. Thin. Ascetic. The kind of face a saint or martyr might have, or a man racked by inner tensions.

She looked down at Nick, crouched at her feet. His face was hidden from her but already she knew it by heart. There was a small hollow in his chin that she longed to touch. She imagined the two of them in bed together, imagined how she would kiss his body for hours, pressing her lips to his flesh, pressing herself into him, making of the two a one. When he stood up, his expression was stern, the features concentrated, giving nothing away. She did not yet know him well enough to judge whether he was worried about something—or perhaps afraid.

"Shall we go?" she asked.

"No. Not yet." With an obvious effort he dragged his attention back to her from wherever it had been. Gesturing over his shoulder, he said, "Sorry. Hospitals always affect me badly."

"Me too. Particularly that one. I think it must be the accumulation of deaths," Frances said.

Nick shivered. "What it must have been like in Florence's day is unimaginable. I'd much rather have been killed outright by a cannonball than rescued and brought in to be nursed under the conditions they had to put up with then."

"Amazing, isn't it, how primitive medicine was until very recently?"

They sat for a moment on a wall, under the mild wintry sky. A group of small girls in white blouses and dark blue skirts went by, two by two, with a couple of nuns bringing up the rear. He watched them without expression, his face chilly. When they had passed, he took her hand. "Fran," he said softly. "Frances."

She felt heavy, pregnant with the anticipation of love. Not today, perhaps. Not next week. But sometime, inevitably. Looking sideways, she saw the darkness of stubble along his jawline, the straight drop of his hair into his neck. Not especially good-looking, she told herself, yet entirely beautiful. He turned to look at her and caught his lower lip in his teeth.

Slowly, she turned back to the view. Neither of them spoke. Neither of them smiled.

■■

"Are you ever frightened, Fran?" They were in the Haci Emin café at Dolmabahçe, the little rococo structure which had once combined both a shrine and fountain and was now neither of those things. He held her hand, smoothing down the fingers as he spoke.

"Not really," she said. "Not so far. But then I haven't really had occasion to be. Footsteps behind me when I come home late at night, or turbulence when I'm on a plane. Otherwise not. Are you?"

"Often. When I was in the army, we did a tour of duty in Northern Ireland. You always knew that if they ever caught you alone, you'd had it." Wind tossed the fir trees behind the café and pushed through the grilled screens. He sounded desolate.

"Anyone would be frightened in a situation like that."

"You can't imagine what it's like to live in an atmosphere of constant hatred. To live always on the knife edge. Sometimes you get so— so exhausted by it all."

"Is that why you got out?"

"Got out?"

"Of the army."

He shook his head. "No. Not really." He lifted her hand slowly to his mouth and kissed it, watching her as he did so. It was difficult, suddenly, to breathe.

■■

Nick said she must buy a kilim to take back to England. They were to meet at three o'clock outside the covered market. Frances arrived thirty minutes early, thanks to a more than usually intrepid taxi driver. She stood watching the crowds, feeling part of the humanity which surged about her, yet outside it, isolated by foreignness, by love, by language. While she waited, she held her shoulder bag close to her body. She had lost her house keys somewhere on that first ferry ride with Nick, and never wanted to go through the hassle again of trying to replace them in a city where little English was spoken. For a week she checked the whole flat every time she came home, wondering whether the thief had used them to get in and steal one or the other of their absent landlord's possessions. Or the drugs. Or even the gun, still stashed away in its embroidered pouch. Nothing ever appeared to have been disturbed. A couple of times she was absolutely certain that someone had been in there, but she was unable to analyze why. She remembered the man who had run down the wooden steps as she turned the corner. Could it have been him? When Nick eventually found the keys caught in the lining of her bag, she felt she had been ridiculously paranoid.

In the distance she saw Nick coming toward her. He had not noticed her yet. She lowered her head to hide the emotions which flooded across her face. Three weeks had gone by since their first meeting and so far he had not even kissed her. But they both knew they were only putting off something that was as inevitable as the rising of the sun. Perhaps tonight . . . She had already planned to let him know that Anna was away, gone to the Princes' Islands with chinless Peter's dishy brother.

When she looked up, Nick had disappeared.

But that was impossible. He was supposed to be meeting her here. He *must* have seen her. She checked her watch: 2:40. Admittedly there were still twenty minutes to go, but since they were *both* early . . . She stared at the people moving busily about her. No Nick. There was a side turning he could have gone down, a couple of doorways into which he might have ducked. But why? Walking toward the spot where she had last seen him, she frowned. Perhaps he had gone into the bazaar to buy something. There were eleven entrances to the place, after all. But why would he do that, since they were to go around it together?

She went into the covered market. The place was such a wilderness of alleyways and boutiques that the chances of catching sight of Nick were slight. For a while she wandered through the noisy bustle, refusing the little cups of apple tea that were thrust at her by traders anxious to sell her everything from handbags to genuine Turkish antiques. Passing a tiny perfume shop near one of the exits, she heard voices from behind a curtain of swinging brass chains.

"*Je vous assure qu'il est ici.*"

"*Il n'etait pas là, au rendezvous.*"

"*Je l'avais déjà vu, moi-même.*"

"*Mais j'attendais presque deux heures.*"

"*Qu'est-ce que vous voulez que je fasse? Je ne suis pas la mère de ce type, quand-même.*"

"*Oui, oui. Vous avez—*"

"*C'est déjà assez dangereux, vous savez.*"

"*Je le sais bien.*"

Although she spoke perfect French, she decided she must have misheard. The conversation sounded like something out of a spy novel. Someone was known to be here in Istanbul, yet he had not arrived at some meeting place where he was expected. The situation was "dangerous."

One of the voices had sounded a bit like Nick's. It was difficult to be sure since the conversation was conducted in whispers. She decided she must be wrong. She might not even have heard the exchange in the first place, had it not been that her ear was always alert to the sound of her mother's native language. There was a young girl behind the little counter near the door; Fran thought of asking if a foreign man had come in during the past five minutes or so. In the end, shrugging to herself—and shaking her head at the man across the way offering her an unbeatable bargain in leather coats—she walked back to the place where they were supposed to meet.

At three o'clock precisely, Nick appeared, coming from the opposite direction to where she had first seen him. His face had that closed look she was learning to associate with something bothering him.

"I'm sorry," he said, as soon as they were near enough to speak, "but I have to fly back to Paris this evening."

She said nothing. They had been going to spend the rest of the day together. Perhaps even the night. Her disappointment was too great for words. She wanted to make a scene, to burst into tears, to scream four-letter words—not at him, but at the Fates which so constantly frustrated them.

"I'm sorry," Nick said again. He put his arms around her and held her tight against his chest. "Don't look at me with such sad eyes, my love. I can't bear it."

It was the first time he had used an endearment to her. She tried not to think of the elaborate bed where she slept, the sheets she had changed that morning, just in case, the fresh flowers she had bought at the little stall across the street.

"How much time have we got?" she asked.

"Just a couple of hours." He took her hand. "I'm devastated, Frances. I'd hoped that tonight . . ." He let the sentence dangle, looking deep into her face until she dropped her eyes.

"So had I," she said.

They found an open-air café and ordered tea, sitting side by side. Frances remained silent. Three weeks—and she was no nearer to knowing him than she had been the first time she had met him. Heedless, the world went on around them, while her chest felt tight with the words she had hoped to say to him when they lay naked together between the jugs of flowers. Here, clothed, public, she could not leap the barriers between them, nor bridge the gulfs.

"Talk to me, Fran," he said. He looked quickly at his watch.

"About what?"

"Anything. Everything. Just don't be unhappy or I shall feel even worse."

"What can I say?" She did not look at him.

"All right. I'll pick a subject." He stared at the wall behind her head. "I know. Tell me about your father. For instance, what did he think was the best piece he wrote?"

"You probably know he won his Pulitzer for the dispatches from Seoul," Fran said. Once she would have felt uncomfortable discussing Tom. Today he seemed neutral, separate, a subject that could safely substitute for the emotion that hung unspoken between them. "But I think he was proudest of some of his investigative pieces. Uncovering corruption on Wall Street, for instance. That insider-trading stuff—I know he got a kick out of that. He hated fraud, excess, people who already had too much trying to get even more. He hated the unfairness of the self-perpetuating systems which govern us."

"He did some pretty hard-hitting articles on terrorism and government collusion, didn't he?"

"Violence for the sake of violence and governmental hypocrisy: he loathed all that."

"I suppose he had a whole lot of private sources keeping him in touch with things: all the different groups with interests in kidnapping and so on."

"Yes. I keep meaning to go through his papers, but I've never quite been able to. . . ." Fran's voice quavered. She felt tears brim and tried to keep her eyes wide enough so they would not spill over.

One did. Nick leaned forward to wipe it away with a finger. He put his thumb on the softness under her chin and turned her face to his. As usual, his expression was serious. "You don't think I *want* to go away from you tonight, do you?" he asked.

Avoiding his gaze, she said, "Have you ever been married, Nick?"

"No."

"It's unusual these days to find a man your age who isn't, or hasn't been."

He picked up a long-handled spoon and twisted it between his fingers. "My line of work," he said. "It doesn't exactly fit in with a wife and children."

She laughed. "What?"

"It wouldn't be fair. You never know what might happen."

"I hadn't realized that selling wine was such a hazardous occupation," she said lightly.

For a brief moment he stared at her. He angled his head back, as though trying to find a shadow that would hide his face. "You know what I meant," he said. "Today was a prime example. Whatever plans you make, you never know when they'll have to be canceled at a moment's notice."

"Yes." She wanted to say: *That's not what you meant at all.*

He took her hand. "It's one of the reasons, Fran, that I've . . ."

"Held back?"

"Yes. I don't want you to get hurt."

"Isn't that a decision I should make for myself?" Frances said. She smiled at him.

Briefly, he closed his eyes, as though the light was too strong. "You can't decide without knowing all the facts."

She leaned against him and kissed the corner of his mouth. He sat very still, enclosed in himself. "I think I already have enough to go on," she said, and kissed him again as he slowly shook his head.

■■

Anna decided she was going to move in with Alan, Peter's brother. "He's moving to a bigger place in a couple of weeks, so I'll go then. But only if you're sure you'll be all right on your own."

"What will Andrew Watson's cousin's friend have to say about it, if I stay on alone?" called Frances from the kitchen. She was piling *taramasalata* onto a dish and trying to do something artistic to it with parsley. People were coming in for *mezes* that night, before they all went out to eat at the little restaurant nearby. Nick had been invited along but had refused since he had a late business appointment. It bothered her that he had never seen the place where she lived. Nor invited her to see his.

"Don't give it a thought, darling. He wants someone to house-sit, right? It's not going to make the slightest difference whether it's me or you. After all, he's never clapped eyes on either of us. Are you sure you don't mind staying here on your own?"

Anna was in the middle of her daily workout. Sweat gleamed lightly on the skin above her breasts.

"Of course not," Frances said. "I'll be fine."

"Perhaps you could persuade lovely Daniel to move in with you."

"Who's Daniel?"

"That man you've been seeing. The ex-army chap."

"His name's Nick," said Frances From a cupboard she took glasses and bottles.

Anna wrinkled her brow, one leotarded leg high above her head. "I'm sure someone said he was called Daniel. . . . Anyway, the man you've been mooning over for the past six weeks."

"Perhaps I'd rather be on my own."

"It's about time you consummated the relationship, isn't it?"

"You've really got a nerve." Fran came into the room, wiping her hands on a tea towel. She dug a foot into one of Anna's firm thighs. "Besides, how do you know we haven't?"

Stretching like a cat, Anna said, "It's the same as pregnancy: you can always tell." Her hair flamed against one of the overstuffed cushions on the floor.

"Sometimes—like with those pregnancy tests—you can tell wrong," Frances said. She tried not to mind that nevertheless, Anna was right.

"Uh-huh. You haven't got the glow, darling. The inner glow." Picking up a can of Diet Pepsi from the floor, Anna sucked at it lengthily. "It would be a good idea if he came here actually. You'd be safer. I mean, they found those two guys with knives in their ribs practically around the corner. And there was that chap they fished out of the harbor the other day."

"It's hardly the same," protested Fran, laughing. "He was an arms dealer or something."

"That's beside the point. Why not ask Nick? If you don't, I will."

Would he come? Fran's body ached at the thought of Nick with her, the two of them together in these rich warm rooms full of painted flowers, closed away from the rest of the city. The Garden of Allah, she thought, as a gust of wind from the balcony caught the brass lanterns and set them swinging, and lifted the silken carpets gently away from the walls. For the first time she noticed what they had hidden until now: a stain of spreading black mold.

■■

She sat opposite Nick on the terrace of a restaurant on Istiklal Street, where they had often dined before. They ate *imam bayildi,* grilled bluefish, crusty bread. The candle between them highlighted the planes of his face. The air was turbulent tonight, blowing leaves and ragged moths past them into the darkness. His face was sadder than at their last meeting, and more anxious. She told him that Anna was leaving and saw how his face closed up while he evaluated the information.

"Will you look for someone else to share the place with you?" he said, finally. He stared down at his wristwatch and back up to meet her eyes.

"I don't know. I like being on my own."

"Will you be safe?" he said. "Some of those carpets are worth a fortune—not a small one, either." Between the two of them the candle flame swayed, leaving a thread of black smoke hanging in space. He caught her glance and added, "From what you've said, the place must be a thieves' paradise."

He was right, of course. "The only thing that really bothers me is the way it creaks at night," she said.

"I suppose that's because it's made of wood. We used to have a wooden holiday place when I was a boy, on the beach near Brixham. The noises it made sounded like gunshots sometimes."

Crumbs scattered across the tablecloth as she broke a piece from the thick-crusted bread beside her plate. "Perhaps I *ought* to look for someone to share it," she said. "As a matter of fact, one of my pupils asked if I'd like to set up housekeeping with him. I could always say yes." She widened her eyes at him and gave her most provocative smile.

"Are you trying to make me jealous?"

Carefully she touched him on the back of the hand. By now, she had learned that she must not overstep the invisible boundaries he had drawn between them. More than that, she must not even indicate she knew they were there. Sometimes she thought that if she made a sudden movement, he would be gone, loping back into the jungle out of which he had strayed.

"I'm not pressuring you in any way whatever," she said. "I know you like your privacy."

"It might be very convenient." He interrupted before she had finished speaking, as though he had been considering something else. "It's about time I moved, anyway. I just wonder how safe it is."

"Safe?" She laughed. "With you there, what else would it be?"

The gray eyes assessed, calculated, refocused. He gave one of his rare and delightful smiles. "Do you really want me to move in with you, Fran?"

Her heart began thumping. She pulled her silk-fringed shawl closer around her shoulders and turned her head to the rest of the room. "Nick," she said quietly. "Darling Nick, you know I do."

When they had swallowed several little cups of thick sweet coffee, they stood together looking out across the Golden Horn to where the mosques glowed quietly in the darkness behind Topkapi.

"It's like a fairy tale," Nick said. "Fantastic. Unreal. And yet underneath all that beauty . . ." He put his arm around her. His hand curved over the smaller dome of her shoulder for a moment, enclosing it. A finger brushed delicately across the front of her blouse. Then abruptly he turned her toward him. "I've been so careful," he said desperately, talking into the soft spaces under her ear, his mouth tugging gently at her hair as he spoke. "I've really tried. I didn't want this to happen, Fran, for both our sakes." He moved his head so that their mouths met.

"What to happen?" she said. She wanted him to say it.

"I didn't want to fall in love. Not with you. Not with anyone. It's not fair. I can't . . ."

"Is love so terrible?" she whispered.

"You don't realize . . . I shouldn't allow you to get involved."

"What are you talking about?" Against her breasts she could feel the strong erratic beat of his heart jumping inside his chest.

"Shhh," he said. For a moment their lips lay together as lightly as honey in the comb, then he was kissing her roughly, almost brutally, like a man deliberately starved, as though he could never kiss her enough. Somewhere deep in his throat he groaned, small, despairing noises that vibrated against her jaw as she tightened her arms around his neck. Her need for him was too strong for her to wonder why.

■■

But why should she have wondered? How could she possibly have known? She simply did not have enough information to have foreseen any of it. If she had had even the slightest inkling of what lay ahead, she would have been prepared for disaster when it came, and thus better able to cope. Later, she wondered whether he assumed that she knew more than she really did. But like the mothers, sisters, daughters, and wives of those who commit terrible crimes, it did not occur to her that someone she knew so intimately and loved so well could be anything other than what she then believed him to be.

■■

"Excellent idea," Anna said, when Fran told her that Nick was going to move in after all. "And if you want my advice . . ."

"I don't."

". . . when he gets here tonight, don't hang about." She shrugged into her coat as a car horn sounded outside in the street. "That'll be Alan."

"I'm not going to lower myself to ask what you mean by that remark."

"Oh, Fran." Anna put her hands on her friend's shoulders. "Are you happy?"

"Of course I am."

You don't seem to be. Love affairs are supposed to be *fun,* Fran. But you and Daniel—"

"Nick."

"Nick—sorry—seem to be so serious about everything. And he's so—so fearfully intense."

"It all depends on your definition of love, I suppose," Fran said.

"He doesn't seem to be around much, does he?"

"I love him," Fran said.

"Well, that's all right, then." Anna sounded doubtful.

"Yes." Fran kissed her, hugging her longer than necessary, as though reluctant to let her go through the door and away. "Enjoy yourself."

"Believe me, I shall."

"And when he throws you over for a younger woman, there'll always be a place for you here. At least, for the next few weeks."

"Oh Lord, yes. I'd forgotten about the chap who owns it. He'll be back at the end of next month, won't he?"

The car horn bleeped again. Anna picked up most of her bags. Fran took the rest. "Don't worry," she said. "I'll leave it spick and span for him to come home to. And if I find his private diaries, I promise not to read them."

Anna leaned out from the passenger seat. "Say that again, with your hand on your heart."

"Do I have to?"

As the car pulled away, she heard Anna's ironic laugh.

She went back into the house, using the front door. The smell of sandalwood clung to the fat curves of the banisters and drifted up behind her into the gallery above. For the rest of her life that smell was to make her feel again the sense of anticipation she knew then, the powerful tightening of the nerves at the thought of being alone with Nick at last, the stills of the two of them loving, learning, tasting, touching, naked together, his hand on her breast, her hand on his thigh, her mouth on his body, his body inside hers, which flicked continuously across her brain.

Coming back into the flat, she heard the telephone ringing. Even before she picked up the receiver she knew what she would hear.

"Miss Brett?"

Her heart dropped. She felt her shoulders sag, but forced herself to stand upright.

"Miss Brett?" She had heard the soft anonymous voice before.

"Yes."

"I'm ringing on behalf of Mr. Nicholas Marquend."

"I thought you might be."

"He asks me to tell you that he has been called away to England on urgent business. He should be back by the end of the week—on Friday, he thinks. He is terribly sorry." The voice was clearly reading from a piece of paper. "He asks that you will forgive him and says he will telephone you the minute that he returns."

"Thank you," Fran said quietly. Even as she spoke she was wondering why she should be thanking someone who had just smashed her dreams.

She was about to replace the receiver when the voice spoke again. "Miss Brett."

"Yes?"

"He asks me also to say that you know how he feels."

"Thank you," Frances said again.

Around her the flat throbbed like a beating heart. Not tonight, then. But soon. Next weekend. Perhaps she could find out the arrival times of flights from London and go and meet him. If she closed her eyes, she could almost see him, almost capture the way his eyes narrowed when he was surprised, his nervous habit of glancing at his watch, the loneliness which sometimes lurked under his cheekbones. Nick, she thought. Do you know how I feel? How much I want you, how hard it will be to get through the hours until you ring me? Do you know how much I love you?

■■

His telephone call never came.

3

TAKE EACH DAY ONE AT A TIME,
you told yourself.

So you did. Then found that you were living in a limbo. The immediate past had been wiped out. There was no future. Not without Nick.

Time is a great healer, you told yourself.

You didn't really believe it. But you waited. The minutes turned into hours, the hours into days and then weeks. You discovered that when your heart breaks, it is not just a question of the simple agonizing snap, a sound you hear over and over again in the darkest parts of the night. It's more the feeling at the back of the head that there is not enough oxygen in the world to fill your lungs, so huge are the breaths you need to take if you are still to function. It's more your heart floating away from you across an ocean of tears into some vast, unknowable space, splitting again and again into smaller subsidiary pieces like some monstrous form of asexual reproduction until the world is a whirling mass of broken hearts.

Don't think about him. Forget him, you told yourself.

Except you couldn't. It wasn't just the sense of loss. There was the rejection to contend with. The feelings of inadequacy. The humiliation of having so nakedly displayed your love for a man who obviously didn't want it. The determination that *next* time . . . except you couldn't imagine that there would ever be a next time. Besides which, it was *this* time you wanted, this time, whatever it was, whatever it might have been. Even though Nick had not felt the same way. Obviously. Otherwise he wouldn't have walked away like that without a word, without a note. Just some phone call from a subordinate.

Over and over again you went through the sequence, lacerating yourself, Nick rushing out the door, already late for his plane to London, stopping at someone's desk, frowning at his watch, saying something careless on the lines of: *Oh Lord, I forgot. You'd better call this number and make my excuses, I'm sure you can think of something, you're always so tactful in these situations,* and then that knowing male smirk, the exchange of raised eyebrows, secret grins. Every time Fran thought of it, she blushed, a total body surge of heat that rushed up from her stomach. The embarrassment. The humiliation. Oh, God, how could she have been so naive as to believe that Nick cared for her, that he felt for her any of what she had felt for him?

Then there were the self-lacerating thoughts. If only I'd been different, if only I'd done this or hadn't done that, *then* he wouldn't have left me. And the self-reproaches. And the realization that there was nothing much, really, for him to walk out on, since they were still at the beginning of the things that might have been. If she hadn't been so pushy, been so all over him, hadn't embarrassed him to the point where he'd eased himself out of a difficult situation, had found it easier to leave without bothering to say good-bye. Oh, God. Never again, she told herself. Never ever again.

Stop brooding, you told yourself.

But how could you help it? You brooded. You cried, under the painted blooms and silken covers you might have shared with Nick. You looked at yourself with disgust: tearstained, self-pitying, a rejected woman bewailing a faithless love. All the music of Istanbul mirrored your mood, mocked you. *Yesterday, all my troubles seemed so far away, now I need a place to hide away,* floated from the waterfront cafés, and *Help me make it through the night.* Yearningly, the tinny transistor by the door of the barbershop wondered *Are you lonesome tonight?* and because you *were,* because you knew you always would be, tears pricked your eyes with luscious agony as you hurried past, even though you knew they were no more than hackneyed songs celebrating the commonplaces of lost loves and shattered dreams.

■■

How long did it last? It could have been weeks. Or months. It felt like always. It felt as though there had never been anything but the gut-wrenching loneliness and the self-loathing.

But *Life goes on,* you told yourself.

That was the great thing about life. It went on. Carrying you with it, forcing you to smile and be polite to strangers. Forcing you to tamp down your inner aches while you elucidated yet another tricky

English idiom to Mr. Yildiz, agreeing that while you could indeed say *He has far to go,* and you could also say *He is going to go far,* they did not necessarily mean the same thing though at the same time they could possibly, in certain circumstances, do so.

Until there came the day you found yourself, instead of returning to your misery, looking with mounting irritation at the plump little man sitting across the table from you and wondering whether he sat up all night searching through phrase books to bring difficult points of verbal idiom to your attention, and whether it was some kind of displacement activity designed to avoid going to bed with a wife he had learned to loathe, or a deliberate dig at you, or merely a subtle form of sexual harassment, something you had not hitherto considered but which, now you came to examine it, the suggestive smile on his face as he watched your patient explanations rather clearly implied.

You wanted to shake him until his beautiful teeth rattled. And suddenly you were into the second stage. You realized that you could live with a broken heart. That you could function. That the body's capacity to bear pain was boundless.

And once you realized that, once you'd tested the limbs and shaken the extremities, and tried out the spare parts and found everything was still in good working order, and nothing was irretrievably damaged, you were well into the third stage.

That was the one where you stared at yourself in the mirror a lot and decided that despite the fact that your major organ had been ruptured, you weren't bad-looking. The one where you told your reflection that there were other men around, thank you very much.

The one where you started to get angry.

■■

Ah. Good. Because once you got angry, the scars began to form. That was the first phase of stage three. You decided that if Nick Marquend showed up on the doorstep, you would spit in his eye. If he telephoned and declared his undying passion, you would hang up on him. Men were a despicable and cowardly lot on the whole, and the most cowardly, the most despicable of them all, must surely be Nicholas Marquend. You wanted to point out just how much grief men handed out to women—had *always* handed out—and how women were no longer prepared to put up with it because they were beginning to see that they deserved better. You spent some weeks in that state, accepting invitations, going out, wishing he could see you doing it, so that he would know how little you were affected by his desertion. And once the scar tissue had covered up the wound, so that only occasionally did the bruised bits of you give a shattering twinge, you moved into the next phase.

You wanted to find Nick Marquend and tell him just what you thought of him. You wanted to point out that it would have been kinder, let alone more mannerly, if he had taken the trouble to tell you that he wanted to break off the relationship. You wanted him to know just what it felt like, being left hanging like that without a word. What it felt like, waiting for the telephone to ring, or the mail to arrive, catching glimpses of what might be him on his way to see you but never were, making excuse after excuse for why he didn't call, didn't come, didn't write.

Not that I care, you told yourself. *Not that I give a damn. But my time in Istanbul is nearly up and before I go back to London, I'd really like to get hold of the jerk, the bastard, and tell him exactly what I think of him.*

Having told yourself that, it seemed like a good idea, a *healing* sort of idea, to do just that.

· 4 ·

Finding Nicholas Marquend.

It sounded easy. A couple of phone calls and the thing was done. Except that it wasn't.

Anna was no use at all. "Darling, I really don't know where Peter met him," she said, pausing as they walked across the Galata Bridge. Her face was brilliant against the collar of her fox-fur coat. When Fran had finally been ready to tell her about Nick, she had listened without comment, then dragged Fran out to wander through the city as they had done on their first arrival.

"But it was at his flat that I met Nick."

"That doesn't mean a thing. Somebody probably brought him along."

"Who, though? He didn't seem to be with anyone."

"Perhaps he gate-crashed the party. People do it all the time."

"He didn't look like a gate-crasher to me."

"Honestly, Fran. Gate-crashers aren't a *type*. They come in all shapes and sizes."

"I mean that he seemed to be there in his own right," Fran said, thinking back to that first meeting. "As if he'd come deliberately."

"Perhaps someone he knew said there was a party going on and he ought to come. You know what it's like when you live abroad. The ludicrous need for your own kind that comes over people."

"Which someone?"

"How should I know?" Anna stroked the collar of her coat. "If you remember, I was busy making eyes at Alan." Behind her, on the farther shores, all around the Horn, the hills glowed with the last fox-red leaves of autumn.

The tension in Fran slackened, moved by the harmony between the red-haired girl and the leaves and the pampering fur. "You look beautiful," she said. "Are you in love?"

"Madly, darling."

"With Alan?"

"Of course. I'm thinking of getting engaged to him, actually."

"That's wonderful, Anna."

"Let's hope Alan thinks so when I tell him. Which had better be soon. He's being posted to Washington next month. I think I'd make rather a good diplomatic wife, don't you?"

"No one better," Fran said. "If anyone could prevent the outbreak of World War Three, it's you." She forced herself to smile.

"I thought I'd put it to him tonight, as a matter of fact. See what he thought of the idea," said Anna. She laughed, throwing her hands apart. "I hope he likes it because quite frankly, darling, I'm absolutely head over heels."

"I'm glad for you," Fran said.

"Look at this." Anna dug a paper package out of her bag. She unwrapped something lacy. Around her the crowds paused momentarily.

"Remember where you are," Fran said. "Women are supposed to be decorous and discreet, not brazenly waving garter belts about."

"Heavenly, isn't it?" Anna said. "It's amazing the effect a simple garter has on the average male."

"Put it away," Fran said, laughing. "About half a dozen average males are being amazingly affected right this minute. Anyway, you don't need any props: you're gorgeous enough as it is. Alan will jump at the chance to sweep you off your feet."

Anna sighed deliciously. "He did that the first time we met. Oh, Fran. Everything's really rather perfect, isn't it?"

"Not for all of us," Fran said lightly. "I hate to break into your idyll with my boring problems, but surely Alan must know where Nick came from."

"I'll mention it tonight," Anna said. "If I remember."

"Before you propose?"

"Absolutely."

"What about his brother? Peter?"

"Peter's already gone back to London. Does it really matter?"

"Yes," Fran said, "it really does." Not just for her, but for all the countless other women, all the Aimée Dubucqs, then and now, caught up in the slipstream of men's lives, dragged along behind them, offered no explanations, no apologies, bartered with, mistreated, despised.

Anna's face softened. She closed her hand gently around Fran's arm. "What good will it do, even if you do catch up with him?" she said. "If he's gone off you, making a scene about it won't bring him back."

"I don't want him back."

"Then why bother trying to find him?"

"I suppose I need to." Fran shrugged, trying to make light of it. She thought of the fathers who regularly featured in the newspapers, unable to accept that the deaths of beloved children in distant lands might have been simple accidents, the consequences of bad luck or too much alcohol or someone else's carelessness. They sacrificed their jobs, their mortgages, their marriages, in order to prove that the balcony fall, or the hit-and-run, was part of a larger conspiracy. For a while their haunted, obsessive faces appeared in the media, pictured as they left yet another inconclusive postmortem, or after yet another confrontation with bureaucracy, growing thinner with the passage of time, gaunter, accompanied by paragraphs hinting at increasing madness, increasingly narrowed perceptions. Would she, too, grow into one of those unquiet people, endlessly trying to change what had happened by denying that it had done so, or, when the undeniable fact had to be faced, that it must have happened some other way, that someone must be to blame, that no god could have been cruel enough so randomly to snatch away the life of their beloved child?

She reminded herself that it was anger which fueled her. And a desire for some kind of reparation, for justice, for a wish to make Nick, if nothing else, apologize.

But she knew it was more.

If she could see his face once again. Or his eyes cold upon her, scarcely showing the fire behind. *Then* she might believe that it was over between them. . . .

"Sweetie, when love's gone, there's nothing in the entire world that's going to bring it back," Anna said. "Nothing. Much better to be dignified about it, not to show him that you care."

"I know that, Anna."

"And a kick in the teeth is all part of life's rich wotsit," continued

Anna. "One broken heart is par for the course. Look at me: I've had a lot more than that in my time."

You're stronger than I am, Fran wanted to say. *You're more habituated to love and its consequences.*

Around them pushed the homegoing crowds, heading for the concrete suburbs of Goztepe, Fenerbahçe, or Kadiköy. The shoeshine boys called for customers, humping their brightly painted boxes through the press. The water sellers clanged their brass cups. In the cafés people sat reading newspapers, drinking glasses of tea, shuffling the backgammon men, waiting for the rush hour to ease. The breeze off the water blew salty and cold around Fran's neck, making her shiver.

She watched a flock of birds lift themselves out of the choppy waves and lumber into the air, flapping toward the land on the far side of the bay. Lights were coming on, twinkling under a heavy sky. By now there would be snow on Mount Ararat. She shivered again. The air smelled of winter.

■■

Anna rang her to say that Alan had been so excited at the thought of marriage that he had been rendered impotent. "It was rather sweet," she said.

"I'm sure it was," Fran said. "If a little disconcerting."

"Only temporarily, of course."

"What about the erotic magic of your garter belt?"

"It put new life into him," Anna said. "Eventually."

"You'll have to be more careful in the future," said Fran, "if good news has that effect on him." The two girls laughed.

"I remembered to ask about Nick Marquend."

"And?" Fran tried hard to keep the wild-eyed note out of her voice.

"Nothing. Didn't know who I was talking about, at first. Then he said he thought he might possibly be something to do with selling French wines."

"And naturally you asked him whom for."

"Naturally. But he couldn't remember, any more than you can."

"Darn it."

Sometimes Fran felt she had read the label of every champagne bottle in Istanbul. Not one had so far jogged her memory. Yet she knew Nick had mentioned the name of the company he worked for, during that first evening. At least ten times a day she asked herself how she could have forgotten such a vital clue.

"But that girl I told you about," continued Anna, "the one who thought she knew our landlord . . ."

"Yes?"

"You could ask her. I'm sure she's the one who told me he was called Daniel. Maybe she knows something."

"What's her name?"

"Sylvia something. I'll get her address for you."

■■

Fran took the bus into one of the newer suburbs. It turned out that Sylvia something was sharing a flat with two other girls, a Canadian and a Californian. It was the Canadian who told her to come along any time after six, by which time Sylvia would be back from her secretarial job at the university. The streets here were broad and anonymous, tree-lined. She had been in this part of the city with Nicholas once; she remembered the pale villa behind a basin of flat water and how he had taken her arm as he stopped to admire the garden. Farther on, modern streetlamps shone starkly on slabs of undecorated concrete. Washing hung from small balconies. The sounds and smells that made Istanbul so individual and exciting were muted here, reducing the area to an ugly, faceless zone that could have belonged equally well to Cairo or Frankfurt or Tokyo.

Sylvia had, it appeared, just arrived home. She was the kind of girl Fran usually tried to avoid. She had seen too many of them, talking of trivialities in overloud voices, reminding people irresistibly of their mothers. When Fran asked about Nick, she produced a cold assessing stare, not exactly hostile but clearly far from friendly.

"Yeah," she said carelessly. "I know who you mean."

"Have you seen him recently?"

"No. Why should I? He wasn't a friend or anything."

"Anna said you called him Daniel."

"Yeah, well. This girl I went to school with was out here and her brother came to visit her once and he said he'd been to school with him. Daniel something—I don't remember exactly what."

"But when I met him, he called himself Nicholas Marquend."

Sylvia was too well brought up to say "So what?" Her body language said it for her. "I don't know," she said. "That's what my friend's brother said. We were sitting in a café once when this Daniel or Nicholas or whatever went by."

"What did your friend's brother actually say?"

"Something like 'Look, there's Daniel Doodah'—I can't remember the surname—'Gosh, I used to go to school with him.' Something like that," Sylvia said with exaggerated patience. "He didn't get up and run after him or anything. He said the Daniel person had been much older than him, anyway. And then when I went to that party at Peter's place, there he was. I saw him talking to you, actually, after he'd asked Anna if you were Frances Brett."

"You mean he already knew my name?"

"He seemed to. I was talking to Anna, and he came over and asked about you."

"What exactly did he say? Something like 'Who's that girl over there?'"

"No, actually, more like 'Am I right in thinking that's Frances Brett over there?' Along those lines."

"And?"

"Anna said it was. And he said something like 'I met her father once.'"

"Anna didn't tell me."

"Yeah, well . . . Perhaps she didn't think it was all that important."

But it was, Fran thought. Because it meant—did it not?—that Nicholas/Daniel had come to the party knowing already who she was. Had come, perhaps, specifically to meet her. If that was true, why?

"I suppose your friend's brother didn't know anything else about him, did he?" she asked.

"If he did, he didn't say so."

"Thanks anyway."

Awkwardly, perhaps realizing that she had been less than gracious, Sylvia offered Fran a drink—gin, or tea, or something. Fran refused. She needed to think. She walked toward the bus stop through wet, featureless streets, trying to avoid coming to any conclusions.

■■

Increasingly it appeared that unless she remembered the name of the firm for which Nick worked in France, she was not going to find him. Rerunning in her mind the details of their all too brief time together, she could see how odd it was that she knew so little about him. Even odder that she, the perpetually inquisitive, had been content to let it be so. Why hadn't she asked more questions? Why hadn't she wanted to learn everything about him that she could, the way that lovers usually did?

Looking back, it seemed incomprehensible. Yet there was something about Nick that made queries unimportant, unnecessary. He had a way of sliding away from requests for information that she had found rather endearing, not realizing then that she would never learn the answers. It struck her, for the first time, that the concrete information she possessed about him was absolutely minimal. A firm of champagne makers in France. Growing up in a village near Bath. Sandhurst after public school—she didn't even know which one. It was as though the man had cast a spell on her, suppressing her normal curiosity.

She tried not to think of him somewhere in the wintering city with another woman, one who was wiser than she about hiding her love. The waters of the Golden Horn slapped against the anchored seacraft, gray and chilled, and behind them the farther shores were dulled. In the cafés old men huddled over oilclothed tables, playing cards, drinking tea, bathed in a kerosene-yellow glow as the afternoons faded into early dusk.

She went back to the places where she and Nick had been. Was she hoping that the same fate—if fate it was—which had thrown them together would cause their paths to cross again for one last time?

Perhaps. But fate did not oblige. One day she took a taxi to the rococo cafe at Dolmabahçe and sat alone among teacups in an empty room. Once she took the bus southward, through villages where in summer camels swayed between tractors, past dead fields of sugar beet and sunflowers, past veiled women walking slowly along the edge of the road, past houses where a bulbous green bottle cemented into the roofs indicated to would-be suitors the presence of a marriageable daughter.

The roses in the flower gardens were dead. At Usküdar, the tombstones in the English cemetery leaned protectively above their graves. The ranks of dead Crimean soldiers stretched away from her: lieutenants, captains, majors, once splendid in scarlet and spurs, now part of history. Standing between the trunks of thin leafless trees, Frances thought: *And now I live and now my life is done.*

She walked back toward the ferry. She saw the nuns again, shepherding their charges. Today the little girls wore winter coats. Some had cherry-colored scarves around their necks. On the way, she passed the arched gateway where, when she had come before with Nick, a stranger had emerged, and caught her eye, and gone. The heavy wooden door was closed tight. There was a small window beside it, thickly grilled. A brass plate was set underneath with something engraved on it in flowing Turkish script; beneath it, in upright capital letters, were the words *The Phoenix Foundation.* Though the name was distinctly secular, from the look of the place she assumed it was some kind of religious organization. That would perhaps explain the man's martyred face, the haunted eyes. A religious community, she decided, men living quietly in prayer, contemplating the sins of the world from an oasis of peace. *Get thee to a nunnery.* She heard, as she rounded the corner, the muted sound of a bell.

■■

Rain fell daily from aluminium-colored skies. Her time here was drawing to an end. Soon the landlord would be back to claim his treasures: the jade boxes, the silken carpets, the flower-painted bed. The spires of Istanbul thrust blackly into the sodden air. Over mosque and palace, roofs seemed diminished, the winter light flattening the full-bellied curves. Fran drew herself inward, miserable, preparing for her return to London. The days had been golden once. Now, like the domes, their former gleam was dulled. The patches of damp behind the carpets on the wall of the flat were spreading, giving off a fungus smell that the pastilles she burned in a tiny brass lamp could not disperse. There was damp, too, in the bedroom, creeping between the vivid flowers, lifting the pigment away from the wood.

Her private pupils brought her presents: handkerchiefs, bottles of lemon-scented cologne, sweetmeats in little wooden boxes. The gifts were wrapped in paper, each one with a lucky azure-blue bead

tied on with ribbon. The secretarial school arranged a farewell party
for her. Some of the girls cried.

Anna and Alan gave a party too. "Not an engagement party,
darling," said Anna. "Just a party party. Alan's madly formal about
these things. Announcements in *The Times,* and asking my papa for
my hand and all that sort of thing. Until then, he won't let me celebrate properly."

When Fran arrived, formal Alan stood near the door in T-shirt
and jeans, clapping people on the shoulder, raising his glass, smiling.
Give him ten years and his hairline would be nearer the back of his
neck than his forehead, the space between his eyebrows would contain a frown, the stomach would swell gently over his waistband. Not
like Nick. Nick was the sort whose figure would remain the same,
whose hair would always be thick, even when it had turned to gray.
Forlornly she pictured an older Nick taking his daughter down the
aisle of a little country church, triumphant because he was able to
wear the same morning-suit he had been married in. She did not
bother to imagine a wife for him. It was bad enough that she would
not be Fran.

Several of the faces in the room were familiar. Anna made
friends easily, Alan assiduously. Frances worked the room, smiling,
greeting, avoiding the glass-filling waiters hired for the evening.
Where she could, she brought Nick into the conversation, hoping to
find someone who knew him. Nobody did.

She saw Sylvia, supercilious in a corner. Sylvia beckoned her
over. "I met the man who owns the place you and Anna shared," she
said. She tripped a little on the words.

"Is he nice?" Fran didn't care much. She knew he could not be.

"Rather beautiful, in a weird sort of way," Sylvia said. She was
drinking something sweet from a small glass. "Amazing eyes, he's got."

Fran would normally have been interested in learning more about
this man she felt she already knew well. Tonight she was more intent
on gleaning what scraps she could about Nick. "Dangerous to know, I
should think," she said.

"He's got lovely hands, too. He could have laid them on me any-
time." The girl's expression was loose, uncritical. Her drink had trailed
an oily coating down the inside of her glass. Fran moved away.

■■

Two days later, she woke abruptly out of sleep. "Pierrey," she said into the darkened room. "Pierrey et fils." The name of the company Nick worked for. She got out of bed, shivering in the cold, the marbled floor numbing her feet. But there was no listing under the name in the telephone directory. Fran was not discouraged. Tomorrow morning she would put a call through to the French telephone exchanges, demand to speak to him, ask for his address. Pierrey. So she wouldn't forget it again, she wrote it down on a piece of paper and propped it against the lamp.

The line to Paris crackled and whispered. Guessing, she gave directory assistance a starting point: Epernay. As well as being half French herself, she had once written a feature on champagne for the in-house magazine of a large insurance brokering firm. She knew that most French champagne was made in the area between Epernay and Reims. After a ten-minute wait, the line filled with sea swells and the crunch of dragged-back shingle. She tried again. This time the operator came back with a number and an address. Pierrey et fils, Lavandière, near Reims, France.

She thought about it. Wind blew up from the waterfront and in through the gaps around the window. The rose-silk carpets on the walls stirred. If she called the Pierrey people and Nick was there, what was she going to do? Harangue him over the telephone? Definitely not. She wanted him to understand that his sudden silence had been cruel, not kind. She wanted him, she supposed, at least to say that he had not wished to hurt her, that he was sorry. What she must not do was to behave like a woman scorned, nor rant, nor weep.

She wanted rational debate. She wanted dignity. She knew she should leave it be. Nick had made his choice and abandoned her: she ought to accept that.

But why the hell should she? Anger flared again. It was a rotten, miserable way to treat another human being, a person to whom you had once been close. He had said he loved her, had he not? He had appeared to want her.

Anna was right, of course. Love grown cold could never be rekindled. But perhaps there would be another Fran in Nick's life one day, whom he might treat differently, with more respect, if Fran now let him know how she felt.

She dialed the number. Her wrists trembled. Her heart bumped about in her chest. Suppose, just suppose Nick himself answered, what would she do at the sound of that dear and familiar voice? The receiver at the other end was lifted and a woman's voice answered.

"I'd like to speak to Nick Marquend," Fran said. Her French was fluent and idiomatic, indistinguishable from that of a native speaker, but she chose to speak in English, and emphatically, remembering the distance between them.

"Who?"

"Nicholas Marquend."

There was a silence. The woman said, "I think you must have the wrong number. This is Pierrey et fils."

"Yes. And I'm trying to trace one of your employees . . ." Was he an employee? Or a director? She could not remember—if she had ever known. ". . . Mr. Nicholas Marquend."

"I don't know anyone called Nicholas Marquend," the woman said.

"Are you sure?" Fran said.

"Ben alors . . ." The woman made an exasperated sound. Fran heard her speak to someone else in the room, imagined the frown as she turned to the other person, her husband, perhaps, pointed at the receiver in her hand, indicated that some importunate wrong number was on the phone. A man came on the line.

"This is Philippe de Pierrey," he said. He spoke in English, not bothering to hide his irritation. "You wish to speak to Nicholas Marquend?"

"Yes. Is he there?" Fran's chest squeezed together.

"Where are you speaking from?"

"I'm in Istanbul."

"Istanbul?"

"Yes. He—Mr. Marquend told me he worked for you."

"There is a mistake, madame. Perhaps a wrong number."

"He told me quite definitely that he worked for your firm," said Fran. "He's English."

There was a pause. The man spoke again, delicately, defensively. "You said Nicholas Marquend?"

"Yes."

"No one of that name has ever worked for us," the man said. "You will have to try elsewhere. I'm sorry."

"So am I," she said.

She hung up.

■■

She went back to the Grand Bazaar. Plunging through the noise and color, past piles of elaborate enamelware, past jewelers and diamond merchants, past interiors that glowed with shimmering silk carpets, she found again the little perfume shop. Inside, so many different scents were mingled that the air almost vibrated. The dark girl who had been there before was gone. In her place was a man, white-shirted, small, his head balding. He had both hands flat on the counter and was reading a newspaper. When she came in, he looked up and smiled, at the same time pushing the paper out of sight. The skin of his face was almost oriental in its smoothness.

"Yes," he said. "Can I help you?" He waved a hand at his stock of glittering gold-topped bottles. He picked one up from in front of him and squeezed the netted rubber bulb attached to it, releasing a cloud of Guerlain. "We have all the famous names."

His voice was familiar—and, for Fran, equated with disappointment. But hope filled her, the first since the last time she had seen Nick. She was certain this was the man who had telephoned her so often to say that Nicholas would not be able to meet her after all.

"You *can* help me," she said eagerly. It was the only positive lead she had had in all the time she had searched. "I'm trying to find Nicholas Marquend."

The man's impassive face wrinkled suddenly, ruffling like the surface of a pond, then smoothed out again. "I beg your pardon?" He raised his hands in the air, as though cupping an invisible beach ball.

"Perhaps you know him as Daniel."

He shook his head. "I speak little English," he said apologetically.

Fran knew he must be lying. She repeated what she had already said, in French. If the black eyes narrowed momentarily, it was so briefly that she barely had time to register it. Glancing toward the brass chains at the back of the shop, he shook his head. *"Pardonnez-moi, mademoiselle."*

For a moment, she was tempted to push through the swinging metal curtain to search the rooms beyond. But what would be the point? It was hardly likely that Nick would be hiding back there.

"If you see him," she said, raising her voice, "please tell him it is absolutely vital that he get in touch with Tom Brett's daughter."

The shop owner remained impassive. "You wish to buy?" he said. "Patou? Givenchy? Dior?"

"No, thank you." Fran tried to catch his eye, without success. "Please pass on my message."

∎∎

For the moment there was nowhere else to go. She had never been to where Nick lived, somehow assuming that he stayed with friends or moved around between hotels. At home, she sat and watched the slight rise and fall of the hanging carpets, as though the whole apartment sighed. She recalled Nick's voice remarking on their value. *Some of those carpets are worth a fortune—not a small one, either.* He'd never been here. How had he known?

Through the window a pale sun gleamed, the first for days. She opened the shutters wider to catch whatever warmth there might be. She remembered the man who had stood below her, months ago, and the irrational urge she had felt to gun him down. Like a kick-start to the brain, she recognized him in memory. That angled glance, that shadowed face. It had been Nick who stood there. What had he wanted?

Another thing: the keys she had lost. It was Nick who had found them, caught in her bag—or so he said—though she had emptied the thing at least a dozen times. The feeling that someone had been in the flat while she was out returned, and with it a flush of embarrassment that swept through her body like fire. Was it possible? Had Nick deliberately sought her out in order to get into the flat? Was that what the whole thing had been about? Cocaine, not love? Had she been used, her emotions coldly manipulated? She remembered again how he had stepped out onto the balcony at the party where they met, not like someone merely seeking fresh air but primed, a glass in either hand, one for himself and one for her, the woman occupying the flat he wished to search while its owner—the man with the compelling eyes—was abroad. Had she been set up in some way?

The small jade casket was still in the closet in the room that had been Anna's. She took it down and opened it. The gun was still there, wrapped in the half-moon-embroidered velvet. She held it in her hand, feeling anger beat at the edges of her brain. Thank God she had not found Nick. Nick, who was so clearly something more than she had at first thought him. For a moment the desire for violent revenge blocked out rational thought. There was a thesaurus of words for women like her. Dupe. Gull. Mug. Sucker. Painful though it was, she had to accept that he had wanted something, and had used her to get it.

Knowing that would make it easy to forget him. To get on with her life.

Which was what she was now going to do.

· 5 ·

THE VOICE ON THE OTHER END of the telephone had sounded cool. So cool that it verged on rudeness. Not to be wondered at, Fran told herself, sucking in her cheeks as though that would make her car as well as herself look thinner as she edged it between a semi piled high with car bodies and a light-flashing maniac in a BMW trying to pass on the wrong side. Not to be wondered at, perhaps, when the person she was about to talk to had just won an award from a group promoting small rural business ventures. She'd noticed the same note in the voices of all the women she was interviewing for this particular feature: "Women Who Win" or something similar. They were busy people by their very nature. They had not won their awards for being nice to pushy hacks on the phone.

At least Alicia Forrest had offered to give her lunch. That was something. People were not always so hospitable. Fran held tight to the steering wheel. As she was about to swing past the small white van in front of her, it had pulled out without signaling. Adrenaline still thumped through her veins as she now watched it doggedly try to overtake a refrigerated truck, regardless of the faster cars lining up behind it. She hoped it would be a decent lunch, with possibly a drink beforehand if not during as well. She'd need a drink, after two hours of this kind of motorway driving. A truck roared up in the left-hand lane with a groaning of air brakes that made her VW vibrate. Its tires stood higher than the roof of her own car. She would be offered sherry, she told herself. In heavy cut-glass. *Dry* sherry. Alicia Forrest definitely had a dry-sherry voice. She hoped she would not get lost: the directions she had been given made it fairly clear that the Old Vicarage was not easy to find.

"It's very isolated," Mrs. Forrest's thin, well-bred voice had said. "If you land up going past the drive of Fantocks, you'll know you've gone too far." She obviously didn't care terribly whether Fran went too far or not far enough or, for that matter, didn't show up at all.

"Fantocks?"

"It's the riding school farther down the lane." Again Mrs. Forrest's brittle voice made it clear she had much better uses for her time than discussing the whereabouts of her home with a complete stranger.

Fran was not worried. She was good at her job. Much better at free-lancing than she'd ever been as a sub. Editors liked her work and the fact that she delivered it on time, so that she was virtually given a free hand when she rang up with ideas for commissions. She liked that, liked being answerable only to herself. There were times when she wondered whether she was turning into the hard-shelled kind of journalist she so disliked, times again when she wondered whether she was asking herself the right questions, but that was usually around three-thirty in the morning, and nearly always after she'd had one more glass of wine than was strictly wise. Whether it was interviewing, fact-gathering, or investigation, she had an ability to find something in even the most hackneyed of subjects that others had missed. Plus—and in journalism it was a big plus—a warmth of personality that encouraged people to tell her things they normally kept to themselves. Her unusual, slightly quirky perspective and individuality of style had made the Frances Brett byline almost superfluous. She had gone free-lance on her return to London six months ago, kicking off with a couple of travel pieces for the *Telegraph* and building up from there. As happened in the world of journalism, one thing always seemed to lead to another, enabling her to keep up the flat in Notting Hill Gate, run the car, and buy hideously expensive tickets to the opera once a fortnight or so. What more could one want?

One could want a lot more.

One could want, for instance, a man who had walked out of one's life nine months ago and never come back. A man for whom, try as one might, one couldn't help feeling something that one knew, despairingly, sickeningly, was as close to love as one had so far known.

She turned off the motorway. Soon she was driving between high hawthorn banks frothed with white blossom, beyond which lay fields of palely ripening barley. The ditches on either side of the road were thick with grass that seemed greener than in the Home Counties. Yellow flowers grew in it. Birds dashed from one side of the lane to the other in front of the car's hood. Gnats hung in see-through clouds above the foaming hedges. Tranquillity covered the fields like thin-spread honey. The scene had a charm that was specifically English. To Fran, daughter of an American father and a French mother, brought up in countries where rurality was wilder, less domesticated than this, there was something alien and etiolated about it. Her father's long secondment to the London office of the International Press Bureau had coincided with her own important school years from eleven to eighteen; although school holidays were mostly spent in her parents' home in France, she had been educated for the most part within the English system. She had not once considered herself as belonging to it. With it, yes, but never of it.

"Turn right immediately after the Garden House Hotel," Mrs. Forrest had said, her voice tinged with impatience, hinting at urgent business calling her elsewhere. "You can't miss it; there are no other houses for miles. Keep going after that until you pass the convent. You'll recognize it by the bell tower—a sort of Victorian brick thing with a little copper roof. Greenshaw Lane is the second turning on the left after that."

The Old Vicarage lay tucked back behind beech hedges and a lawn edged with close-cropped yews, as Fran only discovered when she was passing Fantocks Riding School. The lane was too narrow to turn in, so she had to back up until she reached the long white gate and the granite block with the name of the house carved into it. She suspected that the fact it was sunk into its patch of mown grass at an angle that made it almost impossible to read from the road was a deliberate ploy to deter unnecessary visitors.

She motored carefully up the short, curving drive, to avoid scattering gravel onto the lawn. That was the sort of thing which made prospective interviewees very sniffy; she had learned some time ago to treat graveled drives with respect. She pulled on the handbrake and climbed out of the car. A Volkswagen was probably the least convenient car in the entire world for a long-legged five-foot-niner like herself, but it had been her father's car and that was enough. She knew she would never change it until it fell to pieces about her. Sometimes, even after all this time, she fancied she could still smell his tobacco or catch a hint of the special aftershave they used to make up for him on the rue de Rivoli.

The front door of the house opened. A woman stood there,

watching her. Walking toward her, Fran began rapidly taking mental notes. *(There was nothing in the least countrified about Alicia Forrest, recipient of this year's Rural Businesses Award . . .)* Impeccably dressed: plum-colored silk blouse, tweed skirt in matching tones, cardigan of the same color around the shoulders. The woman's hair was freshly done, and there were amethyst studs in her ears. Fran, expecting someone younger, was impressed. Sixtyish. Very smart. Businesslike, but not off-puttingly so. It was not until the first favorable impressions had been formed that you noticed the walking stick of inch-thick polished hickory on which she leaned, and the almost imperceptible jerk of the hip as she moved.

The woman smiled. Put out her hand.

"I'm Alicia Forrest," she said. "You must be Miss Brett."

The house was pleasant, easy, country-house predictable. The two women walked through to glass doors at the rear which opened onto hedged grass, lichened balustrades of stone, a weeping willow leaning over a large square pond full of reeds. Beyond lay meadows full of wild flowers—part of Mrs. Forrest's stock-in-trade. Women moved slowly among them, flat wicker baskets over their arms. All they needed were sunbonnets made of dimity to qualify for the Far From The Madding Crowd Award, Fran thought. She could smell gentle things: grass, water, herbs, a drift of honey. In the distance, a bell tolled.

"Over there are the drying sheds," Mrs. Forrest said, waving toward a series of long wooden huts of creosoted wood. Her business involved dried flowers, beeswax candles, herbal essences. Once a one-person concern, it now employed over thirty locals, mostly women. Fran was quite happy to postpone the interview. Until lunchtime, they talked about other things: the apple crop in the orchard, the price of curtain material, the way the sun caught the dark blue iridescence on a mallard's wing.

Fran had been aware of inspection, the woman weighing her up before handing over the information for which she had come. Doing some covert inspecting herself, she understood perfectly that should Mrs. Forrest decide against it, that information would not be forthcoming. Meanwhile, she squirreled away the details that would later give the interview its individual personality when she came to write it.

She had guessed right. Before lunch Mrs. Forrest offered her sherry so pale in color, it might have been river water, so dry in flavor that the edges of her tongue curled. They walked together into the dining room. Unlike most formal rooms set aside for eating, this one seemed lived-in and warm. The heavy sideboards and glazed cabinets smelled faintly of lemon-scented polish. Portraits of other generations hung on the walls; there were photographs in silver frames on a small table by the window. Its narrow curved drawer was half open; she could see another photograph frame lying inside. Everywhere there were spectacular arrangements of dried flowers, fruit, vegetables, grasses. They reminded Fran of Flemish still lifes: riotous, overabundant, uncontrolled. Yet the woman who had created them seemed the essence of self-discipline.

A bottle of chilled white wine stood on a silver salver. Pouring it, Mrs. Forrest asked if Fran knew much about wine and seemed relieved when Fran said she did not.

"My son did, of course," she said. "As did my . . . husband." A spasm flicked at one corner of her eye. "So much pretentious snobbery seems to have attached itself to the subject. I find it rather spoils my enjoyment."

"It's the way their nostrils expand that I can't bear," Fran said. "If someone like that takes me out to dinner, I'm always tempted to order something really low-life, like cherry soda." She smiled. Smiling might be part of the good interviewer's technique but with Fran it was always genuine. She liked people because she believed that, on the whole, people were likable.

"I do so agree," Mrs. Forrest said.

Their eyes met across the dining table, mutually approving, two women sharing a ruefully remembered experience. Yet the approval was for something more than a shared scorn. Fran was aware of the woman's liking for her, but also of something else, something mesmeric, compelling, out of the ordinary. It was perhaps the first time, apart from with her mother, that she had found such accord with a woman of an earlier generation than her own. There had been a teacher at school, a don at university, but behind the friendliness of both was a professionalism that kept them at a distance.

Mrs. Forrest's eyes were gray, very clear, and so intense in color that they were almost blue. Fran found herself meeting them head-on, confronting them far more frequently than was usual between new acquaintances. They could have been the eyes of a sixteen-year-old except for the skin around them, which was dark and discolored, the lids reddish as though permanently stained with tears.

Fran encouraged Mrs. Forrest to talk about herself. Before she drove down here, she had memorized a list of questions. Most of the information she gained by asking them was never used, but it helped to have a whole picture of the person she was profiling. "Your family . . . ?" she prompted, waiting until the overalled woman who had served them with an excellent *boeuf en croûte* and fresh vegetables, followed by Stilton and homemade blackberry-and-apple pie, had returned again to the kitchen.

"I have no family." Mrs. Forrest looked beyond Fran to the wall where various portraits of men in military costume were hanging.

What was this? Fran wondered. She'd already mentioned . . . Probing delicately as a dentist, she said, "I thought you spoke of a husband. And a son."

On the other side of the table Mrs. Forrest turned her full gaze on Fran. And suddenly Fran felt as though an iron claw had grabbed and squeezed her insides. She was aware of breathlessness and a sense of coming danger. *Leave it,* something told her. *Drop the whole thing. You'll regret it if you don't.*

"I did," Mrs. Forrest said shortly. "They're both dead."

"I'm really sorry," Fran began. "You must be—"

"Both murdered."

"Murdered?"

"My husband died from a heart attack brought on by the news of my son's death. Whoever was responsible for the one was equally responsible for the other."

"Please don't talk about it if you would rather not," Fran said. The other woman's shoulders were shaking under the softness of her cardigan. She thought how easy it was to catalogue someone as a type, as a paradigm of class and income, instantly recognizable until a second glance showed you something quite different. For gradually, astonishingly, she was coming to the realization that under Alicia Forrest's predictable upper-middle-class surface, underneath the smooth tweeds and the plum silk, the courtesy, the well-bred small talk, she seethed with rage—crawled with it the way rotten meat acquires a heaving coat of maggots.

"I don't mind in the least," Mrs. Forrest said. She took an apple from the Royal Doulton fruit bowl in the center of the polished dining table. "I've lived with it for long enough now." Quietly, pausing now and then to cut the apple into minute portions with a silver knife, she told Fran what had happened.

■■

Eight or nine months earlier, while Frances was still in Istanbul, the Forrest murder had attracted a lot of media attention. The victim had been the only child of a military family vaguely connected to nobility. It appeared that young Captain Forrest was one of the golden ones: successful, good-looking, well off. By all accounts he had been a good man, a fine man, as well. The accounts had come from school friends, colleagues, the local vicar, his military superiors. After public school, he had spent nearly ten years in the army before resigning his commission a year before his death. No motive for his brutal killing had even been produced. Because of his service links, the media had tried to whip up some antigovernment hysteria by hinting at sinister behind-the-scenes activity on the part of the security forces. It was suggested that the murder had been espionage-related, possibly even engineered by one of the lesser branches of Military Intelligence. Captain Forrest was known to have handled sensitive documents. There had been a mysterious trip to the Middle East immediately before his resignation. The allegations had so little substance that even those left-wing MPs who maintained their credibility by embarrassing the administration of the day were unable to make anything of them.

The only certainty was that Captain Forrest, recently returned from Paris, had been standing at the bar of a pub in South Kensington when he had been called to the telephone. A few minutes later, after unhurriedly finishing his drink, he had left, exchanging a few unremarkable pleasantries with the landlord. Nothing more had been seen of him until two hikers, sheltering from a downpour, had come across his freshly dead and horribly mutilated body in the ruins of a fowler's hut on Romney Marsh. His arms had been stretched out on either side of his body and fixed to the floor by nails driven through his hands. His feet, tied together, had been similarly anchored by a metal stake driven through both ankles. He had then been tortured to death. The head had been beaten with some kind of heavy iron bar until it was crushed almost flat. Before his hands were nailed down, the fingertips had been dipped in acid. The victim had been alive and fully conscious throughout. The shock of the discovery had caused Colonel John Forrest, his elderly father, to collapse with a heart attack, from which he never recovered.

Public imagination had been caught by the fine-boned military face which appeared for days in the papers and on the small screen. The religious symbolism of the semi-crucifixion, heightened by the presence of a sponge with which the murderers had wiped away the blood of their victim, had been relentlessly commented on. The police were still no nearer to finding out who was responsible than they had been when the body was first discovered.

■■

"How perfectly dreadful for you," Fran said. "That's such an inadequate thing to say, but I can't think of any words that wouldn't be." Wondering what it must be like to lose such a son, she fingered the edge of his mother's sorrow like a tailor feeling the quality of a rival's well-made suit. Was it anything like the pain she had felt when Nick walked away from her life?

"At least you *said* them. You'd be surprised how many people—friends—couldn't even say that much. It's as if the fact of my son's murder tainted *me* as much as those who did it."

"Are you sure it was your son?"

"Of course."

"But the crushed head, the"—Fran swallowed—"the fingertips obliterated. Surely there must be some doubt."

"None at all." Mrs. Forrest turned her head away fastidiously. "Despite the injuries the pathologists were able to confirm the identity. Quite apart from the fact that he . . . the body wore my son's clothes, there was an appendectomy scar and another scar on his knee which he got from falling out of a tree when he was twelve. And his things were there—his wallet, a diary, letters addressed to him. And the gold pencil he was given for his twenty-first birthday. No, I'm afraid there was no doubt."

"You must feel very bitter."

"Bitter?" Mrs. Forrest curled her tongue around the word as if it were new to her, a concept she had not hitherto considered. Or else one so familiar she no longer gave it any thought.

"Do you ever want revenge," Fran asked, to fill the gap. Although she held a pencil and a reporter's pad, there was an unobtrusive tape recorder on the table. While it caught the words of their conversation, she made other notes in a modified shorthand.

"Revenge." Again the woman considered the word, looking not at Fran but into some quietly boiling place inside herself.

"The person your son went off to meet must, after all, have been responsible, directly or indirectly, for . . ." Fran held her pen over the lined pad on her knee, knowing the answer, waiting for the predictable response. People in a situation like this always came up with the same reply: *No, I don't feel any bitterness. No, I don't hate them. I feel sorry for them. I forgive them.*

Such forbearance made no sense. It was natural to want revenge for a wrong done you. Waiting for Mrs. Forrest to reply, Fran thought back to the more spectacular murder cases since her return from Istanbul. From what wellspring of charity could you dredge up forgiveness for the man who raped and strangled his own stepchild, your six-year-old daughter? How could you not feel bitterness toward the couple who forced your bank manager husband to open his vaults for them, then left him to die of exposure on a snowy hillside? Or the brother-in-law who slowly poisoned your beloved sister in order to claim on the life insurance policy he'd taken out? Yet incredibly, time after time, that was what the bereaved were reported as saying. Did they, *could* they mean it? Or was it some received answer, some need to behave acceptably in the face of adversity, a British desire not to make a fuss?

Mrs. Forrest looked down at her hands, twisting a diamond-and-amethyst engagement ring round and round on her finger. She was still attractive, still taking care of her appearance. She was a striking woman, no question. She must have been beautiful once.

"I had it all," she said suddenly. Her eyes narrowed, as though attempting to contain a force that might otherwise explode into the quiet drawing room and destroy it. "Everything you're supposed to want. Youth, money, looks. Love. My husband. My glorious child." She spoke the extravagant word unselfconsciously.

Fran nodded. She waited. She had discovered long ago that waiting produced the best results. The fewer questions you asked, the longer the silences you left, the greater the need the interviewee felt to fill them. Nature abhorring a vacuum, as always.

"I had no idea it wasn't allowed," Mrs. Forrest said.

"Not allowed?" Fran reached unobtrusively for the volume knob on the recorder. The other woman's voice, though still clear, had dropped until it was almost inaudible.

"That if life granted you favors, you'd eventually be required to pay for them. I just didn't realize."

"Perhaps everything has a price tag," said Fran.

There was a portrait of Alicia Forrest over the elaborate mahogany mantel, affectedly Gainsborough in style. Dressed in something undefined and white, she leaned against a tree, a cloud of black hair around her head, her eyes huge. It must have been painted twenty years ago, maybe twenty-five. The edges of her had still been soft then, you could tell. Soft, and woundable.

"But how cruel to make my son pay," Mrs. Forrest said, leaning forward. "When I would have been glad to—so glad, if I could have spared him . . ." She stopped, biting her lip. Then she said fiercely, "There's something they never tell you."

"What's that?" said Fran. There had been sunshine somewhere beyond the French windows leading out to the garden. Now the light contracted as clouds gathered slowly above the house and drifted across the lawns. With the illumination gone, the room seemed to shrink, constricting her. Fran was aware of turbulence close at hand, of tumultuous emotion reined in.

"That when it's all taken from you, when you lose it, the good times you were allowed to have are no compensation for the loss."

"It's supposed to be better to have loved and lost than never to have loved at all," Fran said.

"What nonsense." Mrs. Forrest stared at Fran as though she must be mad. She was straight-backed, her chin held high, and it was easy to visualize the military men who had littered the branches of her family tree, the long line of colonels and generals that had ended so abruptly with her son, Daniel. "They try to persuade you that it is, of course, but as usual they're lying to you. I find that so very unfair." She picked up the heavy walking stick which leaned against her chair and balanced it across the arms, gripping it until her knuckles bulged through the thin skin of her hands.

"So you have no wish to forgive," said Fran. Stupid question. The woman was burning up with hate, no more forgiving than Othello had been. Except that whereas Othello had been caught in the grip of unreason, this woman had every reason in the world not to condone the wrong done her.

"Forgive?" The woman stared at her. *"Forgive?"* She squeezed the walking stick again until her wrists trembled with tension. "To forgive such people would be obscene."

"After all this time, perhaps . . ."

"Are you married?" the woman asked harshly.

"No."

"Do you have a child?"

Fran shook her head hard. To have a child she would have to provide herself with a husband first. Over the years, various men had applied for the position. Until Nick, there had never been anyone she could think of as a permanency.

"Then you cannot possibly understand," said the other woman. "You can't know the sense of . . . of snuffed-outness that my son's death brought me. The sense of my own mortality. The desolation of knowing that after me there will be nothing. The line ended, gone." She stopped abruptly. The silence was full of tension. The air seemed to quiver.

Fran felt chilled. There was something terrifying in Mrs. Forrest's intensity. "Your son didn't marry?" she asked.

"No. But there was a girl . . . recently. Someone special, so I understood, though he only mentioned her once. Someone he might have . . ." The sentence fell, uncompleted. After a moment, she continued: "He was very choosy. There had been another person some while before, but I never met her. My son did not often talk about such things with me." Mrs. Forrest slowly lowered her eyelids. It was a reaction Fran had seen before. To women of her generation, sex was as dirty a word as any Anglo-Saxon four-letter monosyllable. "I gathered that the earlier relationship was painful to him. He must have decided not to put himself in the position of being hurt again."

"Were you surprised when he left the Army?" Fran said. She could guess the answer, but people liked to follow known paths. They often led to uncharted patches of soil where she was able to mine journalistic gold. Her eye was caught by a painting of a plump man in a buff-colored frock coat splattered with medals, a plumed hat under his arm. In a family with such a military tradition behind it, Captain Forrest's decision to become a civilian again must have had the destructive force of a hurricane.

"Yes." Again there was the slow covering of the eyes, as though to conceal an unacknowledged hurt. "But if his reasons for resigning were . . . sufficient, it was not for us to question them."

There was another long silence. Then Mrs. Forrest carefully replaced the walking stick against her chair. She sighed. "You asked if I feel bitterness, a need for revenge. The answer is yes. Decidedly yes. I will never forgive, never forget what happened to my son."

Fran's heart lurched. Her chest seemed too small to contain it. Why? She looked around the room, taking in the well-groomed furniture, the flowers, the silver-framed photographs, the solidity of it all. It was as though, for a second, she had been picked up by something unseen, and shaken. As if she was being ordered to pay attention.

"When they told me he was dead," Mrs. Forrest continued, "I felt quite literally as though I had turned to ice. Most of me still feels like that." She leaned toward Fran. "Someone deliberately destroyed him and, in doing that, destroyed me. Would *you* forgive?"

"No," Fran said. "No. How could I?" As she spoke the innocuous words, not meaning them, her mind already on her next question, she suddenly realized that she *did* mean them. If anyone had harmed Nick, she would have felt the same way. She might do so even still, though by now scars had formed over her wounded heart. She had absolutely no doubt that Mrs. Forrest meant exactly what she said, that if she could find them, she would do unto the men who had killed her son exactly as they had done unto him. You don't have to be sincere yourself to recognize sincerity when you see it. Any more than you have to be insane to recognize insanity.

What bothered her was not so much that she had felt that same insanity in herself, as that she knew it would take very little—almost nothing—for her to give in to it, to run screaming out into the world, ready to destroy in the name of vengeance.

Mrs. Forrest stared at her hands, smoothing the shell-pink polish on the nail of her index finger over and over again. "I died when I found that he had died," she said. "When I realized that in spite of all my love, I'd not been able to do for him the things mothers do for their children. Shield them. Protect them. He was gone, snuffed out like a candle. That's what they say, isn't it? That's exactly what it felt like. The helplessness . . . I'd always been used to having what I wanted. Nobody had ever denied me anything. And—and then I didn't even have my husband to help me through the horror." She touched Fran's arm. "That shouldn't be forgotten: whoever took my son from me also took John."

There was a pause. Fran wished herself anywhere else in the world than in this room so full of suffering. Through the open windows she heard the slow sound of a bell drift across the fields. That must be from the convent she had passed on her way here. She considered for a moment the ordered peace of the cloister. *Get thee to a nunnery.* What woman had not at some time felt that the cloistered calm of a convent might be a solution to her problems?

"I wouldn't be human if I didn't want revenge. Such a basic need, don't you think?" Mrs. Forrest continued, the cultured voice remote. "You break my toy, I'll break yours. You kill my son, I'll kill yours. Very clean, very simple. Oh yes, I want revenge. And please, Miss Brett, don't think I mean justice. Justice would simply send those responsible to jail for a few years, if it ever caught them. That's not good enough—not after what they did. I'd like to see them suffer. I'd like to hear them scream as they made my son scream." She brushed a hand across her forehead and turned her head away. "Say all that in your article, if you want to."

"An eye for an eye," Fran murmured. She wanted to touch the other woman's hand, put an arm around her shoulders, offer comfort. There was none she could give. Death was irrevocable. Who could comfort when there was no possibility of change or recovery?

"And a truth for a truth. Except in my son's case, no one ever discovered the truth, did they?" Mrs. Forrest stood. "I'll go and make the coffee, shall I? We could take it outside."

She left the room. Fran could hear the rustle of silk from under her clothes. She walked around the edge of the table, idly wondering for whom the widowed Alicia Forrest now dressed herself in silk underwear. The family photographs stood phalanxed beneath the window. A lady would simply have walked past them; nosy Fran did not.

Yet it was more than curiosity that made her stop. She found herself almost—except it sounded so definite—*commanded* to pause. She picked one of them up and examined it: a much younger Mrs. Forrest in a long skirt sat sideways on grass, a baby on her knee. She picked up another: a snapshot of a man in a dark suit and bowler hat, carrying a briefcase, turning to wave. The husband, probably. She felt again the loneliness of the woman who had been doubly bereaved. She imagined the funeral, Mrs. Forrest walking behind her son's coffin like an automaton, her face yellow under a black pillbox hat. Poignant glimpses came to her: a gray churchyard on top of a cliff, yew trees pitching back and forth in the wind from the sea, a bugle call winding into the dank air, tears on men's cheeks. And the mother, with her son's military greatcoat over her arm, one hand moving convulsively over the khaki cloth as clods of earth dropped into the grave.

Ignoring the nearest photographs, Fran pulled farther out the half-open semicircular drawer in the table. A framed portrait lay on its face. She picked it up and turned it over.

■■

Afterward she would remember the moment as pivotal, the last completed fragment of time before things changed, the final point after which the old life, fragile as an egg, cracked and disintegrated, and painfully gave birth to the new. She stood, the black-and-white print in her hand, seeing it yet incapable of understanding it. The face, expressive under a square-peaked cap, eyes shadowed, leaped out at her, reviving all the doubt and confusion she had tried so hard to bury.

Nick's face.

She couldn't take in the ungraspable facts. However long she stared at it, it would never make any sense. Except that it made too much. Once again she listened to Mrs. Forrest's voice relaying the facts of her son's death. Such ugly facts, they were; such unspeakably unbearably ugly facts. She pushed them away from her. If she thought about them, she would go mad. And strewn in among them, like flowers scattered on mud, were all her memories of Istanbul.

· 6 ·

THE ELEGANT DINING ROOM
moved in and out of focus as Fran tried to find a point on which to fix.
She knew she was in shock. She wanted to scream, but sounds
wouldn't come. She wanted to weep, to vomit, to run, but her body
was numb. Again, she tried to assimilate what the photograph was
telling her. She stared down at it in her hand. Was this some error,
born of her longing for Nick? Had she mistaken an illusory resemblance for a genuine likeness?

But there was no mistake. She knew the face as well as her own:
the fanning sweep of the eyebrows, the deep indentation at one side
of the mouth, the cold gray eyes. It was Nick.

Why was his picture here? What coincidence of time and place
had brought her to this house, to someone who must know him, who
might at last, be able to tell her where he was? And even as she asked
herself the question, the answer—cruel and fantastical—swept over
her. Impossible, unbelievable as it seemed, somehow Nick Marquend
and Mrs. Forrest's son must be one and the same person.

If that was true, then he was dead.

Murdered.

■■

Later, when the violent conclusion had been reached, when life had
settled into its new routines, she was to wonder at the element of
chance involved. If she had not had the idea for the magazine article
. . . if Alicia had not been one of her chosen interviewees . . . if
Daniel had been some other woman's son . . . Later still, though
unwilling to believe it, she nonetheless came to accept that forces
stronger than she could have imagined were at work. And in the end,
of course, she was finally able to see that some sort of justice had been
done.

■■

"My son." Mrs. Forrest watched her from the door. "Daniel."

"What?"

"Captain Daniel Forrest," Mrs. Forrest said. She carried a tray with cups and silver jugs. "That was taken about three years ago." Fran's brief flare of hope that this was nothing more than a photograph of a well-loved family friend died quickly. Some instinct warned her not to tell Mrs. Forrest that she knew her son. Or that she had loved him.

"I'm sure I've met him somewhere," she said carefully. "Only I had the impression he was called Nicholas Marquend."

She saw how Mrs. Forrest's hands clenched around the edge of the tray. Her face changed, paling suddenly, the color draining from her mouth. Did she have a bad heart, or some chronic condition made worse by stress? Would it be best to leave the subject? Not yet, Fran decided. There were still urgent questions she wanted to ask. She followed her hostess into the drawing room, showing nothing of the shock which still churned her stomach. When they were both seated, Mrs. Forrest poured coffee carefully into bone china cups. Her hand shook as she passed one over to her guest.

Fran said, "What did your son do after he resigned his commission?" She was amazed at how calm she sounded. *Your* son. As if Nick was no more to her than a name from a newspaper column.

"He went to France," Mrs. Forrest said. She seemed more composed now. Perhaps she had temporarily shaken the hatred out of her system. "To work with a winegrower. A small family concern called Pierrey et fils."

Fran remembered the deep French voice of Philippe de Pierrey insisting that he knew no one called Nicholas Marquend. Why had he done that? Because the person working for him had been called Daniel Forrest, obviously. "Winegrowing seems an odd follow-on to Military Intelligence," she said.

"What would you recommend as being more suitable, Miss Brett?" asked Mrs. Forrest sharply. "Hiring oneself out as a professional killer, perhaps? Applying for a job as a spy, a cheat, a destroyer of other people's lives and reputations? That's what Intelligence seems to mean these days "

"What made him choose that particular firm in France?"

"The Pierreys are old friends of ours. When my son said he wanted to work out of England for a while, they were glad to give him a job. As I said to you earlier, Daniel had always been interested in the business of winemaking and selling. He even had an idea he might one day set up as a wine merchant." There was a faint tone of disapproval in her voice. Like a whisper, Fran remembered Nick's voice, saying, *God, the strength of maternal ambitions.*

Mrs. Forrest's face suddenly crumpled. "Oh, my boy," she said. "What they did to you." She waited, eyes closed, controlling herself. Then she looked squarely at Fran. "I do want to hurt them, you know, whoever they are. I feel quite vicious about it. I would have no compunction in turning them into the abject, whimpering things they must have turned him into."

"You don't know that they . . ." Fran did not want to hear about it, did not want to be forced into thinking about the circumstances of Nick's death.

"I know," Mrs. Forrest said. "I went and looked at the place where he—where they found him. It looked so ordinary. So . . . *ordinary.*" Tears sheened her eyes. "All I could think of was my son . . . in there, helpless with his murderers"—her voice broke— "knowing he would die, that they'd never let him get out alive, that there was no hope."

Fran reached across the coffee table between them and took her hand. The amethyst ring felt cold against her fingers. "There's no need for you to talk about it." She heard Nick's voice again: *You always knew that if they ever caught you alone, you'd had it.*

Mrs. Forrest shook her head. "No." Her voice was almost a whisper. "In a strange way, it helps."

"You keep referring to 'they,'" Fran said. "Do you have some reason for that?"

Subtle as smoke across a distant landscape, Mrs. Forrest's face changed. "No one on their own could have done what was done to my son. There had to be someone else involved. The phone call was nothing more than the bait needed to lure him away."

She looked out into her garden. Behind oak branches, the sea showed, caught in a cup of West Country hills. It was clear that the peaceful prospect brought her no inner calm. "Kill him, yes. You might almost say they were entitled to do that. He had been a soldier; he might have expected it."

"You think he was killed because of something he knew?"

"I think it's likely. But to torture him. For so long. The cruelty of it. The horror." The big eyes stared at Fran. "He was my son. Oh God. My beloved son." She bent her head again, twisting the ring, then slumped back against the cushions of her armchair. Once more she turned her old-young eyes toward Fran. Something burned behind them like a pilot light. "I could pay to have them hunted down," she said. "I can certainly afford it."

"If the police couldn't find out what happened . . ." said Fran. Like half-set gelatin, she felt her own anger stir inside her, rocking against her heartstrings. Someone must know who had killed Nick— and why. There had to be a reason. It ought to be discoverable.

"Merely finding them wouldn't help. It probably wouldn't be satisfactory." Alicia Forrest stirred against the chintz covers patterned in fading swags of roses. "People like that don't deserve a quick death. I would want to kill them myself. And I don't know if I could manage that."

"I wasn't here when it happened," Fran said, "but you told me earlier that the papers had suggested your son was involved in some way with the sale of classified information. Is it possible they were right?"

"Absolutely not."

"How can you be sure?"

"Because I brought him up myself. I know what I put into that little boy to make him into the man he later became. It would have been quite impossible for him to betray his country."

"If you'll forgive me," Fran said gently, "wouldn't the mothers of Philby or Burgess have said the same?" She did not feel gentle; she felt violent, murderous. Her hands curled involuntary.

"Let's talk about your business and the award," she said, changing the subject. She even managed to smile. "That's why I came down here."

■■

This new information changed everything. Nick had not abandoned her, after all. He had been prevented from returning to Istanbul.

By whom? And why had the police not found out who killed him?

Back in London, she began haunting the newspaper morgues and libraries. In all the cuttings she read, he was referred to as Daniel Forrest. She remembered Sylvia talking of the friend's brother who had known him as Daniel at school. It was a discrepancy she could sort out later, though for the moment it made no sense.

Meanwhile, she read everything she could find about the murder of Captain Daniel Forrest. She was used to digging into other people's existences in order to familiarize herself with them. As always, when researching her subjects, she found herself sucked temporarily out of her own orbit and into theirs. While the summer slowly passed, her own outlines blurred, as though viewed through a Vaseline-covered lens. The people close to Daniel, people whom she still knew only through the printed word, accumulated thickness and solidity. She felt herself trapped in the skeins of lives that were not hers.

Poring over the police reports and newspaper files, she mused on murder. What led up to that most irrevocable and irreparable of acts: the removal of life from its rightful owner?

She had never thought deeply about it before. She had never had to. In the past, the media had presented her with the deed and she had passively accepted it. Now she realized that nothing, particularly no crime of violence, could be seen as isolated. No case was complete in the here and now, but stretched back to a beginning connected to the present by a tangle of causal threads, each of which twined through a life to meet in that single cumulative moment of forceful taking.

Where, she wondered, were the beginnings for Nick—for Daniel, as she must now learn to think of him? Were they in Istanbul? In France? In the quiet country house where he had grown up? In Alicia herself?

At night she dreamed nebulously of blood and sacrifice. Once she dreamed of Daniel. Not of Nick, the dark, handsome man with whom she had fallen so suddenly in love, but of Daniel, the soldier. In the dream, his eyes watched her from under the brim of his peaked hat, his face expressionless yet so mutely, hauntingly pleading that she woke with tears in her eyes. "Yes," she said into the darkness of her bedroom. "Yes, I will, yes." Molly Bloom's famous last words. Yet she knew in the dream that what she was agreeing to was not the act of love. Or, if so, it was love in so distorted a form that it was unrecognizable.

She was overwhelmed by a sudden sense of enormous loss. Her body began to shake. Sobs broke inside her like waves crashing on some distant shore. Since coming back to London, she had not cried. Now the tears came again, as they had in Istanbul, a torrent of grief rushing from her, leaving her dry. When it was over, she thought that she would probably not cry for Nick—for Daniel—again.

Occasionally she dreamed, hideously, of his terrible end. She heard the thud of the hammer that must have pushed the nails into his hands, experienced his terrible helplessness, knowing that the rest of his life was to be short and painful beyond bearing. In this dream there was always a figure, black-robed and without a face, standing above her, like an executioner from the Inquisition. She could see its intently serious expression as the cruel work was done. None of the features was recognizable.

■■

She immersed herself in work. There were two interviews still to complete for the "Winning Women" feature. She had to finish an article on the London Season for British Airways' *High Life* in-flight magazine. A German publication which often commissioned her work had asked her to cover some of the fringier Paris collections. She was writing a travel piece on Istanbul and also doing some research on the Campion exhibition about to begin in Paris. In addition, one of the glossier U.S. magazines wrote to say that after her last article had appeared, their reader response, in the form of letters to the editor, had risen to twice its usual volume. This could not fail to be good news for the magazine's owners, in view of which she had but to name her price and they would be happy to print whatever she wished to write for them. They were particularly interested in women's issues. *Black* women's issues? Black *European* women's issues? Particularly if she could find a glamor slant. Fran could take a hint. She made notes. There was a newly elected MP, the first black woman to take her seat in the House of Commons. There was the female barrister in Switzerland who had just won a spectacular amount of damages against one of the biggest pharmaceutical companies, and a Bradford woman who now had a million-pound turnover a year after starting a cosmetic business from her kitchen. There was also the beautiful French model, Sola, who was currently adorning the covers of half the fashion magazines in Europe, which would slot in nicely with her visit to the autumn collections . . .

■■

Mid-July passed into late July, July into August. August in London was hot. Tourists crowded the public places. Picture postcards arrived from friends vanished on holiday to mountain or jungle, to white Caribbean beaches or the blue seas of southern Europe. Fran read them, hardly able to recall the names they were signed with. For her, the simmering London streets, the heat-hazed parks, boiled with emotions she had never experienced before. Having assimilated the fact that Nick—Daniel—had been forcibly prevented from returning to her, rather than choosing not to, she had been released from the cloud of depression in which she had been floundering since her return to London. Knowing that she had not been rejected, after all, enabled her to look back at the times with him in Istanbul and reperceive them in a sunnier light.

It also gave her something that she was aware she had been lacking. She now had a sense of purpose. Because she knew that, if for no other reason than curiosity, she was going to look further into the horrific murder of Captain Daniel Forrest, even though he was dead and the urgency had gone.

The only logical way to find out what might have happened was to retrace the last months of his life. She wrote notes to herself as thoughts, possibilities, questions, occurred to her, pinning them up on the board above her desk, next to a postcard from Rome. It showed a detail from the Sistine Chapel: God reaching one almighty finger toward Man, His magnificent yet infinitely vulnerable creation.

What she proposed doing would mean a return to Istanbul. She told herself she could handle it, not find it too traumatic. After all, time had passed. Besides, her visit to France would provide a breathing space in which to absorb the idea. And as well as her journalistic assignments, she would be able to visit the people at Pierrey et fils. As far as she could tell, that was where Daniel had been just before he went to Turkey.

She would also have to speak to Alicia Forrest again sometime.

Not sometime—now.

She pulled the telephone toward her and dialed.

Alicia's voice sounded remote, as though she was thinking of other things: peaceful things like meadowsweet, knot gardens, beeswax. "Yes."

"It's Frances Brett."

Silence. Tiny sounds of electronic impulses urged themselves back and forth between London and Devon.

"I interviewed you recently," Fran said. "Do you remember?"

"Perfectly." Another wait. Then: "Are you, by any chance, connected with Tom Brett, the journalist?" Alicia said sharply.

The late journalist. The late, great journalist. "I'm his daughter," Fran said, as evenly as she could.

There was hostility in Mrs. Forrest's voice. "I dislike being used," she said. "You came down here and deliberately used my . . . my grief, and my loss, for some ephemeral purpose of your own. I loathe it, this trading on other people's suffering. Vultures. Jackals. You're all as bad as—"

"I came down to interview you as part of an article, exactly as I explained," Fran said. "I had no idea you were Nick's—Daniel's mother, none at all."

"What did you call him?"

"Nick. Nicholas Marquend. That's what he called himself in Istanbul."

The pause was so long that Fran wondered if Alicia had simply put the receiver down on a table and gone away. The silence stretched between them until Alicia spoke again:

"You're the girl, aren't you?" she said harshly. "The special girl he told me about?" Her breathing was breaking down into little inward gasps, like the aftermath of tears.

"I would like to think so," said Fran. "He was certainly very special to me."

"Why have you rung me?"

"I was wondering if you would send me that photograph of him that you have. The one in the dining room."

"Why?"

"Because *someone* must know what happened. I'd like to have something I could at least show around, in case people recognized him. Incidentally: does the name Nicholas Marquend have some special significance? I noticed your reaction when I was talking to you before—it obviously means something to you."

"They're Daniel's middle names," Alicia said. "Marquend was my maiden name."

"There's more to it, isn't there?"

"I don't know."

"I see." Fran had the feeling that Alicia knew more than she was saying. For the moment, she let it go. "Anyway, I'm not going to let him just die without at least trying to find out the reason. He deserved far more than that."

"Yes, he did."

"And I think I know one or two things about him that perhaps the police don't know."

Alicia let out her breath in a long sigh. "If I were younger, I would join you," she said. "I'll send the photograph—and a couple of other things that might be useful. And, Frances . . ."

"Yes?"

"Would you come down and see me again?"

"I promise."

■■

She bought her plane ticket to Paris. Then found herself dragging her feet, reluctant to do anything further. She ought to be setting up interviews over there, telephoning people, calling her mother. Analyzing her own feelings, she decided she was actually afraid of what she might discover about Daniel's affairs. By conferring on herself the role of investigator, she could be about to release some kind of genie. Everyone knew that it was infinitely easier to get a genie out of a bottle than to put him back into it. And something told her that any genie she released was likely to be malevolent, vicious. Not at all the kind who went around providing handsome dowries for indigent peasant brides and changing humble cots into palaces.

She thought about Nick Marquend and Daniel Forrest. Had anyone else, besides herself, known that Daniel was in Turkey under an assumed name? Why had he chosen to do that, and if she told the police what she knew, would it make any difference to their investigations?

The photograph sent by Alicia arrived. With it was a small red-leather-bound address book.

This was found in his pocket, she wrote, *I imagine the police contacted everyone. . . . Perhaps you could return it sometime. Good luck, my dear.*

Searching through it, Fran found her own parents' address in France, and underneath it, in pencil, her Istanbul telephone number.

For the hundredth time, she looked through the yellow Kodak packet which held her photographs from Turkey. So few of them contained Nick. Usually she had to be content with snapping him while he was asleep or sunbathing. It was almost the only thing that visibly annoyed him: being photographed. She'd have put up with his anger and snapped away nonstop if she'd known how short a time she would have with him. If she had only realized they would not have all the rest of their lives.

Later, she was to realize how innocent she had been. How foolhardy. But at the time, it did not seriously occur to her that there was any danger to herself in what she planned to do.

-- PART -- TWO --

ALEXANDER, SOLA, PHILIPPE

ALEXANDER

• 7 •

PROMPTLY AT ELEVEN, THE DOOR of the boardroom on the twenty-second floor of the Pfluger Building on Sixth Avenue opened. The Director came in. As if they had been rehearsing for weeks, the twelve people seated around the long slab of polished amboyna rose to their feet like well-trained chorus girls. In a spontaneous gesture of admiration, they began clapping and continued to do so until the Director had pulled out the chair left for him halfway along the table and sat down.

He gave a slight bow. His brilliant stare moved around the table, holding each person momentarily in a glance of intimate complicity. He smiled at all and at none, and laid his leather document case on the table. "Thank you," he murmured modestly. "Thank you very much."

He addressed them for a few moments before turning to the man on his right. "Jeff?"

Jeffrey Leeming Pedersen, one of the top officers in Pagnell/ Waterhouse, an investment partnership with head offices on Wall Street and subsidiaries in Los Angeles and London, cleared his throat. He began to work aloud through the sheets of figures which lay in front of him while his colleagues followed in their own copies. Between them, the nine men and three women were worth several billion dollars.

While Pedersen talked, the Director allowed his gaze to drift outward to the panoramic view of Manhattan which lay beyond the windows. The city was alien to him—most places were—but it was essential to the Organization. Like the Stock Exchange or the Chase Manhattan Bank, the people here were as much part of the financial structure of New York as the moneyed network that radiated out from its center to all corners of the globe. Three of those present might almost be said to *be* the Stock Exchange and the Chase Manhattan.

These were father figures to a whole society, earnest people who controlled a large proportion of the nation's visible wealth and felt deeply the responsibilities such a role carried with it. For the most part, they were Old Money. Their ancestors had come to the New World, made fortunes, set up trust funds, established their families in society. Barring disaster, their children and grandchildren were ensured a financially trouble-free future.

They were people who had grown up with money: they respected its power the way they would respect the power of some elemental force like a volcano or a hurricane. Money had meaning for them as an organic entity in itself rather than for what its possession could achieve.

After the initial recruitment, the Director left the monetary affairs of the Organization in the hands of his accountants in each country. Money itself was not what he wanted—he already had more than enough for his own needs—so a visit once or twice a year was all that was needed from him in order to keep the investors happy. He listened to Pedersen's patrician accent listing profits and investments for the past quarter. The accounts the Organization held in banks throughout the world were not as solid as they should have been: he frowned. Something was slightly out of kilter here and he would have to have an intensive session with Jeff later.

He glanced around the table again. The facts and figures being quoted were not what they had expected to hear and his was by no means the only frown. The Director had found that Old Money often possessed a great deal more than bulging share portfolios and a line of credit that could finance a small nation. There were the bubbleheads, of course. But on the whole, Old Money tended to have both brains and education: he anticipated a stormy discussion once Jeff had completed his presentation.

He had snared them by appealing to their dormant sense of adventure rather than their higher instincts. Old Money was often Bored Money. He had offered a vicarious chance to live dangerously. He watched them now without appearing to do so. They looked predictable. The men wore conservative well-cut suits from Brooks Brothers and Saks. The women were expensively dressed and maintained, coiffed and jeweled in a manner which clearly indicated their wealth without in any way diverging from tasteful discretion. None of them looked as if they knew how to sweat. None of them appeared ever to have stepped outside their class or expectation.

With a couple of exceptions, none of them had. Their problem, and the reason why they were here today, was that for none of them did life hold any surprises. Recruiting them had been easy, a simple matter of selecting names from the Forbes 500 list. But income was only the first of many criteria. Once he had made up his short list, he had researched each individual exhaustively.

He smiled at them again. Each one represented a personal triumph; a chase in which his will had finally overcome theirs. Sometimes he almost thought that the pursuit was more exciting than the purpose behind it. Targeting his quarry, stalking it through the ballrooms and salons of high society, netting it in spite of initial suspicion, the exhilaration of finally landing it: these were increasingly what gave him his kicks.

Rain had washed the sky beyond the window to a dirty gray and slicked the tops of nearby buildings into the darkly mottled glisten of a seal riding a wave. He could have been watching a black-and-white movie from the twenties; the jumbo jet moving silently from one side of the view to the other, toward Kennedy, added a futuristic rather than a contemporary note to the scene.

In a moment he would present his own report. The members of the board would listen closely to the list of successes their money had contributed to. When he spoke of future schemes, he knew that he would see the light of admiration in most of their eyes. More than that: affection, even infatuation. But for the moment, he had no time for either, whether given or received. And if he had, it would not be among those present, though he was well aware that all the women and three of the men would have been happy to be very much more than affectionate, given the chance.

Not that he cared anything for admiration. It had come his way in the past too easily for him to value it except as the lubricant with which he smoothed the way for the furtherance of his schemes. He was aware of his own charisma; he had seen its effect often enough to realize its worth. As Pedersen droned on, the Director began to feel bored. The people around him were too acquiescent. They presented him with no challenge. He glanced in turn at the women. Two of them were over sixty; the third was probably ten years younger. No challenge there, either. Sexually, he had nothing against older women, but it was type that he looked for. None of these was the right one. If he were that way inclined, the men were more promising: two of the nine were slim and dark, but he knew that one of them was recently married and the second living with a partner who had already developed full-blown AIDS.

Keeping his eye on the smoke trail behind a jet that was heading west, he reflected that while he had no fear of death, he hoped that when it came, whatever gods there were would see to it that his was quick. He had watched too many of the other kind, too many slow extinctions, made more agonizing for the victim by the knowledge that there was no hope of a last-minute reprieve.

They were all looking at him now. Pedersen had completed his report. He had not paid as much attention as he might; it came to him now that it had been less satisfactory than the last time he was here. Funds had been diverted to projects which had failed to produce the required return; there had been some unaccounted-for drains on resources. He should have listened more closely; he had always preferred to leave the financial aspects to the money men, knowing that his own talents lay elsewhere.

Looking around at faces which reflected the figures they had just been hearing, the Director smiled again. Deliberately he notched up the warmth of his personality, bathing them in it. He caught and held the gaze of each in turn, knowing how unsettling they found the color of his eyes, a silvery blue which was at odds with his complexion and which they were never absolutely certain was natural. He slowly removed his speech from his document case, taking his time, keeping them locked into himself by the sheer force of his presence.

Power. The ability to manipulate. They gave him a pleasure far more intense than money ever could. More intense than sex, or even love. Most loves, that is.

He pushed back his chair and rose to his feet. Speaking from a position of height increased the sense among them of his apartness, his superiority. That was what they wanted, these bored rich people: someone they could believe in. A new Messiah. Him.

"Ladies and gentlemen," he began. "Since we last met together . . ."

Standing, he noticed something he had failed to see before. In a corner made darker by the right angles of the dark wood paneling, it was almost invisible. But to the Director, the details were not important. He could have drawn it in his sleep.

There were only five of them in existence. What strange quirk of fate had seen to it that there should be one here, confronting him, when there were so many other places in the world for it to be? Was there some kind of meaning, some kind of portent, to be attached to its presence in this room today?

His delivery faltered. When his audience glanced up at him, surprised, he paused, shook his head self-deprecatingly, smiled slightly. Bending over the silver tray in front of him, he poured sparkling mineral water into a glass, added a lemon wedge, lifted the lid of an ice bucket and removed two ice cubes which he dropped carefully into the glass. His movements were leisurely. He used the ritual to calm himself, consciously making time for his breathing rate to drop.

He did not look again at the piece of sculpture on its polished marble column. It had not been there last time he was here; next time he would be prepared, or Pedersen would have moved it out to his home in Westchester County. Like many of those around the table, Pedersen was a patron of the arts. He collected sculpture. It was not really surprising that sooner or later he would have acquired a Hugo Campion.

The Director began speaking again, his voice flowing smoothly on, pausing here and there for well-timed laughs, rising for extra emphasis, dropping to a passionate request for further support for the Organization during the coming year. Only the youngest of the three women was aware that he was less controlled than he seemed to be. Something was bothering him. Did that, she wondered, make him more, or less, dangerous?

But even she was not privy to the turmoil inside the Director's head. The bronze on its plinth brought back so many memories that he would rather be without . . .

■■

He was always glad when Leyla, tiring of wherever they happened to be, decided it was time to return to Paris. The house in Kent, like the rest of England, was too cold. The flat in Istanbul was too modern; even as a very young child, he was offended by the contrast between the historic city and the stark gleam of black calfskin and smoked glass. It was as if in furnishing it, Leyla was willfully mocking the traditions from which she sprang, deliberately thumbing her nose at someone. When he was a man, he told himself, he would own a house in Istanbul, a proper house, furnished with suitable things, like his father's. He always loved going there: it was gracious, full of objects that brought the past into the present and gave it reality. Leyla did not often allow him to visit his father.

Paris sat somewhere in between Turkey and England. Although it seemed to rain there more than anywhere he had ever been, it was a containable city. It kept its hand on the traditions of the past, yet happily embraced the new. Even in the fashionable part where he and Leyla lived—on the Ile St. Louis, along with high-powered childless couples and fashion models and people in the media—there were still plenty of old inhabitants shuffling in and out of their houses, or sitting in the little park at one end of the island with their poverty-marked faces lifted to the sun.

Later, at school in England, when he listened to the other boys ask their Father in Heaven to give them their daily bread, it was always those old people that he saw, tottering back from the *boulangerie* in their bedroom slippers with the day's supply of *baguettes* under their arms.

■■

He leaned over the narrow balcony of the *appartement*, fingers gripping the decorative wrought-iron swags of the rail. There was scarcely room for the pigeons out there, let alone for a boy. How terrible it would be if the whole fragile structure broke away from the front of the building and plunged into the street, carrying him with it. Or if he leaned over too far and overbalanced, to go tumbling down to the pavement like a doll, his head smashing open against the curb to spill his brains out into the gutter. Would there be time for him to scream? On the television, the bad guys who fell from great heights usually gave a long, wailing shriek before the final unheard thud of their bodies hitting the ground. He thought that probably it would not be like that; the force of falling would send so much air rushing into his lungs that he would drop in silence, unable to make a sound.

He sniffed the compound of river water and coffee and gasoline fumes overlaid with strong French cigarettes and a tang of excrement that made up the scents of Paris for him. There were others, of course. Cooking smells from the restaurants. Soot in the métro, though Leyla said he imagined it because the trains were all electric now. Flowers in the market on the Left Bank. Old stone and incense in Notre Dame, and the curious extra ingredient which he would much later analyze as the distillation of need, given off by those who had come to ask something from God.

The angles of Leyla's shoulder blades were impatient under her little cotton blouse with the white embroidery down the front. That meant she would be sharp with him. He held tighter to the thick iron wreaths. Perhaps she would nip him, seizing the tiniest piece of his arm between her long nails and pinching until he bit his lip and tears rose in his eyes. Or she would grab his hand and drag him for hours along the boulevards, in and out of the *grands magasins*, dashing through the Louvre or the Musée de Cluny, always going faster than his nine-year-old legs could manage so that he streamed along behind her like the tail of a comet. Or maybe she would pull his hair, jerking it cruelly just when he least expected it, when he was off guard, looking at one of his books or through a window or, if they were outside, at the river or the way people crossed the road at busy intersections, weaving in and out of each other like an intricate braid.

Across the way he could see the man who lived in the apartment opposite theirs; standing behind the floor-length drapes, he was watching Alexander as he fitted a cigarette into a long green holder. He often stood there, his hair standing about his head like a halo; Alexander suspected he did not know he could be seen. Something about him, a sense, perhaps, of witness, somehow reassured.

She came to the open windows and stood behind him. He tried not to tense. Suppose she threw him over the balcony rail. He knew she was quite capable of it. Surreptitiously he moved a foot forward and lodged it between two leafy swirls. That might save him, if she should take it into her head to push him.

"We're going to an exhibition," she told him. Her face had the shiny look it wore when she was disturbed about something, as though it had been brushed with a glaze, like one of the *tartes aux pommes* in the patisserie across the street. He was frightened when she looked like that: it meant she was at her most destructive. In this mood, he had several times seen her take something from one of the tables or the cabinets and deliberately smash it on the floor. He remonstrated with her once, saying the things belonged to his father, not to her; she had put her small hands around his throat and squeezed until he lost consciousness.

Sometimes he felt as if he had spent all his life at exhibitions, standing beside Leyla, no more than her shadow, listening while people paid her elaborate compliments, watching when they looked at her as though she were a sorbet they wanted to dip a silver spoon into. They never noticed him; occasionally he wondered if he was invisible. They would ask her out, want to take her to expensive theaters or for cruises on yachts, but she always refused. Afterward, she would fling herself about whichever house they were in at the time, pounding the cushions, crying that she was bored to death. If he asked her why, in that case, she did not go out with those who asked her, she would sometimes look at him from under her eyelids and show her white teeth. "Because they want me to," she would say. Because he was a child, not yet analytical, there had seemed nothing strange about her response.

At other times she would grind her jaws together, saying they were all the same, all too old, all sheep, all dull, saying that she longed for someone different, someone out of the ordinary, someone with spirit. "Besides, they are so coarse," she told him. "So bristly. I hate the way their beards push through their skin." She touched his soft cheeks, stroking them, running her hands over his face. "Not a bit like you."

"An exhibition?" he said now. "What of?"

"Sculpture," she said. "Bronzes, mostly. But some wood, some marble."

"Who is it?"

"An Englishman," she said carelessly. "Hugo Campion. I've never heard of him."

"I have," he said. "I read about him in a newspaper. He's supposed to be very good."

She laughed. "Little wiseacre."

■■

If only he had realized. Given some warning, he might somehow have been able to stop it. Might have pretended to be sick or something, clung to his bed with his eyelids drooping so that she would put one of her small hands on his forehead and murmur "Poor little boy," and stay at home.

Not that he could have bet on it. The chances were that she would simply have locked him into the *appartement* and gone off without him. And once she and Hugo Campion had met, it was too late. He acknowledged that right from the start. He'd been there, hadn't he? He had seen that explosive joining of glances: hers dark and almond-shaped, Hugo's palely blue, round, deeply intense in his red English face. It was he who had been holding Leyla's hand at the time, wasn't it? He who felt the sudden force thud through her slight body. She had gripped his fingers until he almost shrieked as Hugo came up to her, took her arm, said he wanted to sculpt her, and would tomorrow be all right for him to begin?

And perhaps he was the only one to understand how it had happened, how Leyla had stopped in front of a bronze, had reached out to stroke the strong, smooth shape, had nodded to herself as she found the sculptor's biographical notes in the front of the catalogue and then looked around the gallery until she found him. Afterward, when he could be more dispassionate about it, he decided that having found her target, she must have brought Hugo to her side by sheer willpower.

Hugo looked much more like a farmer than a sculptor. His hands were big, the fingers broad and thick at the tip. There was always a suggestion about him of cowpats narrowly avoided, of udders recently pulled. His nails were seldom clean. Watching them on Leyla's body— on her arm, her shoulder, or cupped around the bone of her jaw—he wondered that she did not mind. She was usually so fastidious.

The rest of that summer seemed to be spent in Hugo's rented studio near Montmartre. It was very like the set in a production of *La Bohème* that he and Leyla had seen in Rome once: big and empty, with a large north window which flooded the room with cold blue light. While Leyla posed, he would fill in the waiting time by reading enormously. The H. G. Wells science fiction stories, a lot of Agatha Christie, *Great Expectations* by Charles Dickens, most of the Leslie

Charteris books. They were all in English because Hugo spoke no French. He once told them that at school he had been considered really thick. Putting her tiny hands on either side of his body, Leyla told him that he was *still* thick, thick like a hippopotamus.

Hugo loved that. Larger than life, he roared and sang through those weeks, his shirt off, sweat rolling down the ginger-yellow hair on his broad chest as his thick fingers handled the clay. He was pink all over, where he was not red, as though he had too much blood in his body and it had seeped out to stain his skin. And for hours Leyla stood before him, a long stretch of silk chiffon winding down her body between her almost nonexistent breasts and around the back of her buttocks, to reappear across her thighs. It left her virtually naked.

He knew Hugo wanted her. He watched covertly the way Hugo's gaze was drawn to the place between her legs. He saw how Hugo's loose canvas trousers bulged sometimes, and how his eyes would flick across to where he himself was sitting with his book and maybe a can of Coke or Fanta. Hugo wished him absent; sometimes he himself felt like that about Leyla. She was very beautiful, he knew that. Not like a woman, though. More like a little girl, not much older than he was himself. She wore tiny undergarments, and dresses which seemed no bigger than a doll's when she took them off and hung them up in her closet. If she was in a good mood, she would let him sit on the edge of the bath while she lay back in the foam from one of the bubble-bath preparations she used. He had seen the pinkness of the place between her legs because sometimes she told him to dry her after the bath. Nobody had ever explained why, but he knew it was a special place, both for her and for him. Sometimes she even told him to touch her there. It felt soft and floppy, rather like he did when he was not stiff. Leyla told him to move his fingers about and feel the place; she said it was important for him to know about women. She wanted him to be a good husband, she said—not like his father had been. She wanted him to love women: she said that most men did not. They might say they did, but what they really meant was that they wanted to fuck them. He would be much happier when he was grown, she told him, if he liked the women he fucked. It was a funny word, and he was never quite sure what it meant, though he could tell it was something impor-tant. When he asked her once, she had laughed and said she would show him one day, but he would have to wait until he was a *little* bigger.

Although Hugo wished he was not there, he knew that Leyla wanted him to be. He made it safe for her to flirt and move her eyes about and smile at Hugo. He guessed that Hugo wanted to fuck Leyla but with him there, Hugo could not do so, whereas if he was not, she might have to, even if she did not wish to.

When the piece was finished, and cast, Hugo gave a party. Lots of people came to the studio and smoked the heady French cigarettes that he loved to smell. They drank a lot of wine, except for Hugo, who drank Scotch whisky. There were dishes of things Leyla told him to hand around among the guests. The bronze stood in the middle of the room, under a cloth.

Hugo gave a little speech. "This is probably the best thing I've ever done," he said. His pale blue gaze found Leyla, who was wearing a very short dress of floaty pink material. "But I've never before had a model like this to work from. She has inspired me."

There were dealers in the room; Leyla had told him about them. One was from Rome, three from New York; there was a Frenchman and two Englishmen. Everyone leaned forward as Hugo took one corner of the cloth between thumb and finger. The Frenchman's mouth was wet. "Ladies and gentlemen, I ask you to raise your glasses to— Leyla!" Hugo shouted. He whipped the cover off and showed them what lay underneath.

Not a woman so much as the suggestion of one, yet unmistakably Leyla. Curves, smoothness, long lines flowing from one plane to another. It made you want to touch it. It made you need to experience it. It was very simple and entirely beautiful. Looking at it, and then at the way Leyla stared at Hugo, he felt the premonition of disaster.

■■

Leyla sent him to Istanbul to stay with his father. He enjoyed that. There were always women about in his father's house who spoiled him, who deferred to him because he was a man. In the evenings, when his father came back from work, the two of them would sit together and talk about things while the women came in and out with food. Afterward they brought scented water in a bowl and dried his hands for him on a thick towel.

His father took him sailing for a week, in and out of the islands. In the afternoons, the yacht was anchored near land and they would go ashore to eat. A table would have been set up under the pine trees and food prepared for them by one of the servants, who had come by car. There would be grilled sardines and fruit and thin strips of lamb basted with a spicy sauce and aubergines baked with tomatoes. It was the kind of food he loved, the kind that Leyla would never let him eat. The hot resin smell of the trees suffused those afternoons, mingling with the smoke from the grill and the tang of the sea. His father talked to him a lot—about books he had read, about the heyday of the Ottoman Empire, about the things a man was able to do if he had money, about a man's duty to help those weaker than himself, to look after his womenfolk. He never talked about Leyla.

When he went back to Paris, he found that Hugo Campion was living in the *appartement*. He slept in the same bed as Leyla, now. He was too big for the place, always knocking into tables and leaning back in the delicate chairs until the backs cracked. He was too loud. The *appartement* was no longer peaceful. Always it seemed full of the noise of Hugo, the clodhopping feel of him. Leyla did not seem to mind Hugo's bristles, which often went unshaven for two or three days. He found little round pellets of clay ground into the precious oriental rugs, which had dropped from the folds of Hugo's clothes or the soles of his boots. Hoping obscurely to undermine the interloper, he showed them to Leyla, but either she just laughed or else she pinched him in the old vicious way and called him a sneak.

The rest of the time she ignored him. He missed her ill-treatment. At least she had noticed him then. Now she treated him as her admirers used to: as though he were invisible. She was different. She laughed. She told him Hugo was the son of an English baronet and related in some complicated way to royalty. He was not very interested. In a corner of the salon stood the *Leyla* bronze; every time he passed it, he was reminded of the change Hugo Campion had brought to their lives.

He waited for something cataclysmic to happen.

■■

Toward the end of August, Leyla told him he was to go away to England. Hugo had arranged for him to go to his old school but before that he must attend something called a prep school.

"Why must I?" he asked.

"I don't know," she said impatiently. "It's what boys do."

"English boys."

"Yes."

"But I am not English."

"You will be soon." She stared at him. She had on her varnished look. He knew he was annoying her.

"How can I be English?" he said. "I do not wish to be English."

She smiled; her teeth were sharp. "Hugo is going to adopt you. He will be your father. We are going to live in England, with Hugo."

He sensed abysses into which it would be all too easy to plunge. He was aware of an absence of bridges, of rope ladders, of twisting vines up which, once fallen, he might painfully climb again to the top. Tears came into his eyes and rolled down his cheeks. "I don't want to," he said.

Behind her, the highlights on the bronze statue shifted as Hugo came into the room, intercepting the lamplight, casting his big shadow across the two of them.

"Have you told him yet?" he said.

"Not quite."

Hugo turned to him. "What's this?" he said. He was in his working clothes: a dark red smock over a thick sweater, clay-spattered espadrilles, corduroy trousers. He came nearer. "You're not crying, are you?" With an obvious effort, he softened the natural loudness of his voice. "That won't go down too well at school, you know. Boys don't cry."

"Yes, they do," he said. "I'm crying and I'm a boy."

"*English* boys don't cry."

"I'm not an English boy," he said. He felt the helplessness of being a child, his impotence against the vast strength of the adults who had charge of his life.

"It's probably best . . ." Hugo said, squatting down close to him so that his chest seemed to fill the world. "I mean, if you take my name. You don't want to be different from the others, do you?"

He stared. Up until now, he had thought that difference from others, uniqueness, was a quality to be prized. Was this large Englishman telling him he was wrong? "Yes, I do," he said. He looked at Leyla. "Leyla doesn't want me to be a sheep. She doesn't like sheep."

Hugo laughed hugely. "Who's talking about sheep? I'm just trying to point out that the average public school boy is a conservative little reactionary. Give him something strange and he'll tear it to bits if he can. It's like birds: aren't they supposed to peck to death the ones who aren't the same as the rest of them?"

"Darling, I know nothing whatsoever about birds," Leyla said. She opened her almond eyes at Hugo and he got up and went over to stand behind her. He put his big hand on her shoulder and she touched it with one of her own small ones. Behind them, the statue seemed to smile, mocking him and his helplessness. It occurred to him that its place in the flat was more assured, rested on more solidity than his own. It seemed the ugliest thing he had ever seen.

"You'll be able to play games," Hugo said. "Rugger, cricket—things like that. Instead of skulking around the flat, you'll be out in the open air. You'll enjoy it."

"What is rugger?"

"It's a game with a ball. An oval ball. You run with it, up and down. Kick it." Hugo stopped, helpless to explain rugby football to this small foreigner.

The only games he had ever played were checkers and, later, chess. He could not conceive of rugger, but he knew he would hate it. Running around with a ball, falling over: it was not his idea of fun. He and Leyla had skiied at Gstaad one year, but luckily she had hated it even more than he had, and they had gone back to Istanbul early.

He was terrified at the thought of the new school. They were going to send him away to a foreign country, among people who might, in some way, kill him for being different. He dreamed that night of monstrous beaks snapping, nipping at the flesh of his arms, tearing at him with jagged bills until he bled to death. He woke to hear Hugo's rumbling voice. He was laughing, the noise filling the bedroom where Leyla slept, and spilling out into the passage like a cloud of black smoke.

School. Games. England. Above all, an absence of Leyla. Under the covers, he wept bitterly.

· 8 ·

TO THE LEFT, THE TOWER OF BIG
Ben and, beyond it, the dome of St. Paul's dominated the oyster-pink
sky of early dusk. The windows of Lambeth Palace across the river
pricked into light as the October evening came down on London. In a
room overlooking the Embankment, a number of people waited at a
rectangular table of polished mahogany, talking quietly to each other.
The conversations covered the theater, music, the latest exhibition at
the Royal Academy, the proposed addition to the National Gallery.
No one mentioned the recent Stock Exchange scandal, though two of
those present were intimately concerned, nor the massive hike in the
cost of electricity which would considerably affect the income of the
three of them who owned stately homes. Although these were influential people, cultured, concerned, and wealthy, only four of them approached anything like the kinds of incomes their counterparts in
New York could command.

The heavy oak door opened and the Director came in. He paused
just inside the room, until they had all turned toward him, then
moved toward the empty chair set halfway down one side of the table,
welcoming each one individually. They returned his greetings in a
manner whose restraint gave an ironic twist to his acknowledging
smiles.

They had behaved exactly as he expected them to. Naturally they
did not, unlike their American colleagues, rise to their feet. To have
done so would be most un-English. There was also the fact that three
quarters of them disapproved of or even outright despised him on a
personal level. In the small, class-ridden world of English society, his
family history had been a matter of discussion for more than twenty
years. They or their sons had been at the same schools or university as
he; some of their daughters had fallen in and then—to the relief of
their parents—out of love with him. Nor did they see any reason to

rise for someone who was considerably less well off than they were, and not even English, to boot.

He waited while they settled back into their chairs. Of all his various trophy rooms, this one gave him the most satisfaction, representing as it did the results of his most careful maneuvers. Not one of these people had been easy to net: each had taken months of careful planning to beguile into the Organization. So he was particularly perturbed to feel among them an undercurrent of alarm, a sense of all not being well. He glanced at Jeremy Sutton, wondering what was wrong, but the accountant failed, as always, to meet his eyes.

"Thank you," he said. He spoke for a while in a firm, well-modulated voice. Deliberately, he talked for longer than was necessary, giving them the full impact of his impeccably upper-class accent, hoping to calm the flutters of disquiet. Two days ago, in New York, he had felt the same unease among the board members there: clearly something was going badly wrong—but he was not going to let them see his own anxiety. Finally he turned his clear blue gaze to the man on his left. "Jeremy, perhaps you would like to give us your breakdown on the quarterly figures."

Jeremy Sutton cleared his throat. Youngish, plumpish, he shuffled his papers about, avoiding the Director's eye. He always seemed ill at ease when the two of them were together, despite the fact that he was a respected figure in the City, that his position as an accountant with his family's merchant banking firm was impregnable, that his wife was the second daughter of a fecund peer, and his two sons were already attending the same prep school as their father—and the Director— with Eton to follow. It pleased the Director to see Sutton behave like a bumbling schoolboy, as though there were some unfinished business between them, some wrong to be righted which he had not yet fully understood. Now, he tapped together the papers he held between his hands and began to review the Organization's quarterly finances for the benefit of his colleagues. No one would have guessed from his uneasy comportment that he was much sought after as a guest speaker at City functions, as much for his wit as for his elegant concisions.

As he spoke, the Director watched a flock of seagulls rise suddenly from the cold river and sweep past the windows. Their wings were tipped with gold as they skimmed toward Ludgate Hill. The clouds piling in from the west were tinged with the bonfire glow of a myriad neon streetlights, and, above them, a single star blinked in the darker evening sky. He heard Sutton stumble over a simple sentence, clear his throat, start again.

As Sutton's voice faltered a second time, the Director felt a surge of power run through him like an electrical charge. Whatever was wrong—it was clearly something to do with the financial rather than the organizational side of things—he knew he could put it right. Or see that Jeremy did. Certainly whatever it was must be smoothed over. And no one was better at that than himself. Manipulation: that was what it was all about. Bending others to his will was heady stuff. Particularly where Sutton was concerned. The man was uncomfortable, thrown off balance, and could not work out why. Perhaps he would have to get rid of Sutton, make a public example of him. Nothing would give him more satisfaction. The Director had changed considerably in the twenty or so years since he and Sutton had been schoolboys together. Sutton had forgotten those days; he knew that he himself never would.

■■

The wood crackled as a thin blue flame crept like a mouse around the huge pile of timber, stopping here and there as though trying to decide where to start nibbling. They watched in silence, openmouthed, breath hanging in front of their faces, solid in the frosty air. Above their heads was the guy, arms outstretched, crucified on a couple of two-by-fours provided by the caretaker. It was dressed in an old jacket of the Headmaster's, with one of his unmistakably home-knitted scarves around its neck. A crude facsimile of his features had been produced by one of the arty boys in the top form. ("Ha, ha, Beamish. Most amusing . . ." the Head had said, smiling thinly as he passed through the front hall, as though it had never happened before, as though the whole school didn't know that his wife kept a supply of old jackets bought at jumble sales which were donated with apparent reluctance from his wardrobe for just this occasion every year.) A quantity of soft white cotton sprouted from beneath a tweed cap similar to the one the Head wore occasionally while gardening after lunch on Sundays. The likeness achieved, though recognizable was, as the Head dryly pointed out, considerably short of amazing.

The flame darted upward, catching at some dried leaves still attached to a branch of beech. There was plenty of wood this year: the groundsmen were still clearing up after the autumn's big storms. For a moment the leaves glowed, stretched themselves as though on the rack, then fell back into ash. The little flame burrowed farther into the bonfire, looking for sustenance, searching for the paraffin that the Art Master had sprinkled liberally on it just before school supper.

The boys were beginning to grumble.

"Not as good as last year, sir."

"I reckon it's not going to catch light at all."

"Hope the fireworks are better than this."

"Bit of a washout, isn't it, sir?"

Suddenly, flame and paraffin met. There was a small whoosh of sound at the heart of the pile, and the interior began to catch, sending blue flames leaping up inside its center toward the tattered trousers of the guy. The boys began to cheer. So did the Art Master. Campion realized that for a moment the man must have had visions of the whole thing turning into a complete fiasco, the bonfire failing to light, the boys turning on him and the Old Man hauling him onto the carpet to explain why he hadn't done a better job, especially when he'd spent the past three weeks telling everyone how expert he was at fire lighting.

The rising flames sucked at the damp wood, flaring when they found the paraffin, grabbing at cardboard and bits of old furniture that had been tossed onto the pile over the past few weeks. The Art Master began to move around the perimeter, distributing sparklers and admonishments.

"All right, Riseborough; you know perfectly well you're only allowed two."

"Woodrow, you've got three there; give one of them to Macdonald."

"Don't be more of a fool than necessary, Jackson, you're a bit old for that kind of behavior."

The boys chattered and pushed each other about. At the edge of the crowd, Campion stood by himself. He knew that his solitude worried the masters; only the other day, the Chaplain had called him in and talked to him frankly about making friends and learning to get on with the others ("School is a rehearsal for life, Campion . . ."). Nobody seemed to realize that he *preferred* to be alone. He had no need of other people—particularly not of these boys—to reinforce his version of himself. *Shows a disconcerting degree of self-possession for an eleven-year-old,* the Head had written on his last fortnightly report. Leyla had probably crumpled it up and thrown it into the fire.

The Art Master came by. "Here you are, Campion," he said. "Don't set yourself on fire, for God's sake." He moved on with his box of sparklers to the next noisy group.

Campion held tightly to the two he had been given. In a minute a member of staff would come around with matches to light them, and they would spit and spark, spewing incandescence as the boys twirled them round and round, drawing spiral patterns of brightness on the blank air. Campion wished someone would invent a longer-lasting sparkler. No sooner had the snowflakes of white fire erupted into the darkness than they were gone. That was why he preferred the steadier glow of the bonfire. It was well alight now, the flames hot and red, the wood roaring as it was consumed, sparks leaping into the black sky above. Smoke swirled and dipped. The heat advanced toward him like a wall. The other boys began stepping back, especially when the rising wind tossed the smoke this way and that, snatching it out of the faces on one side of the fire to sling it back into those on the other. Each time it did so, the boys made the most of it, coughing themselves hoarse and pretending to suffocate. One of them was staggering about right now, clutching histrionically at his throat before falling to the muddy ground and going into exaggerated spasms of agony.

"Sir! Sir!" the boys called. "Jackson's choking to death, sir."

"Shall I get Matron, sir?"

"Will his parents sue the school if he dies, sir?"

Although they were the big boys, the ones who would be sitting the entrance exams for their public schools next term, they seemed incredibly juvenile to Campion. Half of them weren't even looking at the fire. Some were trying to stick lighted sparklers down each other's collars. Several were lobbing surreptitious jumping jacks in the direction of the Headmaster's daughters and a couple of the female domestic staff who were clustered to one side. Campion despised them. No true man would try to frighten women in such a way. He watched with contempt as the Chaplain dragged Jackson to his feet and thumped him on the back, telling him not to be such a silly little idiot.

The wind pushed at the fire and sent the whole thing leaning toward Campion. Heat scorched his face. Sparks landed on the sleeves of his regulation navy-blue anorak, and he brushed at them absently, narrowing his eyes to peer directly into the glowing heart of the bonfire. It was like a different world in there: soft crumblings of burning ash, tumbles of fiery heat-whitened wood, red-hot edifices of branch and twig collapsing into each other with little spurts of flame. Was hell like this? He thought of the phoenix, rising again out of its own ashes, of salamanders, of steel swords thrust into the tempering flame, of the glassmakers in Venice where he and Leyla had watched a molten drop of glass slowly blown into crystal. Fire was the very soul of life, he told himself. He hated it here: the cold, the damp. In Paris it rained even more than in England, but it never seemed as wet. Beneath his Wellington boots there were soggy wet leaves, and under them, the cold muddy grass at the edge of the games pitch. Ahead of him stretched years of schooling, punctuated with the torture of rugby. *Football then was fighting sorrow for the young man's soul—Mr. Matthews, the man who taught English, had read that to the class last week with some sardonic comments about the souls of the particular young men in front of him at the time. The other boys had found it amusing. Campion had not. It said exactly what he felt.*

Two of the thirteen-year-olds strolled past. He hoped they wouldn't stop. He didn't like either of them much, though Forrest, the Head Boy, was very popular with the younger boys.

"*You're a new bug, aren't you?*" *the Head Boy asked.*

"*Yes.*"

"*Come from abroad, don't you?*"

"*Yes.*"

"*Do you know what this is all about?*"

"*Uh—yes.*" *Campion wondered why he should ask. Everyone knew about the man who had tried to blow up the English Parliament.*

"*What then?*" *the other boy—Sutton—asked rudely.*

"*Guy Fawkes.*"

"*Oh.*" *Sutton turned to the Head Boy with an overdone look of surprise.*

"*What's wrong?*" Campion asked. He decided he loathed all boys, even though he was one himself, but particularly Sutton. When he was thirteen, he would be a lot more mature than any of these idiots.

In fact, he already was. He knew he was looking disdainful. He also knew that was why people like Sutton disliked him.

"Oh, nothing, nothing." Sutton laughed in a hateful sort of way.

Campion started to turn away. He wasn't going to play their stupid childish games.

"It's just," Sutton said, "we didn't think you'd bother to turn out for an occasion like this." He waved a gloved hand around to indicate the invisible woods beyond the football pitches, the Victorian Gothic of the school buildings crouched in the darkness, the other boys.

Campion could feel rage begin to boil somewhere in his chest. He knew already what Sutton was going to say. He wished he were a dog or, better still, a wolf. He would leap at Sutton, sink his fangs into him, tear out his throat. He could feel the easy soar from the ground, the muscles bunching together, his haunches tight, his tail down as he bared his teeth ready for the snarling grab. How surprised Sutton would be, before he started howling and sobbing for mercy.

"Well," said Sutton. "I mean, you're not, are you?"

"Not what?"

Sutton looked quickly over his shoulder to make sure the Head Master wasn't in earshot. "Not English, you stupid black cretin," he said quietly.

"Come on, Jem," Forrest said uneasily. In a school with an increasing number of boys from what the staff called developing countries, racist comments were definitely not acceptable. Besides, although he was not sure why, he felt vaguely sorry for the new boy who had not yet made any friends. He could remember all too well his own first term at school.

Campion's anger subsided abruptly, as though someone had turned the gas down to simmer. One of these days he thought he might use his anger to do something really spectacular. Meanwhile, there was more to be gained from apparent indifference. For the moment, he had to decide whether to refute Sutton's charge or coolly agree with it. Which would work best? He could try using reason, pointing out that while *black* might be a useful adjective to describe, say, Wako Major and, even more so, Wako Minor, whose mother came from a darker-skinned tribe, it was hardly suitable for someone like himself. Or he could remind Sutton that for centuries his ancestors on both mother's and father's side had been lawmakers and politicians in the powerful Ottoman Empire. He decided to keep quiet and smile his most superior smile. For some reason, that always irritated them more than anything else.

Sutton's face darkened. "Did you hear me, dickhead?"

"Yes, thank you, Sutton. I say, Sutton."

"What?"

"May I borrow your deodorant?"

Forrest tried not to grin, even though Sutton was his friend. Everyone knew how easy it was to make him rise to the bait about the way he stank, especially after games. Something to do with his hormones, Matron said. On the other hand, new bugs couldn't go around cheeking prefects like that.

"Shut up, Campion," he said coldly.

"Yeah," Sutton said. "Stupid wog bastard."

"I'm sorry," said Campion politely. "What did you say?"

"You heard, wog."

Campion gave his arrogant smile again. He turned back to the fire, apparently unconcerned. But the pleasure had gone. Wog? Was he a wog, whatever that meant? And did it matter? It was not a word he had heard before, but there was no need for it to be explained: he could tell that it reinforced the differences between himself and the likes of Forrest or Sutton. For the first time, he realized that while he relished his own apartness from the herd, he did so because he himself chose to be separate. Being excluded was quite different. He whispered his name to himself. His *real* name.

The remains of the guy perched in the middle of the flames, its blackened arms outstretched on its blazing cross.

■■

Leyla had promised to take him back to Paris for the half-term holiday. He had not realized just how much he had been looking forward to it until she told him carelessly that they would not be going, after all.

"Why not?" He was in bed. He held tightly to the sheets which covered him. He would not let her see how his heart plunged. Being here, in this English place, surrounded by possessions that were not theirs, he felt even more alien than at school.

"I forgot about it," she said.

"We could still go, now I've reminded you."

"I don't want to." She sat down on the edge of his bed and touched her stomach. "Traveling makes me feel sick."

"It never used to."

"Well, it does now."

"Why?"

"Because I'm pregnant, if you really want to know." She stood up and put her hands on her tiny waist. "God, how I hate it all: getting fat and ugly, and all the pain, and then the ghastly business with the milk." She turned a cold stare on him. "Do you know something?"

Slowly he shook his head. "What?"

"I loathe children."

Methodically he worked through the implications of what she had said. Then he asked, "Do you mean babies?"

She spoke through her teeth. "I mean all bloody children. But especially babies."

"Does that mean you hate *me*?" She had never come out and said so before. He rather wished she would; at least he might then know where he stood.

Perhaps something in his face struck her. She shook her head and tried to laugh. "Of course not you, stupid one."

He did not believe her. "When is this baby due?"

"About five and a half months from now." Getting up, she walked across the room. She lifted a china ornament of a woolly sheep with a tree branching out over its back and put it down again deliberately hard, as though she hoped it might break. He thought it was probably very valuable. "Bloody Hugo. If he hadn't got drunk and careless, this wouldn't have happened."

"Hugo is the father of your baby?" he asked politely.

She whirled, her short skirts flying out. She had changed her hair since he last saw her: it hung around her face in a thick short bob that lifted as she moved, and then settled back into place. "Naturally he is, you damned little idiot. Who else would be? We're married now, or hadn't you realized?"

He stared at her. "Yes, I had realized."

Under her yellow top, her shoulder blades protruded spitefully. When she turned again, he noted that her breasts were fuller than he had ever seen them. The middle part of them was stiff, the way they were when he had touched her in the bath. "I hope to God it's a boy," she said. "Then I won't have to do this ever again."

"You already have a boy."

"*I* do. Hugo doesn't. Somebody has to inherit all this." She waved a thin arm angrily at the bedroom with its fine pieces of furniture and heavy brocade curtains. Not a boy's room at all. Nor like the room kept for him in his father's house. Her wave encompassed the rest of the grand house and, beyond it, the whole of Eastholme, the estate in the Cotswolds which had so suddenly become Hugo's after the unexpected death of his elder brother.

"I thought," he said carefully, "that he had adopted me."

"He has."

"Doesn't that make me his son?"

She snorted. "Not really. Only in name."

He was so glad to hear her say it that he almost could not breathe. Tears of gratitude came into his eyes. Careful not to let her notice, he said with nonchalance, "I see."

Leyla's dark eyes narrowed. "You can't possibly have imagined that you'd inherit Eastholme, could you? They'd never allow it to pass to someone like you, someone who doesn't have the Campion blood in his veins."

As a matter of fact, he had assumed that as he was now Hugo's legally adopted son, he would automatically take on Hugo's responsibilities when he grew up. The news that he would not both liberated and angered him.

"Leyla," he said.

"Yes?"

"What's a wog?"

"You are," she said. "And I am."

"Why are we?"

"Because we're unmistakably foreigners, not only by birth but in looks too. Black hair, brownish skin: that means wog. I'd never realized what it meant to be different until I came here. Nobody in Paris ever for a moment . . ." Her voice faded. She looked down at the rings on her tiny hands. "You wouldn't believe what I've had to put up with since I moved here."

"What sort of thing."

"Insults. Rudeness. Things you're too young to understand."

"Who's insulted you?"

"All of them. What Hugo calls the Establishment. They're not all that keen on him, either. A sculptor, for goodness' sake. But since he came into the title, they've had to put up with him. It's me they can't take. I'm the one who gets treated like a leper."

"Do they matter much?"

"They shouldn't." She pushed angry tears out of her eyes. "But they do. God, how I hate them, especially the women. So dull, so self-satisfied. They live through their husbands; they don't seem to do anything for themselves. It's all gardening, a little social work, the village church. The Christian so-called religion . . ." She made a spitting sound. "How I hate all those cruel icons of theirs: saints being tormented on red-hot grills or with their eyes plucked out. And look at the Crucifixion: it's an image of violence and death, not of peace and love." Her face crumpled and she looked as he had never seen her: helpless, bewildered. "What really makes me laugh is that it's the ones who go to church most regularly who treat me worst."

He thought of his father, and the impeccable courtesy he always showed toward the wives of his friends. He felt a pang for the dark warm eyes and soft voices of the men in the country where he came from. In the grate beneath the marble overmantel, the fire collapsed into itself. Leyla jumped up from the edge of the bed and dropped more coal into it, delicately picking pieces from the polished brass scuttle with a pair of tongs. He thought how beautiful she was, how graceful, her slender body poised, her dark profile edged with the fire's red glow. He wished passionately that she loved him.

"So we shall not go to Paris," he said.

She was angry again. "Didn't I just say so?"

"I could go alone," he said. "Marie-Claire could look after me."

"Marie-Claire has gone to visit her mother in Marseilles. The *appartement* is shut up for the winter."

"I should like to visit my father, then."

For a moment she looked at him without speaking. Then she flew across the room and leaned over him. Her dark eyes seemed to have points of fire in them. The chain around her neck glittered; the opals which hung from it sparked with the movement of her voice. It was the piece of her jewelry he liked best, knowing his father had given it to her. He would never have admitted to her that seeing it comforted him, gave him the momentary illusion that whatever his father had done to make her so angry, to make her hate him, had now been forgiven. It was the great unacknowledged dream of his childhood that the two people who had given him life would eventually come together again.

Now rage had made Leyla almost incandescent, like the sparklers he had held in his gloved hand on Guy Fawkes Night. He felt that if he let her see how frightened he was of her, she would kill him. Grabbing his jaw in one hand, she squeezed until he thought she would crack the bone.

"Visit who?" she demanded, teeth clamped shut behind her lips.

"My *real* father."

"Hugo. Is. Your. Father. Now." Each word was rammed at him with brutal force.

"No."

Whatever she did to him, he would not admit anything else. His father was gentle and sweet-voiced, nothing like red-faced Hugo, with his dogs and loud laugh and thick clumsy hands. Leyla's newly rounded breasts hung above him like golden apples. He wondered what she would do if he took one of them in his mouth and gently bit into it. He wished she was not so entirely beautiful. He felt himself stiffen under the sheets. He wished he did not love her.

■■

The baby was not a boy.

He did not see her until she was four months old. Leyla gave birth to her after he had returned to school for the summer term. The Headmaster called him into his study to give him the news, adding that Leyla had undergone a difficult labor and needed to rest. The Headmaster found it awkward to talk about such things to a child, not sure to what extent the communal store of received sexual inaccuracies that the boys bartered among themselves had filtered through to this particular one. Labor: did he understand what that meant? Or what had caused it in the first place? He found it vaguely disturbing that neither Sir Hugo nor his wife wanted the boy to return to East-holme for the vacation weekend: it would surely have been natural to show him the new baby.

Campion was a serious child, the Head reflected, and dauntingly self-contained. Clever, too. Although English was not his first language, he would undoubtedly get a major scholarship to whichever public school his family had selected for him. Because the Head was a conscientious man and genuinely fond of his young charges, he encouraged his staff to keep him informed of those boys who seemed in any way different from the mainstream. He had already been told by his secretary that Campion's only mail, in the three terms he had spent at the school, had been postmarked Istanbul. As far as he knew, Campion had received no telephone calls. There was obviously a degree of emotional neglect there. Tempering the usual heartiness of tone that he adopted when addressing the boys, the Head explained that Sir Hugo had considered it best that Campion remain at school during the weekend off, and that special arrangements would be made for the half-term holiday. He found himself trying not to feel sympathetic, aware that pity was something this boy would furiously resent.

The half-term arrangements involved Campion's traveling in the care of Forrest, the Head Boy, as far as Bath. There, Forrest's mother was to collect them and drive Campion to the house of an elderly cousin of his father's. He was acutely aware of being a nuisance to everyone. His face stiff with pride and mortification, he spent most of the journey from Paddington staring out the window. He could tell Forrest was making an effort to be friendly, even going so far as to invite him to use his Christian name.

"Though not when we get back to school, of course," he added.

"All right." Forrest had probably forgotten that he had spoken to him only once during the whole year, and that he was unlikely to have the opportunity or the desire to do so again before the end of term, when Forrest would be leaving for his public school.

"You're awfully lucky to have a new baby sister," Forrest said.

"Am I?" The green English countryside moved past the window, the foreground very fast, the distance more slowly. He saw sheep, cows, broad flat rivers cutting between meadows. He yearned for the landscapes that had been his until Hugo came into their lives: the minarets of Istanbul, Paris with its sand-pathed parks and stone ponds; Rome—even the formal gardens of the beautiful Queen Anne house in Kent. At Easter, Leyla had said she was going to sell it. He did not think his father would allow that: he had often said it would be his when he became a man.

"I wish I had a sister," Forrest said. "Or even a brother. I'm an only child."

"So am I."

"Not anymore."

"No. I suppose not." Campion wondered without much curiosity what the new sister would look like and whether she would make any difference to his life. He decided she probably would not. Observing the undulations of a willow-lined river, Campion reflected that Hugo had already made all the changes it was possible to make. The worst, of course, was taking Leyla away from him. The little, that is, that she had ever allowed him to have.

"What's she called?" Forrest said. A paperback copy of *Great Expectations* lay on the seat beside him.

"Who?"

"Your sister."

"Oh." Campion wished he would stop talking about it. He looked indifferently out the window. "I don't know."

"What!"

"I don't know."

"Seriously?" Forrest seemed amazed. "You mean your parents actually haven't told you?"

"No. Not yet."

"Don't they write? Or telephone? Or haven't they decided what name to have?"

"Not really." Campion did not wish to say that Leyla never wrote —and, naturally, neither did Hugo. His father did, regularly, but to explain that would mean explaining about Hugo and the adoption. A blush began somewhere under his shirt collar and moved up across his face. To a boy like Daniel Forrest, the notion of a family which did not maintain the normal links with one of its members was obviously inconceivable.

"Sounds a bit like my father," Forrest said gruffly. "He's in the army. They're always posting him abroad, and he never gets round to writing." He, too, looked out at the passing scene. "Not much," he added.

Campion could tell he was torn between being kind to a person whose family obviously neglected him and being loyal to his own father, who probably wrote to him once a week from wherever he happened to be.

As they ate the packed lunch provided by the school, Forrest picked up his book and waved it at Campion. "Have you read this? We're doing it in English."

"Yes, I have."

"That's jolly good for someone your age. Especially . . ."

"Especially what?"

"Well, I mean, you live abroad, don't you? And speak French and everything. According to Mr. Matthews, Dickens is a very English writer."

"I enjoyed it," Campion said, "though it was rather long." He did not add that it had helped to get through the long hours in Hugo's studio while he worked on the *Leyla.*

"Most of Dickens is," Forrest said. "Did you know that Estella means a star?"

"No."

"Mr. Matthews says it symbolizes the distance between Pip and Estella—that she represents something Pip can never attain." Forrest paused, setting his head back on his shoulders and giving the younger boy a secretive glance from under his brow. "Actually, I think it's rather a sad book."

"Yes," Campion said. For him, Estella had Leyla's face. He remembered poor Pip being pressed to the hard pincushioned breast of Mrs. Joe Gargery, and the fire which had destroyed Miss Haversham along with her cobwebbed wedding cake and mouse-nibbled curtains. "Very sad. There's a lot of mist in it, isn't there. Is that symbolic too?"

"Absolutely," Forrest said. "Hiding the truth and things. According to Mr. Matthews."

At Bath, Forrest's mother met them. She whirled her son into her arms, kissing him again and again. "Daniel, darling!" she exclaimed. "It's so marvelous to have you home again."

"And terrific to be here after lousy old school," said Forrest.

"You can't imagine how much I've missed you," his mother said. "Especially with Daddy gone." She hugged her son again and turned to Campion.

"This is Campion, by the way," Forrest said.

"Hullo, Campion. I'm delighted to meet you." Mrs. Forrest

laughed, holding out her hand. Happiness burst out of her, quirking up her lips, curving her cheeks. Every time she looked at Forrest, she smiled. She had big gray eyes and was beautiful. Not like Leyla but in the English way, with bones that lay under the skin like smoothly sculpted stones. She asked if Campion had enjoyed the journey and whether he was hungry.

Campion told her he was not. He tried to remember the last time Leyla had kissed him.

Driving through the outskirts of the town, Mrs. Forrest said over her shoulder, "You must come over one day during the holiday. Daniel's all alone and I'm sure he'd love to see you."

"Of course," Forrest said. Reverting from the responsibilities of his position at school to being someone's son, he seemed softer and smaller. Campion sensed kindness and good breeding in both the Forrests, a wish to make him feel welcome. Although he had never consciously considered such concepts before, he now saw them as eminently desirable.

"Thank you, I would like to," he said. He knew he sounded stiff and cold, but he could think of nothing worse than people feeling sorry for him. He had seen it before: nobody ever understood the relationship between him and Leyla. If he was forced to spend the day at Forrest's house, did that mean he would have to invite Forrest to Hugo's house some time? Next weekend off or something? Leyla would not like that. He was deeply discomfited.

"I'll give your cousin a ring," Mrs. Forrest said. "The Headmaster gave me her telephone number, just in case. Perhaps you could get a bus out to us, and I'll drive you back."

His father's cousin was plump and old, dressed in black with many silver ornaments, like the women he had been used to in Istanbul. Three or four female friends exactly like her were in the drawing room when he arrived; all of them swooped down to kiss him and exclaim at his resemblance to his father. Not a bit, they told each other, like his mother. He sensed their disapproval of Leyla.

Surrounded by their loving concern, it did not occur to him to wonder why there should be this little pocket of Turkish women living in the West of England, nor to ask where their menfolk might be. He was lulled by the familiarity of the house, though he had never visited it before. It functioned in rhythms he was used to. He ate alone—the kind of dishes that his father ate—while the cousin and one or more of her friends attended to his needs. At night he slept in an important bed covered with lace-edged pillows. Pictures he recognized hung on the walls: the same sorts of pictures were in his father's house. He felt himself relaxing for the first time since he had come to England.

When Mrs. Forrest's telephone call came, the cousin was delighted to accept the invitation on his behalf. Forrest's house was much nicer than Hugo's, though not nearly as grand. The Old Vicarage stood at the end of a lane, surrounded by fields full of wild flowers. The kitchen smelled of baking apples.

"Why don't you boys walk the dogs," Mrs. Forrest said. She wore an apron over her dress. "Lunch will be ready when you get back."

Campion followed Daniel single file along the edge of a field. Somewhere, distant cows lowed quietly. A blue haze hung over hedges that were full of strong-smelling white blossom. It was deeply peaceful.

"Do you play table tennis?" Daniel asked over his shoulder.

"No." Campion never felt inadequate, nor did he now. Daniel Forrest probably did not do many of the things *he* could. It was a matter of chance. "I play chess, mostly."

"You ought to join the school chess club."

"I didn't know they had one."

"It's gone off a bit this term, now Jonathan Cooper's left."

"I should like to learn to play table tennis."

"We'll have a go after lunch. Look, there's a hare." Daniel pointed across the fields to where a copse of pine trees began. "See him?"

"No."

"Look." The older boy put his arm around the younger and turned his face in the right direction. "See? Sitting up against that dark bit where the trunks all merge together."

"Oh, yes," lied Campion. He breathed in Daniel's warm smell: soap and fresh-ironed cotton and thin boy's sweat. He wondered if he himself would have the same scent when he was older, on his way to being adult.

They continued around the field. "Have you got a gun? Do you shoot?" Daniel asked.

"Shoot?"

"Rabbits," Forrest said. "Crows. Things like that."

"No!" Campion was shocked. "You shoot them? Kill them, do you mean?"

"Yes."

How could anyone deliberately aim a gun at something, squeeze a trigger, send death hurtling toward something small and defenseless? "I should not like that at all," he said, realizing how disapproving he sounded.

Daniel did not appear to mind. "On a farm, you have to. Pigeons, for instance—they can destroy an entire crop."

"It's murder," Campion said.

"Not when what you're killing is vermin," said Daniel with certainty.

After lunch, the two boys crossed a cobbled yard to what must once have been a stable and climbed dusty stairs to the loft above. Remnants of straw lay in corners. There was a sagging sofa, shelves full of battered children's books, two or three boxes of old toys. A limp-armed cloth doll in knitted soldier's uniform sprawled over the arm of the sofa. A rubber bat swung from the ceiling, its harmless teeth bared in a snarl. A Ping-Pong table, covered by an old army blanket, took up most of the available space. Pulling off the blanket, Daniel set motes tumbling through the disused air to settle back onto the moth-soft piles of dust which covered everything in the room. He tugged open the windows, dislodging the small corpses of cocooned flies and desiccated wasps.

"Phew," he said. "It gets pretty messy in here while I'm away." He blew at a pile of comics, lifting a wave of gray dust into the air. Campion had never seen anything so unkempt and neglected in his life. Sun slanted in at the open windows. Across the fields, a bell sounded. The long, slow note dragged through the heat toward them, trailing over the hedges and meadows and the thin-trunked pine trees like a ribbon.

A flash of illumination, a microsecond of total comprehension, passed through Campion and was gone. He knew that had he been able to grasp it, he would have understood the entire universe and the meanings behind it. He was deeply aware, not of happiness but of contentment. Although this was England, and alien, he was for once part of it; he belonged, if only for this single moment, in this particular place.

At the same time, in the yard below, car doors slammed. A voice called. Someone came stamping up the wooden stairs, shouting Daniel's name. "My mother's taking my sister for her riding lesson and dropped me off here. Hope you don't mind."

Campion recognized the voice. It was Jeremy Sutton.

Coming into the room, Sutton continued, "My mother did ring, but the line was engaged and we couldn't wait." Looking at Campion, he said coldly, "Hello." He moved around the table to stand beside Daniel. Shoulder to shoulder the two older boys stared at him.

He was alone again. Dispassionately, he anticipated that it would always be like this. Even welcomed it.

· 9 ·

GRAY SATIN SHEETS, THE WOMAN thought. Her mouth twisted as she remembered the buttery feel of them under her hips, her body spread out on them, as though she were a piece of meat prepared for consumption. She'd had the devil's own job getting hold of them in the first place. Vulgar, yes. Gray satin could hardly be described as anything else. But then the Director *was* a trifle vulgar, was he not? That was why she found him so terribly exciting. God knows Jacques had been anything but, his face so long and mournful and so indescribably well bred that it was a surprise when she discovered how vigorously and often he liked to make love. It was such a pity that he was so bad at it. Perhaps his mistress had enjoyed it more than she. Poor Jacques: she still did not understand why he had made such an extraordinary gesture. At least he had left her with three titles, no children, and a fortune. There was not much else a woman widowed in her early forties could ask for, especially when the Director was in Paris.

She glanced around the much-mirrored room. The constant honking of car horns outside in the Place Vendôme eased off for a moment, like the collective hush that sometimes comes over cicadas on a hot afternoon. What would the rest of them say if they knew what she and the Director did after the meetings? What would they say to the tall black candles which waited in their silver holders beside the bed, and the champagne in its bucket and the dreadful satin sheets? Even more, what would they say if they could watch as he removed his clothes with that exquisitely torturing slowness of his and then flung her so violently, so passionately, onto the bed? Thinking of it, while opposite her Gilles Laforêt droned on, quoting statistics and figures and balances, she had to clamp her lips together in order not to moan aloud with anticipatory pleasure.

She had never asked if there were other women. She didn't really want to know. Nor even cared, if the truth be told: the Director was fantastic to take to bed, which was all that mattered. Her friends were well aware, thanks to her discreetly indiscreet hints, that she had a lover; she had no wish to jeopardize her position in society by allowing them to see the kind of man he was. With those oriental looks, that definitely non-European coloring, he would never do in the salons of the *haute monde,* despite his connection to some branch of the English aristocracy. Besides, he was so much younger than she was. People would laugh behind her back. Accuse her of cradle-snatching. Call him a gigolo or a toy-boy. So far, the luxurious intimacy with which she surrounded him when he was in Paris had seemed to satisfy him, along with the insatiable physical desire she had no difficulty in demonstrating. But sooner or later, it was bound to occur to him that they never went out anywhere together. She dreaded the day he suggested they dine out at Maxim's or the Tour d'Argent and she had to refuse: it would mean an end to the affair if he realized why. After which there would be the inevitably frustrating chore of looking for a replacement.

Still: it did not appear to be a problem that need concern her for the moment. She brushed hair away from her face; it was a new style, perhaps a little young for her, but she had thick hair and her coiffeuse had assured her she could carry it off. She hoped the Director liked the color. She had spent some time that morning with her chef, putting together a menu that would combine artistry with moderation: her lover was a man of abstemious habits. She hoped he would like the gift already lying on the satin pillows. Hideously expensive, but worth every centime. She tucked her mouth in once more, thinking of how, after they had dined in the intimacy of the small salon rather than the formal dining room, he would grab her hand as he had so many times before and drag her into her bedroom, already pulling at the zipper of his trousers. And then . . . Marvelous!

She remembered so clearly the first time they had spoken to each other some three or four years earlier. Arriving late at the dinner party, she found that the other guests had already formed their temporary social liaisons. She had disliked the way they looked at her, complacent in their togetherness while she, the newcomer, the widow alone, was left on the outside. Gilles had steered her across the salon, where they stood drinking aperitifs. "Someone I want you to meet," he had said. "This man could change your life."

"But I do not wish my life to be changed," she told him. "My life is eminently satisfactory." She brushed his cheek with her hand, unflirtatiously. Gilles was an old friend.

"It will be more so." His hand was on her elbow. "As always, Henriette, you look ravishing."

"Thank you, Gilles." She had taken the glass of chilled vermouth that was offered on a tray.

"Yellow is a good color for you." He stroked the pleats of her long silk skirt with a connoisseur's fingers. "Gallini, yes?"

"Of course. I rarely wear anything else." The first sip of wine burnished her taste buds; it was a moment she had always relished, the evening before her, and Jacques—so often detained at the bank by some business or other—not at her side to shut her off from whatever promise it might hold. That particular evening, Gilles had led her across the room to the fire which burned beneath the elaborate marble mantel. A man had turned, held out his hand. Gilles had introduced them—it was as simple as that.

She'd seen him before, several times, at Gilles's larger gatherings. She herself had always been too busy being charming, being Jacques's wife, to spare time for the young medical student who usually stood alone, or listened, with head courteously bent, as some woman chattered about nothing. Then Jacques had . . . died, and for a while there had been no partying. This was the first time she had actually stood face-to-face with him.

It was the eyes that astonished her. They were quite wrong with the type of face which contained them. Gazing into them, she had felt herself being hooked, played, reeled in. She had gone along with it, enjoying the expert manipulation as she allowed herself to be pulled into the shore. Gilles had seen to it that she went into dinner with him. He had spoken of injustice, at some point; at another, of collective duty, the responsibility of the rich. She had listened with only half her mind, wondering what the body beneath the dinner jacket was like, imagining it already in the peach-colored light of her bedroom. He put a hand on hers as his voice changed, as his eyes compelled her to listen to his description of natural disasters on the other side of the globe. "We need to be able to provide instant help," he had said. She had nodded, only half listening, thinking of other things: of his beautiful hands on her hips, of his eyelashes brushing the tips of her nipples, of his body jerking into orgasm inside hers. "An organization set up internationally . . . permanent salaries . . . time is vital . . . we who have so much . . . impossible to imagine the suffering . . ."

What was he? Why did he tell her these things? At the head of the table Gilles watched her, his handsome face bland with satisfaction. She had agreed to a further meeting; eventually—after consultation with her accountants—let herself be persuaded into financial commitment. She had been astonished to discover that Jacques had been on the board and had been happy to take his place there. In her drawing room the next evening he had wasted no time, telling her that but for the fact that Gilles's table had been laid with an irreplaceable antique dinner service by Limoges, he would have taken her there and then among the silver and crystal, in front of her friends, not caring what they thought.

"What about *my* thoughts?" she asked.

"You wanted it as much as I did," he said.

"Such conceit." There had been a catch in her throat as she laughed, knowing even before he lifted her skirt that this would be lovemaking of an exceptional order.

■■

Why do Frenchwomen spend so much time changing the color of their hair, the Director wondered coldly. She had dyed it lighter, almost blond, fluffed it out like a soap opera star, made herself totally undesirable as far as he was concerned. He had found her useful until now, even entertaining. Her reaction, for instance, when he had jokingly told her he preferred to make love on satin sheets. It had been the second or third time they had slept together: she had not known him well then, had not wanted to offend him by mocking such vulgarity. And the gifts she gave him, gifts he did not want and had no use for: heavy gold watch straps and silver hip flasks and the like, as though he were a gigolo. Because of the difference in their ages, she was embarrassed to parade him in front of her friends, which suited him perfectly—he knew far too many people in Paris as it was.

Her legs had struck him first: stockinged in navy nylon and ending in dark blue suede shoes that did flattering things to her calves. Her legs first; after that, the raindrops shining in her hair. She was old enough to be his mother, but that had not been a drawback. Quite the opposite, in fact.

Until now. Tonight he would leave quickly when the meeting was over, before she could reach his side and give him her usual low-voiced invitation, her eyes already anticipating his acceptance. He knew Gilles wished to speak to him—he could use that as an excuse. And he had a great deal to worry about at the moment. As in London and New York, there seemed to be a substantial drain of resources, without any particular project apparently being responsible. Although finance was not a subject on which he was at all knowledgeable, it was clear that a radical audit of the Organization's complicated interests would be necessary in order to track down the source of the losses. On the other hand, he had no wish to offend Henriette, or risk her resignation from the board. There was too much potential benefit to the Organization from her contribution, and she was not a stupid woman. Something must be done. He would have to play it carefully, close to the chest.

From the start, she had been harder to net than he had antici-pated. Gilles Laforêt had said of her: "Clever, my dear. And, now that Jacques is dead, underoccupied—there are no children. She's too clever, really, for the life-style she has chosen. Immensely rich, of course; that goes without saying. I doubt if you'll have any problem."

Yet, after the preliminary rounds were over, she had been shrewd. When he called—on her invitation—at her fashionable apart-ment, she had wanted to see balance sheets, had asked for itemized accounts of expenditure, demanded copies of receipted bills. It had taken all his skills to persuade her to stay with them, as he explained again the Organization's particular function. Her face, in the half-light of early evening, had caused his heart to flutter. For an instant, there had been the possibility of a dream about to be fulfilled.

Very discreetly the Director glanced at her, caught her eye, turned on the blaze for a second or two. He watched with satisfaction as a tiny smile flickered across her face, lifting one side of her mouth. She looked down at her lap, then back at him. She ran her tongue over her lower lip, like some cheap floozy. She was the sort of woman who assumed that a man's behavior was ruled by his groin. He supposed she was not to know what had attracted him in the first place. Her dark, almost black, hair had been part of it. So had the slim boyishness of her body. But more than that had been the fleeting likeness he had caught the first time he saw her, something about the line of the cheekbone, the shape of her eyelids, which had immediately suggested someone dear and long lost.

■■

"What's she called?"

"Amy."

"Aimée? That means 'loved,' in French."

"I know it does."

"I thought you didn't like babies."

"I don't. Hugo does, though. This one, anyway." Leyla looked indifferently down at the child asleep in her elaborate cot. Campion thought he had never seen anything so beautiful in his life. She had tiny little eyebrows which lay feathered against her forehead. Her skin was golden brown, dusky, like Leyla's. When he put a finger softly to her cheek, it had the same moist feel as peeled mushrooms. One hand was curled into a little fist beside her ear. Her bottom stuck up into the air beneath the embroidered quilt which covered her. He wondered what color her eyes were, and whether she would look like him one day. He wanted to pick her up and kiss her.

"She doesn't look a bit like Hugo," he said.

"Not much fun for her if she did," said Leyla. "Poor little thing: I expect Hugo's precious Establishment will make her as unhappy as they've made me, just because she's dark, just because she's different."

He longed to ask if he could take the baby outside, push her around the garden paths. Without formulating the thought to himself, he knew that if Leyla realized how much he wished to do so, she would prevent him. He turned away, pretending lack of interest. "Does she cry a lot?"

"Not too much, thank goodness. It hurts my breasts when she does."

"Oh."

"Horrible. They start to leak. It was the same with you. The sooner I can get her onto a bottle, the better." Leyla opened the front of her blouse. "Look. Have you ever seen anything so hideous?"

He took in the two swollen breasts. Blue veins ran across them. The nipples were very dark. A drop of milk slowly appeared on the end of one. "I think you're leaking now," he said. It amazed him to think that once he had closed his mouth around her and drawn sustenance from her body.

"Suck them," she ordered.

"What?"

"Suck my breasts," she said.

He hesitated.

She came closer, her eyes slitted, hissing through her teeth, "You used to once. Such a greedy little monster: you didn't hold back then."

Her eyes were large and shining. He moved closer to her. During the summer he had grown. He was the same height as she was, perhaps a little taller. Staring into her eyes, he put his hands out and gently cupped them around her breasts. They were warm and solid. He squeezed softly and saw milk run between his fingers.

"Suck them," Leyla said fiercely, her teeth clenched. "Go on, damn you."

Slowly he lowered his head. When he moved his tongue across the nipple, it felt hard and rubbery. Leyla gasped. Not for the first time, he was aware that something about her was distorted, off-key. He sucked at her, trying to remember what it had felt like to be as small as Amy, tucked in close to Leyla's warm side, hoping to recapture helplessness. He tasted sweetness in his mouth. Mother's milk. He pulled away, but Leyla gripped either side of his head between her hands, keeping him there. "Oh God," she said. Her voice was a whisper.

Somewhere below, Hugo called. They heard his feet ascending the oak staircase. For a moment, Campion was afraid she would not let him go, that Hugo would find them there. But she dropped her hands, turned away from him, rebuttoned her blouse.

He leaned over the cot. Amy had not moved. Little snoring breaths bubbled out between lips crinkled like fallen petals. Something moved in what he thought was his heart. He felt soft with it, and strong.

"Pretty, isn't she?" Hugo strode across the room to stare down at his daughter. He put a hand on her raised rump, covering it completely. "What are you planning to do with yourself until school starts?"

"I thought I'd work on some chess problems in my room," he

said, moving slowly toward the door. "My father gave me a book of them while I was there."

"Jolly good."

"*Who* did?" Leyla said. Her voice was fierce.

He stopped, turned, caught her eye. "You know," he said. "My father." For the very first time in their relationship, he felt that he was the stronger one. When he was younger, she might have pinched him, come up behind and knocked him violently from his chair. Now she stayed beside the empty fireplace, her black eyes full of rage.

"No," she said.

"No what?"

"No chess today."

"Why not?"

"You can take the baby out for a walk."

"I don't want to."

"Just a minute," Hugo said, frowning. He smelled of whisky. "Don't they teach you any manners at school? That's no way to speak to an adult."

"Sorry," Campion said.

"Take the baby out," repeated Leyla. "I'll call the nursemaid—"

"Nanny," Hugo said.

"—she can get Amy ready."

Somehow he had made her do what he wanted. It was almost his first victory over her. Later, he would analyze how it had been done, so that he could use the techniques again.

■■

To himself he called her Aimée. Beloved One. Beloved Female. He loved her. He knew that he would happily give up his life for her. He fantasized the house on fire, smoke pouring from the roof, timbers falling inward, and himself dashing into the blazing inferno to rescue Aimée from the flames, only to succumb himself as he handed her into safety. He rarely dared display his love; if Leyla knew, she would find a way to forbid it. Happiness was something of which he had been aware in an impersonal way: hitherto it had had meaning for him purely as an intellectual concept. Now, with Aimée, it became real. The love he felt was untinged with the fear that always hovered when he was with Leyla. He was able to laugh without worrying that whatever had made him laugh would be denied him. When Aimée's fingers closed around his, his chest contracted. When she put her arms around his neck, or pressed little wet kisses to his cheek or laughed, he felt as if he would explode like a firecracker. From the start she was slight, without any of the chubbiness that goes with early childhood. Standing with her in his arms in front of one of the long mirrors which were all over the house, he rejoiced in the likeness between them.

■■

He passed, via the Common Entrance examination, on to Hugo's former public school. His reputation as a chess player had gone before him. Asked one day in class to read the part of Malvolio in *Twelfth Night,* he displayed a talent for translating words into emotion he had not known he possessed. The boys around him were impressed. Word spread. Thereafter, he was earmarked for the plum parts in any school production. He learned how easy it was to manipulate an audience. Putting on the role of someone else, he felt liberated from himself. He played the part of young Marlow in *She Stoops to Conquer* with a comic hesitancy and assured timing that caused the head of drama to talk about RADA or the Central. He began to realize, as the terms moved past him, that by the school's standards, he was a success.

In the holidays, he spent all the time he was allowed with Amy. Leyla was frequently in London. She had bought a flat in Bloomsbury, somewhere behind the British Museum. Knowing now what *fucking* meant, he wondered whether she had a lover. Or many of them. The thought was less painful than it would once have been, and yet not so. He thought of Hans Andersen's Little Mermaid. He would gladly have walked across sharp knives for Leyla had she asked him to. He knew that she never would, that she did not see him as someone worth asking a sacrifice from.

Quite often he and Hugo found themselves eating together silently in the big dining room, after Amy had been put to bed. Both reared with a tradition of good manners, they tried to talk to each other but without much success. They had so little in common: only Leyla, really. Since the two of them found conversation difficult, Campion would have preferred to read as he ate but he sensed that to ask permission would be to bring Hugo's wrath down on his head. English gentlemen did not behave in such a way. Especially not when such large sums had been expended on their education. He thought often of his father, with whom conversation never flagged.

Hugo did not seem happy. He drank large amounts of whisky before dinner and more during it. When Leyla was at home, she seemed to tolerate his drinking, refilling his glass herself when his hand shook too much to control the bottle. As time went by, his face, already highly colored, grew redder, webbed with the thin threads of broken veins. His pale blue eyes developed the liquidity of a dog's. He sat for hours every evening in the study, the decanter at his side, staring at the *Leyla* on its plinth. Passing the door, Campion occasionally heard him talking to it, his voice a mumble blurred by drink. Campion wanted to tell him that the more he drank, the less time Leyla was likely to spend with him. It seemed an obvious enough equation; nonetheless he felt himself incapable of offering such advice. He remembered, with a chill, how Leyla had looked across a Parisian art gallery and drawn Hugo to her side.

Amy was Hugo's solace. The absence of her mother did not appear to worry her: Hugo was enough. As a baby, she lay in his arms, staring up into his increasingly ravaged face. As she grew older she spent hours sitting on his knee in her bright little dresses with her cheek pressed close to his. Her dark eyes loved him. Watching them together, Campion did not feel any jealousy. Hugo was, after all, her father. He was very much aware of how strong a presence his own father was in his mind. It was right that children and parents should gain nourishment from each other. He wondered if Hugo ever remembered Paris, and Leyla whirling like a brightly painted top through the summer days. In recent years, Hugo had spent almost no time in the studio which had been built for him in one of the barns. His agent came down frequently, urging him to work, reminding him of exhibitions planned, of commissions accepted but not yet completed. Reading the newspapers, Campion discovered that the price of Hugo's work was escalating as word spread that he was finished, artistically. He wondered what the *Leyla* would fetch now.

Amy walked and talked early. Hugo took to going around the estate with her each day, her hand in his. She was fascinated by everything, from the bull which lived behind thorn hedges in the Half

Acre to the combine harvesters which arrived at the end of every summer to tear the wheat stalks from the ground and magically turn them into grain. Her voice was like a cricket's, high and chirping, constantly asking questions.

Hugo bought her a rocking horse, grand in the Spanish manner, a dappled gray with a beautifully tooled saddle of soft red leather. She named it after a horse that featured in many of the stories Hugo made up for her, which had belonged to his grandfather. Once it was installed in her nursery, she spent hours rocking back and forth, dreaming.

Most days, before dinner, before Hugo had really begun to empty the whisky decanter, she sat within his big arms and repeated for her father's benefit what she could remember of nursery tales Campion had read to her earlier. Her glance always included her brother in their circle. Afterward, he was to remember that the three of them had achieved a kind of peace together on those evenings without Leyla.

One rainy afternoon, when she was around four years old, Campion found a catalogue of a forthcoming auction of modern sculpture at Sotheby's. Amy was delighted. Although Campion was teaching her, she could not yet read. She ran her stubby fingers over the illustrations and laughed aloud. One in particular caught her fancy; it did not come as much of a surprise to him to see that it was a piece by Hugo. He told her so, pointing to the letters of Hugo's name and spelling them out for her. He had one arm around her, his hand splayed across the delicate bones of her back. Her fragility made him aware of his own strength. If he wanted to, he could crush her completely. He realized that since her birth he had been released in some measure from Leyla. The fear which, looking back, had always been so much a part of his childhood, had dissipated. It was still there, lurking on the edge of his consciousness, but he could hold it back now, not be overwhelmed.

That evening, as the three of them sat around the fire in the study, Amy questioned Hugo about his work in her shrill insect voice. She wanted to know why he no longer seemed to do any. She brought the catalogue and put it in front of him, turning the pages until she came to the illustration of his work. Hugo's face lit up. He put down his glass of whisky. As Amy's had done, his fingers caressed the pictures. It was the first time Campion had seen any kind of similarity between father and daughter.

"Look," Hugo said, "over there." He pointed at the *Leyla,* which stood against the wall. "I made that for your mother."

"Make something for me," Amy said.

"All right."

"Promise?"

"Absolutely, darling."

He started the next day. It was the beginning of his resurrection.

■■

When Campion was sixteen, his father decided to spend some weeks in England. It was a long time since his last visit. For the past five years, the house on Romney Marsh had been let out to tenants. Now arrangements were made through the estate agents for it to be prepared for him to move into with his son. He arrived just before the end of the summer term and traveled down to see Campion in the school's production of *The Merchant of Venice.*

Campion played the part of Shylock for poignancy, softening the Jew's harshness, emphasizing his loneliness and bewilderment, his wistful desire to belong, an alien in a hostile land. His Shylock trod a minefield littered with usages and customs that he did not understand; his own, when he attempted to impose them, were despised. His "Hath not a Jew eyes?" speech rang through the school theater with a passion that sprang from personal experience.

Toward the end of the play, with Shylock humiliated and rejected, he looked out into the audience from under the shaggy eyebrows that the makeup crew had affixed to his own with spirit gum, and saw Alicia Forrest wiping tears from her eyes. It was a moment of great power. He knew then that he could conquer the world if he had a mind to. He looked forward to introducing his father to her afterward. It was the first time in his school career that someone of his own had been there.

"You were brilliant," she said at the reception held afterward on the lawn of the Headmaster's house, as boatered boys milled around her taking cakes and tea to their parents. "Absolutely marvelous." She held his hand between hers and smiled at him before turning to his father. "You must be incredibly proud of him."

"Extraordinarily so." His father touched his shoulder. "But then I always have been."

"Are you thinking of taking it up as a career?" Alicia said. "Daniel tells me that you're absolutely certain to get a scholarship to RADA." She and his father looked at him, faces inquiring.

He shook his head. "No."

"It seems a pity to have such talent and not to use it," Mrs. Forrest said.

"Yes, maybe."

"You're probably making the right decision. Acting is a precarious profession, or so we are led to believe," she said. Her eyes strayed, looking for her own son. Campion could tell from their sudden glow when she had picked Daniel out from among the other boys. "What will you be going into?"

"I have decided to be a doctor," Campion said.

"Very wise," said Mrs. Forrest. "Much safer than acting."

"That's not why I wish to take it up."

"Doctors are among the blessed of the earth," said his father. His dark face was proud. Campion had not told anyone until now what he planned to be. Leyla and Hugo were not interested; Amy was too young to wonder.

"Of course," Mrs. Forrest said. "I did not in any way wish to imply anything different." A flush rose on her face. Campion thought she looked good with the color in her cheeks. She was a very attractive woman. Looking forcefully into her eyes, he smiled and saw the color deepen.

"And your son, Mrs. Forrest?" his father asked. "What will he do now he has left school?"

She laughed. "He's earmarked for Sandhurst. I'm afraid both sides of the family, Marquends and Forrests, have gone for soldiers for as far back as anyone can remember."

"A respectable career," his father said. Campion knew that the words did not echo his thoughts. Killing others for a livelihood was not a choice he would have wanted his own son to make.

"We're proud of him," she said quietly.

"He's the head of the school," Campion said, sensing his father's reservations and not wishing Alicia Forrest to be hurt. "Good at just about everything."

"Not like you, though," Mrs. Forrest said. How did she know? He had not spoken to her since that prep school half-term five years ago, yet she seemed to have been aware of him. Had she asked Daniel how he was getting on, perhaps; kept tabs on him through the year? She had probably been to other end-of-term plays. He wished he had known. This was Daniel's last term: she would not come again.

It occurred to him that perhaps it was a good thing that Leyla never came to these affairs: he was gladder to be here with his father than he could have imagined.

Mrs. Forrest rummaged in her handbag and produced a camera. "As this is the last time we shall be here, do let me take a picture of you both."

He stood next to his father, feeling his arm around his neck, while Mrs. Forrest clicked the shutter. He was moved by the possessive pride in his father's face, and by the pleasure he himself took in that possession. His own personality bloomed inside him like a flower hitherto insufficiently watered.

■■

At the end of the first week of the holidays, he and his father spent a few days in London. His father had business to conduct during the day, so Campion wandered around the city on his own. He felt like a foreign tourist, though he had lived in England for nearly six years now. He walked around Kensington, along the Embankment, through St. James's Park. He went to the summer exhibition at the Royal Academy. Coming out, with the sun beginning to drop behind the black-tiled mansard roofs, he heard an oboe winding through a piece of classical music he did not recognize. Telemann? Purcell? The moment was loaded with significance: happiness dropped over him. He felt he had managed to steer a course through the treacherous seas of life and reach at last a safe landfall.

He visited the famous sights: Buckingham Palace, the Tower of London, Trafalgar Square. One morning, coming out through the big wrought-iron gates of the British Museum, he thought he saw Leyla across the road. She wore peacock-blue leather trousers over a white leotard. A handbag of matching quilted leather was slung across her narrow body on a long golden chain. Keeping back, he followed her across Russell Square into the elegant Georgian streets of Bloomsbury.

She must be heading for her flat; although he had never been there, he knew the address. Seeing her unexpectedly, he was able to assess her like a stranger. Unlike a stranger, he felt a surge of longing so total that he leaned for a moment against the railings of the nearest house, afraid he might fall down. Not once had he ever asked—of himself, of her, of God—why she had not loved him. He was intellectually aware that he was not unlovable; quite the opposite. Yet, because of her, he would always feel himself to be so.

At a house with an elaborate fanlight and brass numbers fixed to a freshly painted green door, Leyla stopped. She stood searching for a key in her bag, then looked up at the second floor. There were long windows, guarded by plain rods of iron. At one of them, a boy stared down at her. The boy was like Campion, maybe a year or two older. Black hair, tawny skin, good mouth. Seeing Leyla, he smiled, lifting one hand in greeting. She blew him a kiss. For a moment she stayed there, looking up at him. Campion heard her laugh before she took the three shallow steps at one stride, turned the key in the lock and went inside.

The boy's eyes caught Campion's. He grinned. Campion walked on by, pretending not to notice. His face was hot. Who was this boy? Possibilities overwhelmed him. Perhaps Leyla had friends staying with her. Perhaps the second floor flat belonged to someone else—but he knew it was not so. For a second of shock, he had even wondered whether the boy was Leyla's son. Impossible. The boy had been naked. He had waved with one hand. But with the other he had deliberately begun to stroke his groin.

What horrified Campion most was how like himself the boy looked.

· 10 ·

GILLES LAFORÊT FAVORED SHELLEYAN
hair, pink shirts, and double-breasted suits in fine English worsted. He
stood in one now, shaking the Director's hand with both of his. A
bracelet of heavy silver links jangled on his wrist. Not gay, the Director thought, smiling down at him; I know he's not at all gay, but he's
not rabidly heterosexual either.

"As always, a very efficient summation, Gilles," he said, thinking
how effortlessly continental tailoring made even the most benevolent
of men look like gangsters.

"Do you think so?" Gilles made some play with the much-used,
dimple in his right cheek.

"I should not say so otherwise."

"But we have problems, yes?"

"Do you know why?"

Gilles shook his head. "I've been over and over the figures and I
can't see what's wrong. If it didn't sound too absurd, I'd say someone
is deliberately trying to sabotage our efforts."

"Why would anyone want to do that?"

"Exactly. That's why I call it absurd. It may prove to be a simple
accounting error, in the end." Briefly Gilles touched the younger
man's cheek. "Shall I see you tomorrow evening, *cher ami*?"

"Tomorrow?" The Director frowned.

"Did I not tell you? I shall be entertaining a few friends. In the
country."

"I'm not sure that I—"

"You must come. I absolutely insist." Gilles leaned one manicured
hand on the table beside him while with the other he stroked the
Director's sleeve.

"I have no time for parties, Gilles. You know that."

"But there will be people there it is important for you to meet." A
man with a passion, Gilles reflected, is always easy to manipulate.

Once he, too, had felt as passionate and determined as the Director did now. It was difficult to remember what about, or whom, but he distinctly recalled the emotion. These days, it was all game-playing, all sleight-of-hand. Looking at the younger man's face, remembering the evangelical enthusiasm of his address an hour ago, he wondered if there was not the stuff of martyrdom about him. Not that the Director could be called saintly, no matter which way you defined saintliness—not that that stopped the wilder elements of the press from using the word. Certainly no one could accuse the Director of neglecting the sins of the flesh—one or two of them, at any rate. Perhaps knowing what they were and then renouncing them made a man purer in the end than an innocent ignorant of them from the first. How long would it be before the Director's present fanaticism was overtaken by the caution of middle age? Prudence was the old man's curse, Gilles reflected; prudence and mistrust. He disliked very much the insistent approach of old age. However hard one fought against it, the passage of time was not gainsayable. He knew that he was a good decade from being considered old; well-muscled, fit from regular workouts at the gym, against the odds he was keeping it at bay.

"What kind of people?" the Director said.

"The very kind you wish to impress. And—after the figures we've just heard—that you *need* to impress. A minister, two industrialists, a newspaper editor. Even a couple of members of France's semiredundant aristocracy. Plus a charming widow with whom I am half in love myself. She will be bringing her charming daughter with her. At least"—Gilles paused to light a cigarette, drag in a breath that made him cough, blow smoke out into the room—"since the mother is charming, I assume the daughter is as well. Perhaps she would do for you, *cher ami.* She is half English, like yourself."

"I am not." The Director was annoyed. "And I dislike the English intensely, as you know."

"This girl is the daughter of Tom Brett, the American journalist who was so unfortunately caught in the cross fire in . . . where was it? Libya? Palestine?" He paused. "No, I mean Beirut."

"I see." The Director frowned. "Is Henriette invited?"

"Yes." Gilles paused, making an effort not to look sly. Another of the irritations of being elderly was the loss of control over one's expression. What had once been engaging, too often these days appeared fatuous; the confidential now seemed merely shifty. "She does not know I was also going to ask you."

"Would she come if she did?"

"Why not? You met at my house, if you remember."

"She is terrified that if we meet in public, people will instantly put two and two together and tear her credibility to shreds."

"How odd . . ." Gilles paused, fluffing his fingers through his romantically flyaway hair. "When she has none."

"How unkind you are, Gilles. Always the *bon mot* rather than the *mot juste.*"

"That's why I have so many friends." Gilles smiled, remembering too late that nowadays, if he was not careful, his smile showed yellowed teeth and too much gum. "Tell me, are you tired of her?"

Was he? The Director considered. *Tired* was the wrong word, implying overindulgence, satiety. It was simply that he now realized that whatever he had been looking for in her did not exist—had never existed. "Not tired," he said slowly. "Simply . . . mistaken."

"You must not seem to abandon her, my friend. Women should not be humiliated," Gilles said. "And this one has much to offer the Organization. It would be a pity to antagonize her."

"I have already realized that." Across Gilles's shoulder, the Director saw Henriette moving toward them. Backlit from the window, her hair seemed even blonder. Any resemblance he had once imagined had now vanished. "I shall be there, at your party," he said quickly, avoiding her eager eyes.

"Good. You will drive down, yes?"

"Yes. Let Henriette know, will you?"

"All right."

"And try to track down that discrepancy in the figures as soon as you can."

"Of course."

"Thank you, Gilles."

As he turned away Gilles said, "It's not the only thing you have to thank me for."

It was true. Thinking back, he remembered one particular time, six years earlier . . .

■■

Paris in November. Crisp. Chilly. Campion was twenty-one and this was the first time he had been here when the gutters were clogged with slimy leaves not yet swept away, and steam rose in pantomimic clouds from the métro ventilators. In this present cold snap, the color had leached out of the city. There was ice at the edge of the river, which flowed sometimes black as mud, sometimes white, reflecting the clouds. Stripped of their leaves, the trees cast complicated patterns darkly against the snow-heavy sky. Black barges moved like coffins along the surface of the water.

Campion released the catch of the French windows and stepped out onto the narrow balcony. Cold air rushed at him, making him shiver. It seemed a long time, a lifetime, since he had been a child here, sniffing Paris into his lungs, clinging to the thick ironwork tendrils of the balcony rail for fear that Leyla would push him over to his death. In the street below him, an old woman in a shapeless cardigan came out of the *boulangerie* with half a dozen sticks of bread and slapped away along the pavement. From somewhere nearby, the smell of fresh-roasted coffee seeped into the frosty air. Nothing much had changed since his childhood.

Wrong.

Everything had changed.

In the apartment opposite his own, a man and a woman stood embracing. Campion watched them with interest. The woman was tall, well groomed, wearing a skirt and jacket with a blouse that tied abundantly at the neck. From the way she turned her head to avoid damage to her makeup, he deduced she was off to work. The man was shorter than she, still in an elaborate dressing gown. When the woman had gone from the room, the man opened the windows and stepped out onto his own balcony, pulling cigarettes from a pocket and lighting them with a gold Dunhill he removed from a small suede bag.

Catching sight of Campion, he blew smoke into the air. "Ah," he called. "The medical student."

It was the first time in all the years that any neighbor had spoken to him. "How did you know that?" Campion said. For a moment his mind ranged over subtle Sherlockian clues: a special flattening of the fingertips, perhaps; a hospital pallor; the scent of formaldehyde.

"My dear, I've lived here for thirty years. I know everyone. I'm Gilles Laforêt, by the way." He gestured with his cigarette, as though he would have shaken hands across the gap which divided them. "And you?"

"Alexander Campion." He said it without thinking.

"English?"

"No."

"I didn't think so. Where is your pretty mother these days?"

"She lives in England now."

"It's a long time since we saw her."

"She no longer comes to Paris. At least, not to this apartment."

Not now that I have been banished from her, he thought.

■■

During his last year at Cambridge, he spent the Easter vacation at Eastholme. Next term he would take his finals; providing he passed, he would be off to Paris for the beginning of the university semester in the autumn.

Amy was eleven. Sitting at the book-strewn table in his bedroom, he watched her from the window as she sprawled in jeans and sweater on the stone balustrade, reading the stern volumes she had removed from the library and carried out into the chilly spring sunshine. She had confided in him one breakfast time that she *adored* Dickens.

She was tall now, taking height from her father, but she showed none of his clumsiness, nor his porcine pinkness. Campion loved to see her in motion, exulting secretly in the way her limbs extended from the elegant litheness of her body, the way they carried her forward, or brushed the dark, glossy hair back from her face, a gesture she made twenty times in every hour. Sometimes, looking up from his books, he saw her in the distance, riding her pony; he remembered her as a child, astride the nursery rocking horse.

He wanted to touch her thin shoulders, so like her mother's yet so entirely lacking Leyla's furious impatience; he wanted to feel the softness of her budding breasts, and stroke the smooth skin beneath her jaw. His desire for her, analyzed and broken down, was simply the need for human contact. What he desired above all was that she, so much beloved, should touch him back, should hold him, should tell him, as nobody yet had done, that he was loved.

Leyla was often away from the house. Hugo, though moving constantly in a whisky haze, was working hard, spending his days in his studio. His eyes sought his daughter's whenever they were in the same room together; he looked to her for the approval that he wanted from his wife. Campion was not yet wise enough to see how closely their needs—his and Hugo's—paralleled each other.

Hugo was called away to a series of meetings in London and decided to stop overnight rather than make the journey twice in one day. "It's about an exhibition they want to set up in New York," he had told Amy. "If it comes off, I'll take you with me."

Campion, stretched in a chair, saw with a pang of fierce envy how her dark eyes lit up. "New York!" she exclaimed. "Wowee! Can we go and see the Statue of Liberty?"

"Of course."

"And Fifth Avenue?"

"Anywhere you want." Hugo's eyes, heavy in their loose sockets, promised her the entire North American continent.

The night he left for London, Campion and Amy sat together in front of a log fire. The television rolled some program made up of banalities and audience laughter across the screen. She snuggled up to him on the sofa and he slipped his arm around her, hugging her close.

"Honestly," he said, after a while. "This is the most appalling brain-softening rubbish I've ever seen."

"I bet you watched much worse than this when you were little," she said.

"Ah, no." He shook his head. "I was not allowed."

"Didn't you have a television, then?" She looked appalled.

"Of course. But usually I read instead." He did not say that Leyla had enjoyed forbidding him to watch anything she thought he liked. Rooms full of pinches, of trepidations, of deliberately inflicted miseries, came back to him. "I did not have fun, the way you do."

"Come on," Amy said, grinning. "You'll be telling me you grew up in a cardboard box next."

"What?" The joke, if that was what it was, eluded him.

"It doesn't matter." She knelt up beside him and looked closely into his face, frowning a little. "You're terribly handsome, you know."

"Am I?" He laughed a little, pulling her against him, wanting the closeness, yet made uneasy by it. He could feel the curve of a beginning hip; already her body was turning into a woman's.

"Yes. At least, *I* think so," she said seriously.

"Thank you, Aimée."

She stayed close to him. He could see one of her eyes, so close that its size was distorted; it seemed to him he could plunge forever into its soft depths. "I love the way you say my name," she said. "You don't say Amy, like everyone else." Her eyelashes butterflied his cheek.

"That's because I'm not English." He turned his face toward her. His lips brushed inadvertently across her mouth.

She leaned forward and kissed the side of his face. "I love you," she said.

"And I you."

"I wish you came home more often."

"It's"—he did not want to hurt her by saying that it was not his home, that it had never been intended to be—"difficult finding the time. Medical students have to work awfully hard."

"Sometimes it's so awkward." She wrinkled her mouth.

"What is?"

"Living here. Daddy, for instance. He drinks such a lot: it makes him a bit sort of funny, sometimes. And Leyla's never here. I don't know what she does up there in London."

Campion thought he did. He tightened his mouth. "I'm here now."

"And I'm glad."

At ten o'clock, he looked at his watch. "Time for bed, Aimée," he said.

She did not argue. "Okay. Come up and kiss me good night, will you?"

"In fifteen minutes."

When he went upstairs, she was still in the bath, lying half submerged, staring up at the ceiling. Her hair had been tied up on top of her head with a rainbow-colored ribbon. The sight of her thin halfway body, no longer a child's, yet still far from being an adult's, moved him unbearably. Briskly, he pulled out the plug, found a towel and held it out to her.

"Come on, *ma petite*," he said. "You're supposed to be in bed."

Docilely she stepped into the waiting folds and let him pat her dry. Her dark eyes were pensive. "I always used to think that everything turned out right," she said. "But it doesn't necessarily, does it?"

"Not always." Under the towel he could feel the curve of her buttocks.

"What do you do when it doesn't?"

"You adapt. You learn to live with it." He did not wish to talk about such things, afraid she would turn to Leyla and his relationship with her. Afraid, too, that lingering here with her was somehow wrong. She was not a little girl anymore. He felt his cheeks grow hot. "Come on," he said roughly. "Where's your nightdress?"

"Under my pillow."

He followed her into her bedroom. By the side of her bed, she dropped the towel and began to pull her nightdress over her head. It was tied at the neck with pink ribbons: they tangled with the one in her hair. With her arms in the air and her head covered, she began to giggle helplessly.

"Help!" she said. "I'm stuck."

Campion drew in a deep breath and advanced toward her. "For heaven's sake," he said. He lifted the nightdress to restart the operation.

"Help!" she said again, falling toward him. She leaned against him, shaking with laughter.

Hugo came into the room and stopped short. Behind him was Leyla. She ran forward, pushing past her husband. "Get your hands off her!" she screamed. "Get away from her, you pervert!" He turned, the hem of his sister's nightdress in his hands, feeling sick, knowing that Leyla had found the weapon she had looked for all his life, the weapon that would kill him at last.

She had turned to Hugo. "Thank God we came back," she said, one hand on her heart. "I knew something was wrong." Her eyes gleamed with malice as she rushed past him to Amy and tugged down her clothes. "Did he hurt you, darling?" she crooned. "Did he *touch* you?"

Amy struggled out of her mother's arms. Her face was red. "Of *course* not," she shouted. "Of *course* he didn't."

Over her shoulder, Leyla spat at Hugo, "She's probably too afraid to tell the truth."

Campion moved slowly toward the door. Amy screamed at him. "Tell her, Alexander. It isn't what she thinks."

He said nothing, wondering how she could already know about such things.

"Say something, Alexander. Tell her." Amy collapsed on her bed, weeping. The nightdress had rucked itself up over her immature hips.

Leyla tugged it down. Her face was controlled, chilly. "I know what I saw," she said. Her black eyes stared into her son's. "I've always been terrified he would turn out as perverted as his father."

Campion would not look at her. He passed Hugo, who still stood red-faced and stupid, just inside the room, trying to take in what was happening. Campion said nothing, made no denial. What was the point? Leyla had what she wanted; she had taken a plowshare and beaten it into a flaming sword. She would see to it that he and his sister would never be free together again. She would destroy his love, and take pleasure in the destruction.

What made it all so unbearable was that in a way she was right. Although he had done nothing, God only knew how much he had wanted to.

■■

"Ah." Laforêt leaned over his balcony. *"Au 'voir, chérie. A bientôt."* Foreshortened, the woman who had emerged from the entrance at street level looked up at him and waved. She carried a briefcase of brown alligator skin with gold clasps. He looked across at Campion again. "And did the marriage to the big Englishman succeed?"

Campion did not answer for a moment. This stranger seemed to know a lot about him. Finally he said, "That would depend on your definition of success."

Laforêt's face changed: the mouth pouting, a dimple showing in one cheek, the eyes crinkling. "My dear, it sounds terrifically intriguing. However"—he brushed a hand down one of the velvet revers of his dressing gown—"one is scarcely dressed for an exchange of confidences. Why don't you drop over tonight? We could have a drink. Do say yes."

Campion thought he might enjoy a couple of hours with someone who could not exactly be classed as a stranger, even if this was the first time they had met. "Thank you," he said.

"Around eight," Laforêt said. "There may be other people arriving later. You won't mind, I'm sure." He gave a complicit smile, as though he had known exactly what Campion had been thinking about him and, with a wave, stepped back into his own flat.

■■

It was the first of many parties that Campion was to attend in the big Laforêt apartment. Gilles, he would learn, was a genuinely happy man. He loved women—all women. He also loved men, not sexually but as friends, nor was he ashamed to say so, to say "I love you." After the years of English schooling, Campion found such openness exhilarating. In Gilles's company he felt some of his secretiveness seep away, as though the older man's liberal personality was causing hairline fractures in the seals around his heart. Despite an opulent lifestyle, Laforêt was far wealthier than he needed to be, nor was there any reason why he should not continue to be so until he died. Although, he told Campion, he had originally trained as an accountant, family money had eventually made working for a living seem redundant. It was in his drawing room that Campion first began consciously to appreciate that money, the independence it bestowed, was like having a third hand. With the essentials taken care of, you were free to get on with more important things than mere self-survival.

That first evening, crossing the shuttered street, he was still wary. A manservant opened the door to him and led him into the big salon. Gilles was alone, drinking brandy in front of an open fire. Only one lamp was lit. It threw strange shadows from the bronzes with which the room was filled: rearing horses, men in armor, pagan youths standing naked beside tree stumps, helmeted goddesses. A profusion of gilt, of decorated porcelain, of mirror and silver and patterned fabric, crowded the available spaces. Campion was too inexperienced to recognize the expectant readiness of a place shortly to be filled with guests.

Gilles opened champagne. "We must celebrate," he said.

Taking the narrow crystal glass, Campion said, "Celebrate what?"

"Your first time here. I hope sincerely that it will not be your last."

They tipped glasses together and drank. Campion felt himself loosen. He sat opposite Gilles, staring into the fire, content not to speak until his host wished to.

"So." Gilles raised his brandy to his lips. "The sculptor still breathes life into clay, does he?"

"Sorry?"

"Monsieur Campion. Does he not still produce those glorious pieces? I must confess I have seen little of his work recently. Has your beautiful mother not inspired him to even greater heights?"

"Sir Hugo has more or less given up sculpting," he said lightly. "The demands of his estate . . . Perhaps you did not know that he inherited when his brother died. It is a big responsibility."

"And are there children from this so . . . inapposite marriage? Do you have a hundred small half-siblings to hang around you when you return to the house of Monsieur Campion?"

"No," he said. For a moment, his inner self strained at the padlocks which confined it. *To tell someone. To be able to tell someone . . .*

"That is sad," said Gilles. "I have no children myself, nor ever wished for them, but that is more because I have never been able to give up all women for one. Had I done so, then children would have been the natural result. As it is . . ." He gestured delicately at nothing in particular. "As it is, I have friends instead."

Even after three years of reading medicine at Cambridge, Campion was not accustomed to alcohol. The champagne he had drunk lay warmly within his body, loosening the joints, slackening the ligaments which bound his limbs to his torso, relaxing him. "How did you know I was a medical student?" he asked.

"My dear, a man of my age and wealth must occupy his time somehow. I have no job, no family. When I am not entertaining my beloved friends, or being entertained by them, I spy on my neighbors. I used to watch you as a child, clinging to the balcony opposite. Especially when the pretty little mother appeared."

Campion said nothing. Almost he could feel again the cold iron against his fingers, the cold fear in his heart.

"One was never quite sure that she would not do some violence," Gilles continued gently. He did not look at his guest. "One was never absolutely certain that irrationality would not finally conquer. Once one had realized, one made sure, always, that one could be seen, watching."

Campion said, "I saw you sometimes."

"You were not meant to." Gilles turned the glass in his hand. Reflections from the fire danced on the cut-glass facets and struck flickering highlights from other objects in the gloominess of the room beyond. "When you returned last year, alone, and grown so big, so handsome, I set myself to find out why you were back here. It really wasn't difficult."

"You made inquiries?"

"Some. For the rest, I observed. The white coat you sometimes throw over a chair when you come home at night. The books you study. The long hours you appear to work. And then there are the young people—your fellow students—with whom you spend time."

Campion straightened in his chair. "How can you know about them? I never invite them home. Have you followed me?"

"A couple of times, while walking near the university, I have happened by chance to see you."

"Isn't that taking spying on your neighbors a little far?"

"A little, perhaps. Not too much." Gilles spread his arms wide, smiling like a cherub. "But do you grudge me this? I have so little else."

It was difficult to feel annoyance. Leaning back, Campion said lazily, "What else do you know about me?" He wondered at an existence so empty that it should need the meat of other lives to flesh it out. Why should his hitherto unknown and anonymous neighbor go to such lengths to find out about him? He was not yet sufficiently acquainted with Gilles to appreciate his enthusiasm for the business of living, or his genuine fondness for and interest in his fellow men. Yet even during that first meeting, new possibilities glittered at him. Dimly he perceived, through the older man, that there were lives based on affection rather than fear, existences not trammeled by ungiving. It seemed many years since he had last loved anything: incredulously he realized it was possible that he might one day love again.

"I suspect, for instance, that you have been quite deliberately stunted," Gilles said.

Surprised, half laughing, Campion said, "What?"

"Emotionally, I mean. Perhaps you have not yet realized it. I also know that you have not yet begun to enjoy, to accept, to give."

"How can you possibly know such things about someone you've never met before?" Campion found himself blushing without knowing why. "Did you deduce them, too? You cannot have observed them."

"It's amazing what you can see through a window," said Gilles. The doorbell rang.

The people he met that first time were representative of those he was to meet over the next few years. Rich, for the most part, and very influential. United in the warmth of their feeling for Gilles. Laforêt never spoke again of Leyla, yet Campion knew they both shared a knowledge of her. It became a comfort to him to know that if he needed to tell someone about the horror which, even after all these years, still swelled inside him, Gilles was there. It made the burden of his loneliness much easier to bear. It occurred to him that, until now, he had never had a friend. There was Amy, of course. And moments, during his schooldays, when he and Forrest might have . . . but circumstances had not made that viable.

It was at one of Gilles's parties that he first noticed Henriette de Tresail. She and her husband arrived late, shedding apologies. They had been to the theater and there were no taxis because it was raining. Drops of water sparkled in her black hair as she brushed at it with her hand. Her dark eyes crinkled as, shaking with sudden laughter, she described how they had splashed through the puddles, had reached a taxi at the same time as a fat old man in a dinner jacket, had wrenched at the handle and jumped inside and roared away, leaving him impotently raging. Leyla's eyes used to crease in the same engaging way when she laughed.

Though they did not talk together, Campion watched her. Later, Gilles held him back when the other guests had gone. "Have a nightcap with me."

"All right, but a quick one. I'm on duty at the hospital tomorrow night."

The two sat down on either side of the black marble fireplace. "She is old enough to be your mother," Gilles said. "Not only old enough, but like enough."

"Who is?"

"Henriette. The one who came late."

"So?" Campion ran a finger around the rim of his glass.

"So perhaps that is why you could not take your eyes off her."

"I saw no likeness to Leyla."

"She is very rich. Her husband is the Comte de Tresail."

"The banker?"

"Yes. Were you aware that in spite of that, poor Henriette is lonely?"

"How could I be? I didn't speak to her."

"But you wished to."

"Possibly." Campion did not explain that it was Henriette's likeness to Amy that attracted him, not any similarity there might have been to Leyla.

"It shall be arranged."

"Don't be ridiculous, Gilles. I can arrange my own rendezvous, when I wish to make them."

"After the first time, yes."

Campion flushed. What else had Gilles observed from his vantage point? Or, rather, not observed? "What do you mean?"

"I cannot be sure," Gilles said. "But I would guess that you are a virgin, yes?"

"That is my business."

"Of course. I merely wish to state that Henriette would do very well if you would like to change that state of affairs."

■■

Much later, after the Organization had been set up, after Jacques de Tresail had blown his brains out and Campion had changed from medical student to director of the Phoenix Foundation, Henriette did very well indeed.

■■

At his father's invitation, Campion spent the summer in England, in the house on the marshes. His father said, "I intend to visit your mother. It has been a long time since we met."

For a second, a flame of hope flared in Campion's heart, then died. It was too late for the reconciliation he had longed for over the years. By marrying her, Hugo had made sure that Leyla could never return to his father.

He wanted to go with him, to see Amy. He knew that Leyla would poison the visit, make elaborately sure that the two of them would not be alone together. Perhaps if he spoke of his love for his sister, his father might help. He opened his mouth to say something, to request, perhaps even to demand, that the separation Leyla had forced on them was brought to an end. He longed to see his sister; the force of it licked at his nerve ends like flames. *She had no right. . . . It was cruel, cruel.* Inside him, emotion boiled like heating water. He did not recognize it as a need for tears.

He went over to his father and put an arm around his shoulders. He was the taller now; he looked into his father's warm brown eyes and felt, as always when he was with this gently, kindly man, a vast rush of love. "Father . . ." He felt awkward, his repressive English upbringing too strong for him to give way to displayed emotion, visible tenderness.

"Yes?"

"I've wanted . . . all these years I've wished . . ."

"Yes, my son?"

". . . so much to be with you."

"And I with you." His father's hand caressed the back of his neck. "Always I have longed to be with you."

The two men smiled at one another, each recognizing the other's pain.

■■

In London, walking through the Burlington Arcade, he passed a jeweler's shop. In the window was a pendant—fire opals set in gold—almost identical to the one Leyla wore. He bought it as a gift for Aimée; twisting the stones to catch the sparks at their heart, he thought of it around her neck, between her young breasts.

He was in the garden when he heard the telephone ringing inside the house. After a moment, the woman from the village who was acting as temporary housekeeper came out to him, walking between the low box hedges which guarded the flower beds full of lupins and lavender. She told him he was wanted on the phone. He could see from her mouth that she was distressed, but he did not stop to question her. He walked ahead of her along the brick walkway toward the cool darkness of the house, brushing past the fuchsia bushes loaded with red-hot blossoms. The apples on the little tree were hard and round: there would be a big crop this year although the tree was still young.

Big shapes of chintzed chairs rose out of the dimness. He stumbled between them, half blind from the bright light outside. The telephone was in the hall. He lifted the receiver. Sun streamed through the stained-glass panels in the front door. The fiery reds and oranges fell onto his hand and his bare leg.

Scorching him.

Searing him.

Enveloping him in flames. His hand tightened around the jeweler's little leather box as he listened to the voice on the other end and heard what it was saying.

SOLA

• 11 •

SHE NEVER MINDED THE FITTINGS.
The hours of standing still while the seamstresses fussed around,
adjusting here and pulling there, the tiny tugs as they positioned the
fabric into Gallini's intentions gave her a chance to go away for a
while, back where she wanted to be. Today she stood serenely while
they manipulated about her an evening dress of glacé-kid leather, as
soft and fluid as silk, peacock green, intended to cause a sensation at
the season's first White House ball or Elysée Palace reception. Patiently she turned when instructed, raised an arm, shifted a leg. Otherwise, she was not there. If asked, she could not have described
either the color or style of what she was wearing. Not even the fabric,
although the rich scent of the leather hung just within reach, mingling
with the acrid smell of the seamstresses' sweat and the odor of new-
baked bread from the patisserie on the other side of the road.

She wore a run-down pair of high-heeled shoes in order to repro-
duce the thrusting bodylines around which the dress was being
shaped. Leg-warmers of garish knitted wool kept her legs warm during the fitting sessions. Even in summer the Gallini studio, situated at
the top of the house off the rue Montaigne, was chilly. Yet Sola hardly
felt the cold.

*The garden bloomed in perpetual summer, the borders neat, the
lawns green, tight-packed with grass between flower beds where each blossom stood as it had since her first entranced sight of it. Beside the brick
paths grew thick white lilies, lupins, lavender. There was a little apple
tree, wooden tubs with bay trees on either side of the gate that was never
opened, neatly trimmed box hedges which gave off a dark aggressive smell
in the heat. No roses—they were too voluptuous—but white daisies
massed against the brick walls and fuchsias hanging over the pathways. It
was always sunny in the garden, always warm. Sometimes a small sea-*

breeze blew, ruffling the tall trees on the other side of the wall, making the lilies sway. It was the only place where she was happy.

Sometimes she thought she would like to have become a nun. The cold, quiet peace, clean light falling onto bare stone floors, the routine, the sense of safety. Yes, she'd happily have joined a contemplative order. But they'd never have her. Not after the things she'd done—been forced to do.

How often she had told herself that Mary Magdalene had been forgiven. More than forgiven, loved. But how much worse her own sins were than anything the Magdalene might have done. It was only logical to assume that a person who committed unforgivable sins must, ipso facto, be unlovable.

She stood, scarcely moving, shifting her weight infinitesimally from one foot to another while the women adjusted the hemline, hissing between their teeth as they folded the supple leather in their cream-softened hands. It was a trick she had learned that third winter after Mikkele went away to Germany. She'd learned fast. She'd had to. At thirteen years old, there had been no alternatives. Or so she had presumed when Kemal had explained it to her in his soft voice, holding her hand while she wept for a life she sensed should not have been so brutal. That was not, indeed, for other, luckier ones.

She turned her head slowly to watch her image in the glass. Professionally she noted the way her head sat on her body, the outline of her almost nonexistent breasts. She knew, without any conceit, that physical perfection such as hers was rare, as was the astonishing beauty of her dark severe face. Only a year ago, American *Vogue* had launched it as "The Look of the Decade." Flawless skin the color of tea without milk, soft pink mouth like a kiss come to life, huge eyes, a body that people wanted to run their hands over. She was aware of these things as fact because she was a professional, and because so many people had told her they were so.

Nicole, from the publicity department, appeared at the door of the big cold room. In Sola's opinion, Nicole had more chic than most women. More chic than quite a few of the professional models, too. Though she was too short for regular modeling, she sometimes showed Gallini's less spectacular numbers to private buyers. Designs from the *haute couture* houses were intended more for an ideal of femininity than for the imperfect bodies of its actuality. Since working here, Sola had divided her own sex into two groups: the ones like herself, and the real women, the ones who had jobs and brought up families. She was part of a group that was mainly rich: Italian princesses, *le tout Paris,* the third wives of American millionaires or English pop stars. They seemed not to worry that their diet-starved figures and haggard faces had nothing to do with womanliness. To Sola, they were merely breathing dress-rails on which to hang the clothes for which men like Gallini made them pay through the nose. Nicole was not like that. Her slim figure was natural rather than acquired. There was something sad stashed away inside her, Sola often thought. Probably the husband about whom she sometimes, but not often, talked—about whom Sola never asked. You had to respect other people's privacy if you wanted them to respect your own.

Nicole had people with her: two women, three men. Buyers, were they? Or journalists? The latter, probably. At this time of year, with the collections on show, there were always such visitors. Besides, the buyers went in for a certain chic, if only to establish their own credentials; journalists did not have to. One of them, a tall, dark-haired girl with the kind of clothes that Sola automatically tagged as English, stared at her then spoke to the publicist, who nodded. Sola let her eyelids droop to disguise the irritation she felt. More interviews, no doubt. Further repetitions of the story of her life—or the version of it that Sola produced for public consumption. It seemed incomprehensible that anyone would want to read it yet again. She watched them pass between the aluminum dress racks where the canvas *toiles* hung like shrouds. She hoped they would not come over to her, ask questions, take notes, their eyes greedy on her body as though she was no more than an object, no more than something to be used and paid for and forgotten. She hated the look journalists always had, of cold detachment, indifference. The indifference of others brought back the past too painfully.

The dress swirled as one of the seamstresses rearranged the tiny painstaking folds on the hip. Sola looked down at the woman's bent back, the freckles on her hands, the dusting of dandruff on the shoulders of her blouse. The woman was what—forty-five? Fifty? It seemed unimaginably old. Sola knew that she herself would never be that old. Long ago the scars had formed over the wounds left by the loss of her mother and of Mikkele, but it would take no more than a pinprick to pierce the tissue and then the grief would ooze from her again like pus, until she drowned in it.

The incongruity of the older woman's shabby black clothes in this room dedicated to the highest of high fashion, the smartest of unnecessary chic, never failed to sadden Sola. Her own mother had been a seamstress before the disease stopped her working. That was how Sola always saw her, sitting in the chair with the high back, shrinking with the passing years, her body growing ever more twisted, blue eyes liquid with unspoken pain. As a child, Sola had often stared into that yellowed bloodless face and wondered why she was dark-haired with black eyes and skin the color of burnt toffee, while Mikkele was so much lighter of complexion. He had explained about genes and chromosomes and dominant characteristics; she, through some genetic lottery, took after the Algerian father they had never known, while he had inherited more of their mother's coloring.

Their mother had been tall once, as high as a tree, Mikkele said. The two of them had loved to walk down the cobbled streets between the shabby wooden houses to the markets, watching her ahead of them, her round hips swaying from side to side under the loose garments she always wore. Coming back home, uphill, she would lean into the angle of the slope, the heavy basket of bread and vegetables dragging her to one side, the jangle of her bracelets loud in the silence of early afternoon. Around them, the city grew modern, leaned toward the West, toward England, toward America, but her fair-haired mother still clung to the traditions of the remote village where she had been raised by her peasant parents. . . .

On her knees, the seamstress behind her grunted, tugging the fine tough fabric at Sola's waist. The girl stood quietly while the woman's fingers stretched and smoothed. Gallini had a great line in melodrama, and all of them knew that the slightest deviation from his intended effect was liable to produce a comprehensive selection from his vast range of hysterics. It was worth taking an extra half hour over the fitting to avoid that. Gently Sola clenched her teeth together, grinding the thoughts of the past into obscurity. Bad days, worse nights. Block them out. Pretend they had never happened. Don't let anyone know about them, ever.

Consciously, she let her strained shoulders droop. She breathed in, slowly filling her lungs, willing herself back into one of the gardens.

Deep breathing relaxed the muscles and reduced the inner tension. She'd learned that in her yoga class. Until recently, it had worked. Now, with the new pressures, it was helping less than it used to. She wondered where she could go next. Over the last few years she had tried almost everything in her efforts to get away from the past: booze, drugs, psychoanalysis, drugs again. Even sex. But all they had done was open wider the chasms she had hoped were closed, and instead, shown her with terrible clarity where the demons lurked.

For a moment the visitors were lost among the long tables stacked with fabrics and the dress forms ranged like ceramic Chinese warriors against the wall. Then they reappeared, moving away from her down the room. Their voices were swallowed by the leaning rolls of silk and brocade, of fine cashmere and tweed, by the swathes of material which hung everywhere. Their images, mirrored in the long looking-glass walls, moved too, faintly blurred by the angle of reflection. Nicole spoke to them earnestly, her sleek blond head nodding, the nodding repeated in the mirrors.

Sola closed her eyes and breathed in slowly through her nose. A garden, any of them, she did not mind which. Like Alice, she only had to look into a looking glass to be lost in another world which had nothing to do with this. Colors swirled inside her head, took on shape and meaning: blue of sky, green of grass. She found herself in a garden she had visited last year, when Gallini had taken some of them over to London.

She walked slowly along gravel paths toward a box hedge where lupins bloomed above massed clumps of alyssum and daisies. There were no real seasons in her gardens. Flowers grew as and when they pleased. Gardens were long-term investments. Creating one was like working in the dark, blinkered, the darkness pierced by impulses of light which would be the future. She had smelled orange blossom and lilac then, swooning with the sweetness of the scent. Not now. This time there were roses, too: open, sweet-scented, white and cream and yellow—but she did not care for roses anymore. Not after . . . Carefully she pushed the memory out of her mind, and selected somewhere else. Apple trees, the blossoms dancing against a blue sky, pure, virginal, impregnable. Daffodils delicate under gnarled black trunks, bearded irises warm among speared leaves.

When she opened her eyes, Nicole was approaching the raised plinth on which Sola stood.

"Don't forget the photographers will be here immediately after the lunch break," Nicole said.

Sola shook her head. "I hadn't."

"And there's a woman journalist from England who wants to interview you sometime tomorrow. If you don't mind, I've given her your home address. There won't be time for her to talk to you during the day."

"Do I have to?" Sola said. She drew her beautiful brows together and slammed down the shutters inside her head. She hated interviews: people always asked the same questions: *Is it true you met Gallini at . . . ?* and *Do you find your ethnic origins a help or . . . ?*

"She's doing a series on black women in high-powered jobs," said Nicole.

"Do I count as black?"

"Of course," Nicole said reprovingly. "The word is used much more generally these days. She wants to hear something about your life as a top model, but from a different perspective. Apparently she's not particularly interested in the glamor aspect."

"That's a change."

"Quite. Just make sure you mention Gallini as often as you can."

"Must I see her?"

Nicole stared at the tiny platinum watch set with diamonds which she wore on her right wrist. "Of course you must." She looked up at the model. "Don't worry about it, Sola. You'll be fine."

Sola watched thoughtfully as Nicole walked the English girl away from her toward the door. Her ruler-straight brows lay against her skin as though embroidered in black silk, each delicate stitch clearly defined. For a moment she thought of feigning illness tomorrow, but she was under contract to Gallini and he would throw several of his celebrated fits if she refused to do an interview.

Which brought her to the other matter: the man. Her eyes went to the tall windows at the end of the room. She could see the black roofs of the houses opposite, a ginger cat lying against the railings of a narrow balcony, a depressed rubber plant put out for the air. He had been there again last night, on the other side of the street, standing back in a doorway as she came out into the chill evening wetness of Paris in a rainy September. There had been fog around the lamps. The outlines of buses farther down the boulevard were blurred, impressionistic. She could not see him clearly, yet she knew he was waiting for her. She had felt a chill in the middle of her spine. For years men had stared at her, but there was something different about him and the way he had watched her: not so much frightening as disturbing. There were always the kooks in this kind of game; she knew that. Always the perverts hanging about, fingering themselves through the pockets of their trousers, ringing up during business hours to make obscene suggestions about the girls, trying to con the receptionist out of home phone numbers or addresses. It was one of the hazards of being beautiful. But the man who had waited for her yesterday and the day before—she knew perfectly well he was wait- ing, although he pretended to be nothing more than a passerby—did not have the air of one who needed furtive sex. Even in the dark, she could see that he was too sure of himself for that, too much in control.

What terrified her most was that although she had not seen him full face, she knew she had seen him before. But where? Was it in Istanbul? She chopped the thought off as viciously as an ax-swinging executioner. She almost never gave the city its name; doing so gave it a substance she wished to deny. Without a name, her own past was made more nebulous, which was how she wanted it to be. It was safer that way.

Whoever he was, could his presence here be simply a coinci- dence? Or had he tracked her down, deliberately sought her out? Her nails dug into the palms of her hands. All she wanted was peace. All she wanted was the quiet of a garden where she could be alone. She had been innocent once, until forced into a way of life which had haunted her ever since. Was it fair that she should go on suffering for something that was not her fault? Like the past, the world crowded in on her.

Yesterday he had almost spoken to her. Soon he would. And what would she do then?

Turning her head, she saw herself receding through an infinity of mirrors, each reflection more indistinct than the last. Tall, dark, un- smiling, with the huge eyes and rounded vulnerable forehead of a baby. People often forgot just how ruthless babies are—have to be—in order to survive.

Her solemn face stared back at her. She had not wept since the day of her mother's funeral. Not once—though God knew there had been reason enough. Nor had she ever smiled. People—her mother's cousin, the nuns—had urged her so often, pointing cameras at her, asking if she liked this or had enjoyed that and she always said, "Yes, thank you. Yes, I did," because it was the truth. She had not liked to disappoint them, but they seemed unable to understand that smiling would not make it more true.

Looking at her reflection, she wondered which one was the true Sola: the vulnerable or the strong? Was there ever a truth, or was there merely the suggestion of it? She knew that the persona she presented to the world was false in every way except in the fact of its existence. And in its memories. Nothing could ever change the past.

• 12 •

HER TENTH BIRTHDAY WAS THE
day when everything had seemed to alter. When she was older, she
could look back and realize that nothing is ever that cut-and-dried.
Journeys need time to prepare; arrangements have to be made. It was
obvious, later, that things had not suddenly all changed on that particular day. Mikkele, for instance, must have been laying plans with her
mother and uncle well before that. There must have been letters to be
written and documents to obtain: work permits, passports, resident
visas. But as far as she was concerned, Mikkele went to Germany on
her birthday and nothing after that was ever the same.

He announced that he was going when her mother had finished
putting away the plates and cups and was sitting with Mehmet in the
other room, drinking the bottle of wine that Mehmet had brought.

"Tonight Mehmet and I are going away," he said.

"Away?"

"To Germany."

"Why didn't you tell me?" she asked. Her birthday slipped away
from her, its colors suddenly turning gray.

"I'm telling you now, sweetheart."

"But you can't go," she said. "You can't leave us alone."

"I have to. Mehmet and I are going to find work," he said.

She was glad about that. Work meant money. And money meant
presents like the necklace of glass beads he had given her, each one
the color of the sky in summer before the sun has fully risen. "That's
good," she said doubtfully.

"I hope so." Mikkele looked through the doorless opening into
the second room. "You know I don't like to leave you and our mother
alone. But Mehmet says there is plenty of work in Germany. We can
send you money. And when we come back, we shall be rich enough to
buy a little business."

"A fruit shop?" she said. She had always wanted to have a shop like the one in the small bazaar, where cascades of tangerines and peaches and melons spilled out of baskets onto rush mats, beautiful and reassuring, a promise of endless plenty.

Mikkele smiled. "Maybe a fruit shop. Or maybe carpets. Or perfumes. Anything you like."

Round-eyed, she stared up into his pale eyes. Six years older than she was, he had already reached most of the height he would have as a man.

"Perfumes? We would be like Kemal Effendi then."

Mikkele's face clouded. "We shall never ever be like him," he said shortly. *"Never."* For a moment he looked in silence at his little sister's face. She was small, underdeveloped. Not really much bigger than an eight-year-old. Perhaps she did not get enough to eat. Or the nuns had somehow brainwashed her into thinking that she would be in a better state of grace if she mortified the flesh: ate less food than she wanted, or gave hers away to someone in greater need than herself. Like his sister, he had been brought up as a Catholic. It was a faith that he had found difficult to sympathize with and impossible to follow. There were so many illogicalities. Why, for instance, should there be more rejoicing over one lost lamb that is saved than over the ninety and nine who struggled to be virtuous? Why was prayer more likely to reach the ear of God if the petitioner knelt upright on a hard stone floor than if he used a hassock?

He knew all about the nuns who taught his sister, and the thousand inducements to guilt that they practiced. Solange's aptitude for asceticism worried him. Once he had woken in the night to find her sleeping on the bare floor of the room they shared. Although it was the middle of winter, she wore only a thin cotton nightdress and her covers were still on her bed. Once, he had seen her hobbling home from school like an old woman, her face screwed up with pain from the stones she had put in her shoes. When he remonstrated, she lifted her face to his and said, "Sister Véronique says Our Lord's sufferings were far worse than anything *we* could ever experience."

"You are so little."

"Sister Véronique says we must mortify the flesh for the glory of God."

What kind of a God asked little girls to wear stones in their shoes? "There are many names for God," he said. "And many ways to glorify Him."

She was too young for him to explain what he had realized some time ago: that most of us are not called upon to sacrifice ourselves for an ideal, and that if we were, if martyrdom was the general expectation, then an event such as the Crucifixion would lose its supremely symbolic appeal. He had made his own choice of ideal a couple of years ago; if it led to martyrdom—as he had so often been warned that it might—he could be thankful that at least it would not take one of the sadistic Christian forms. Commitment to terrorism meant that he had lived long enough on the edge of fear almost to welcome the possibility of a clean bullet through the heart or an exploding bomb. Capture and torture were eventualities he preferred not to think about.

Looking at Solange's face, he felt a pang of misgiving. His mother's illness was beginning to take hold—it was one of the reasons he and Mehmet had decided to go to Germany. Would she be capable of protecting this little innocent one? Already men stared after her in the street. Suppose he was not able to return for a year or so: who would take care of his sister? He thought of Kemal, their landlord, and his uneasiness grew. The man was always at their apartment, being overfamiliar with their mother, staring at Solange, attempting a brusque kind of friendship with Mikkele himself. Once he had offered him two or three days of rough gardening work, and, when Mikkele accepted, for the sake of his mother and sister, had come down in person to drive him up to his villa in the hills . . . but it was best not to think of that.

He could only warn the women against the man and his reputation; he dared not do more. To show open hostility to a man like Kemal could put the two of them at risk. They might even find themselves turned out onto the street. Or worse.

Mikkele did not wish to think about what worse might mean. Kemal's reputation was well known. The upper levels of the city's society admired him as a reputable businessman who supported local charities and gave generously when help was needed, but many of those who lived further down the scale feared him. Even if they had never seen him, they knew of him. It was rumored that he was heavily involved with many of the city's more lucrative crime rackets. Most said nothing when confronted with his thugs: they found life hard enough already without the extra burden of the violence, extortion, and intimidation that were an essential part of Kemal Effendi's stock-in-trade.

The disease which was attacking his mother was slow. She had explained it to him but he had not wanted to hear about the way her tall, well-loved body would gradually disintegrate. It was only necessary to seize on the fact that she was not going to die—at least, not soon. In a year or two they would have accumulated enough savings to come home again, to buy the things she would need, to pay a woman to come in and look after her while Solange continued her studies.

It was his mother's prime obsession that her children be decently educated. Education was the key to the door that would lead the two of them to freedom, to a better life than the one they had been forced to live since his father's death in an accident at one of the quarries north of the city. Not that they were desperate: with the compensation his widow received, and the money she was able to earn as a seamstress, they had managed. But the money was beginning to run out, especially as the disease was making it harder for her to work. It worried him. Earlier in the year, Kemal had raised his rents; not a lot, because that would not accord well with his public image, but enough to cause hardship for a number of the families living in his apartment buildings.

Many other children in the same building were taken out of school at the earliest possible moment and set to work at anything—market stalls, picking over the fleeces which came into the city from the countryside, running errands, or sweeping café floors—in order to bring money into the household. Mikkele and his sister were often jeered at by the street urchins as they set off in the mornings in their neat school smocks. Mikkele did not mind leaving school. By most standards he was already well educated—the monks had seen to that —and besides, he had long since outgrown the childish world of rules and books. He had stayed on only because the leader of his terrorist cell felt it provided good cover for his other activities, and allowed him to slip into places to which entry might otherwise be barred. He knew that for him, what he had undertaken for the cell so far was only the beginning: as soon as he had raised his sister, seen her into a good job as a secretary, maybe in one of the foreign banks on Istiklal Caddesi, he had plans of his own.

■■

For Solange, Mikkele's departure had been traumatic. One moment they were a unit of three, close-knit and loving. The next, it was as though a desert wind, laden with scouring grains of sand, had swept over them, leaving only the bare bones of the family they had once been. Until he was gone, Solange had not realized to what extent Mikkele was the pillar propping them up.

Sister Véronique had called her into the parlor. Outside the heavily grilled window was a paved courtyard with a rectangular pool in the center. Although she had never been out there, Solange was sure there must be fish in the water, flitting like gold and silver shadows between the thick stems of the water lilies. The rough white walls were crowned with orange tiles the color of the cinnamon they sold from huge baskets in the Spice Market. Fig trees threw shadows which Solange thought must be as big as ogres' hands. In niches cut into the walls stood statues of saints and, at one end, in a kind of grotto, the Blessed Virgin Mary herself, hands clasped together as she gazed upward toward heaven.

Sister Véronique smelled of rose water. She put both her hands on Solange's shoulders. "You didn't tell me your brother had gone away," she said. Her eyes were very sad.

How to explain that you had not thought a person as . . . as *elevated* as Sister Véronique would even care to know you *had* a brother, let alone that he was off in Germany earning money so they could one day have a fruit shop? Or maybe a perfume shop.

She cast down her eyes. *"Oui, ma soeur,"* she said. Sister Véronique must always be addressed in French. She came from a place called Paris and was always saying she hoped they would go there one day since it was the most civilized city in the world.

"You should have told me," insisted the nun.

Under the heavy cotton smock she wore to protect her school uniform, Solange felt her muscles tighten with the anticipation of fear. That particular note in the nun's voice meant she was angry—no, not angry so much as grieved over something one of her pupils had done.

"I'm sorry, *ma soeur.*"

"It sounds as if you were trying to keep something from me, Solange—as if you were trying to deceive me."

"No," Solange said. She tried to keep the desperation out of her voice. She had noticed in the past that any appearance of fear only grieved Sister Véronique more, because it showed a lack of desire to reform.

Silently she prayed that if she was to be beaten, it would be on the hands. She could hide her hands from her mother; it was much harder to disguise the fact that sitting down was painful. Besides, Mikkele had taught her to rub methylated spirits into her palms. It toughened them up so the ruler hurt less. "No, truly I was not. It was just . . ."

"Just what?"

"I did not think you would be interested, *ma soeur.*" As soon as she had said it, Solange knew how angry, how *grieved* this remark would make Sister Véronique. She stared at the floor, noting the twin curves of her feet in their black uniform shoes against the edge of the richly patterned carpet. It was bordered with a fringe of blue and gold and red, each silk thread ranged exactly parallel to its neighbor.

Sister Véronique clapped a hand to her chest as though she was trying to restrain her heart from leaping out of her breast from sheer indignation and sorrow. "Not interested, Solange? Not *interested?* How can you say such an extraordinary thing to me?"

Solange murmured. She could feel her backside tightening with terror.

Inside Sister Véronique's chest her breath wheezed and groaned. She pressed both hands against the front of her habit. "You know how much the welfare of my girls means to me," she said. "To say otherwise is a cruelty which I had not expected. Oh, Solange, Solange, you have grieved me. To be cruel to others, even out of thoughtlessness, is a sin." Her voice suddenly changed. "Which sin, Solange?"

"Pride, *ma soeur.*" Solange hoped she had picked the right one. In the panic which filled her, she could scarcely concentrate. Among the older girls it was different, but she had learned that for girls of her own age the sin they were most often guilty of was pride—followed closely by greed. And not telling Sister Véronique about Mikkele could scarcely be labeled greedy—unless it was a spiritual greed, a desire to keep for herself the information that she should have shared.

She squeezed her nails into her palms. *The hands, please,* she begged silently. She did not dare look up at the figure of the Sacred Heart which stood in a corner of the room. Tears were already forming in her eyes. It always hurt so much: that first vicious stroke which for a second you scarcely felt, until the pain washed through you, aggravated by the second and third. She tried to calculate how many strokes she would receive. Not telling them about Mikkele was surely a very minor sin, wasn't it?

Without moving her head, she watched Sister Véronique walk around behind her desk and open the big drawer in the middle. She took out a thin white stick, tapered at one end like a conductor's baton. *The hands, the hands* . . .

The nun tapped the stick into her palm, and smiled. "You have grieved me very much, Solange."

"I am truly sorry, *ma soeur.*"

"The only way to drive out sin is to punish it, Solange. You understand that?"

"Yes," whispered Solange.

"Hold out your hands, child. Both of them."

Solange stretched out her arms to their full extent, palms upward. Sometimes Sister Véronique could make you stand like that for as long as ten minutes. The ache would sometimes have bitten deep into your shoulders before she started to use her stick. After that, of course, everything was focused on where it landed. Solange felt her chin quiver.

The nun stepped forward and raised her arm. Then, abruptly, she lowered it. "I am failing you, Solange, by not dealing with you as God would have me do. I beg you to forgive me if this once I neglect your soul."

Solange heard only enough to realize that, for some reason impossible to comprehend, she was to be let off. For the moment, the cause of the relief was irrelevant. The ache in her upper arms was already excruciating; all her fingers trembled violently.

"Yes, *ma soeur.*" She hardly dared breathe for fear of again arousing the nun's grief.

"The fact is, I have received a visit from a friend of your family. He tells me he has been keeping an eye open for you and your mother, now that your brother has gone. Do you know to whom I refer?"

"No, *ma soeur.*" What friend? Her mother had no male friends, beyond Mehmet, who was her husband's brother and had always visited them once a week until he went away with Mikkele.

"Surely you must know Kemal Effendi."

Solange wanted to say that there must be some mistake. Kemal was not a friend of the family but their landlord. Some instinct made her keep quiet. She sensed that for some reason of her own, Sister Véronique would not wish to have this pointed out. "Yes, *ma soeur.*"

"He has asked if we would allow him to take you out for a ride in his car this afternoon. I have given the matter some thought and decided that in view of your circumstances, it might be of benefit to you. You may therefore present yourself in the front hall at three o'clock."

■■

It would be many years before Sola was to question just how much the nun had known.

Much later she would remember the new piano in the music room, or a glittering pair of candlesticks on the altar in the chapel, and wonder what they had cost and which of the other girls like her who had waited for Kemal in the front hall had paid the price for them.

Twice a week, Kemal would turn up at the big iron gates of the school and take her away with him. "For tea," he would say, or "For a little drive." And lowering his voice to a murmur, would add confidentially, "She will be safe with me, *mes soeurs.*"

The nuns would nod, glancing at each other beneath their pale eyelids. To what extent were they aware of events outside the cinnamon-tiled walls? Did they have any notion of the crimes attached to Kemal's name, or did they truly believe in the public persona he presented, as philanthropist and benefactor? They knew that Solange's father was dead, that her brother had gone abroad to work, that the mother was dying of some incurable wasting disease of the muscles. In a cosmopolitan city such as this, the child's background need not necessarily be a barrier to a job, respectability, a decent life. Yet, worldly beneath their black habits, they knew that it probably would. Perhaps they genuinely believed that if Kemal Effendi took an interest in her, she might have a better chance to get on and for that reason were always delighted to send little Solange Bonami off in his care.

"So handsome," they said, pushing her hair back under her school hat, brushing at her white blouse and blue school skirt. "Such a good man," they whispered, tying her scarf of cherry wool around her neck.

■■

Sola loved everything about him from the beginning. He smelled rich. There was tobacco in the smell, and a perfume with citrus and musk in it, clean starched cotton and thick leather. For the rest of her life, Sola would see him again in her mind's eye whenever she smelled lemons. That first afternoon, she climbed into the car beside him and felt immediately at ease. He was big. Close to, she could see a dimple in one cheek, the indentation of pockmarks beneath his eyes, the flash of a gold tooth when he smiled. She had seen him before, of course, though she had only observed him from a distance. On his once frequent visits to their apartment, she had never dared do more than peep around the door at him; in addition she had often noticed him walking through the city streets surrounded by his men, seven or eight of them at a time.

That first day, he took her to a café and sat drinking tea with her while she ate sweet sticky cakes. Once he leaned forward and wiped a drip of honey from the corner of her mouth. He smiled at her. People passed their table, nodding, calling out greetings. Sometimes they stopped to hand over money or envelopes to him. Sometimes he would call out a name and a passerby would come over and listen while he spoke in a low voice, then go.

That first day, he told Solange about his own little girl, who had died when she was eight years old.

"You remind me of her very much," he said. "For her sake, I hope you will be my friend."

To Solange, it was a novel idea that a grown-up should ask a child to be his friend. "Of course I will," she said. She saw herself taking the place of his lost daughter, just as he might replace her lost father. She felt very proud, sitting there in public with him, and hoped that people would notice and wonder who Kemal's friend was.

"That would be very kind," he said.

"What was her name?"

"Uh—Yasmin."

"That's a very pretty name," she said politely.

"She was a very pretty little girl," he said, "but not as pretty as you are." He looked her over. "How old are you, my dear. Eight? Nine?"

"Ten," she said. "A month ago today."

"A month ago? Then you must allow me to buy you a late birthday present."

"Oh, no." Though no one had ever explained to her exactly why not, she knew that she must never accept presents from men.

"Why not?"

Rapidly she decided that the nuns would hold more weight with him than her mother. "Sister Véronique would be cross."

"Sister Véronique?" He laughed, the gold tooth flashing at the back of his mouth. "She most certainly won't."

He obviously did not know the nun very well and Solange felt tense with anxiety. On the one hand she did not wish to offend this kind man who had no family of his own. On the other, she dreaded the thought of grieving Sister Véronique. She stared at him, her eyes huge and worried, trying to think of something that would convince him.

He put one of his hands over hers and closed it protectively. "Please, Solange, let me do this. It would give me so much pleasure." His eyes were large and dark and seemed to grow suddenly moist. She guessed he was thinking of dead Yasmin. "I promise you I'll have a word with Véronique. You'll see: she won't even mention it to you."

Solange had never before heard the nun's name without its prefix. In an odd way it removed her mystique, reducing her to ordinariness. Until she left school, Solange was never to fear Sister Véronique quite as much again. That was one of the many things for which she was grateful to Kemal.

Later, as a damaged adult, what she hated most was that whenever the concept of "Father" came to mind, it was Kemal who rounded out the notion for her. His smell, his feel, his arms around her, always signified the fatherness of "Father" in the split second before she kicked it away, out of her head, out of her heart.

■■

The pattern of that afternoon was repeated for several weeks. Kemal would collect her from the convent and drive her off into the city, each time to somewhere new. They would eat sweet cakes at a café. He would buy her some small present, repeating how much pleasure it gave him since he no longer had a daughter of his own. He would then drop her off at the school in time for her return home at the normal time. Solange never told her mother of these outings.

Then one afternoon, on a day of gray skies and rain, instead of taking her to a café, he drove her to a house set in the hills above the city. The grounds were surrounded by walls inside which grew a thick hedge of cypress. The house was cream-colored and wide, with curved orange tiles on the roof, which glistened in the rain. There was an air of rejection about the place, perhaps because so many of the windows were shuttered. There were roses everywhere, white ones, their scent filling the air, their petals scattered like snowflakes on the gravel. A fountain faltered in front of the house: a single jet that rose from the center of a shallow stone basin. Solange shivered at the chilly, unforgiving look of the low-slung clouds reflected in its ruffled surface.

There was no one else in the house. Kemal took her upstairs into a long, dark room full of books and pictures and mirrors framed in gold. There was a bed against the far wall; at first glance it seemed as big as the entire flat where she and her mother lived. There were big soft pillows embroidered in white silk, and a shiny coverlet with beautiful roses all over it, red and yellow and pink and some tight little buds with hairy green leaves around them.

Kemal told her he had to talk to someone on the telephone, and until he came back, she was to get on with her schoolwork. Opening her school bag, she sat down at a table whose surface was made up of tiny squares of stone all fitted together to make a picture of a bearded man standing on a shell in the middle of some waves and holding a three-pronged fork.

After a while, Kemal came back. He brought tea with him, rose-colored in a thin pot of green china. Rose against green: was it pretty or not? She could not decide. Although the tea tasted vaguely unpleasant, and much too sweet, she drank it to please him. He sat down in a chair and watched her. She pretended not to notice, knowing he must be thinking of his own lost little daughter.

"Solange," he said. His voice sounded husky. Her heart constricted with pity for him.

"Yes." When she glanced up at him, she saw tears on his cheeks.

"Come over here."

Obediently, she pushed back her chair and walked toward him. At the same time he stood up. He picked her up in his arms. "Do you know why I have brought you here?" he said, holding her close against him.

She shook her head, feeling her hair catch on the roughness of his chin.

"Today would have been Yasmin's birthday," he said. "You have been a good friend to me, little Solange. I was so sad until I met you. Now you have taken her place for me."

She could feel him trembling. She pulled her head back away from his and smiled at him. There was something hot and strange about his eyes and the way his mouth moved. He kissed her cheek, pressing his lips hard against her soft skin. He snuffled his nose under her chin, tickling her so that she giggled hard enough for him to lose his hold on her. He shifted, grasping her more securely, and she felt his hand under her short school skirt. It closed over her buttock, enfolding it.

She felt warm and comfortable; her limbs seemed too heavy for her to lift. He walked slowly over to the bed and laid her down on the big soft comforter. For a while he talked of Yasmin, sadly, telling her what he and Yasmin would have done had she still been alive. It was nice, pressed up against him in the half-dark; she felt warm and safe. He shifted so that he was half-lying, one arm under her shoulders, the other between her parted legs. As he talked, he caressed her under her skirt with gentle fingers. He told her how happy he was to have her there beside him, that it was like having his daughter back again. So when he asked her, a little later, to let him see her naked, she complied. Again he spoke of Yasmin, of how he used to kiss her, like this, and like this. Solange was glad to let him kiss her in the same way, if it made him happy.

When he lowered his head and began to suck at her, she felt soft and swollen with love for him. She opened her legs as wide as she could for him; she turned onto her stomach so he could cup her small buttocks in his big hands, slide a finger slowly in and out of her. She was glad to know how fathers were, never having known her own. Even his weight on her, pushing gently up inside her was surely nothing more than a measure of his affection, a way he could truly love her as though she were his own child.

Or so she had believed.

After that, when he picked her up from school he would drive straight to the house. There was never anyone else there. He would always talk of Yasmin. While they waited in the big tiled kitchen for water to boil for tea—sometimes green, sometimes rose—from a cupboard he would take cakes of honey and nuts and thin layers of pastry which she would greedily devour.

What made Sola so angry later, whenever she allowed herself to think of those days, was that she had genuinely loved Kemal. Even at ten years old, she had known it was not the kind of love she felt for her mother, or for Mikkele. It was a love compounded of possibilities, of delicious tremors that she ought to have been too young to feel, tremors that she was later to recognize as being purely sexual. At the time, she felt she would truly have died for him, had it been necessary.

Even after he changed.

She could smell drink on his breath—she could tell it was something stronger than wine, though she was too young to know exactly what—when he picked her up. As she sat in the car beside him, he put his hand on her thigh and squeezed it hard. When they reached the house, he went straight up to the big room with the bed, not bothering to see whether she followed him. She did, of course—she would have followed him to the edge of the world if he wanted her to. As soon as she came in, he kicked the door shut. He picked her up and threw her onto the bed, pinning her down with one hand while he fumbled with the belt of his trousers. Then he flung himself across her body, forcing her legs so far apart that she cried out in bewilderment . . . before bewilderment turned to fear as he bit and chewed, turning her roughly over, jabbing into her again and again as she gradually came to understand, through the tears and the screams, what the relationship between them really was.

Much worse, was her own realization that deep down, somewhere unacknowledged, she had always known.

■■

It was too late by then. There was no way she could have told her mother the truth. Young as she was, she could see that there was no escape from the economics of their situation. Perhaps if she had spoken out the very first time—but then she had had no idea that it was the first time of anything—or told her mother that she had been taken from the convent by the landlord. But it was too late. She had only wanted to be loved. Now, if the two of them were to live and be fed, she must submit to Kemal's will. There was no choice.

So she submitted, particularly since he had pointed out that if she told her mother he might find himself obliged to put the rent up again.

Dumbly, she also submitted the first time they found another man waiting for them at the villa. A man with the overstuffed pink skin and huge body of a scrubbed pig; a man who smelled, whose flesh shook when he walked, whose small eyes gleamed when, at Kemal's order, she silently undressed and lay down on the bed and, in hatred, let the man do to her what she had let Kemal do out of love.

And again she acquiesced when, the next time, Kemal told her to scream as though what the man did hurt her. She never told him that it really did.

There were many other men after that. She learned to swallow the screams that would rise in her throat while they violated her still undeveloped body—unless Kemal ordered otherwise. In the end, it was pride that kept her silent under the pain. Scream, shudder, wince, and she showed the pig-men that she was something more than a mechanism through which they obtained gratification. They were perverts, but not sadists. They did not like reminders that she was a human being like themselves. Their guilty glance avoided hers. She knew they spoke to Kemal of it because his kind eyes would shut down and something cold and alien took over. Those were the nights she remembered in dreams for the rest of her life.

Once, Kemal had given her a gold star on a pin, saying it was a prize for diligent work. Her by now misshapen mother had cried with pleasure when she saw it, turning it over and over in her crablike hands. Believing it to have come from the nuns, she had not, of course, known exactly what it was her daughter worked at so diligently, and no one was likely to tell her. Why had she so easily accepted what she perceived merely as Kemal's generosity? Had she never asked herself why a man with his reputation would send them food and allow them to stay on in the apartment at so low a rent? Why should she imagine that Kemal would come so often to visit them unless he was getting something out of it?

If she had asked, Solange, even then, would have told her. When she finally died, Solange was often to blame her for not recognizing what was happening. She *should* have realized, should somehow have risen from her bed to call the cops and save her daughter from Kemal.

■■

One afternoon, Kemal told her that a very important man would be waiting for her at the house. Whatever he wanted, she was to let him do. He opened the glove compartment of his car as he drove and took out a box.

"That's for you, little one," he said, in his gentle voice. "But you must work hard for it. And not mind if he hurts you a little."

Dumbly, Solange had opened the box and found a little moonstone set in gold which hung from a golden chain. She looked at Kemal and wanted to say that no betrayal that might happen in the years to come could ever be as great as his betrayal of her love for him. She longed to tell him that nonetheless she still loved him, still wished she could be his own little daughter and sit on his knee surrounded by his strong arms, as she used to. She said nothing.

The roses were in bloom again, as they had been the first time she came there. The smell of them now made her feel ill, associated as they were with afternoons of pain. In the hall, a man was sitting. He rose when they came in. The hat he wore hid most of his expression, but she could see he had a secret face as she walked past him to the foot of the stairs. With the shutters closed against the afternoon sun, the hall was gloomy. The man spoke to Kemal in a language she did not understand, though from her lessons, she guessed it to be English. He was younger than the men who usually came to the house. He sounded curt, as though he disapproved of Kemal, perhaps even disliked him. He did not appear to be afraid of him, though Solange knew that most people were. She felt herself flush with shame as he glanced beyond her up the curved staircase to the half-open bedroom door, gesturing angrily. He understood where she was going. Silently she prayed that he would not hurt her too much.

· 13 ·

ANOTHER TYPING CLASS WAS over. The little group of girls burst through the convent gates and out into the city, chattering with relief at their release. Behind them, the big wooden gates slammed shut, leaving the nuns to their unsullied silences until the next morning. While the others giggled away along the street, Solange stopped, pretending to search through her school bag for something, until they had gone. These days, she avoided her fellow pupils. It they came too close, they might deduce what she had done on those afternoons with Kemal, or smell on her still the rank perfumes of sex. It was better to keep away from them.

This particular day, the street was empty by the time she again started along the sidewalk. She set off in the direction of the bridge, hoisting her bag over her shoulder. If her mother was not too ill, she would soon be able to get the domestic chores out of the way and get on with her homework; if she was quick, there might still be time to look again through the new book Kemal had brought back from his last trip abroad. It was all about English gardens; even though she suspected he had not bought it with her specifically in mind, that did not detract from the pleasure it gave her.

A man turned out of a side street and came toward her, then, seeing her, slowed down. She drew in her breath, feeling her heart lurch. Was it one of the pig-men?

From across the road, he called to her. "Didn't I see you once at Kemal Effendi's house?"

She shook her head.

"Yes, I did," he said. "Some months ago. I was waiting in the hall when you came in."

Again she shook her head, pressing her lips shut. He was right. It had been nearly a year ago, yet she still remembered. There had been something strange about that afternoon. The man in the hall had never come up to the bedroom where she waited, though eventually

Kemal himself had appeared. She knew enough about him by then to cringe as he came toward her. She could tell he was angry: his mouth was set in a thin line, and his normally gentle voice was harsh as he told her to gather her things together because they were leaving.

She had asked no questions: she had learned not to. Through the window she could see the day fading across the fountain and the garden, and farther off, the lights of the city. Had the man in the hall decided that he did not want her? If so, what would Kemal do to her? Perhaps he would stop coming to the convent to collect her. She hardly knew what her reaction would be. Relief, of course. On the other hand, never to see him again . . .

She was old enough now to know what he had done to her, passing her around as a favor to what she guessed had been business colleagues or friends. Yet because he was all she had known of fathering, she loved him still—when she did not hate. There was something sweet and soft about him, like a juicy peach or a ripe melon. She loved to drive about the city in his car, smelling him, feeling the stuff of his suit as her hand surreptitiously brushed against his sleeve. She loved the way his dark eyes filled with concern when she told him of her mother's condition. He had begun to give her extra money occasionally, telling her to buy something special for the invalid. Once, dropping her in front of the apartment building where she lived, he reached into the backseat for a blanket of fleecy blue wool.

"For your mother," he said.

She started to thank him, holding his hand between hers. He put a finger across her lips.

"She must be looked after," he said. "She is very ill. Does your brother say when he will return from Germany?"

"Not yet."

"It should be soon, I think. Write and tell him so. It is a man's duty to care for his womenfolk."

At the time, his statement held no irony for her. Later, she was to wonder how he reconciled such a sentiment with his treatment of her.

■■

Shortly after this, she began to menstruate. Because the other girls had whispered about such things among themselves, she was aware that at fourteen she was later than most of her contemporaries. She waited with terror for Kemal to find out. When he did, his reaction surprised her. Instead of anger, he showed concern, almost affection. He kissed her gravely on the forehead and held her against his heart. Later, as an adult, she would realize that she could not have been the first child drugged and abused by him—nor the last. Somehow, though, she had succeeded in arousing in him something more than perverted desire. Where before he had posed as a father in order to gain something from her, now he began indeed to treat her as a daughter.

He asked her what she intended to do when she left school. He told her that she must train for something, learn a skill. At this time she was still small, her new breasts no bigger than soft buttons on the front of her body. He told her that when she was older, he would pay for her to attend one of the secretarial schools in the city.

"Meanwhile," he said, "Véronique has decided to introduce a typing class for some of the girls. I have told her you must join it."

"Typing? On a machine?"

"Yes, stupid one. Where else? Not that secretarial work is only typing out letters. A good personal assistant is worth far more than her weight in gold."

She twirled around in front of him. "How much would I weigh in gold?" she said.

"Not much, my rosebud. An ugly, skinny little thing like you wouldn't weigh more than twenty copper coins." He reached out his arms, smiling at her. "Come here."

She did so, nuzzling against him while he kissed her cheek. His lips lingered close to but finally avoided hers. "Not even thirty?" she said.

"Not even twenty-five." He held her away from him, between his knees. "If you work very hard, I might even make you my secretary. Would you like that?"

"Very much."

"You could come abroad with me, to France, to England."

"To America, too?"

"Even to America, if you wanted. But you must study hard at school, and learn everything there is to learn." His hands cupped her buttocks. She liked the feel of them on her body. She leaned forward and kissed his mouth.

"And you can start practicing by tidying up some of my papers for me. It will be good practice for you. I might even pay you for it."

"Me? I'm not the right person."

"You are. Do you know why?"

"Why?"

"Because I can trust you."

"Suppose I make a mistake?"

"Then I will beat you," he said solemnly. She did not think he meant it.

■■

"What is your name?" The man stood in front of her. His Turkish was overlaid with an accent she recognized as English.

She considered. There seemed to be no harm in telling him. If he knew Kemal, he was not exactly a stranger. "Solange Bonami," she said at last.

"That sounds French."

"Yes. My father was Algerian."

"So you speak the language?"

She nodded, giggling a little. "Better, I think, than you speak Turkish."

He did not smile. In French, he asked, "Do you have time for a glass of tea?"

She put down her school bag and tightened her red woollen scarf. It was colder now, the year turning into late autumn, the winter ahead already warning of its approach. She knew she ought to say no, but surprisingly she felt no fear of him. "All right."

As they walked side by side toward the Galata Bridge, he explained that his name was Nicholas Marquend, that he was from England, and that he was working temporarily in Istanbul, selling wine.

He found an empty table at one of the cafés halfway along the crowded lower level and they sat side by side, looking out over the water. A ferry slowly nosed up to the little pier and docked, picking up passengers, letting more off. At the railings in front of them, boys leaned over, dangling fishing lines.

"Are you related to Kemal Effendi?" Nicholas Marquend said.

"Oh no." She glanced sideways at him. "He's . . . a family friend."

"You must tell me about him."

"You are his friend, too, aren't you?"

He hesitated. "More of a business acquaintance, really."

"Oh." She watched one of the boys busily hauling in his line, encouraged by envious cries from his friends. Was it possible that this Nicholas Marquend did not know about her true relationship with Kemal? Could it be that he saw her as nothing more than an ordinary schoolgirl; had she misinterpreted his inquiring glance in the gloomy hall of Kemal's villa a year before? The possibility exhilarated her: his apparent ignorance of the truth freed her. She felt as though she were a bird that had miraculously struggled out of the hunter's net and soared up into the bright air.

"I don't know a lot about him," she said cautiously, "but he is a very generous man, very good to my family."

"Really?" Nicholas Marquend sounded disbelieving. "What about his own family? There is a son, isn't there?"

"I don't—yes, probably." Although this was news to her, she realized how odd it would sound if she appeared to be unaware of the fact. "I know Kemal Effendi had a daughter once."

"Did he now?"

"Yes. She was called Yasmin. I haven't ever met the son."

"He doesn't live in Istanbul," Marquend said. "I understand that he and his mother moved abroad some years ago."

No wonder Kemal often seemed so sad. To have his daughter die, and his wife and son abandon him. "Poor Kemal," she said.

Tightening his mouth, Nicholas Marquend said, "Do you meet many of his friends? What sort of people come to his house?"

She looked away across the water, watching a tanker slowly push away from the jetty and negotiate its passage into the shipping lanes between the busy ferries. She felt herself flushing. "Business people," she said. "Important business friends." In truth, Kemal had often told her to be particularly nice to a man because he needed a favor from him, or he expected an advantageous deal to be completed.

"I'm new to Istanbul, you see," Marquend said, as though his questions required some explanation. "I need to build up my own contacts."

"But Kemal is not in the wine business."

"He knows a lot of people." Leaning forward, Marquend gave a twisted grin, as though he were not used to smiling. "To be honest with you, I've heard that he's influential in the city and I'm hoping he'll help me get established here. So the more I know about him, the more chance I have of finding the best way to persuade him to give me a hand."

She nodded. Although she knew she ought to get back to her mother, she was enjoying herself too much. The Englishman obviously thought she was an important person in Kemal's life; she searched her memory for him, digging up snippets of information that he might find useful. She told him of Kemal's trips abroad, of the important people who wrote to him, the names of colleagues, and was pleased when he wrote them carefully down.

■■

When she finally returned home, darkness had fallen across the city. She would have to give up any thoughts of reading tonight and concentrate on completing her homework. She ran up the steep hill toward the flats, turning for one last look out over the roofs below to where the Golden Horn glimmered between the sheltering shores of Europe and Asia. Lights lit up the night. In the harbor she could see boats illuminated with colored bulbs. Golden specks moved slowly in the darkness, signaling the movement of craft across the water. A wind blew up the street toward her, stirring the washing on the balconies. She shivered and went in to prepare the evening meal.

A stranger was in the kitchen. He sat on one of the two plastic-and-chrome chairs, the one with its seat repaired with sticky tape. He was bearded and even under the rough pea jacket he wore, she could see he was strong and well muscled. For a moment she stared at him. Then she threw herself into his arms.

"Mikkele!"

Instead of kissing her, he held her at arm's length, frowning. "Where have you been?" he demanded. "You should have been home hours ago. A child your age, wandering about in the dark . . ."

"I'm fourteen," she said. "Not a child any longer."

"All the more reason to be careful."

He had not looked at her properly. He had not seen the person she had become during his years away. "Aren't you glad to be home?" she asked.

"Of course. It's just . . . I hadn't realized how ill our mother was." He gestured toward the bedroom. "Mehmet and I set off as soon as we received your telegram. We got here this morning. We've been traveling all night—I'm tired."

"What telegram?"

"It said she was dying. We left at once."

"I sent no telegram."

He pulled the cheap white form out of his pocket and smoothed it out on the plastic tabletop. "Look."

Solange remembered the conversation she had had with Kemal about her mother. She guessed it was he who had sent it: with his connections it would not have been difficult to find out where Mikkele and Mehmet were working in Germany. Knowing Mikkele's former attitude to their landlord, and uncertain of the alien he had become, she did not say so.

"It's signed with your name," Mikkele said.

As he spoke, Mehmet appeared in the doorway. He looked haggard. He shook his head at Mikkele before holding out his arms to Solange. She sensed that something terrible was about to happen. Once again her life would change. Alarmed, she ran past him into the bedroom. A faint light burned beside her mother's bed. Even in the gloom she could see that the spirit which inhabited that twisted body propped up on pillows was slipping fast away. She knelt beside the bed, holding her mother's wasted hand. It felt like the claw of one of the yellow chickens they occasionally bought in the market: bony, unfleshed, dead. There was an olive-wood rosary on the bedpost: she touched the plain wooden cross which hung from it and began to recite a prayer. "Holy Mary, Mother of God. Blessed art Thou . . ."

Was it because she had stopped to drink tea with the English stranger? Was it because she had deviated from the path of duty that her mother now lay at the point of death? Rationally, she knew it could not be, that her mother's death would be the culmination of years of suffering, that it could have happened yesterday or next month and could not be attributable to her own neglect. She reminded herself that for some time she had assumed control over the household, that she had cared for her mother as well as she could, and at the same time kept up with her schoolwork as her mother wished. Nonetheless, guilt consumed her. She had known she should come home before now, yet she had stayed with Nicholas Marquend—she had enjoyed being with him, telling him things that would be useful to his business.

The room smelled faintly of oranges. Raising her head, she saw what she had not noticed before: an elaborate basket of fruit beside the bed. Mikkele and Mehmet must have bought it with the money they had earned in Germany. The lamplight shone on grapes and tangerines, on peaches and the polished skins of apples. There was even a mango. Her mouth filled with longing.

"Don't die, Mother," she whispered quickly, pushing her face into the counterpane. "Don't die—not today." She was ashamed of herself for the thought. But if it had to happen soon anyway, tomorrow would do just as well, and she would then be absolved of the sin of matricide.

■■

During the years that he had been away, Mikkele had grown into a man. Watching while he paced up and down the pitted linoleum of the kitchen, Solange wanted to ask him how it had been there, in Germany—what life in another country than theirs had been like. Had he gone overland? And if he'd gone by sea, had there been typhoons, whales, sea serpents, mermaids? Had he seen coral strands, dragons, oysters full of pearls, turtles big enough to ride like a horse?

She had read about such things, but dared not ask as Mikkele beat his fists against the wall in protest at the cruelties of fate. Instead she sat clutching her rosary, muttering prayers, while in the bedroom, women attended the body of their mother, washing the shrunken limbs, trying to straighten the deformed spine for display in the coffin which rested on chairs against the wall.

Solange could not feel any grief. For too long now her mother, the person she once loved, had been absent. Her place had been taken some time ago by an entity for whom even the simple act of breathing was an effort, who needed help to perform the most basic functions. She had never grudged giving the assistance needed, never complained about the double load of duty she carried. But now that it was over, she could acknowledge to herself that more than anything else, she was relieved.

Once she might have tried to explain this feeling to Mikkele, knowing he would understand, but the grim-faced man who stalked about the house was not someone she could imagine turning to for comfort. He had changed too much; fingering the carved wooden beads of her rosary, she acknowledged to herself, with a sense of foreboding, that he no longer practiced the faith in which he had been raised. She herself had gone to Mass every day since his return, praying for her mother's soul, and that of Mikkele.

A week had passed since she had sat in the café with the Englishman. She had gone to school each day until yesterday, when the doctor had told them that death was imminent.

Now, tears rolled down her brother's cheeks as he held forth to his uncle about the sorry conditions in which his mother had died. There was a newspaper on the table which he stared at as he passed and repassed; the front page held a picture of a plane hijacked by terrorists, shimmering in the heat of some Middle Eastern airport.

"It's always the poor who suffer, always the poor who pay with their health, with their bodies, with their lives." His voice was strained and passionate, and he slammed the table with his fist. "Look at this. Terrorism will always flourish where there is poverty and injustice. Look at it. The Americans, the British . . . Even people in this very city. The rich, the indifferent . . ." His hand came down again on the newspaper photograph. "Look! They talk of international cooperation against the threat of violent men. Can't they see that only when you cure the disease, will you destroy the symptoms? Until then . . ."

Solange heard Mehmet answer, his voice placatory. Mikkele spoke again, more softly. She heard Kemal's name. What was he saying? Whatever it was, she knew it would be contemptuous and hating. This new Mikkele frightened her. She clutched the roughly carved beads between her fingers and tried to concentrate on the soul of her dead mother, soaring heavenward on its journey to a place near the right hand of God.

But her thoughts refused to remain dutifully fixed. Instead, they hopped about inside her brain, darting from her typing class to Kemal, from the mango still in her mother's room to the way Mikkele's eyes had burned when he looked inside the book on English gardens and saw what was written on the flyleaf. It would be impossible to tell him what had happened to her since he had been gone, or to explain that Kemal was not really the monster he took him to be. She touched the little opal pendant which had been her mother's and now hung around her own neck next to the moonstone he had given her. What was going to happen to her now? Would Mikkele stay in Istanbul to look after her, or would he return to Germany?

She hated herself for hoping that he would.

■■

"He says I must never talk to you again," she sobbed. She felt Kemal stiffen and his arms tighten as he held her close.

"What have you told him?" he said. She could tell he was anxious.

"Nothing, except that you are my friend."

"What did he say to that?"

"He said I had no need of such friends. He threw that book you gave me into the harbor. He said it was tainted. He spoke of blood money."

Kemal did not answer. He rested his chin on her hair. She wriggled around. "What does that mean, Kemal? What is blood money?"

Kemal did not answer directly. Instead, he said, "He sounds like a man with some dangerous views. He should be careful who he repeats them to."

"Do I have to do what he tells me?"

"He is the man in your family."

"But if I am not to speak to you, how can I be your personal assistant?" Solange loved that phrase. Each word, separately, carried resonances of warmth and caring. Personal. Assistant. Together they exemplified everything she felt for Kemal.

"Perhaps when you are sixteen, and old enough to think for yourself, we can talk about it again. Until then, you must listen to what your brother says."

"I don't want to live with Mehmet's cousin."

"Your brother is your guardian now. You must obey him."

"But I love you, Kemal."

He held her close. "And I you, little one. But one day, you will grow up and not think so kindly of me. You will think that your brother is right."

■■

Mikkele settled her in with Mehmet's cousin, an elderly lady who ran a boardinghouse in a part of the city where she had never been. When he kissed her good-bye, she was glad to see him go.

She did not recover from what she saw as Kemal's betrayal. In her view, he had abandoned her to the boardinghouse cousin and she could not forgive him. Several times she had tried to contact him, by letter or telephone. Once she paid a taxi to drive her to his villa in the hills but eventually told the man to let her out, getting panicky at the cost. It was as if the intimacy she and Kemal once shared had blown away like snowflakes in a gale. She gradually began to realize exactly what he had done to her. She started to hate him.

The memory of the pig-men grew larger in her mind, along with the pain. The remembrance of those warm afternoons with Kemal faded like the patterns on sun-bleached chintz. Clearly they had meant nothing to him, after all, or he could not have deserted her like this. Her body became hideous to her as she remembered his hands touching her; when she remembered the other hands as well, she was filled with bitterness. How would anyone ever look at her, how would she marry and bear children, if what she had done in such innocence became known? It would all have been easier if she had not still loved Kemal. She wanted to be able to hate him cleanly and forget him gradually. But hatred could not flourish properly while it was entangled with love.

She understood that if she could keep her past locked inside herself, then no one could use it against her. Secrecy was the only way, her doorkeeper against further intrusion. The less she spoke to others, the less chance there was of an inadvertently betraying word. Keeping herself aloof would be her best protection.

Mehmet's cousin cooked well and plentifully. Solange began to grow. With height she gained strength, emotional as well as physical. Knowing herself to be already wicked, she also began to rebel, questioning the world about her, daring to wonder whether things had to remain absolutely as they were. She asked herself if God existed and when the lightning bolt failed to strike her dead for her heresy, decided that perhaps He did not. In the mirror her face stared back at her, solemn, unsmiling, a woman's face now, almost unrecognizable as the big-eyed child she had once been. Kemal used to call her ugly; even though he had not meant it, she now told herself that he was right. Although she knew she was not hideous, her distorted vision told her that she was. Like an anorexic, she was aware of the contradictions she presented herself with.

■■

One afternoon, as she walked through the bazaar, she saw the Englishman again, outside a perfume shop. She remembered his name: Nicholas Marquend. She was nearly sixteen by then, tall, thin, her dark coloring emphasized by the white dress she wore. She knew she looked older than she was. She greeted him, glad to have even this vague a link with Kemal. As before, they drank tea together. Although he managed to smile at her, he seemed bleak and distant; she was astonished to see the same cold look in his eyes as in Mikkele's.

He told her that he had been away and was now back for a while. He said that business was good. She was too proud to ask if he had seen Kemal; her heart sank when he volunteered the information that Kemal was spending a lot of time abroad at the moment, mostly in Paris. Always, in some corner of her mind, she had hoped that she might unexpectedly bump into him, but now she realized it was unlikely.

After that, they met quite often. Although no formal arrangement was made, she would pass by the perfume shop two or three times a week, and he would usually—but not always—be there. It occurred to her that he might be falling in love with her. No longer a child, she sensed a loneliness in him that matched her own.

She talked to him of her feelings of frustration, sometimes so strong that they threatened to overwhelm her. She complained of the tedium of living with Mehmet's cousin, her wish to get away from Istanbul. When he tentatively suggested that they might go down to the southern coast for the weekend, she agreed to do so. She was under no illusions about why he wanted her company, but told herself that if he was using her, she also was using him. She knew that he would probably try to sleep with her. If he did, she would not stop him. What would be the point? She had no honor to maintain, no virginity to defend. Besides, if there was no God, there could be no sin. Bitterly, she realized why Kemal had no longer used her once she became a woman. There would be too much scandal if a convent girl became pregnant; too many questions would be asked.

"Where would you like to go?" he said.

"Kelkan," she said. Kemal had taken her there once. They had arrived on his boat and eaten in the restaurant of a hotel. She carried with her a photograph of the two of them sitting at a table on a terrace overlooking the harbor: it was the only one of him that she had.

She did not protest when the Englishman booked a double room for the two of them, nor did she tell him that she had been there before, with Kemal. They ate lunch on the terrace; cypresses cast thick shadows across their table, like black cigars. She held herself inward, watching him across the table. He asked her again about Kemal: she told him sadly that she had nothing to tell. One of the roving photographers who swarmed around the tourist areas climbed the steps from the beach and began to snap the diners with a Polaroid camera. Nicholas shaded his face with his hand, motioning the man not to include him. When the picture was placed on the table in front of Solange, she picked it up. The photographer had disobeyed Nicholas. She slipped it into her bag, next to the one of Kemal. It struck her as amusing that the two photographs were almost identical: only the man was different.

After lunch Nicholas suggested that they go upstairs and change into swimming things. In their room, he watched her undress. She took off her white frock, shaking it in the sunlight which came through the shutters. She heard his quick breath as he walked through the bright shadows toward her, took hold of her, laid her gently on the bed. He was quick. She was glad about that, because she felt nothing. The weight of his body on hers reminded her too vividly of the past. If he had taken a long time, or tried to please her, she would have found it unbearable.

"You are very beautiful," he said.

She turned her head away so he would not see the tears which came into her eyes.

That evening, they walked along the quay. Astonishingly, Kemal's boat was tied up to a pontoon in the harbor. Was he on board? She felt sick with excitement and desolation; she smiled up at her good-looking companion as if she loved him, hoping that if Kemal noticed her at all, he would see that she did not care that she had been abandoned by someone she had once trusted.

Over dinner, they drank a bottle of French wine. Nicholas told her that one day he would like to grow grapes, produce good wines as well as sell them. He spoke of France, of California, rolling the lovely names of grapes around his tongue. She did not say much. It was better to let him talk. The wine slid slowly through her body, melting her. She was frightened to open her mouth, in case she let out too much that ought to be concealed.

He told her he must go and talk to someone but would soon be back. Restless, she walked down to the harbor again. There were lights shining on Kemal's boat: her body felt sore with longing for him. She walked nearer, intending to look through the portholes to see if she could catch a glimpse of him; as she did so a dark shadow detached itself from the shadows and slipped away. It looked like a man; something about the way he moved made her certain that it was Nicholas. Why would he be spying on Kemal? She said nothing when they met again at the hotel.

In bed that night, he again made love to her. "So beautiful, so beautiful. . . ." he murmured against her breast.

"Yes, yes," she said, pretending to feelings she did not have. She traced the line of his ribs with her fingers, touched the dark hair of his crotch. She wondered if he felt anything more than she did. When he had finished, she lay against the pillows, softened by what she had drunk, defenseless. She wanted to tell him about Kemal, about what had been done to her. The words gathered in her throat, waiting to be spilled in front of him like a libation. His hands moved over her skin, harvesting her. As he opened her body and entered her again, his cold eyes did not smile.

He came, jerking a little, making sounds of pain. After a while, he leaned his head against her shoulder. "Talk to me, Solange," he said.

"What about?"

He shrugged lazily. "Your friend Kemal?"

She realized that his casual tone was only a pretense. She knew she should be discreet, that he had brought her there for a purpose which had nothing to do with herself and that could be dangerous to Kemal, but before she could prevent them, the words tumbled out. Phrases, sentences, whole paragraphs ran from between her lips and spread themselves before him. It was like vomiting. Gasping, she tried to stop but could not. After a while, he began to stroke her, as though he were calming a terrified animal. When she had finished, she was trembling.

"That explains . . . one or two things," he said.

His face was terrifying. She could not tell if the anger and disgust it showed were directed at her or not. She thought: *Who is this man? What does he want?* He continued to stroke her in silence until she fell asleep.

The next day, he asked her whether she would like to stay, or would prefer to return to the city. She said she would stay. They swam and sunbathed, and took an excursion bus to see some ancient ruins. What she had said was not mentioned. He did not touch her again.

Back in the city, he drove to the house of Mehmet's cousin. Leaving the engine running, he lifted her hand to his lips and kissed it. "Good-bye, Solange," he said. "And thank you."

She could not meet his eyes. She opened the door of the car and got out. "Thank you for . . ." She could not finish the sentence.

"Solange," he said. "Life is not all unhappiness."

"I am not unhappy," she said.

"I'm glad."

She watched his car pull away. When she reached the room where she slept, she opened her bag. There was money tucked into the side pocket, more folded bills than she had ever seen. And both her photographs were gone.

■■

She told the nuns that she would leave the convent at the end of the current term. In the final week, Sister Véronique called her into the parlor.

"I am instructed to tell you that an account with the American Bank has been opened in your name," she said.

"What do you mean?"

The nun unlocked a drawer in her desk and produced a checkbook. "This is for you. I am also to remind you of the secretarial course you planned to take." Her voice deepened. "You are to know that a post as a personal assistant will be found for you, once you have qualified."

Kemal!

She could almost hear him saying it: personal assistant. Although she had not seen him for almost two years, he must have been thinking of her, as she had of him. She felt weak with longing for him.

Sister Véronique was pushing the sleeves of her habit back from her wrists. "I would be failing in my duty if I did not emphasize what a lucky chance this is for you," she said. "A girl like yourself, untrained, unqualified, with, to be blunt, so few expectations, would otherwise find it hard to make her way in the world."

It had never occurred to Solange that her expectations were anything but boundless, though she said nothing, merely nodded.

"I need not tell you that with the necessary qualifications, you could work anywhere you wished," the nun continued. "Abroad, for instance. You could go to London. Or even America."

"What about Paris?"

"Why not? Your French is excellent and you are a clever girl. And as I have told you before, Paris is the most civilized of cities."

There were hairs on Sister Véronique's chin, three of them, coarse and black. Solange looked past the nun at the little courtyard beyond. Above the wall there were minarets and the onion dome of a mosque. She was tall enough now to see that the water in the pool was thick and green, matted with weed. No fish could have survived there. The plaster saints in their niches were peeling. The Blessed Virgin still gazed toward the skies, but there was mold along the folds of her once blue gown.

"Yes. It might be a good idea for you to spend some time away from Istanbul before you settle down to bring up a family. When you have completed your secretarial diploma, I can give you the names of a couple of hostels run by good churchgoing people where you will be well looked after, if you do decide to go to Paris."

Paris. All her life it had been dangled before her by the nun, a prize to which she had never thought to attain. Now it beckoned, within her reach. A new life, she thought. No one will know who I am there: I can start again, I shall be free.

"Thank you, *ma soeur*."

Three days later, she had emptied the bank account and was on the train to France.

PHILIPPE

• 14 •

OVER BEYOND THE HILLS THERE was a storm rising. Comte Philippe de Pierrey could already feel the ripples of it, the tiny pulses of cold air pushing toward him from the mountains, pressing the vine leaves nearer the soil from which they sprang, making them shiver. For the moment the sun still shone, but by early afternoon there would be rain unless the winds swept the clouds on by.

The back of his neck ached. He stretched his arms out in front of him, lacing his fingers together to ease the tension in his shoulders. It had been the kind of morning he disliked: too much desk work, an acrimonious discussion with the *maître de chais* about two of the seasonal workers caught shoplifting in the nearby town, a client storming in to complain about a recent consignment, a salesman trying to sell him something from his latest brochure. With the phone calls as well, there had not even been time for midmorning coffee.

Distantly, on the road which ran around the lower rim of the hills, a blob of color appeared. Yellow. Like mimosa, he thought, or a duckling, newly hatched. He raised the binoculars which hung around his neck and focused them. Far away, a small yellow car scurried between the fields of vines, almost drowned in the shimmer of heat which rose from the crowding leaves. At this hour of the afternoon, there was no other traffic on the road. Most sensible people were still at lunch.

Was this Englishwoman—Frances Brett—sensible? Probably. She had rung him the week before, from England. "I'm a free-lance journalist," she had said, barely bothering to introduce herself. It had been early, before he had had time to pour his first cup of coffee. She spoke unusually good French for an English person. A kind of vivid energy ran through her conversation like a seam of gold. "I wonder if you would allow me to come and talk to you."

Her voice was low-pitched and warm, with a soothing quality to it that brought back to him a sudden brief memory of childhood baths and the roomy laps of nursemaids.

"Why?" he said. With one hand he reached for the coffeepot.

"Château de Pierrey is one of France's leading champagne producers, isn't it?"

"Not quite," he said. He stretched his hand toward a cup, but it was out of his reach. Silently he cursed.

"No?"

"You should have done your research better," he said. Sometimes he surprised even himself with his bad temper. "We are not, and have never claimed to be, one of the leading producers of champagne."

She tried to interrupt but he pressed on, annoyed at being telephoned so early in the morning, annoyed at the distance between himself and the coffee cup. "What we *do* claim to be is a producer of one of the leading champagnes."

There was silence on the other end of the telephone.

"The difference," he said tetchily, "should be obvious. Even to a journalist."

"Yes, well," she said, ignoring his tone. "Champagne: it's a glamor subject. You don't need reminding how much of the stuff the English drink in a year."

"No."

"And I'm sure you wouldn't mind the publicity."

"We don't need publicity," he said. He knew he sounded absurdly stiff, and even just plain absurd. *Everyone* needed publicity; it was increasingly one of the essential ingredients in maintaining business growth. *Free* publicity was an extra bonus. "The reputation of Pierrey et fils speaks for itself."

"Of course it does," the woman said. "That's why I should like to talk to you."

"We are busy people," he said firmly. "I'm sure you can find other producers willing to see you." He was puzzled. He had spoken to this voice before, some time ago, he was sure of it.

"Monsieur de Pierrey, I can't force you to see me," the woman said briskly. He saw her in spectacles secured, perhaps, by a cord around her neck. She would wear some kind of slim skirt, he decided, creased across the thighs by sitting for too long, and good teeth that protruded ever so slightly. "But it does seem shortsighted of you not to allow yourself to be included in the article I'm preparing. After all, if I may say so, however prestigious the reputation of Pierrey et fils, it is not yet Roederer or Salon le Mesnil."

"Very true," he said irritably. He could do without this kind of aggravation so early in the morning. "Nor does it aspire to be."

"Surely, monsieur le Comte, you have more ambition than that."

Of course he did. In fact he had plans that would startle his staider colleagues, once he was in a position to implement them. Whenever that might be. Both of the widows were still going strong, although his grandmother would be eighty-one this year. They were a formidable duo, Geneviève and Laure, his mother and grandmother. Together they ran the family concern, as they had done for the last thirty years. Although little known outside France, the small and increasingly prestigious *maison* produced one of the most stylish and delicate of champagnes. The heavy green bottles had been familiar to connoisseurs for over a century: the gold-bordered label, the line drawing of the vines with the hills behind, the words *PIERREY et fils* in bold black lettering. Sometimes Philippe saw the label as symbolic: the capital letters representing the widows, the lower case standing for him, the *fils,* the final flourish who represented nothing more than the family's continuity.

Although he was nominally in charge of the day-to-day administration, there was no question that Pierrey et fils belonged to the widows Pierrey. Sometimes it seemed that he was in the same position as an heir-in-waiting, such as Prince Charles of England, or one of those unfortunate Ottoman princes Mihri had told him about, who found themselves locked up for fifty years with only deaf-mutes and sterile concubines for company while they waited for a throne.

"Besides," the Englishwoman said coaxingly. "I *want* to include Pierrey et fils in my article."

Fatally, he had hesitated. "Well . . ."

"Tuesday afternoon," she said. She had a trick of bypassing the circumlocutory politenesses that he had come to associate with the English. There was none of the usual Will-that-be-all-right? and Would-you-mind-if? Just the straightforward statement *Tuesday afternoon.* He elaborated on his mental picture of her: she would be small and determined with blond hair curling around pink cheeks. She would wear a demure blouse, be cool like an iceberg.

Not a bit like Mihri, his mind added quickly, before he could stop it.

"What time?" he said. It was not what he intended to say.

"Three o'clock?" The statement was only marginally a question.

"Tuesday?" She would have one of those deep, soft bosoms, too, like so many Englishwomen.

"Yes."

With a time specified, again Philippe had hesitated. Could he now baldly say that he had changed his mind, that he did not wish to talk to her on Tuesday, at three o'clock or at any other hour of the day? What he *could* still say was that it would not really be convenient; he could perhaps put it off until the following week and then forget about it. He opened his mouth.

"Au revoir," the woman said. Before he could reply, she had hung up.

She must have taken his silence for agreement. "Damn you," he had said into the dead receiver. He had no means of contacting her. He shrugged. Sometimes events overtake us. This was clearly one of them. And it said something for her that she had known about Pierrey et fils in the first place. It said quite a lot. He had reached for the coffeepot.

■■

He lifted his glasses again. Miles away, the little yellow car still moved like an exotic insect between the wide spread of leaves. He felt that Mademoiselle Brett had stolen a march on him; when she arrived, he would be cool with her. He would pretend to be less fluent than he really was—as he ought to be, after those schoolboy summers spent at the Forrests' house in Devon. They seemed a lifetime away now, a place apart from this, held still entire in his memories like feathers trapped in ice.

■■

The week before his fourteenth birthday, his mother had called him in to the small salon. She and his grandmother were seated on either side of the empty marble fireplace in a pair of matching *fauteuils* that

■

made his back ache just to look at. Nothing in the room had changed for as far back as he could remember, apart from the Ronson table lighter, the original of which an absentminded Texas millionaire had put in his pocket while arranging for a hundred cases of the Pierrey Brut to be flown over to celebrate his wife's fiftieth birthday. The air smelled of the surreptitious cigarettes which the widows allowed themselves after lunch; two each, smoked with the awkwardness of teenagers. They thought he didn't know.

"We have been talking," his mother, Geneviève, had said, looking across at Laure for approval, as she always did. "Soon you will be a man."

He was well aware of the fact. He wondered if she knew just how much of a man he already was. He hated to think what she might say if she were to find out—God forbid—what he and Monique Villeroy, the sixteen-year-old daughter from a neighboring estate, had been doing last time her parents brought her to lunch.

"Yes," he said. It was one of those statements to which there was no adequate response. Besides, he had learned a long time ago that agreement saved trouble. It was already clear to him that sooner or later he and his mother would clash spectacularly; since that would be a clash he intended to win, he meanwhile agreed with her when he could.

"One day you will be running Pierrey et fils on your own," she continued. His grandmother nodded.

"I know," he said. He smiled at them both.

"We therefore think it would be a good idea for you to go to England."

"Why, particularly?" He was tremendously excited by the prospect, though he showed nothing of it. The logic behind their thinking escaped him for the moment.

"To study the language, of course. When we are gone and you are in charge of all this"—Geneviève waved a vague hand around—"you should be able to talk to the English and American customers in their own language."

It seemed unimaginable to him that either of them would one day be absent from Lavandière—or from himself. At least, not both of them at once. He could see that his grandmother's death must occur in the not too distant future, but a Lavandière without Geneviève seemed like a contradiction in terms. He tried to visualize it, but let the thought go. At fourteen, death was something his imagination could not encompass, nor had any particular wish to.

"I should enjoy seeing England," he said, injecting what he hoped was the right amount of pleasure into his voice.

"But you will not be there for enjoyment," Geneviève said reprovingly. "You must work hard."

"*Very* hard," his grandmother echoed in the high faint voice that always reminded him of dolphins calling to each other through the deep oceans. "For the sake of the House."

"Oh, I will," he said, his voice eager, but not too eager. His grandmother watched him steadily through her gold-rimmed spectacles, faintly smiling. "When am I to go? And where?"

"Arrangements have been made," Geneviève said. "At the beginning of the summer you will fly—"

"I would *much* rather go by boat," he said. "I'd like to see the white cliffs of Dover."

"Whatever for?" She looked at him with that absent gaze of hers.

He knew she would not understand if he spoke to her of bluebirds and Vera Lynn. Perhaps she had never even heard of Vera Lynn. Nor ever ascended the broad-stepped ladder into the extensive attics that stretched beneath the roofs of Lavandière. But he had. It was while rooting around among the old dress-forms and trunks full of papers that he had found the wind-up gramophone and the stack of 78rpm records. There had been something magical about turning the handle, about slipping one of the discs out of its sleeve, about setting the needle arm at its edge and listening to the thin sea-voices of people called Marlene Dietrich and Edith Piaf, the weedily macho tones of a male choir singing *Auprès de ma blonde,* or the tinkling music of prewar films by Carné or René Clair. It was like a ribbon connecting his own present to someone else's past. He hoped very much that some of it was his father's past.

In among the pile were three or four English recordings. He would never forget taking one of the heavy black discs from its faded brown paper cover and listening to a heart-wringing voice sing of country lanes and a tomorrow when the world would be free. Vera Lynn: she came to mean England to him, and courage, good-byes, though the war was over long before his own birth. He liked to think of his own father listening, as he was doing, crouched up here under the roof, under the strutting feet of pigeons and the rough scent of wood. One of the records contained speeches by Winston Churchill. He could not understand everything the slurred, sleepy voice was saying, but he had enough English to be moved by the drama of the words spoken: . . . *We shall never surrender . . . This is not the end . . . we shall defend our island whatever the cost may be . . .*

He could not imagine explaining to Geneviève the feeling he had for a people and a country he had never seen: a tiny island somewhere to the north, where a queen still lived in a palace guarded by beefeating soldiers in bearskins, a race that could not cook but had produced Shakespeare and beaten off the Germans in the war. Nor that its value lay in the contact it gave him with the father he had never known. So he had never asked specifically if these records had belonged to his father: he preferred to believe that they had than to know that they had not.

Now if he said the boat was more romantic than airplanes, she would tell him he read too many novels. "I would see more," he said lamely.

"Possibly," she said, speaking in dismissive tones and adjusting the heavy gold cross at the throat of her high-necked white blouse. "Your grandmother suggested that we contact a distant cousin of the family—some people called Forrest who live in the southwest of England. Madame Forrest has said she will be delighted to have you to stay for three weeks this summer. Then when you return, her own son can come back here with you and learn some French."

"An excellent idea," his grandmother said in her subaqueous whistle.

"There is a son?" said Philippe.

Geneviève looked down at the letter in her hand. "He's called Daniel. He's the same age as you, a little older perhaps. I hope the two of you will get on together: he could be a great help in teaching you to speak English like an Englishman."

His grandmother said, "And what shall you be doing this afternoon, Philippe?"

"I'm cycling over to the Villeroys'," he said. "Monique has invited me to swim in their pool." It was by no means all that she had invited him to do, but he had no intention of telling either of them that. A blush spread across his face: he could feel his forehead start to glow with sweat and terror. *If they ever discovered that he had touched a girl's breast* . . . His fingertips burned.

"And then?" Laure asked.

He looked away from her. "Uh—I haven't really thought yet."

"Remember, my child, that wasted time is lost time."

"Yes," he said, trying to appear virtuous. Why was it he always felt compelled to pretend he was something other than his real self when he was with the two of them. He loved them both, as far as they allowed him to, but it seemed to him that the person he was bore no resemblance at all to their expectations of him. Had they ever seen him as he really was? The persona he attempted to adopt when he was with them was totally alien to him: an uncomfortable blend of the Spartan boy with the fox under his cloak and a saintly prig like Little Lord Fauntleroy.

Outside, crossing the big hall, he wondered how different things might have been if he had not been an only child. If there were other children in the family, perhaps Geneviève would have been forced into a more maternal role, instead of channeling all her energy into the production of champagne. But she had remained a widow since Comte Antoine, his father, had been knocked down and killed by a drunken taxi driver while on a visit to Paris. Philippe had been five at the time and could only dimly remember the big man with the red face who laughed a lot for no apparent reason.

He wondered what this English Daniel would be like. He hoped they would be friends.

He would never for a moment have considered himself as deprived, yet after only a day in the Forrest household, Philippe was aware that his own matriarchal family seemed to be missing some vital ingredient that he was much too inexperienced to be able to name. He envied Daniel Forrest his easy intimacy with his mother, as well as Mrs. Forrest's obvious delight in her son. Philippe himself had never felt unloved; it was merely that any demonstration of affection had always been frowned upon by the two widows, whereas Alicia Forrest touched her son constantly: hugging him, kissing the top of his head as she passed, taking his hand.

Those summers in Devon became the focus of Philippe's adolescence. When he was not anticipating his next visit there, he was

reliving the last one. England was everything Vera Lynn had led him
to expect, and more. Sailing with Daniel out of Brixham harbor; Oxford quadrangles; the Tower of London; green rivers and flower-filled
meadows; bacon and eggs. The images, nostalgically dazzling, flickered endlessly through his mind. It was as if he were watching them
on the broken stereopticon he had found in the attic. When he asked,
Laure told him it had been his grandfather's when he was a boy. On
one of Daniel's reciprocal visits to Lavandière, the two boys had spent
an entire week putting the apparatus in working order again then
watching the jolting images appear: horses jogging up to fences and
unsteadily jumping over; circus riders twirling hesitantly on the backs
of zebras; an Indian in a blue cotton turban climbing jerkily up a rope
and disappearing.

He realized Daniel's value as a friend when he played him the
Winston Churchill record. "Fantastic," Daniel said, awestruck. "It's
what the history master at my school would call living history. Listen
to that voice. In a way it's a pity we aren't at war anymore."

"You're going to be a soldier, aren't you?"

"My family always have been."

"But do *you* want to be?"

"I think so," Daniel said. "Yes. Play that Churchill thing again."

The years of those summer weeks with Daniel seemed to have
filled most of his adolescence. When he later came to reckon them up,
he found there were only three.

■■

His last summer in Devon, the weather was cold and wet so he and
Daniel had spent most of their time in the old hayloft converted by
Colonel Forrest into a playroom. Dust lay thickly everywhere. The
ceiling was supported by rough-hewn A-shaped beams against which
the damp-stained plaster had bulged. An ancient chesterfield, leaking
straw and horsehair, its springs long since gone, sagged against one
wall. Bookshelves hung lopsidedly between two doors which opened
straight out into space. Lying about were tennis racquets, a croquet
set, a medieval toy castle complete with incongruous World War I
soldiers. A battered cupboard had been full of boxed games: Ludo,
Monopoly, Snakes and Ladders, checkers. Whatever they played,
Daniel always won, but Philippe never minded. There was a particular

thrill in sliding down the luscious curves of some startling red-and-green-patterned serpent while the rain drummed against the roof. That gave him more pleasure than winning ever could.

In the early evenings, the sun occasionally broke through the clouds to fill the air with gold. He remembered dust motes silently falling from the beams, the bounce and skitter of Ping-Pong balls, the staggering piles of old comics, the way the light lay along the barrel of the air gun hung on the wall. It was on just such an evening that they'd seen the hare sitting motionless at the edge of a little copse of pines, its ears pink-edged in the setting sun.

When Daniel had taken aim and fired, Philippe thought he would be sick.

He moved the binoculars higher. A kestrel hung above the long rows of vines, its wings vibrating so lightly, it seemed to be motionless, all its power distilled into maintaining mobility. He wondered if whatever small creature it sighted among the leaves was aware of death poised so high above it, whether there was a microsecond of recognition before the neck-snapping thunderbolt swept out of the sky. Had Daniel felt any primeval sense of doom, that final morning of his life? Any presentiment that this would be the last time he scraped a razor blade across his cheek and felt the tiny resistance of bristle against tempered steel? And if he had, what could he have done? How would he have chosen which of the day's activities, both planned and random, to avoid? Where could he have begun to alter time's itinerary in order to escape death?

He could not. No one could. Not Daniel. Not Antoine, his own father. Not fieldmouse nor shrew, nor the innocent hare on the edge of the pine copse that Daniel had shot.

The kestrel dropped suddenly to earth. Philippe lowered his glasses. He had not thought about the hare for years. Once it had haunted him, huge and reproachful in nightmares, its innocent moment in the sun so bloodily cut short. He wondered whether the assertive Mademoiselle Brett would expect to conduct the . . . interview, he supposed it must be called, in English or in French. *Tuesday afternoon*—he resented the way she had just assumed he would be free to see her, the way she had put down the telephone before he had had a chance to refuse. Mentally, he added five years to the age he expected her to be. Imperceptibly, the glasses he had given her moved more sharply into focus, became steel-rimmed, forbidding. Her full bosom ripened. . . . He would spare her an hour, no more, then send her packing with a couple of bottles of champagne—nonvintage, of course—under her arm. That should keep the wretched woman happy.

■■

The year in which he would be seventeen, Geneviève had announced that some of the great wines of the future would be coming out of northern Spain and that the Pierreys should be in a position to profit. His grandmother, who had learned by then to trust her daughter-in-law's instincts, had hardly quibbled when it was decided to expand the Pierrey interests by the purchase of a part share in a bodega in the Rioja Alta, the finest winegrowing area of Spain. The summers of being seventeen and eighteen, Philippe had spent in Spain.

Was it his age that had made those summers so happy? Philippe had never been able to decide. Certainly he had been aware every day of happiness, of the actual presence of felicity, as though he had been vouchsafed a visitation from a rarely seen saint. Tangibly, he had experienced something that until then he had not known. Nor had he known, until then, how much he desired it, though at almost thirty, he knew enough to be aware that he was not happy now.

In Spain he met, for the first time, women utterly unlike the smooth-skinned expressionless pair who had raised him. So closely had Geneviève grown to resemble her mother-in-law, they might have been sisters, though thirty years lay between them. And although neither of them ever raised her voice, expressed any emotion, wept, or laughed, nonetheless both were filled with such tension, such unbearable frustration, that at times he almost fancied it lay on their cheeks like the bloom on a grape, or like botrytis, a poisoned sweat they could no longer keep within.

By contrast, the women in the household of Don Feliz Torres de Oyon y Castellaña had kept nothing within, or so it had sometimes seemed to Philippe. All day long they sang or laughed or shouted to each other in short soft thumps of speech that began before he was properly awake and went on long after he had fallen asleep at night in the white bedroom at one end of the wide house. Sometimes they wept noisily, tears falling copiously down the fine dark gold of their faces. Sometimes they screamed, fists clenched and pounding whatever was at hand: the table in front of them, their own soft laps, the stuffed arms of the furniture in the drawing room. The screaming was occasionally induced by anger, more often by a fancied injustice, an insult, a harsh word from their adoring lord. For Don Feliz loved all of them: his handsome wife, her two equally handsome sisters, and the four beautiful daughters, of whom none showed the slightest inclination to marry, though there were suitors enough to keep the aunts and the mother in full-time employment as duennas.

Philippe had loved the femininity of it, the glimpse of white frills whisked into work baskets when he approached, the musky scent of overwarm women, the curved bodies, the secret female traces he sometimes caught sight of soaking in galvanized iron tubs. He was aware of hidden pulses beating in the house. He sensed rhythms that ebbed and flowed, washing over and around him as gently as ripples in a pond. For the first time he had understood the simplest of truths: that women were a different species from men. He saw how vast the chasms were that yawned between the two, how entirely other were the emotions which moved women from those which moved himself.

■■

The loss of Mihri, and Daniel's death, had severely shaken the essential structures of his life. Over recent months he had experienced an urgent need to examine, to analyze, the past. Thinking back to those two idyllic summers in Spain, he had concluded that though it was not a peaceful household, peace was the element he had found there.

He lifted his face to the sun, eyes closed. He sniffed. Already the scent of water was in the air, bringing freshness after the long summer's ripening. If wind came, it would bring rain along with it. The grapes, inert among the delicate fan-shaped leaves, would resist it at first, then, when enough water had gathered, they would begin to droop toward the ground. If that happened, they would no longer be usable. He hoped very much that it would not rain. He hated rain. It had rained the last time he had seen Daniel, the day his friend had left for England and never returned.

He frowned. Damn that Brett woman. Why should he be expected to talk to people like her? He had enough on his plate already, with the day-to-day running of the place, let alone all the extra things that fell to him to deal with.

It was difficult to pinpoint exactly when he became aware that the widows had begun to edge him out of the winemaking process and shunt him sideways into administrative duties. Why had he let them? More importantly, how was he going to get back in? He had seen it as a matter of finesse. With Daniel gone, it was increasingly borne in on him that the bludgeon was going to be more effective than the rapier. The confrontation with Geneviève that he had anticipated for so many years was imminent.

Standing up to their combined power had never been one of his greatest skills. When Daniel came to work at Lavandière, he had hoped that together they might . . . but that was over now. Frustration sat on his ribs, smooth as mercury, poisoning his pleasure in the landscape around him.

He forced himself to breathe deeply. You had to keep control—Daniel had taught him that. At all times, you had to be in command of yourself.

In front of him a bee sank onto one of the veined pentamerous leaves, its black legs splayed, each separate hair gold-tipped. Clouds raced above his head, long shadows running ahead of them across the vines to the other side of the valley. The leaves stirred. The bee quivered, gathering its force for the upward plunge back into the air. A few thin grass blades gleamed in the soil beneath the vine. Philippe lifted one of the solid clusters of grapes, each one fecund, pregnant with the wine waiting for release behind the golden green-tinged skin. Its sun-warmed weight hung from the stalk, ripe as a woman with child. Like a woman's breast. Like Mihri's breast, warm in his hands, tender in the dark against his chest, against his face.

· 15 ·

SOMEWHERE UNSEEN, BEYOND green-black pines trees, a bell began tolling. The long, slow strokes circled through the heat, lassoing Philippe with cool images: quiet cloisters, water dripping into mossed basins, stone-flagged halls. There was some kind of monastic settlement at the other end of the valley, though he had never visited the place. Until a couple of years ago, it had been little more than a manor with a private chapel, both falling picturesquely into ruin. Recently, it had been taken over by a religious order and restored. He had never seen any of its members, but imagined sandaled monks mortifying the flesh with hair-shirt cruelty, or quiet-eyed nuns floating through white rooms, ceaselessly praying for a world with which they had long ago lost touch.

Heat scorched his shoulders through his cotton shirt. Beneath his feet the soil burned. Apart from the single bell, the afternoon was quiet, filled not so much with an absence of sound as with a positive presence of peace.

He lifted the glasses again and focused. The duckling-colored car had stopped. With the binoculars, he could read off the "75" on the license plate, but no more than that. As he watched, the driver got out and stood hip-high among the vines, stretching. A woman: he could see her clearly. His throat felt dry and there was a sudden piercing ache in his chest.

She could have been Mihri.

He let the glasses fall. He passionately wished that he could free himself of the pain that living without her entailed. It was not constant: days could pass without the racking, roiling tumult clutching at him like a cancer. But when it came, it was intolerable—and made worse by knowing from experience that if he looked again, the woman from the yellow car would be nothing like Mihri.

Now, as on each occasion over the past months, trapped by his own misery, he repeated to himself the bare fact which though his head had accepted it, his heart—no, not his heart, his soul—refused to believe:

Mihri was dead.

He never deliberately thought about her. He had schooled himself to store her in that same part of his mind's wardrobe where he kept his father. But occasionally wisps of her tumbled out, caught him unawares and had to be stuffed back and the door slammed: her scent, her black-edged eyes, her white undergarments.

It had excited him unbearably, as they walked side by side, not touching, to know that beneath her prim exterior—the neat skirts, the dark high-necked sweaters—there was such an orgy of lace, swelling and spuming over breasts and hips and thighs: panties and garters, petticoats and bras, froths of whiteness against the dark honey of her skin. He was excited in the same way by the white scarf she always wore over her hair; he knew—Oh God, how he knew—the way that same hair looked, loose against her shoulders.

Thinking of it now, he felt the familiar bile of hate rise in his throat. Violence was alien to him; he loathed the fragility of atmosphere that it generated, the sharpness like ozone left in the air after a storm. Violence was emotion hardened into a spiked collar he had no wish to wear. Yet if he could find those reponsible, he was afraid that he might, without thinking about it, murder. In imagination he had lingered over the details, hating himself, hating them for putting such thoughts into his head: he saw his thumbs sink into their eyeballs, his hands rip apart their skulls, the hammer which would crush the soft parts of them, the blowtorch, the knife. . . .

What made it all the worse was that he knew, as certainly as if it had been proven beyond all reasonable doubt, who was behind Mihri's death.

■ ■

Once it had been settled that he would attend the Sorbonne, Geneviève arranged for him to board with an elderly cousin of his grandmother's. The tall house on the Place Henri IV was bleak and comfortless, full of damp smells and gently decaying furniture. The cousin was very similar to his grandmother: tall, angular, sexless. When a fellow student—a girl with long red hair—smiled unequivocally at him across the lecture hall, it was like seeing a semicircle of light at the end of a dark tunnel. Over the months that followed, he realized that warmth and strength and softness had not been attributes specific to the women of Don Feliz Torres; they belonged to women in general.

He also discovered that most women were prepared to lavish all three of those qualities on those they loved. And he became aware of the emotional bruising women suffer from men. He saw that under even the most powerful of female surfaces lay an ego pummeled to wafer thinness, and that in exchange for loving, all they ever asked was to be loved.

Philippe was more than ready to oblige. During his first two years he fell drastically in love at least six times, and even more drastically out of it.

It was partly through the persuasion of one of these women that he had joined a group of self-styled anarchists. But only partly. Mainly, he joined as a form of rebellion, the first he had ever indulged in. It was a way of expressing a desire for freedom from the constraints of his background and heritage and the future that had been determined for him by his father's death. Because even if Geneviève had been inclined to marry again, he, Comte Philippe Antoine de Pierrey, would still have been the heir to the vineyard and its ever-increasing reputation.

However, he soon discovered that these anarchists bored him. He had nothing in common with any of them except the girl who had introduced him to the group; what he had in common with her had little to do with politics. They were sharp, restless people, raised in industrial towns, the sons and the daughters of the professional middle classes, with a contempt not just for the values with which they had been reared, but for almost everything. Gradually, through spending time in their company, he began to realize that each one was an alien, a societal misfit. The thought that *he* must therefore be one, too, displeased him. He was repulsed by the excitement with which they discussed destruction, the way their eyes shone at the thought of the death of innocents. He came to hate the slogan with which members were supposed to greet each other, lifted from the rootless radicals who were their corresponding generation in West Germany. "Don't argue—destroy." Philippe had spent his life helping to nurture, coaxing new life out of the soil each spring, harvesting the fruits in autumn. The message of annihilation went against every instinct he had ever possessed.

"We will overthrow this rotten society and build a new one," they assured each other, yet when Philippe asked how, they were vague about details of the rebuilding. He came to dread the weekly meetings in the room above an anarchist bookshop. A man called Jean-Luc Zulyan seemed to be vaguely their coordinator. He was a student in the medical faculty, though he scarcely seemed to have time for study. He claimed affiliations with the Red Army Faction in West Germany, and Action Directe.

His talk was spattered with references to their "Leader," the founder of the group, who spent his subsidized days traveling across France to set up similar factions in other universities. He was an older student, a *pied-noir* whose father had been beaten to death by the French army in Algiers. Philippe saw him once that autumn from a distance, crossing the campus surrounded by disciples as though he were divine.

With the clarity of the disengaged, Philippe began to realize that the motivation of some of his comrades was less a desire for change than a love of the clandestine and the destructive. Like him, they needed a direction to their purposeless lives, and found it in undercover activities. They sneered at the bourgeoisie from which they sprang, and ranted at the power of the ruling classes, borrowing a revolutionary language from the Red Army Faction, which had risen from the ashes of the Baader-Meinhof Gang.

One evening in October, Jean-Luc produced a submachine gun and insisted that the whole group learn how to assemble and fire it. Philippe was frightened. What had begun as a game had become all too terribly serious. It occurred to him that he might be forced to take part in some operation that would actually leave people dead.

The Red Army Faction began hitting U.S. targets in Europe. Action Directe set off a series of car bombs in the heart of Paris. Jean-Luc was ecstatic. "We must be prepared to die," he told them, his hate-filled eyes meeting each one of theirs in turn. Philippe felt emphatically that he was far from ready for such a drastic step.

When a hand grenade was thrown into a café where students congregated, he was horrified. Though his group was not responsible for the outrage, they were nonetheless delighted; he realized that they were high on the excitement of causing fear in other people; that they were terror junkies. The fact that five innocent young people had died, and scores were injured, meant nothing to them.

"Il n'y a pas d'innocents," Jean-Luc shouted, quoting Emile Henry, who had bombed a Paris café back in 1894, and the others took up the cry. Philippe could not believe in the concept that those who died had somehow contributed to their own deaths.

He became convinced that he himself would never be free of them, and that any attempts to leave the group would result in his own bloody death at the hands of those he had once called comrades. When Jean-Luc told them that the Leader had managed to establish links with the Abu Nidal, Philippe went back to the house of his grandmother's cousin and threw up.

■■

Two years ago, Daniel had said, "Can you take a couple of weeks off?" They were sitting in a brasserie, drinking beer, trying to decide what to eat while around them moved waiters like caricatures, in long white aprons, plates stacked in tiers along one arm. The air was thick with the satisfying odors of fried garlic and spilled wine.

"When?"

Daniel shrugged. He was on one of his periodic visits to Paris. "This month sometime? Whenever you like—but soon."

"What for?" Philippe enjoyed being a free agent. The fact that his student days were over was not so much a pleasure to him as a confirmation that time did indeed pass, that life was moving onward toward a wanted goal. Analyzing his feelings, he had long ago realized he was one of those for whom youth is more of a burden than a delight. The prospect of maturity did not depress him; the gray that occasionally glinted in his dark hair merely corroborated an inner feeling that his happiest years were yet to come.

Daniel was different. He had made a success of being a boy. Even across the divide of their dissimilar language and education, Philippe could see that. Nor did he envy Daniel the fact that he would go on to be a successful man as well.

"I want to go to Istanbul," Daniel said. "I've got three weeks leave."

"All right." Philippe shrugged, raising his glass to his mouth. "Why not."

"It's the most romantic city you'll ever see. So beautiful . . ." Daniel smiled reminiscently. "And the girls are . . ." He shook his head. Beer and emotion drowned the adjectives he might have used, so that Philippe had to guess.

"Easy?"

"No. Certainly not that. Some of them, maybe. But it's a Muslim country. No, I was going to say—"

"Beautiful?"

"More than that. Glowing, perhaps. Like lamps. I can't really describe it."

Philippe laughed. "You've obviously had a close encounter with one or two of these glowing girls."

"Not one or two," Daniel said. "Just one." He spoke carefully, seeming to check each word over before uttering it, as though afraid of revealing something he was not supposed to divulge. It was a way he had. Once, Philippe had asked him what he was trying to hide, and Daniel had stared soberly at him without replying before tilting back his head. Philippe guessed that in his army uniform, this action would have brought the shadow of a cap brim over his eyes and kept his secrets safe.

"Shall I meet her?"

"I doubt it." He watched something on the other side of the room. "She no longer lives in Istanbul."

Philippe did not probe. Despite their long friendship, he and Daniel rarely touched on the personal. Besides, the thought of getting away was exhilarating, even without the prospect of girls who glowed like lamps.

But that was before he went to Istanbul.

Before he met Mihri.

■■

Walking through the curved corridors of the bazaar, he and Daniel passed a little perfume shop.

"I must go in here" Daniel said. "Something for my mother . . ." He stood aside to let a girl step out through the narrow doorway. "You wait here."

"All right."

Philippe was always amenable. Through the window he watched Daniel approach the proprietor, a balding man in a tieless white shirt worn buttoned up to the neck. He moved farther along the row of shops to one where painted ceramic wares dazzled with their color and delicacy. Above his head, subtle as a hint, floated the smell of some spice he could not identify: cumin or coriander? He sniffed, trying to think what it was and where he might have smelled it before.

Behind him, a voice said, "Excuse me."

He turned. The girl who had earlier come out of the perfume shop stood smiling at him, head tilted shyly to one side. Her eyes did not quite meet his, as though they dared not. "Please forgive me for asking: you are English?" she said.

"No," he said regretfully. "French."

She switched at once to bad but comprehensible French. "That is even better," she said. "It would give me such pleasure if you and your friend would have a cup of tea with me." She flicked her hand at a little café farther down. "I need to practice, you see, and it is always so hard to find someone who can help me."

She wore a black polo-necked sweater of very fine wool over a straight black skirt. Although she was clearly westernized, in obedience to Islamic culture her hair was covered with a white silk shawl. He did not know much about the Prophet, but Philippe guessed that he would not approve of the way her clothes emphasized her femininity.

He indicated Daniel, still inside the perfume shop, standing by a curtain of long brass chains. "If you wouldn't mind waiting for my friend . . ."

"Your friend is English?"

"Yes."

"That is good. I can practice two languages at once."

"Are you planning to visit France?"

"Yes. And England. My parents wish me to marry a nice boy, but I say first I must have some freedom."

She had a sensuous mouth: soft and full, long-lipped; it dominated her face, demanding attention. Her eyes, on the other hand, were the most innocent Philippe had ever seen. They were lined with kohl; it was the only makeup she wore. Despite the boldness of her original approach, she did not meet his gaze, dropping hers, shying away from full contact.

Philippe rather wished that Daniel were not there. The three of them sat with glasses of scented tea in front of them, watching the passing scene. The girl was called Mihri. She told them, in scrupulously alternated sentences of French and English, that she was the daughter of a professor of philosophy at the university, that she was twenty-two, that she had a degree in mathematics, that she was working for Turkish Radio. While Daniel asked polite questions, Philippe speculated about the "nice boy" Mihri's parents wished her to marry. Was he merely an abstract, a hope as yet unfulfilled? Or was there an actual nice boy, walking the streets perhaps, at that very moment, secure in the knowledge that one day Mihri would be his?

■■

In her free time, Mihri guided them over the city. For Philippe, memories of that holiday were always to be associated with a crick in the neck. "Look up," she would command them in her soft voice. "Look. Up there." And up he would obediently look, at narrow spires outlined against sunset skies, at elaborate carved ceilings, at Byzantine mosaics of sad-eyed saints and madonnas. She accompanied them to museums, to mosques, to monuments, gently insistent, determined that they should miss nothing. She sat with them while they ate dishes they would not otherwise have tried: spiced sauces, unrecognizable fish, *borek* and *köfte* and *kilic*.

Philippe realized he was in love somewhere between Europe and Asia, as Mihri stood at the rail of a boat which was taking them along the Bosphorus. Her hair suddenly broke free of the scarf which confined it, and whipped back toward Istanbul, burnished and splendid, caressing his face. He was filled with the need to go down on one knee and offer her his heart; tears filled his eyes. He wiped them away, pretending they were caused by the wind.

Daniel must have known how he felt. Sometimes he would go off, saying there was someone he had to see. Then, alone with Mihri, Philippe felt himself expanding, most truly himself. He understood what Daniel had been trying to say, back in Paris: for him Mihri glowed the way alabaster does, lit from within.

He longed to hold her hand; the sight of her arm beneath her blouse, the turn of her head within the white shroud of her scarf, the movement of her mouth, intoxicated him. She was all white and brown; the made-up girls he had known at university seemed brash, their colors strident against the soft charcoals of Mihri. He realized he had been mistaken about love in the past, that only now was he experiencing the real thing.

Taking Mihri home one evening in a taxi, he could refrain no longer from touching her. He brushed her hand as it lay between them. She leaned her head against the back of the seat and without turning her head, looked straight into his eyes. Slowly he bent toward her. Istanbul vanished as his mouth touched hers. A surge of emotion set him shuddering, and snapped the ropes that kept him anchored. He felt himself floating away on an endless sea, his whole body transformed into a single pulse.

Gently, she pulled away from him. Her shy glances avoided him. At her door, he stood staring long after it had shut behind her, until the taximan hooted with impatience.

He felt himself enveloped by her, drowned. Willingly, he sank into a pool of desire. He walked with her through the warm darknesses of the city, sometimes with Daniel, sometimes without, always crammed with longing. They visited Topkapi: the flat pools of the gardens reflected her pale face, her dark hair. Staring with her at the treasures of dead sultans on display, he tried not to imagine what her naked body would look like hung about with jewels. She shimmered beside him, infinitely tantalizing, absolutely needed. Sometimes he thought that if only he could touch her breasts, or put a hand on the softness of her belly, his craving for her might be partially assuaged. Yet he knew this was a delusion: if she allowed even that much contact, he would die if she denied him more.

For the first time, he sensed a roughness, a brutality, in himself that he found alarming. All too clearly, he could imagine a situation in which his need overwhelmed his love: where he would force his passion upon her whether she wanted it or no. Though he had performed the act of sex many times, he was aware that making love to Mihri would be an event of deeper significance than anything he had experienced before.

■■

Mihri took the two men to meet her parents, who lived in a flat near Beyazit Square, close to the Istanbul University campus. From the windows they could see the tops of trees; when the leaves shook, it was as if those inside floated on a swaying green ocean. The philosophy professor was small and plump, his pale immaculate suit worn with careful pride; his wife was shy and shapeless. The two of them watched their daughter as she moved among the books and photographs with which the flat was crowded; their eyes pealed with love and pride.

They all drank tea together, talking of national differences, of democracy, of monarchies. The professor spoke of the Ottoman sultans, whose colorful exploits still informed the popular image of Turkey among foreign nations. From there he moved to the treatment of the Turkish *Gastarbeiter* in Germany, to the intolerance of religions which forbid freedom of expression, to injustice everywhere. In his student days the professor had visited both England and America: without specificities, he indicated his regret that his own country lacked the tolerance for dissent that was a feature of theirs.

Philippe gazed out across the flat roofs of the university complex to where the Beyazit Tower thrust skyward between the trees. When Mihri bent over him to offer sweet cakes, she gave him a glance from her dark eyes that was so full of promise, it was like being handed a wine-soaked sponge: there was no way that he could contain it without losing precious drops.

■■

One afternoon found the three of them in the eastern suburbs. They walked along wide streets of stuccoed villas set back behind walls studded with iron railings. Below them, almost at their feet, it seemed, was a mosque, its irregular roofs a mass of geometric forms. Outside one of the houses, Daniel paused for a moment, irresolute. Turning to Philippe, he remarked that danger was always at its most lethal when disguised as respectability. Mihri-stunned, Philippe did not ask him what he meant, knowing that Daniel would explain if he wished to. Thinking about it later, it occurred to Philippe that this must be the home of the girl Daniel had mentioned when he first proposed the trip to Turkey.

Daniel insisted that they see more of the outlying country, so they left the city and traveled to a port in the extreme south. Tipsy with love, Philippe followed as if sleepwalking where Daniel led, his mind full of Mihri. He barely took in boats, rocks, a square castle falling into ruin. They walked along a stone-built jetty past palm trees and tall square houses. Fresh fish was being fried somewhere over an open fire. Blue water slapped at the harbor wall; beyond it, the sea spread flat and hard toward stony green hills. Shallow working boats banded brilliantly in ocher or scarlet, lined with azure paint, swung against the quayside. Alongside them were modern yachts of fiberglass, achingly white.

Someone called to them.

Daniel stopped and turned.

A voice said, "Good Lord. Is that really you, Forrest?"

Stumbling through the white heat, half blinded by the brilliant light, Philippe heard Daniel respond, "Hello, Campion. How extraordinary to meet you here."

"Less extraordinary than it is for me to meet *you.*" The answering voice was cool, dry. To Philippe's ears, it sounded entirely English and something less than pleased. He blinked; his eyelids felt thick and gritty. Walking slowly toward them was a man, his body still registering surprise.

"Are you on holiday down here?" Daniel asked.

"Partly. My father's yacht is kept down here." He screwed his face up as though trying to remember something. "Or did you know that?"

"I don't think I could have."

Philippe sensed that Daniel *did* know, although he had no evidence for such a feeling except long acquaintance. It dawned on him suddenly that this place had not been chosen at random. Daniel had come here deliberately. There was a new steeliness in his friend that he had not fully absorbed until now. The ears of the shot hare twitched suddenly in his memory.

"Why don't you come aboard," suggested the man called Campion.

"We'd love to," said Daniel. "Let me introduce Philippe de Pierrey."

"Ah." Campion wore white shorts, a faded canvas cap over dark hair. His body was smooth as an olive, unbroken by blemish or mole. He held out a hand. "How do you do?"

"Philippe makes wine," Daniel said.

Campion smiled briefly. "Of course. I recognize the name."

"What about you?" Philippe said politely.

"I'm studying medicine in Paris," Campion said.

"That's where we flew in from," said Philippe.

There was sharpness in the glance Campion threw at Daniel. "All the more coincidence that we should meet here, don't you think?"

"Absolutely," said Daniel. "Is your father here?"

"No. I expect him to join me later in the week," said Campion. He clapped his hands, a faint frown between his brows.

A young man came up from the cabin and was introduced as the boat's skipper. Blue eyes blazed surlily from a bronzed face as he handed Campion a tray of glasses and bottles. To Philippe the two of them at first glance seemed so alike as to be indistinguishable; later, as the skipper moved among them with small dishes of *mezes,* he saw that it was no more than a trick of the light, a movement of the head.

Campion poured drinks and they sat beneath an awning, talking gently. While the other two spoke of England, of Mrs. Forrest, of Paris, Philippe thought about Mihri. As the afternoon wore on he fell into a pleasurable semi-coma, dazed with love, with wine, with the heat. At some point they all swam; at another, food was served. In between, Daniel insisted that Campion's skipper take their photographs.

All around them, jags of gray rock thrust harshly out of the water, hinting at dangerous reefs beneath.

■■

That autumn, Philippe found it difficult to concentrate. Though the widows kept him busy, thoughts of Mihri deluged him. She telephoned one day to say she would be visiting Paris shortly. Hearing her voice on the telephone, he felt giddy. He booked a room in a Paris hotel for her and made business appointments in the city to explain his absence from Lavandière. Possibilities swung from the ropes of his life like charms on a watch chain, golden.

On the way to pick her up at the airport, he noticed that his hands trembled on the steering wheel. The road was up: men in *bleu de travail* moved lethargically here and there; others operated mechanical diggers without enthusiasm. He waited impatiently in the long line of traffic, occasionally banging the steering wheel with frustration. Suppose she thought he had forgotten, or not bothered to turn up. Sweat started up in his armpits. When he reached the terminus, she was waiting, her face calm, the mobile mouth curved in a smile even before she saw him.

"I knew you would come," she said. She lifted her face to his, and he saw what he had not previously realized: that her love was as strong as his own.

"Will you marry me?" he gasped, holding her hand. In Istanbul he had not dared to do so.

"Yes," she said.

"What about the nice boy?"

"Which nice boy?"

"The one that your parents have picked out for you?"

"You are nice enough," she told him.

Driving back into Paris, she sat with her hand on his knee, not speaking. Her hotel was near the university; as they rode up in the lift to the fourth floor she rested her head against his shoulder. Once they were in her room, she ran to the window and stared out over the roofs of Paris.

"I never thought I would be here," she said.

"I never thought you would, either," Philippe said.

She turned into his arms. Her timid eyes slipped away from his. "I think we must sleep together," she said seriously.

"Sometime, yes," Philippe said. His heart thudded violently.

"Now." Mihri began to unbutton her blouse. He glimpsed lace beneath it, the smooth swell of her breasts.

"No." He tried to hold her blouse together, dizzy with desire.

"I want to. I have thought of nothing but this since you left Istanbul," she said. She began to undo his shirt.

Faintly, he fought back into control. "It would be irresponsible of me . . . I could not possibly . . ."

"You are not forcing me." Softly she touched his mouth with a finger. "If anything, it is I who force you. If you had not asked me to marry you, I would not have done this."

Under her skirt there was more lace. She wore black stockings.

He felt his mouth tremble. He realized now that there were some pleasures so intense that they could kill like a thrust from a sword. In the quiet room, his breathing sounded harsh. As he pulled her toward him, anticipation gushed within him like water falling over a weir.

He held her against his naked body, feeling her heart beat against his. Slipping his arm beneath her, he laid her gently on the bed. He could scarcely see, his eyes blinded with longing. He put his hand on her breast as gently as though it were made of spun sugar and felt her stiffen.

"I am a virgin," she whispered into his neck.

He could have stopped then; he could have protected her from himself. But she touched her marvelous mouth to his lips and he was lost, out of control. She was mermaid-smooth, slipping between his hands like river water, turning under him, smiling, flowing over and around him. Once she cried out. When he came, she laughed quietly.

■■

She was to stay in Paris for three weeks and he spent every minute with her that he could. They lay together in the hotel bed as though in a world new found, drinking each other in, making plans, staring for long minutes at a time into each other's eyes. She no longer avoided his glance. Philippe moved through life on the constant verge of ecstasy. The future lolled in front of him like summer ease.

■■

He was walking with Mihri along the Boulevard Haussmann when someone bumped roughly into him. He turned to find himself face-to-face with Jean-Luc Zulyan. The man recognized him immediately. In the years since university, he seemed to have diminished, as though all the body fat had been expelled from his flesh, leaving only bone and sinew. His gaze was deadly with unfocused hatred.

"Philippe!" he said. "How have you been?"

"Fine," said Philippe. "And you?" He wanted to shield Mihri from the eyes of this man who he sensed was terrifying.

"Things are going well. The Leader has been here in Paris recently—you missed a truly inspiring speaker." Zulyan spoke as though the gap since their last meeting had been a matter of a few days rather than a few years.

"A pity," Philippe said, feeling foolish. "But I no longer live in Paris."

"Never mind. Keep in touch with us. We have some terrific plans —a whole new campaign." Jean-Luc rubbed his hands together; the sound they made reminded Philippe of rats in a hayrick.

"We must go," Philippe said abruptly. He took Mihri's arm and turned away into the crowds.

Jean-Luc called after him, *"Il faut épater la bourgoisie!"*

Philippe did not turn around.

■■

He took Mihri eventually to Lavandière, the first girl he had introduced to the widows. Mihri walked between the vines, touching the soft ripe bunches of grapes. Looking back at him over her shoulder, she said softly, "No wonder you are so beautiful, Philippe. This is a beautiful place."

No one had ever called him beautiful. He tested the word in his head: *beautiful.* Yes, with Mihri he was. Her white scarf rippled across her shoulders while the two widows watched from the terrace, smoke slowly twisting from their hidden cigarettes. They did not need to speak of their disapproval of a girl from such an alien culture: it oozed from them like resin. He hardly cared. In the end, they would need him, so they could not afford to reject his chosen woman entirely.

In the car traveling back to Paris, Mihri said, "They did not like me."

"They did," Philippe said. "They loved you."

"But not as your wife."

"They will."

"They are worried that I will not make good champagne."

"That will be my job."

"And what will be mine?"

A thousand clichés clogged his tongue. Love, sweetness, children, the future: he could not speak. Instead, he touched her knee and smiled.

■■

On the Tuesday of Mihri's final week, he had an engagement he could not miss. Mihri wanted to shop so they arranged to meet in a café just off the Boulevard St. Germain, much favored by students who fancied themselves out of the ordinary. It was up a steep flight of stairs; the decor featured huge blowups of black-and-white photographs: Ansel Adams, Dorothy Wilding, Angus McBean. The proprietors, a plump American from Cleveland and his French wife, played Mozart and Bach on an expensive hi-fi system.

The métro was crowded, the trains slow in arriving. Philippe stood smiling to himself at the edge of the platform. Love smoothed away the little irritabilities of life, he thought. Where once he might have been impatient, now he saw the delay as a bonus in which to dream of Mihri. He was half an hour late for their rendezvous by the time he took the métro stairs up to street level. As he ran, making up lost time, he saw flashing lights ahead, heard the whine of sirens, smelled smoke. The street was running with water, huge canvas-covered hoses snaking across it, between the bunched navy blue police cars. A crowd had gathered and was being held back by a length of plastic ribbon tied across the road. Black smoke dribbled from a wrecked building halfway down the street; glass lay sharded in the gutters; he could see a giant photo-exposure of the Rocky Mountains standing on one edge against a wall. The blue intensity of ambulance flashers raked the buildings on either side as stretchers went by, carrying covered burdens. An arm flopped; he recognized the Mickey Mouse watch on its wrist as belonging to the man from Cleveland.

The onlookers stood shocked, words hopping nervously from mouth to mouth: ". . . bomb . . . terrorists . . . fifteen killed . . ."

He knew Mihri was dead.

Even before he saw the bloodstained white scarf which fluttered raggedly from a gaslamp attached to the wall opposite the blown-out facade of the café.

•• PART • THREE ••

FRAN

· 16 ·

EMILIE SAT IN THE LITTLE CONSERVATORY attached to the house at Précy-St.-Léger. On the table in front of her, carnations and pinks stood stork-legged in a round-bellied jar of green glass. She touched one of the sharp-toothed petals with her finger. "I hope you won't be too tired, *chérie*," she said. "I shouldn't be dragging you out to dinner parties the minute you get here."

"I'm not exactly geriatric," said Fran. "I think I can handle it. It'll be great to leave the entertaining to someone else."

"I think you'll like our host," said Emilie.

"Who exactly is he?"

"He's called Gilles Laforêt. Immensely rich."

Fran wrinkled her nose. "I tend not to like the rich."

"Why ever not?"

"They may look out of the same windows as we do, but they see a different view."

"Is that a reason to dislike them? More a reason to pity them, I should have thought." With the tip of her brush, Emilie translated the delicate sorbet colors of the flowers onto the sheet of paper in front of her.

"Except that they always seem convinced of the superiority of their own view."

Emilie laughed. "I don't know what Gilles sees when he looks through the window. I only care that he is kind, as well as rich."

"How old is he?"

"Younger than I am." A faint flush appeared on Emilie's cheeks. "Does that matter?"

"Oh," Fran said. "Oho. You fancy this Gilles, don't you?"

"You're being ridiculous, Françoise."

"Where did you meet him?"

"He came to visit me after Tom—when Tom was killed."

"What?" Fran sat up straighter, frowning.

"That's right."

"He just turned up on the doorstep offering condolences?"

"More or less."

"And you let him in?"

"Why should I not?"

"But he could have been *anyone*."

"Indeed he could, *ma petite.*" Emilie looked reprovingly at Fran. "But in fact he turned out to be Gilles. He had met Tom once or twice. We even knew some of the same people. He owns a little château in the next village: that was good enough for me."

"But—"

"I was glad of his support," her mother said firmly. "And I still am. Please do not mention it again." She dipped her brush into water, shook it, touched it to a cake of crimson, then to another of white.

"All right," Fran said. "If you answer one more question."

"What is it?"

"That break-in you told me about: was it before or after Mr. Laforêt appeared on the scene?"

For a heartbeat or two, Emilie continued to add a faint hint of raspberry to cream-pink petal tips.

"Well?" Fran said.

"After. But if you are seriously suggesting that Gilles had anything to do with it—"

"I'm a journalist, *maman.* I like to get the facts straight. Like Dad did."

"Anyway, nothing was taken. I told you . . ."

"Only because your friends brought you back early and surprised the thief."

Emilie was thinking about it. ". . . at least, nothing that I noticed."

"You said whoever it was had been rooting around in Dad's office."

"Yes. But that was the only indication I found that anyone had been in the house."

"Apart from the garden door being forced open."

"Yes."

"And the fact that someone had tried to break into his filing cabinets."

"Yes."

"And . . ."

Taking a deep breath in through her nose, Emilie closed her eyes. Her mouth trembled as she said: "All *right,* Françoise. Please do not remind me of it again."

Fran was immediately annoyed with herself. A break-in was traumatic enough: the violation of one's personal spaces, the feeling of alien hands on one's possessions; how much more so when it followed on the heels of bereavement. For the moment, she felt she could not pursue the subject further.

Through the doors into the garden, she watched a bird hop busily among the roses, pecking at the dark earth. A trail of small white moths danced slowly among the ripening green-gold pears. She thought, There will be a bumper harvest when autumn comes. And who is this man, this Laforêt? What did he really want? She could see that Emilie was biased toward him, which made it more difficult to question her. Nonetheless, she was not going to let it drop.

She said, "What time are we expected tonight?"

"Eight o'clock."

"So I have time for a bath."

"Plenty."

Fran folded herself upright. As she passed Emilie, her mother said: "I forgot. There's a letter for you on my desk. It arrived a couple of days ago but I didn't forward it since I knew you were coming here."

■■

A buff envelope. An Istanbul postmark. It need not be anything beyond a forgotten bill, a note from one of her pupils. Nonetheless, her chest vibrated with the beat of her heart. She knew it was none of those things. Opening it, she spread the contents on the table in her bedroom. Her unknown temporary landlord in Istanbul must finally have gotten around to forwarding mail that had arrived after her departure. There were postcards from traveling friends who had not realized she was back in England, receipts for a couple of small bills which she had settled before she left, a letter from her American grandmother postmarked months before, an unopened packet of black tights which she could not remember buying. Anna's, perhaps? There was also a sealed envelope with her name and address written on the front.

The knock of her heart quickened. She sat quite still, staring at the black ink, the incisive capitals, the elegant hand. Her name. Her address in France.

It was Nick's writing.

How?

Why?

Deliberately she reminded herself that he was beyond all question dead. Then she picked up the covering letter.

> *Frances Brett:*
> *These must be yours. Probably unimportant and awfully out of date, but thought I'd better send them on. I'd have kept the tights if I ever wore them! The envelope had fallen under the bed—shows what kind of a housekeeper I am that I've only just found it. Thank you for looking after my apartment for me. Next time I'm in England, you must let me buy you a drink. Hope I got the address right: I copied it off the enclosed.*

There was an indecipherable initial scrawled at the bottom.

Slowly, she opened the enclosed envelope. Under the bed? How had it got there? If it was addressed in Nick's—Daniel's—writing, it was a reasonable assumption that he had put it there—except that he had never been in the flat. Once again the suspicions she had felt concerning him: her lost keys, his mention of the valuable carpets on the walls, reminded her that she could not be sure. Had he entered the flat and concealed this envelope in her bedroom for some obscure reason that, because he died before he had the chance, he was never able to explain?

What reason would there be for him to do such a thing?

And how could she have missed it in her last tremendous bout of cleaning before she left? There was scarcely a corner of the flat she had not scrubbed and polished. Certainly none in the bedroom.

For an extraordinary moment, she felt a dead man reach out and touch her. Plead with her. There was nothing of the horror film about it. No clanking chains and rotting flesh. Simply a current of strength from something—some*one*—who had once been warm and alive and now was not. Daniel? She saw for the first time how a life could imprint itself so that although it had ceased to move forward in time, it nonetheless still existed, not in another dimension but solidly in the places where it used to be.

Indefinably, she felt she was being manipulated in some way. By what? Or whom? *See what's in there,* she told herself. *The answer could be inside.*

If so, it was not immediately obvious.

All it contained were three photographs and a paperback in French. *Le Saint à New York*—Simon Templar doing something dashing on the other side of the Atlantic. Fran turned it over. It had a battered quality, as though it had been thirdhand when Daniel acquired it—from a fleamarket, perhaps, or one of the bookstalls alongside the Seine.

She put it to one side and picked up the photographs, just snapshots, poorly developed and fading now. In one, a man sat on a terrace at a restaurant table, with the sea beyond him and a cypress bulging to one side. His hand was up, shading his eyes. Was it Daniel? Fran thought not. Opposite him was a girl, so deeply tanned that she was made to appear almost black by the photograph's unsubtle contrasts.

A second snapshot appeared to be identical: the same terrace, the same girl, the same cypress tree. Only the man was different. This time it *was* Daniel. The girl seemed somehow familiar, though her dark face was too indistinct to be clearly recognizable. She wore a white trilby and a loose white dress that reached to just below her thighs. She was laughing, raising a glass to the camera. Was this the other girl Daniel had been interested in, the one Alicia Forrest had mentioned?

The last photograph was of much better quality. It showed Daniel and two other men. They wore shorts and were standing on the deck of some kind of boat. From the soft-focus whiteness around them, Fran could see that the sunlight was intense and filled with masts. The two unknown men sat on the cabin roof, laughing as people in photographs so often do, the camera recording a moment that ignored all the inner anxieties, the tensions and uncertainties. A little apart, his hand on the helm, stood Daniel, a hat shading his face. Even in shadow the strong features were vivid, intense. He looked very solemn. Fran felt a curious wrench of the heart, seeing that look, remembering how he hated to be photographed. Faintly, in the background, she could see the square outlines of an ancient castle. Where was this taken? And how long ago? Who were they, those men, dispersed now, yet trapped forever by the camera in that single moment, without a past, futureless, even the present gone in the second of capture? What endeavor had brought them together in the sunshine one afternoon of the past? Had they succeeded? Did they like each other? Were they sailing away from the port which was pictured behind them, or had they just arrived? If so, where had they come from? And who had been behind the camera?

She picked up the book again and shook it. Nothing dropped out; no clue in the shape of a long blond hair or a cryptic note. She riffled through the pages but found no markings, no indication as to what it meant. Puzzled, she looked again inside the envelope container. Right at the bottom, attached to the seam, there was a piece of folded paper. Carefully she pulled it out. It was tissue paper, so fine that it was scarcely noticeable—and would not have been unless it was specifically looked for. Fran unfolded it, feeling the thump of her heart. It was a note, a note that rambled, that read:

> *Frances: If you get these, then something has gone badly wrong. I can't explain, but hang on to them. You know more than you realize. Your father will have told you that no experience is ever wasted. Please believe that I didn't want you to be involved and remember, there are many names for God. If things had only been different . . .*
>
> *If you are in difficulties, address yourself to them as your father might have done and you will find that they unravel.*
>
> *I know how you hate clichés, but I can only say: I could not love thee, dear, so much, etc.*

He had signed it, not *Nick*, but *Daniel.*

She breathed shallowly for a few moments, her eyes closed, deliberately blanking her mind. What did it mean? And why had he told these things to her, rather than someone with authority, such as the police? It looked as if he had written the note in a hurry, almost as though he was frightened. And strangest of all was that signature. It meant he must have realized that if she eventually received the package, she would already have found out he was not Nick Marquend, but Daniel Forrest.

Rereading it, she saw that he was trying to make her understand something without explicitly stating what. Was that in case someone else should find the note? She picked up the envelope. She could see no sign that the seal had been tampered with. That might mean exactly that. It might also mean that Andrew Watson's cousin's friend—the owner of the Istanbul apartment—was expert at covering his tracks. But why should it mean anything of the kind? Why should there be any connection at all between him and Daniel? If he had, for some reason, opened the envelope, and the contents had held some significance for him, why would he have sent it on to her? Some things had to be taken at face value: the complete noninvolvement of her former landlord would have to be one of them.

More important to her, at that precise moment, was the fact that Daniel—Nick—had loved her. Or at least implied it. She wondered why it had never occurred to her during those painful last weeks in Istanbul after his departure, to think that something might have happened to him. Was strong, capable Françoise Brett, so much in control, so cool and laid-back, in fact more insecure than she liked to imagine? She remembered the terrible months after her father's death. Perhaps she had subconsciously preferred to believe she had been thrown over for another woman than accept that a second man she loved could have been snatched away from her.

■■

Lying in scented bubbles, Fran reflected again that although she did not for a moment imagine that a rich château-owner would break into her mother's house, it was odd that this Gilles Laforêt should have shown up without warning. It might be as well to check him out for herself; meanwhile, she would keep an eye on him. She wished she had spent more time with Emilie just after her father was killed. She had flown over as soon as she heard the news but had only been able to take a few days off. She could still remember that dazed week, how chill the house had seemed, the telephone constantly ringing. The two of them had sat in the garden for hours. For the most part they had not talked. Occasionally Emilie would sigh, say, "He always . . ." or

"Once, we . . ." and speak for a few minutes about the past she had shared with her husband, before relapsing once again into silence. Listening, Fran had felt deprived at not having the comfort of such memories.

Your father will have told you that no experience is ever wasted . . . She sat up suddenly, water sloshing up over the edge of the bath. Had Tom ever said that? It was the kind of remark he might have made, but she certainly had no recollection of his ever doing so. And if he had, how could Daniel have known about it? Wet, naked, she climbed out of the hot water and ran back into her bedroom.

Your father will have told you . . . and further on, *address yourself to them as your father might have done* . . . What did that mean? Twice he mentioned her father. Like a whisper from a ghost, she remembered Sylvia's careless voice: *He said something like: "I met her father once."*

Water dripped onto the carpet, darkening the pale blue pile. *Address yourself* . . . and *There are many names for God.*

It had to mean something. But what?

■■

In the car, Fran turned toward Emilie. "What does Monsieur Laforêt do to be so rich?"

"Most of it's inherited, I believe. I don't know that he does anything very much, though he has business interests all over the place and sits on a lot of boards. I imagine that sort of thing is fairly time-consuming."

"What sorts of people will be there tonight?"

"They usually seem to be superlative of their kind," said Emilie. "Very rich. Very clever. Very good-looking."

"And which 'very' are you?"

"Very ordinary, I should imagine."

Fran patted her mother's knee. "You may be ordinary to Monsieur Moneybags, but you aren't to me . . ."

"Thank you, *chérie.*"

". . . though I don't exactly know how you define ordinary."

There was a silence. "Your father was not ordinary," said Emilie. "No."

Neither was Daniel. He was cold eyes, bleak mouth, a man who found life too serious for smiling. Yet she knew that, given the chance, the two of them—she and he together—could have burned brighter than any star. *Address yourself to the difficulties* . . .

She was trying to. She thought about the person or persons who had killed him. What kind of mind could listen to the screams of a fellow being and not be moved to compassion? What sort of person came equipped for torture, carrying water and a sponge, carrying acid and the instruments for battering a man's head into pulp? There was only one answer to that: a professional. She shrugged her shoulders hard, several times, to shake off the sudden rage she felt. She wondered what she would do if she ever came across his murderer. Nothing, probably. No sane person could inflict such pain on another, surely. Not in cold blood.

It occurred to her for the first time that there must have been a specific reason for Daniel's death. He could not have been lured from South Kensington to the marshes at random. Someone had wanted something from him. With an effort, she shut off the images of his dying.

Information. They must have wanted information about someone or something. The whereabouts? The identity? The future disposition of. If she could discover who had needed that information, she would probably know his murderer. But first she would have to find out just what the nature of the information was.

And also work out the meaning behind Daniel's letter. Like a badly knitted sweater, it needed unraveling: was that why he had used the word? She would have to tease out his meanings, if she was to achieve anything . . .

Emilie's voice broke into her skittering thoughts. "Fond as I am of Gilles, I don't think I'd invite his friends to dinner with me," she said. "On the other hand, I get a lot of pleasure from observing them. It's something I got used to: there were always so many to observe when your father was still alive. You know how he liked company."

"I remember."

When Tom Brett was at home, the house had fizzed with other people. Journalists, for the most part: foreign correspondents, photographers, those used to traveling light and looking at horrors. People would come for dinner and stay for a week. Men with haggard faces spent hours shaving in the bathroom. Women with sun-strawed hair lingered in the garden, squeezing cream onto themselves and reminiscing with shudders about assignments in Saigon or Iraq. The kitchen was always crowded as they sat around the scrubbed table recalling old friends and hairbreadth escapes. In the evening, they lounged among the cushions in the drawing room, drinking prodigiously before falling asleep on sofas and camp beds all over the house. They laughed a lot—yet, if caught unawares, their faces were sad, their eyes often appalled. Once, passing the half-open door of a bedroom, Fran had seen the photographer, François Vacherot, sitting on the side of his bed, weeping with his hands over his face. And once a man back from covering the Iran–Iraq war had walked through the garden with a glass of Pernod in his hand and cut his wrists in the field beyond.

"Have you given my suggestion any further thought?" she said.

"Which one, darling?"

"About writing Dad's biography."

"Yes, I have. It might be a good idea. He was an interesting man, who led an interesting life. On the other hand, was it interesting enough for other people to want to hear about it?"

"Yes," Fran said. "Definitely yes."

"I might find it too painful."

"You might find it therapeutic. And who else could do it as well? You knew him better than anyone."

Emilie half laughed in the darkness. "How well does anyone know anyone else? There were places in Tom where I couldn't go and things he would never have discussed with me."

"Nonetheless . . ."

"If anyone's going to do it, I know I'm the obvious person," Emilie said slowly. "That's why I've left his office the way it was. When I do make up my mind, everything will be waiting for me."

"I've brought his other papers over from London, so I can help you start sorting the whole lot out, if you want."

"I am not against the idea, Fran. I'd just like to think about it a bit longer."

"Don't think too long. Someone else might sneak in first."

Lights that indicated the outskirts of the next village swung on cables between the shabby trunks of plane trees. Their leaves glowed exquisitely green against the shaded municipal bulbs.

"Fran . . . Something is bothering you."

"Yes."

Emilie slowed the car. "Do you want to talk about it?"

"I don't know if it would help."

"Talking always helps. That's why I like Gilles Laforêt: he listens when I need to talk. Is it love?"

"Is what love?"

"Whatever it is that disturbs you so badly."

Frances laced her gloved fingers together in her lap. Then she said, "Someone I could have loved was killed . . . he was murdered."

"How terrible."

"I only learned about it a few weeks ago. Before that, I thought he had simply walked out on me—except there wasn't really much for him to walk out on. Not then. The way he died was particularly awful . . ."

"Ma pauvre petite . . ."

"The police still haven't any idea who did it. And that envelope you gave me this evening . . . there was a letter in it."

"From him?"

"He's—he was called Daniel. Yes, from Daniel."

"That is bizarre."

"I thought so too. The circumstances are so odd. How could he have known my address here in France?"

"Someone could have told him."

"But who?" A thought occurred to her: Was it possible that there was some connection between Tom and Daniel? "Mother," she said urgently. "Did someone called Forrest ever come to see Dad?"

"Not that I remember."

"What about Marquend? Nicholas Marquend?"

In the darkness Emilie shook her head. "I don't think so."

They turned between tall ironwork gates into a drive. At the end of it stood Laforêt's floodlit château; not a castle in the English sense, rather, a small country house. Cars lined the spread of gravel in front of a double flight of curving steps.

It was less grand inside than Fran had expected. The furniture was, for the most part, antique, good rather than magnificent. Huge sofas piled with cushions. Plenty of books. Objects here and there: rose bowls, pieces of porcelain, a cabinet full of carved ivory chessmen. When Fran looked closer, they were all knights—and all from different sets. It was a subtle touch; wealth underlined rather than manifested, for what ordinary person could afford to buy a whole chess set in order to display only a single piece?

"Miss Brett? I am Gilles Laforêt. What a pleasure it is to meet you."

Fran turned.

Her host indicated the chessmen. "You play chess?"

"Yes. And so, presumably, do you."

"I do indeed." Laforêt smiled at another man who had come up to stand beside him: thirtyish, handsome, aloof. Without appearing to wish to, he compelled the attention. If most of us are pawns, thought Fran, this one is surely a king.

"Alexander, *cher ami,*" Laforêt said. "Let me introduce you to Miss Françoise Brett." His tongue trailed across the sibilants of her name; he had the high, light voice she associated with elderly queers. Yet in spite of that—or perhaps because of it—there was something youthful about him, an eagerness to confront the world, that made him seem younger than the man with him. "This is Alexander Campion. Like you, he keeps a foot on each side of the Channel."

She smiled, held out her hand, shook his. He murmured some politeness. Ordinary actions, part of a ritual gone through a thousand times before with a thousand other people. This time was in some way different.

Not a king, she decided: a knight, riding out to alter the world in some way. But was he Black or White? Whichever one, the man was beautiful: bronze-skinned, dark hair cut short, small ears set close to a finely sculpted head. He gave an impression of delicacy that was immediately counteracted by the strength of his mouth. Alexander Campion. Despite the name, he was entirely un-English. Images swept through her mind: dunes of ribbed sand, barbaric princes racing across the desert with rifles held high in their hands, headcloths fluttering in the speed of their passing, bodies low and close against the streaming manes of their steeds. Easy to imagine this Campion as their leader, his beautiful hands grasping the reins as he twisted in the saddle to urge his men onward to danger, destruction, conquest.

Very slowly, she blushed. His full upper lip curved into a one-sided smile that might easily have become a sneer. She felt that he had

known what she was thinking, and despised her for it. He was undoubtedly aware of the impression he made; he probably had the same
effect on every woman he met.

"Forgive me for staring," he said. "You remind me of my sister."

"Oh." Was that a compliment? She was nonplussed, unused to
being compared to the sisters of men she had just met.

"I am very fond of her." His mouth turned down. "I haven't seen
her for a long time now."

"Ah." Where words ended, his voice was sometimes accented.
Apart from an occasional overemphasized s, it was pure English public
school. Yet he was far too exotic to be English.

"Gilles tells me you are a journalist," he went on.

"Yes. Free-lance."

"And you live in London, I believe."

"Most of the time."

"But you are here now. Why is that?"

"Part business, part pleasure. I'm visiting my mother, who is one
of Mr. Laforêt's neighbors." He nodded: evidently he had already
heard of Emilie. "My father died recently and I've brought over a lot
of his papers for her to sort out. I thought I might be able to give her a
hand. There are also a couple of events I want to cover—some collections and so on. I set up some interviews before I left England."
Conscious of talking too much, Fran added, "What about you? Do you
live in Paris?"

"Not all the time. I have homes in England—"

"Whereabouts?"

"I own a house on Romney Marsh, in Kent. It's let to a film
producer at the moment." He smiled, his blue eyes warm. "Such odd
people. In their way they're as vagrant as any homeless itinerant. But
who am I to make such remarks?" He shrugged. "I too move about. I
also have a home in Istanbul."

Fran stared at him. An invisible net, its meshes stronger than any
steel, finer than the finest silk, seemed to have been cast over her.
Soon the drawstring would begin to pull tight and she would find
herself threshing about in the supple prison, twisting like an eel, unable to escape. Would she be alone or were others also caught in it, of
whom she was not yet aware?

"Istanbul?" she said. It was almost a gasp.

"Yes. My father is Turkish."

"Campion is not your average Turkish name."

"And I am not your average Turk." He smiled again. "Actually, I'm here to visit my stepfather's exhibition. He's a sculptor."

"Goodness," Fran said. "Hugo Campion."

"Yes."

"I'm writing a piece on it for one of the Sunday papers."

"Really? You must allow me to take you round it. I might be able to give you something more personal than the usual press handout."

"I should like that," Fran said. Her mind was already working some of the angles. It could be a better than average piece: the son, the father, the intimate little details that would make a good story. "And are you yourself an artist?"

"Not that sort," he said. "I originally trained as a doctor but I now run a large privately funded charitable organization."

"What kind of charity?"

"It's something like Médecins sans Frontières, if you've heard of that."

"Of course. They're one of the volunteer medical movements."

"I worked with them for several years, all over the world: the Middle East, South America, Africa."

"There are quite a few groups like that now, aren't there?" said Fran. There might be a further story here. "I was reading about a German one recently. And there are one or two in the States, aren't there?"

"Yes, but my own organization is truly international. I wanted to widen our areas of involvement without being limited by lack of funding."

"I thought shortage of cash was a perennial constraint with charitable organizations, whatever country they operate from."

"Not with mine." He seemed almost triumphant.

"How have you managed that?" Fran said, genuinely curious.

He shook his head. "It's too involved to go into here. Perhaps another time."

Alexander Campion did not operate like other people, Fran saw. When he spoke, his face scarcely moved; although he smiled, his eyes did not light up. He's like a statue, Fran thought: a beautiful statue into which no one has yet breathed life.

"How does your group work?" she asked.

"We maintain teams of highly skilled professionals, experts in various techniques of survival and rehabilitation, from nursing skills to psychological counselors. All of them are able to fly at literally an hour's notice to wherever there is a need for our services. Our people are ready to go twenty-four hours a day. As you can imagine, I spend a lot of my time on fund-raising. It's expensive to take highly trained professionals out of the work force and keep them on constant alert, which is basically what we're doing. We've found it's the only way to get the standard of professionalism we want. Sadly, the most dedicated aren't always the most qualified. Not that we only operate in disaster situations. There are the long-term refugee camps, for instance. A whole new field is opening up in preventive medicine. And the AIDS epidemic in Africa has meant the formation of several entirely new units devoted simply to epidemiology."

"What do your teams do when there isn't a crisis?"

"You would be surprised, Miss Brett, at just how often there *is* an emergency in some part of the world or other."

She nodded. He was coming alive now, his hands moving in the air, his face gathering warmth from his conviction.

"Not all disasters receive the publicity that is given by the European press to an Armenian earthquake or a famine in Ethiopia," he explained. "And we also work closely with organizations like Amnesty International."

"What's your organization called?"

"You will not have heard of us. We do not publicize ourselves, except to the relevant authorities."

"Tell me anyway. I'm a journalist and I like to know things."

"We're called the Phoenix Foundation." He glanced quickly at her. "The symbolism of the name should be obvious."

The Phoenix Foundation. She remembered a heavy gate set into a wall, a winter street, her heart lying in her chest like a smooth cold stone.

"As a matter of fact, I *have* heard of you," she said. "There's a branch in Istanbul, isn't there?"

She could tell he was taken aback. Although his face remained smooth, his eyes changed.

"You know Istanbul," he said.

"I lived there for six months."

"Frances Brett," he said. "Of course . . ." He nodded, looking at a place not in the room, calculating something.

"What do you mean?"

He shook his head. "Nothing."

"But you must have meant something. Does my name have some significance for you?"

"Yes." He smiled easily, charmingly. "But it was a different Brett." Taking her arm, he moved her back toward the center of the room. "And did you enjoy your stay in Istanbul, that most beautiful of cities?"

"It was wonderful. I intend to go back as soon as I possibly can."

"Alexander, *mon cher.*" Gilles came toward them and put a hand on Campion's sleeve. "You are monopolizing Mademoiselle Brett. There are others who wish to speak to her."

Following Gilles toward another group of people, Fran wondered whether she had actually liked Alexander Campion. Probably not— but there was no denying his idealism or the fire and passion which fueled him. It was the kind of zeal she imagined a saint might possess. She had read enough, seen too many graphic pictures of the Armenian earthquake, the effects of explosive on the tender limbs of children, the victims of chemical warfare, not to know that those who tended them, often in impossible conditions, were dedicated in the highest degree.

Yet, did she imagine it, or was there something robotic about Campion? It was as though he could switch on and off at will, as though under the smooth glitter of his polished exterior, there was an alien intelligence waiting to be activated. She thought, *He is a manipulator.* Yet in spite of that, there was about him something to which she responded as she might to a child: a reaching out for attention, a need to be soothed.

She was tempted to explore him further. She would think about the possibility of doing a story on him and get in touch later, if it seemed worth it.

She looked over her shoulder. Alexander Campion was talking to a thin woman with blond hair, but his eyes were on Fran. She could not begin to guess what he was thinking.

Watching, noting, Gilles Laforêt said, "Do not worry, mademoiselle. I have placed you next to him at dinner."

The remark irritated her profoundly. Despite his charming manners, the man clearly saw her as little more than a bitch in heat. Was that his attitude to all women, or just to her? She wished she could take him up on it; had she been in England or America, she would have done so.

Twenty-four people sat down at Gilles Laforêt's dining table. The food was quietly superb, discreetly served. Fran was placed between a high-ranking editor of *Le Figaro* and—as Gilles had promised—Alexander Campion. The editor told her, face suitably serious, of the shock her father's death had caused among his journalistic confrères.

"And François Vacherot, too," he said. "Such a loss. Men of their caliber always seem to seek out the most hazardous assignments. I suppose we should not be too surprised when such situations backfire on them."

Fran nodded. If Tom had not deliberately walked into danger, he might be alive today. The longing for him rose sharply inside her.

"And you, too, Mademoiselle Brett, are a journalist," the editor continued. "Are you here to work or just to visit with your mother?"

"Some of both." She explained about the coverage of the minor collections, her appointment to see Sola at the House of Gallini, her intention to visit Pierrey et fils, the Campion exhibition.

"The Phoenix Foundation," she said to Campion, when the editor had turned to the woman on his other side. "In Istanbul it looked like a monastery."

"Perhaps it was."

Fran laughed. "You don't look in the least like a monk," she said.

"Nor is it how I describe myself—it would sound too much like a plea for something we don't want."

"Like what?"

He shrugged. "Pity, perhaps. People always assume that those who have taken vows of religious conviction are celibate."

"Aren't they?"

"Not necessarily."

"That *does* sound modern."

"Why shouldn't it? My foundation has achieved a synthesis of ancient and modern beliefs, the traditions of the past harnessed to the technology of the present to ensure that our work will carry on in the future by being successful now." He tilted his glass at Fran, his expression serious. "How does that sound?"

"Intriguing." It would make a terrific story, Fran thought. Perhaps even a television piece. She could see cloisters, cowls, a lichened sundial juxtaposed with the very latest in medical technology.

"Retreat from the world is not all contemplation and crucifixes these days, you know. It's not even herb gardens and rural possets, though"—Campion laughed—"I imagine a certain amount of quiet posset-making still goes on. It's simply that the members of the foundation have chosen action rather than contemplation as their means of serving God."

"I've never known what a posset is, exactly."

"Curdled milk," Alexander said. He grinned. "Or so I believe. Like Miss Muffet."

"How many centers are there? These monasteries or whatever?"

"We're still growing. So far there aren't more than half a dozen, scattered across Europe, but we plan to expand, particularly into the Third World countries. We add to our numbers every year, of course. You would be surprised at how many people there are who wish to retire from the world and yet maintain an active role in its affairs."

"And where do you place these centers?"

"Wherever we can combine the need for peace with speedy access to a major airport."

"That sounds like a contradiction."

"I suppose it does." He put his glass down. "And *you're* beginning to sound as though you're interviewing me for one of your newspapers."

"Why not?" Fran said. "It's a good idea. I could take the pictures myself."

"No."

"Why not? It would help in your fund-raising, surely. It would make a terrific story."

"No. You are kind . . ."

"Not kind, just a hack looking for a story."

". . . but we are private people. Besides, I prefer my own methods of raising money, and our donors would dislike intensely to have their involvement splashed across the front pages."

"Hardly that, Mr. Campion. A discreet two-page article in some monthly magazine is about as high as it would go." She sensed that he was alarmed. More than alarmed, angry. Better not mention television.

"What does it say in the Bible?" he said. "Do good by stealth?"

"Something like that."

"That's how my board members want it. As far as possible, I prefer to accede to their wishes. Not that it always works. I find that people of your profession are not easily deflected."

She smiled, without any intention of giving up the idea. She would have to look further into it, when she had time.

With the dessert, they drank champagne. Pierrey et fils. Catching sight of the label, Fran realized that occasionally she was able to forget about Daniel. She could be objective about him, about the little they had shared. She no longer suffered from nightmares. Even speaking with Philippe Pierrey to set up their meeting tomorrow had not been traumatic because she was prepared, armored against the name. Seeing it now, unexpectedly, she had a sudden urge to weep. Daniel came back to her, eyes shadowed as the two of them stood looking out over the waters to where Istanbul shone against the dark hills. She remembered his kisses, the sounds of despair in his throat and his arms wrapped tightly around her as though he never wanted her to leave him.

In the end, it was he who had left her. She bent her head. She touched the prongs of her silver dessert fork, pressing the tines hard against her fingertips. If she was not careful, tears would come. *It is not the dead we should feel sorry for,* she thought. *Daniel is at peace now; it is I who am not.*

Nor is his mother, lost and alone. She remembered the tremor of Alicia's hand, the big amethyst ring loose on the papery skin. Someone should go out to root for her, Fran told herself. Daniel's death should surely be paid for, be avenged.

Coffee was served in the drawing room. The large floor-to-ceiling windows had been thrown open: the weather was very warm. When Gilles offered to take some of his guests on a tour of the house, and Emilie joined a group setting up a game of bridge, Fran wandered out onto the terrace overlooking the back of the house. In the distance, the orange glow of Paris lit up the sky. The fragrance of tobacco plants swung nebulously in the air. She heard voices close at hand, their conversation urgent and whispered, but could see no one. From the room behind her came music, soft and dreamy. Closing her eyes, she swayed in time to it.

Footsteps sounded, coming up from the garden. She opened her eyes as Alexander Campion appeared on the terrace. He seemed disconcerted at the sight of her, pausing at the top of the steps. Then he moved unhurriedly toward her.

"May I have the pleasure, mademoiselle?" he said. His arms closed around her like a prison.

Fran smiled against his shirt front. This was a cliché straight out of a cheap romantic novel. For a few moments the two of them moved together in the dark, as close as shadows. She thought, *If this went on for long enough, it would be easy to forget Daniel.* And thought again, *Whatever one's anxieties are, there are always these moments of perilous pleasure.*

Alexander turned her gently to a stop and stepped back.

"Will you tell Gilles that I was called away." The way he said it was a command rather than a question.

Before she could answer, he was walking away from her across the polished parquet floor.

A pity, she thought. She had wanted to talk to him at greater length about his organization; the story was already shaping itself in her head. It occurred to her that it was a long time since she had been in a man's arms.

■■

That night she dreamed again of Daniel's death. The hammer thudded, like the knocks of a terrified heart. The black-robed figure stood beside her, watching. It put a hand on her shoulder. When she turned her head she saw for the first time its eyes, blazing like sapphires in the emptiness that was its face.

• 17 •

*HE STOOD THERE ON THE BALCONY,
the lights of Istanbul behind him starring the darkness around the
broader gleam of the floodlit mosques.*

*"Give me your telephone number," he said. He patted a pocket,
pulled out a small red address book, a gold pencil.*

She told him.

*He wrote the digits down, crossing the seven like a Frenchman.
"I'll ring you in the morning," he said. His eyelashes were very black.*

*The sky darkened slowly. Night blotted out the details of the
bridges, reducing them to a belt of twinkling diamonds between the
continents, between East and West. She felt weightless with the promise of something that was just beginning, so light that if she were to
leap outward into the darkness, it would buoy her up.*

"I look forward to it," she said.

*"First thing." He put a hand on her shoulder and the tremors sang
in her body like champagne. "Will you be there?"*

"Yes."

■■

Through her eyelids, Fran could see that morning had overwhelmed
the bedroom. She did not wish to wake; she wanted to stay there with
Daniel, timeless in Istanbul, at the beginning of it all, before he went
away, before the winter came.

Address yourself, she thought. And as she did so, realized that it
was a word with more than one meaning. She remembered the small
red leather–covered book that Alicia Forrest had sent her, along with
the photograph of Daniel she had requested.

She kicked back the covers. She picked the address book up from
the table by the window and turned to the *B* section. Her parents'
address in Précy had been written in halfway down the page; beneath
it was her own telephone number in Istanbul. When the little book

had arrived from Alicia, she had merely leafed through it; now, the page had new resonances. Daniel had written her Istanbul number down in pencil, yet the French address was written in black ink. She should have realized earlier what that implied: that he already knew about her or, more specifically, about her family—probably about Tom, her father. Which made it all the more likely that—as she had once half suspected—he had come to the party given by chinless Peter, deliberately to search her out. But if he had wanted her to extract some meaning from this assumption, what might it be? The more she thought about it, the more obvious seemed the conclusion: to a greater or lesser degree, Tom Brett must be involved.

But in what?

The answer might lie in her father's papers. They were all stored in the concrete basement room he had fitted out as an office, overflowing from boxes and suitcases. His notes alone filled three filing cabinets; he never threw anything away. "In my business, everything overlaps," he had told her once. "The more I learn, the more I see how the interests of big business and terrorism and wartime economies are part of one vast interlocking enterprise."

To search through them all, not even knowing what to look for, could take weeks. In addition, every scrap would require her mother's personal scrutiny before it could be discarded. And there was always the possibility that something which had no significance for Emilie might be relevant to Fran herself.

Below her in the garden, the early morning sun glimmered flatly among the roses. She went downstairs and spread herself in the hammock suspended between the pear tree and a silver birch. It was cool under the leaves, green and remote. Dew hung from the grass blades: her footsteps followed her darkly across the lawn. Swinging herself with one leg, she turned her concentration to the problem of sorting out Tom's papers. She could not afford to take the time to go through them all—Daniel must have realized that. Therefore there had to be a shortcut. All she had to do now was figure out what it was.

Emilie came out of the house. Her feet were bare, her legs brown beneath a cotton dress. She brought croissants, greengage jam in a dish of faceted glass, coffee. The warm scent of it lay among the ripening pears, sharp and tangy.

Emilie poured from a white pot. "When are you leaving for Reims?" she asked.

"Soon."

"To see this Monsieur Philippe de Pierrey?"

"Yes."

"The maker of champagne."

"That's right."

Looking away, Emilie said, "Is this work, or something to do with the friend you spoke of last night?"

"Yes—to do with him. At least, I think so."

"And you will be back this evening?"

"Yes. It may be late."

"I shall wait up for you."

Fran swung her legs down to the grass. "Mother, did Dad ever say what he was working on, just before he was shot?"

"Not much. Some kind of exposure, I believe. But I don't know whether it was exposing something or someone." Emilie wrinkled her forehead. "I can't remember him saying anything particular about it."

"Could it have been some kind of fraud? Or corruption on a large scale?"

"He hated greed," Emilie said softly. "I do remember that before he left on that last assignment, he was angrier than I'd ever seen him. He kept talking about the manipulation of innocents."

"It's what he hated most: the innocent at the mercy of the ruthless—the kidnappers, the terrorists, the dictators."

"It's not ringing any bells," said Emilie. "Though there is something . . ."

"What?"

"Something. But I just can't recall . . ."

"Keep trying."

■■

Later, in the act of swinging away around the small stone pond in the center of the graveled drive, Fran braked. Her mother still stood on the top step, waving. She was about to be left alone again for the day, and her face had assumed a sadness that Fran imagined had become habitual since Tom Brett's death. She held a camel-hair paintbrush in one hand. Fran thought, *She misses my father fiercely, and always will, but that does not stop her carrying on with her life.*

Daniel had only touched the periphery of her own life; what she mourned in his loss was not so much what was as what might have been. Looking at Emilie, she realized how important it was that she did not allow his absence to dominate her future.

She leaned from the window: "Take care, *maman.*"

"Of course. You too."

Fran had the impulse to say, "I love you," would have done, had it not been for the inhibitions of upbringing. Instead, waving, Fran drove away. Later, she was to regret that, to realize that impulses sometimes have logical roots and ought to be given in to.

She had forgotten just how much at home she felt in rural France. Paris was a city, not like any other but nonetheless sharing the attributes of all: noise, dirt, traffic, crowds. Out here, in the wider air, the harmony between man and environment seemed closer. Last time she had visited the champagne country had been in springtime. The landscape had been sullen then: bare earth, miles of black wire stretching bleakly into the distance, twisted vine stumps viciously pruned. But this late in the year—almost harvest time—the long rows of vines spread lushly toward the milky-blue line of hills which rose on the horizon. Here and there the green was punctuated by dark red tiles, a black-roofed church spire, walls of old stone. A sense of purpose overlay the immediately accessible lushness. Fran liked that.

The expressway turned northward toward Reims. The Pierrey management maintained a small office in Reims itself, close to the cathedral; a secretary told her that Monsieur de Pierrey was at the château, and gave her directions. Ten minutes beyond the outskirts of the town, she began looking for signs to the estate. Half expecting a fairy-tale castle, she was not surprised to see a squat stone building, irregularly disposed among the vines, full of arches and crenellations and unexpected stairways. Many of the former châteaux of this region had not survived the wars which for centuries had spilled across the borders between France and Germany. Crouched so close to the ground, this one seemed to have escaped notice. She got out of her car and looked at it with pleasure. A durable building, built for function rather than beauty.

She strode up the stairs toward the double front door. Would

Philippe de Pierrey make a fuss when he discovered she had come to talk of Daniel rather than of champagne? Would he order her off the premises, shouting about false pretenses? Or should she dissemble: start with the champagne and gradually move on to Daniel? She decided to play it by ear. It would depend on the kind of man Philippe de Pierrey turned out to be.

He opened the door to her himself. "Mademoiselle Brett?"

"Yes." For some reason he seemed somewhat taken aback by her.

He had thought she would be older. This tall vivid girl in her designer jeans and shirt was a far cry from the faded blonde of his anticipations. Her hair was silky in a way that reminded him of water. He frowned at her.

He was younger than she had expected, and less formal than his voice. Instead of a suit and tie, he wore fawn cotton trousers and an open-necked white shirt from which protruded a tangle of dark hair. She sensed sadness somewhere at his core. A man not yet fulfilled, she would have said. She thought, *How many of us are?* And thought further, *Daniel was. And my father.*

She followed him into his office. He showed her a chair, then sat down on the other side of a big partners' desk set in the middle of the room. He spoke briefly into one of the telephones, twisting away from her to do so. The room smelled sensually of Gauloises and food, of wax polish and the intellectual dust of books.

This must once have been a small library. Rows of leather-backed books stood behind twisted brass grilles; a set of oak library steps stood in one corner and there was an old-fashioned lectern near the window. Now, however, in front of the shelves there were computers on modern teak desks, cordless telephones, a fax machine: most of the paraphernalia of a hi-tech, up-to-the-minute industry.

Fran decided she would get a better reception if she came straight to the point. "You will have every right to kick me out . . ." she started.

His eyes were hazel, a warm mixture of green and brown, like good tweeds. They went cold at her words. "Why should I do that?" he demanded.

": . . because I didn't actually come here to talk about Pierrey et fils."

"About what, then?"

"About Daniel Forrest."

He stiffened. "What are you? Police? I thought you said—"

"A journalist—free-lance—as I told you. But Daniel was a—was my good friend. When I heard what had happened, I just felt . . ." She shrugged her shoulders. "That I wanted to find out more."

"Why come here?" Philippe found he was speaking in French. He had not meant to. He wondered what instinct had made him realize, simply from her voice on the telephone, that this woman would mean trouble.

"As far as I can discover, once he left here, he ceased to be Daniel Forrest."

"And became—what?"

"I knew him as Nicholas Marquend."

"Ah." His look was speculative. "It was you who telephoned me some months ago, demanding to talk to this Nicholas Marquend." He pursed his mouth. It was a good mouth, Fran thought. Fine-edged, shaped like a longbow. It looked as though it would like to smile a lot, but so far had little to smile about.

"That's right."

"If I can help . . ." He spread his arms.

The door opened and a woman came in with glasses and a bottle. "Thank you, Marie-Josèphe," Philippe said. He stood up. Deftly he removed the top from the bottle, releasing no more than a smoky puff. He poured a glass and handed it to Fran. "This is one of our blanc de blancs," he said.

"Which means, if I remember my research, that it's blended from white grapes only, right?"

"Yes. That makes it less weighty than traditional champagne, and much more suitable for drinking during the day."

"Isn't any time a good time to drink champagne?"

He smiled. "*I* think so, but not everyone agrees."

They drank in silence. The wine was pleasant, sparkly. To Fran's palate, it tasted very similar to any other champagne she had drunk, but she knew better than to say so. It would be like telling a mother her baby was ugly. Instead she said, "Do you have any idea at all why someone should have wanted to kill Daniel? It must be something you've thought about."

"His death was a complete shock to me," said Philippe. "To all of us here. During the six months he spent here with us, he lived as one of the family. Which, of course, in a way he was. He did nothing that might suggest he was in danger of his life." He stared at Fran. "Surely his death was a random thing, wasn't it?"

"Possibly. But he must have had some reason to have been living under an assumed name when I met him. And he'd come directly from here."

"I noticed nothing," Philippe said again. His manner was cold. Behind the desk he held himself stiffly, almost hostilely.

Fran wondered why. Did he think she was accusing him of complicity in his friend's murder? Or did he simply dislike the fact that she was raking up a past he would obviously prefer not to think about. "Did he go out a lot?" she said. "Take trips and not tell you where he'd been? The clue to his death must surely lie in the last few months of his life."

Philippe tightened his mouth. "He went away from time to time. We weren't keeping him on a leash. His arrangement with us was extremely flexible. He quite often went out in the evening."

"Did he have other friends in the area?"

Philippe thought about it. "He didn't mention anyone in particular," he said slowly. "On the other hand . . . I did receive an impression that he was visiting someone he knew."

"You didn't ask him?"

"Daniel was a very private man. Not someone you interrogated. If he wanted you to know something, he would tell you. Otherwise, you were wasting your breath."

Remembering how little she herself had learned about Daniel, Fran knew that Philippe was right. Nonetheless, she continued probing. "Could he possibly have been seeing a—" she found it hard to say —"a woman?"

"Again, with nothing specific said, I don't think so."

"Why not?"

Leaning back in his chair, Philippe laced his hands behind his head and gave it some thought. Finally, he said, "Partly because he didn't dress up. In fact, quite the opposite. Old trousers, thick sweaters: if he was seeing a woman, it couldn't have been anyone special to him or he would have taken more trouble." Watching the small shift in Fran's face, Philippe was glad to be able to say that. "This is just an impression I received. Naturally I did not monitor his clothes, or anything else he chose to do: as I said, he lived like one of us."

Fran put down her glass. "Did you like him?" she said.

"What?"

"I asked if you liked him."

"Naturally I liked him." Though even as he said it, Philippe realized it was not something he had ever thought about before, simply had taken for granted. *Did* he like Daniel? He must have done. "I was rather a lonely child," he said. "Daniel was my first close friend. When he died, I was devastated." He paused, dragging his memories of Daniel out from their hiding place to give them a good shake. "Of course I liked him. I miss him tremendously. He was my good friend."

"And mine."

"Which is not to say that sometimes one was not irritated by his" —Philippe sought for the right word—"his self-righteousness? Is that what I mean?"

"That's a somewhat negative quality, isn't it? Not one I would have used."

"I don't mean it to be. It's just that Daniel tended to see everything as black or white, with no gray areas, none of those places where right and wrong merge to produce uncertainty."

A bit like you, Philippe wanted to add, *or, rather, a bit like I suspect you to be.*

Self-righteous, Fran thought. Was that what Daniel had been? "I always imagine saints to be like that," she said. "Totally uncompromising."

"And martyrs. I certainly don't see Daniel as saintly. He had a strange brutality about him sometimes," continued Philippe. "I remember once . . ."

"Go on."

"It hardly illustrates what I mean." He was uncomfortable at the effort of trying to explain. "It sounds silly all these years later, but he shot a hare once."

"Why?"

"For no reason at all that I could see." Latent indignation made him seem more human. He laughed, sounding embarrassed. "I mean, obviously, living in the country, I'm not exactly squeamish about killing vermin and so on. I go out with the guns myself, from time to time. But that hare was just sitting there, in the sun, not doing anything. And he shot it."

"I imagine martyrs are always uncomfortable people to live with."

"The rigidity of pure principle. Like your Saint Thomas More. Daniel was rigid in exactly the same way; quite unable to accommodate those who strayed from the code—even though the code was entirely of his own devising. It was a physical effort for him even to speak to people he thought had let themselves down."

"Did *you* stray from the code?" Fran said.

Philippe gave a strange little smile. "I'm afraid I did. Luckily we continued to be friends. But it was with more of an effort afterward."

"Any chance of your telling me what your transgression was?"

Again the shutters fell over his heather-colored eyes. "Absolutely none," he said.

"What exactly did you send him to Istanbul for?" said Fran.

"Istanbul?" Philippe stared at her in amazement. "Why would I send him there?"

"I understood that he was there to open up the market for French champagne," Fran said.

He shook his head. "There's no possible way that Pierrey would be interested in new markets. We have enough trouble filling our orders as it is. This is a very small concern, and we've always concentrated on quality rather than quantity."

So, thought Fran. Daniel had lied about that too. How many more untruths had he told her? And to what end? "But Daniel was still working for Pierrey et fils, as far as you were concerned, when he died?"

"Absolutely. He told us that he would be taking a few weeks off, but as far as we were concerned, he was still one of our employees."

"Where did you think he was, then?"

"In England."

"I see." Fran could feel a headache starting up. Whatever had ultimately happened to Daniel, it did not seem to have originated here.

"Mademoiselle Brett." Philippe leaned his elbows on the desk and stared at her. She could see silver flecks in his curly hair. "Why do you want to know all this? Daniel is dead. We can't bring him back. Should we not let him rest?"

"I have to know."

"Perhaps some things are better left unknown."

"Perhaps." Fran sipped again at her champagne. If there was an aftertaste of raspberries or a hint of toast on the palate, she could not distinguish it. "Didn't you find it surprising that Daniel should have thrown up his army career to work here?"

"Not really. He told me that his stint as a soldier was over, that it was time to get started on another phase in his life. It seemed logical for him to come to us; he had always been interested in the process of champagne making, ever since he used to visit us as a boy."

"Did you ever suspect there might have been another motive behind his decision to come here?"

"He probably wanted a change from soldiering as much as anything else."

"Monsieur de Pierrey, would it be possible for me to see the room he occupied?" Fran tried hard not to sound as though she was pleading.

Philippe thought, *She has a wounded look to her mouth when she speaks of Daniel.* It became clear to him that this visit was more than she had made it out to be—and less. She had loved him; he was dead; now she came as a pilgrim to visit the places where he had once been alive. He stood up. "If you wish."

As soon as she stepped inside the door, she felt him. He was there, implicit in the faintly tobacco-scented air; a palpable presence. Her first quick glance took in the old-fashioned wardrobe of carved walnut, the armchair, the polished secretaire. The room was comfortable—half sitting room, half bedroom—with a view out over the vineyards. A shelf of books stood against one wall and she walked toward it, putting a hand up to her face to hide the sudden looseness of her bones. This had been Daniel's room.

She read some of the titles. Behind her, Philippe said almost defensively, "This is one of our guest bedrooms. We keep it stocked with the lighter kinds of fiction."

Standing behind Fran, he was suddenly acutely aware of the way her long hair lay over her neck and shoulders. He had time to realize what he had overlooked before: that she was beautiful. If she had known Daniel in Istanbul, was it possible that this was the girl his friend had mentioned before—the one who glowed?

Fran felt inexplicably uneasy with him standing so close behind her. She turned back to him, laughing. "I haven't come to examine you on your reading habits," she said. She was overwhelmed with the fact that here, in this room, Daniel had dressed and undressed, had shaved in the morning and brushed his teeth at night, had lived his intimate secret life.

The books were mostly paperbacks, some in English, some in French. She saw a translation of *The Spy Who Came in from the Cold;* Simenon, Rendell, Dick Francis. There were a couple of current best sellers and some thick volumes of classics—War and Peace, Great Expectations. There was a hardback chair placed by the window: had Daniel sat in it? And if so, what would he have been thinking about, sitting here, looking out across the vines to the hills? Or had he been using those high-powered binoculars of his to keep watch on something—or someone?

She looked up at the bookcase. "How many of these belonged to Daniel?" she said.

"Not many."

A haloed matchstick figure postured on the spines of several of the books. The Saint—or, in this case, *Le Saint,* since they were in French. It was years since she'd read one, but she could still remember how exotic he'd seemed, that suave Robin Hood figure with his connecting attics and his contempt for the law. She reached toward one of them.

No!

It was so strong, she half turned toward Philippe.

Not that one!

The voice had no sound, yet she heard it distinctly. Was it Daniel's voice?

She looked at the books again. Which one did he want her to take down? And why? What would she find: a letter, a photograph, something that would point toward his murderer? She hesitated. *The Saint in Europe:* she took it down and flipped through the pages. It was in the same battered condition as the one she had been sent from Istanbul.

"May I take this?" she said.

Philippe couldn't think of any reason to refuse. Besides, why should he? Particularly if she was Daniel's special girl. Unprotestingly, he watched Fran put the book in her bag. He wished that just once he had told Daniel what his friendship had meant to him—but men rarely say such things to each other.

He shepherded Fran back down the stairs and into the office, then sat down again at his desk.

"One last thing . . ." Fran showed Philippe the photographs sent to her mother's house from Istanbul. "Do you recognize anyone here?"

"Not this woman. Nor the other man. This is Daniel, of course." Gently he touched the face of his dead friend.

"What about the people in this one?" Fran pushed the photograph of the boat in the harbor toward him.

Philippe looked down at his own younger face. "Good heavens!" he said. How long had it been: almost three years? It seemed like a lifetime ago. "That's me."

"And this one?"

"Someone Daniel had known at school. We bumped into him in a little Turkish port where we were staying—I can't even remember the name of the place."

"What about the name of the friend?"

"I can't remember that either." He held the snapshots between thumb and forefinger. "Where did you get these?"

"I don't want to go into the circumstances, but Daniel sent me these photographs recently—"

"Daniel has been dead for over a year, Miss Brett." He looked at her with irritating compassion, as though he thought grief might have unhinged her.

"He *arranged* for them to reach me, along with a couple of other things," Fran said tartly. "There has to be a reason why he did that. I've spoken to you and you appear to know nothing. Perhaps this other man knows more. Or—" She stopped, struck by an idea. "Who took the photograph?"

"Some hired hand—the skipper—who stayed below most of the time we were there. This Campion called him up from the cabin to . . . yes: that was the name of Daniel's friend. Campion." Philippe looked surprised at his own powers of recall.

"Are you absolutely sure?" Fran felt the long strands of events plaiting themselves together into an ever thicker braid. Of course: how could she have failed to recognize the man she had met last night.

Two months ago, six months, and it might have seemed like the most outrageous of coincidences that he should have known Daniel. But more and more she was aware of a divinity shaping her ends, and the ends of others. For a moment, fear stirred in her belly. The unknown and the incomprehensible hovered about her.

"Yes. Alexander Campion. Actually, he'd been at the same school as Daniel but I don't think they were friends. He certainly didn't seem very pleased to see us there so unexpectedly. The odd thing is, I never really thought that the meeting was accidental. I think Daniel set it up."

"Why?"

"I have no idea." He looked down again at the photographs. "The other boy—the one who took this snap—I particularly remember him because at first glance, he seemed so like Campion, though once I saw him close to, I realized he wasn't at all. He had light eyes. Very odd, in such an eastern sort of face."

"Campion does too."

"No. His eyes were brown. Just what you'd expect with his coloring."

"But—" Fran was disappointed. For a moment there, she'd been so sure . . . but it was obviously another, different Campion. "I hadn't realized you were in Istanbul with Daniel."

"We had a holiday there together." Philippe sat up, back unconsciously stiffening as memory canceled the liveliness in his face.

Fran wondered what had happened there to hurt him. She got up to go. "Here's my number," she said. "I'll be there for the rest of the week. If you think of anything—anything at all—please get in touch with me there."

She looked into his eyes and away again. She was not sure what she thought of Comte Philippe de Pierrey. He could be no more nor less than he seemed, yet she was acutely aware of things left unsaid, of darkness, even violence, below his pleasant surface.

He saw her out to her car. Before she got in, she held out her hand and he took it. It was strong and firm and, he had already noted, unringed. Her eyes were very dark as they looked into his, with a hint of laughter at the corners that he found disconcerting.

"Were you in love with Daniel?" he asked abruptly.

A few days ago, she might have said yes. Now she wondered if that would have been the truth. She *might* have been in love with him. She was *ready* to be in love with him. Love had certainly been part of whatever relationship they had shared. But the man she thought she knew had not, after all, existed. Whoever she had wanted to love was a chimera. "I don't know," she said. "Perhaps, if he hadn't died . . ." She shrugged. "I don't know."

She drove away into the sea of vine leaves which reached to the edge of the valley. Already shadows lay across the lower slopes of the hills. A bell sounded across the bluing air. On the far side, instead of taking the road toward Paris she turned in the other direction. The bell was joined by others, iron and insistent. Curious, she followed their sound to a complex of buildings: a hall, arched of window and door; a fine old house of mellow brick; what looked like a chapel; a newer block that could have been residential quarters. Set in a brick wall, ten feet high, was a gateway, massively closed.

Driving slowly past, it scarcely came as a surprise to see the plaque set into the wall and read words she had read before: *Fondation Phénix.* And underneath that, in English: *The Phoenix Foundation.*

· 18 ·

BEFORE HEADING BACK TO PRÉCY, Fran stopped in at the offices of the local newspaper. Showing them her press card, she asked what information they had about the Phoenix Foundation. Although they were willing to help, they had little information to offer. The organization was self-sufficient, closed in on itself, wishing to be left alone. What supplies they bought were not ordered locally. Occasionally one or two of them would be seen about the town, distinctive in a rough robe of monkish black. Fast cars occasionally drove at high speed away from the cluster of buildings which were their headquarters. Other than that . . . there were shrugs, outspread hands, the pulling of Gallic faces . . . one regretted but one knew nothing.

She took the drive back to Paris slowly. She kept the car radio on low, tuned to a station playing classical music. On the passenger seat lay the Leslie Charteris book: her thoughts played with it, tumbling it over and over as they tried to work out its relevance. First *Le Saint à New York;* now *The Saint in Europe.* Daniel wanted her to deduce something from the books, but she could not work out what.

The sky above the city was losing its daytime intensity as she left the expressway and turned onto the streets. It would be dark by the time she was home. As she slowed in preparation for a left-hand turn, a battered *deux chevaux* ripped out of a side street and slammed into the side of her car. Luckily the avenue was quiet; although she was shunted across the road and up against an iron-grilled shopfront, she was not hurt. The driver of the little Citroën was Moroccan, unshaven, made foolish by too much wine. Throughout his questioning by the police he sat staring at his feet, occasionally grinning at nothing in particular. None of his papers were in order: it took nearly three hours to sort everything out.

Reaching Précy at last, Fran observed that Emilie had not yet gone to bed, for there were lights still glowing faintly somewhere toward the back of the house. She sat for a moment with the car door open. It was peaceful out here in the dark. Above her head, worlds a million miles away throbbed in space, remotely beautiful. Slipping off her shoes, she walked around the side of the house toward the back garden. The grass needed cutting; the separate blades scratched lightly at the soles of her bare feet. The doors of the conservatory were open. Lamplight spilled onto the lawns, outlining the roses, clinging to the firm shapes of the fruit in the pear tree.

She thought fondly of Emilie, too caught up in what she was doing to be aware of how late it was. It had always been like that: Emilie painting, time passing. Inside the house, she called out. Her mother did not answer.

The sitting room was full of some acrid odor. Thinking that Emilie might have left something on the stove, Fran hurried into the kitchen. It was empty. She took a few minutes to identify the smell as burnt paper. Had her mother already started on the sorting out of Tom's filing cabinets? For a moment she stood in the hall, trying to decide where the smoky odor came from. The basement? Was Emilie down there?

She called again. *"Maman!"*

No one answered.

It was only as she went down the stairs to Tom Brett's basement office that she began to feel something was wrong. The smell of smoke was stronger now. She could see a line of dim light under the door at the bottom of the steps. She opened it cautiously. Cushions of smoke bulged against the ceiling, black billows edged with glassy blue. The thick atmosphere, overlaid with gasoline fumes, was unbreathable. Holding her skirt up over her nose and mouth, she checked the room. Emilie was not there, just the flat charred corpses of Tom Brett's papers. Someone seemed to have sprayed the filing cabinets, the boxes, and the desk with inflammable liquid and set them alight. She backed out, pulling the door to, amazed that the house had not gone up in flames. She ran upstairs, calling her mother's name.

Emilie was in her bedroom. She lay among her pillows, propped against the headboard. She had been tied up; her thin painter's hands lolled from the bedposts, secured by white nylon cord. There were small round marks on the backs of them, where lighted cigarettes had clearly been stubbed out. Her wrists were swollen, her face bruised and dirty. Before she had been struck viciously on the side of the head, several of her ribs seemed to have been broken.

She was still alive. Under the bloodstained cotton of her dress her heart beat erratically and breath rasped unevenly from her throat. Fran dialed the emergency services, emphasizing her mother's head injury. For the moment, she did not undo the ropes which bound her mother, knowing that the police would wish to see everything just as she had found it. Forcing a few drops of brandy between Emilie's lips, she decided coldly that she would give them ten minutes: after that she would make her mother more comfortable and to hell with the evidence.

It was eight minutes, in fact, by the time the first car came up the drive and slewed to a halt at the front door. She heard men's voices, more tires on the gravel, car doors slamming. She went downstairs to let them in. The police were briskly comforting. While the medics attended to Emilie, they went all around the house. Desolately Fran followed. They were looking for further signs of damage, but there were none. Whoever had set the blaze in the office had made no attempt to disguise his intentions: nothing else had been disturbed.

Not wanting to remember Emilie's bruised face and bloodied head, Fran wondered nonetheless why the intruders should have needed to beat her up. If the intention behind the break-in had been simply to destroy whatever evidence Tom Brett might have accumulated against persons so far unknown, why waste time on violence? It should surely have been enough to tie Emilie up and get on with what they came to do as fast as possible, since they had no way of knowing when Fran herself was expected back.

Or had they? The *deux chevaux,* the Moroccan, the hours at the police station: could that accident conceivably have been deliberate— to delay her return home? It seemed very unlikely: had the crash occurred at Reims, it would have been different, but no one could have known when she would pass that particular side street, or, indeed, whether she might not have chosen an alternative route back to Précy.

Unless she had been followed all the way back from Reims.

The thought chilled her; even more so did the realization that if she had been followed *back,* she must necessarily have been followed there, too.

Who had known she intended to visit Pierrey et fils that afternoon? Emilie, of course. And Philippe de Pierrey. Could either of them have passed the information on? She remembered mentioning the midseason collections and Hugo Campion's retrospective to Alexander Campion during dinner. Had she also told him she intended to interview Philippe de Pierrey? There was no reason why she should have done. Yet she had certainly told someone. Her host? She thought not. Rerunning the events of the evening before, she recalled the distinguished features of the *Figaro* editor. She had certainly spoken to him about it. But it was ridiculous—paranoid—to think that he could have had anything to do with either the accident, or the assault on Emilie. What possible grounds could he have?

There was little she could tell the police. The boxes of singed scraps of paper were evidence enough that a crime had been committed, but any suspicions she might have as to the motivation behind it were as yet too vague to be of any help to them in finding the culprits.

Once they had finished their examination, Fran drove to the hospital. Emilie lay in a high bed, her face drained of color except for the bruises along the side of her jaw and the mauve curve of her eyelids. When Fran spoke to her, they fluttered but did not open. The rage that Fran had contained until now sat in the back of her throat, fighting with tears.

The hospital authorities told her there was nothing she could do, so she drove home again through a night that seemed infinitely blacker than any she had previously known. The road took her past the entrance to Gilles Laforêt's place: through the tall iron gates she could see lights on in the ground-floor windows. Back at Précy she went around the house, locking and bolting. Too late, of course, but the simple action gave her an illusion of safety. How would Emilie feel, when she returned to this house that had been invaded by such violence? Fran went upstairs and stripped the sheets from her mother's bed. There was blood on them and more on the pillows. Downstairs, the telephone sounded and she ran, terrified that the hospital had been wrong, that Emilie was sinking into death.

It was Gilles Laforêt. "Forgive me calling at such an hour, but is everything all right?" he asked. "I was driving home a short while ago and thought I saw police cars."

Fran had no reason to doubt his concern—or any to trust it. No reason, indeed, to trust anyone. How easily, she thought, tightly gripping the receiver, is paranoia born. "An intruder broke in and attacked my mother," she said.

"My God, how frightful. Is Emilie . . . ?"

"She's in hospital, unconscious. She was pretty badly beaten up."

"Any other damage? Anything stolen?"

"Nothing—except someone set fire to my father's papers. They were totally destroyed."

"Totally?" Gilles sounded shocked.

"Nothing but heaps of charred paper," said Fran. "Whoever it was did a pretty thorough job."

"But your mother was hoping to write your father's biography, wasn't she?"

"Out of the question now. Not if she was relying on the stuff down in the basement."

"My dear, should you be alone? I can easily come over and fetch you."

"I'll be fine," Fran said grimly. "I doubt if whoever it was will come back again: he's achieved what he came to do."

"Are you *sure* you'll be all right?"

"Absolutely. I've taken a strong sleeping pill." She made yawning noises. "I shall probably be asleep before I make it up to my room."

She went into the kitchen then downstairs again to the basement. The firemen had sprayed the place with foam to prevent the spread of further fire and smoke. She moved one of the heavy filing cabinets away from the wall, shoving and tugging until it shifted, screeching on its metal base. The wall behind seemed smooth, at first sight, undisturbed. She felt along the surface until she found an unevenness in the plaster. Some years ago, Tom had showed her how three or four bricks could be pulled out to reveal a recess. It was a good place to conceal things, he said: not a proper safe and therefore, though less secure, it was also less detectable. Especially since there was a small wall-safe upstairs, concealed behind a painting of a Provençal landscape.

Fran tugged gently at the loosened bricks until they came away from the wall. She pulled out the package which lay in the space they left. Inside, wrapped in oiled khaki cloth, was the service revolver which Tom had acquired during the Six Day War in Israel.

Time shimmered like a mirage. Nothing could have been farther from the lush overripe orientalism of the flat in Istanbul than this soot-stained water-soaked cellar with the single unshaded bulb swinging overhead. Nonetheless, it was as though all the months since Daniel had never been, and she was again unfolding a pouch of embroidered silk to find a gun, surrounded by the silver crescents of Islam.

Carefully she slipped the weapon into her pocket. Tom had shown her how to load it: she took a handful of ammunition from the box which was hidden separately, beneath outdated copies of *The Economist* in the bottom drawer of one of the file cabinets.

Then she turned her attention to what was left of Tom's notes. She was well aware that paper burned erratically; whatever she may have said to Gilles Laforêt, there were probably recoverable items. She pulled rubber gloves over her hands and began swiftly sorting through the sodden mess of ash and foam. She found a notebook, some stapled sheets of which the bottom few had survived, envelopes full of scraps of lined paper, reporter's pads which had not been entirely destroyed, newspaper cuttings. Anything that looked as though it still contained decipherable writing she dropped into the big plastic sack she had brought with her from the kitchen.

As she worked she listened for unusual sounds. It occurred to her that if anyone came down here, she would be trapped: the stairs were the only means of escape. She took the gun from its wrappings and loaded it, laying it on the desk beside her. In so confined a space, the stench of recent fire was overpowering. The back of her throat felt raw and charred.

It took her nearly two hours before she felt she had salvaged everything that might conceivably be of use to her. Wearily, she lugged the bag upstairs, locking the basement door behind her.

It was late, almost dawn. She undid the bolts on the conservatory door and breathed in the freshness of the garden. The clean air gripped her; she drew it into her clogged lungs, face uplifted to the lightening sky. She found a couple of rugs and a pillow and carried them out to the hammock. Wrapping them around herself, she climbed in and set it swinging. Dew fell gently from the leaves above her face. Somewhere a bird offered a tentative line of song to the coming day and fell silent again. She slept.

Emilie was conscious but in pain. "Thank God you were not there too," she said. She sounded hoarse.

"What happened?" Fran demanded.

"They came round the side of the house and into the conservatory," Emilie said. "I was at my painting table, thinking about going to bed."

"Did you see their faces?"

"One of them. The other had a scarf wrapped round his head: I could only see his eyes."

"What did the first one look like?"

"Small. Eastern, I suppose. Certainly not European."

"What kind of Eastern?"

Emilie shrugged and winced. "Not oriental. Arab, maybe, or Algerian. That kind. He must have been about forty, a little man, a bit like a monkey."

"What about the other one?"

"I couldn't really see anything. Young, I'd have said, from the way he moved—but not a teenager. Perhaps in his twenties. Blue eyes, smooth skin." She had the observant eye of the artist, but behind her calm tones there was shock. More than that, there was loss. The world in which she had hitherto moved with confidence had perceptibly shifted: as long as she lived, she would never again feel entirely safe.

Fran took her hand. The cigarette burns were ringed in dull yellow from the ointment that had been spread on them. Below the groove between thumb and first finger the skin showed a few brown marks, the first faint signs of age. "Mother," she said gently. "Did both of them hurt you?"

"No." Emilie turned her head to hide the weak tears which began to fill her eyes. "Only one of them. The other went downstairs after he'd helped tie me to the bed. He kept asking me questions about Tom, what he'd been investigating when he was killed and whether he had another office somewhere else. He seemed to know about the London flat." Emilie's voice quavered like a child's. She clutched at Fran. "Oh, *chérie*, it was terrible. I thought they would kill me. I thought they would . . . do you know what made it so terrible?"

"What?"

"He never raised his voice. He lit a cigarette, and hit me . . . and kept asking and asking, and all the time he hurt me, there was no expression in his eyes. It was like a nightmare."

"His voice," Fran said. "Was there anything special about it? Any accent?"

"No. He spoke in a sort of whisper, in French. The worst thing was that—even while he was—stubbing out that damned cigarette and—and smashing his fists into me, his voice never changed. Not angry, not excited, not vicious, just"—Emilie broke down into weeping, her body churning under the covers—"like a job he had to do," she said through sobs. "As though it was no more to him than just another job."

Fran tried to hold her. "It's over," she soothed. "It's finished."

"How can it possibly be?" Hysteria underlay Emilie's voice, ready to break out and take control.

"Because the police have agreed to tell the newspapers that everything of Tom's was destroyed. If that's what these people came to do, they'll believe that the job was completed, so there'll be no need for them to come back."

"But why do they want Tom's things at all?"

"I don't know. Not yet."

For a moment or two there was silence in the white bare room. Outside in the corridor a stretcher mumbled by on rubber wheels. A nurse starched stiffly past, holding a tray.

Making a visible effort, Emilie said in a low voice, "I haven't told you everything." She rubbed at one of the burns on the back of her hand.

"What more?"

"He asked about you."

"Me?"

"He wanted to know what you were doing here, whether you ever worked with Tom on his stories, why you went to Istanbul."

Fran drew in a deep breath. "That was very stupid of him," she said grimly.

"Why?"

"Because if I hadn't made the connection before—and I might very easily not have done—I've made it now."

"What connection?"

"Between Istanbul and Dad and—and Daniel's murder. I don't know what it's all about but I'll find out. And when I do . . ." She gripped her mother's hands so tightly that Emilie cried out.

"For heaven's sake, Françoise," she said shakily. "What are you thinking? You look so terrifying."

"I feel it, *maman*."

"You must be very careful until these people are caught."

"I will be. Tell me: Which one of them was it who hurt you?"

"The younger one. The one with the scarf over his head."

Fran nodded. "I thought so."

She could see him. She had already dreamed of him. Blue eyes set in emptiness, the swathed head, the casual gratuitous brutality. Unmoved by the beating heart, the sweat of terror, the reduction of a human being into a tortured animal.

Don't.

Don't think of Daniel, spread-eagled on the floor of that grim hut. Don't think of acid and sponges and a man whose voice did not change, whose eyes held no expression even in the midst of atrocity. Driving away from the hospital, Fran wondered whether there was such a thing as pure evil, or whether one always had to make allowances for environmental factors, for parental mistakes. Coldly, she knew now that if she ever caught up with Daniel's killer, or her mother's attacker, she would make no allowances whatsoever. Thick as pus, hatred for whoever had done this to her gentle mother welled up inside her, swelling her throat. She tamped it down. Someday, she might need that hatred; someday she might be able to use the poisons it gave off.

■■

The telephone was ringing as she came into the house. The smell of smoke had diminished but still lingered about the stairwell. She lifted the receiver.

"Yes?"

"Alexander Campion here."

She was not sure whether she really felt suddenly happier, or whether she merely imagined it. "Hello," she said.

"Gilles tells me that you've had some trouble: that your mother was attacked and a fire was started."

"Yes."

"How very dreadful for you."

"Not so much for me as for her," Fran said.

"But she is all right?"

"She seems to be. They broke a couple of ribs, and there's a hairline fracture to her jaw, plus a nasty wound on her head. Other than that, it's mostly severe bruising."

"I was going to ask whether you would like to go round the Campion retrospective this afternoon, but obviously in view of . . ."

"I'd very much like to."

"Are you certain?"

"Yes. I can't be with my mother twenty-four hours a day. And it will keep me occupied."

"That is perfect."

They made arrangements to meet. Then, "Will you have dinner with me afterward?" he asked.

"A drink I would love, but I shan't have time for dinner. I have an interview set up for the early evening. And after that I shall have to get back to visit my mother."

"Of course. We'll have dinner another time." His voice changed. "Do you have any idea why those people broke in? What the motive behind the attack was?"

"Something to do with my father, we think. The fire was obviously intended to destroy all his papers. My mother is very upset: she had hoped to write a biography of him, but it'll be almost impossible now."

"Why would anyone want to do such a thing?"

"He must have had some information that could be dangerous to someone. The intention was obviously to make sure there was no evidence left against them. The pity of it is that we don't know what he was working on when he died."

■■

The Galerie Knabel was off the Faubourg St. Honoré. Campion was already there when she arrived. He smiled, his eyes lighting up at the sight of her; he touched her shoulder. She smiled back, thinking, *He is trying to charm me. Why?* Inside the large main room, the Hugo Campion sculptures had been arranged in groups which were designed to show the sculptor's chronological development.

"You can see the emotional changes that took place in him over the years," Fran said, fascinated by the cleanly abstract shapes dotted about. She held her small tape recorder in her hand. "Look at this: it's quite different from what he was doing earlier." She consulted her catalogue. *"Leyla.* What a beautiful piece of work."

"My mother was the model," Campion said. He did not look at the polished bronze. "It was the first summer we met Hugo, right here in Paris. I was nine."

"Was that exciting? I read somewhere that he's huge—very much larger than life."

"He's a big man," agreed Campion. "He certainly overwhelmed my mother. I was just swept along in the tailwind." There was a passionless quality in his voice when he spoke of his stepfather.

"Is she French?"

"No. She comes from Turkey. She left my father when I was four years old."

"I see. So Campion isn't your real name?"

"It's the name I use, except when necessary. Hugo Campion adopted me."

"And moved you to England."

"Yes."

"Did you find that traumatic?"

"We had led a very nomadic life," Campion said. "Leyla could never stay long in one place." He laughed. "By the time I was seven, I think I had stayed in just about every five-star hotel in Europe."

Leyla. Slim, brown, beautiful. Afternoons in Rome, in Madrid, in Lisbon, barred light creeping through blinds and shutters, heat weighty as water filling the polished spaces. Leyla, slipping out of her bright clothes, walking naked across the floors of double rooms to shower in Budapest, in Seville, in Athens, her small breasts, her fine flat belly, the sheen of perspiration on her gold-brown skin. Those afternoons came back to him like the flavor of coffee: strong and rich, unforgettable.

Always on guard. How many times had he sat on the side of a bed, watching her, his arms rigid, ready, waiting for her, not knowing whether she would ridicule him, or speak softly through her teeth with a noise far

*louder than any scream, whether she would take his hand and dance with
him in the dusky light, holding him close to her warm nakedness, or push
him, pinch him, catch the side of his head with a slap made vicious by her
rings.*

She had terrified him; he had loved her.

Fran moved on around the room to the next piece. "There seems
to have been a huge gap between the *Leyla* and the next group of
work," she said. "Six or seven years. What was he doing in that time?"

"Disintegrating," Campion said.

"Why?"

"Once my sister was born, my mother took a lover. More than
one, I should think."

"Oh." Fran had hoped for revelations, but these insights were
somewhat disconcerting. Would he let her use them in her article?
Probably not: families liked to preserve a discretionary fence around
their skeletons. She was surprised and a little repelled by the cold way
he spoke.

"Hugo took to the bottle," Campion said in his dispassionate way.
"My mother encouraged him."

"Why should she have done something like that to her own husband?"

"She likes to be in control. To have taken a man like Hugo at the
height of his powers, a veritable cascade of creativity, and dam him up
the way she did . . ." His wave included not only the works on show
but all the sculptures Hugo Campion might have produced. "That's
real power."

Fran started to laugh, thinking this was a joke. The chilly look on
his face made it clear that it was not. She turned a page of her catalogue. "What started your stepfather working again?" she said.

The cynical note disappeared from Campion's voice. "My sister,"
he said. "Aimée."

The name dropped into her head like a baited line into a pond.
Her goldfish thoughts darted, nibbling at memory, skimming across
the past. Aimée Dubucq, the Giaour, the foreign Sultana, walking
beside the flat pools above the Golden Horn, plotting her revenge.
Istanbul, curved and watered, cypresses, tiles of a piercing blue, Daniel with his shadowed eyes. Time does not act on memory to soften
the edges, blur the details; if anything, it sharpens them. Emotions

may lose their acid outlines, but not places and people, not if you wish to retain them.

"How did she do that?" Fran asked.

"She asked him to make something for her."

"And he did?"

"Yes. This."

It was another bronze. His fingers caressed the silky lines of the piece, lingering on the suggestion of a baby's rounded, vulnerable head.

For Amy, Fran read.

"Yes. She was four when he did this. She loved it."

"He only cast two versions of it, according to the catalogue."

"That's right."

"I wonder who owns the other."

"Probably some Texan oil billionaire." He smiled at her, and again she was made aware of the deliberate intention to please. "Come and look at this."

He led her over to a sculpture made of steel, polished in such a way that from some angles it looked like glass. Again, in spite of the piece's abstract presentation, Hugo Campion had contrived to suggest an almost representational clarity. A loose bird shape, soft flickers of almost-fire, a head raised to an invisible sky; a plaque on the wooden block which supported it said *Resurrection*.

"It feels so anguished," Fran said. She moved her shoulders about as though to dislodge a burden.

"Being born again in fire is probably rather painful," Campion said, his mouth wry. He took her arm and pulled her closer to him. "Especially when, according to the legends, the fire is made from the ashes of your own father."

■■

They drank aperitifs at an open-air café on the rue Montaigne, sherry-colored St. Raphaël for her, a glass of red wine for him. Both being from cosmopolitan backgrounds, they spoke for a while of the difficulties of moving between different cultures.

"Which of your homes do you prefer?" Fran asked.

"Istanbul, without a doubt," Campion said.

"Why?"

"Perhaps because my memories of the place are kinder than anywhere else."

"How do you mean?"

"My father lived there. I was always happy with him."

She had learned by now that he had a way of saying deeply personal things without altering the tone of his voice, so that at first hearing they seemed to have no more significance than a request for the salt. It was both disconcerting and touching.

"Do you see him often?"

"No." He spoke abruptly; she had a sense of having trespassed. "I always wished to stay with him when I was a child but my mother would not let me. I think now that she left him because he was too strong for her. She couldn't change him, the way she changed Hugo."

"And why are your memories of other places less kind?" Fran asked.

"Mostly because they also contain memories of my mother—of Leyla." He turned his head toward Fran; his deep gaze swallowed her up. She inclined toward him, moved by the bitterness and longing that she sensed in him.

"Were you unhappy with her?"

"I adored her," he said.

She half smiled, raising her glass to her mouth. "Is that an answer?"

"Not really."

"So give me one."

"I—" He looked down at the round tabletop, then chased a grain of sugar around with his finger. "She hated me, I think."

"That's a heavy burden for a child to carry around."

"I didn't realize it until recently." He lifted his hand and flicked the sugar grain away from him. "I still haven't worked out why. What I did."

"I suppose you don't see her much, then."

"Hardly at all. Though as a matter of fact she's in Paris at the moment." He paused and then said, "She used to live here but she moved back to Istanbul a couple of years ago."

"Will you see her?"

"She's asked me to meet her for lunch; I've agreed." Fran saw him try to smile. "One always hopes that things will change, doesn't one? She's a very wealthy woman now, thanks to her family, and has a great many business connections all round the world. She still travels a lot: she told me once that personal contact was the best way to set up deals, much better than leaving things to accountants and bank managers."

"She's probably right."

"Probably. I wish I had more time for it myself but I'm already overcommitted, as it is, hardly able to keep tabs on the day-to-day affairs of my organization, let alone get involved with new ones." He waved at the waiter, indicating their glasses. "For instance, you told me the other night that there was a branch of the Foundation in Istanbul. I'd completely forgotten, though when I checked with the accountants, they told me it had been set up a couple of years ago, with my approval." He gave his warm smile. "In spite of loving Istanbul, I'm afraid I tend to block it out of my consciousness now that Leyla's back there."

"Did you get on with your stepfather?"

"Not very well—I suppose I resented him for taking my mother from me. And in the early years of his marriage, he was so besotted with her that he completely neglected me. Then, later, he did something so unforgivable that I've hated him for it ever since. I don't think I could even sit in the same room with him. Yet I don't suppose he was —is—a particularly bad person." He played with his glass, swirling the jewel-red wine around inside. "It could even be argued that what he did was not his fault, but Leyla's. She may not have actually swallowed the drink for him, but she certainly kept his glass filled."

Despite his good looks and his money, what made Alexander Campion so instantly appealing was his naked need to be loved, Fran decided. In addition, there was the impression he gave of being a man with a secret tragedy locked inside him. What woman could resist it?

He had turned to look at a girl who had come hurrying around the corner. Dark, tall, much taller than Fran. She carried herself as though an invisible cloak swung free from her shoulders. In profile, her face was cut with the same severe beauty as an antique queen's: Nefertiti, Astarte, Cleopatra.

"I think that's Sola," said Fran. "The model."

"Sola." Campion watched the girl as she walked past them.

"The one I have to interview, later."

"She's beautiful."

"Isn't she just?"

"More than beautiful. If I didn't have to get ready for my flight to Sweden tomorrow," he said, his eyes still on the girl, "I'd have begged to come along."

"She probably looks like hell in the mornings."

"Do you think so?"

"It was a joke."

Over her second aperitif, Fran said: "Did you ever meet someone called Daniel Forrest?"

He said coolly, "I was at school with someone of that name."

"He was a good friend of mine," Fran said. "Yesterday, Philippe de Pierrey happened to mention that he'd met someone called Campion while he was on holiday in Turkey with Daniel. I wondered if it was you."

"Pierrey? I don't recall—"

"Champagne."

"Ah, yes." He drank carefully from his glass.

"Was it you they met?"

He had met her for the first time only a couple of days ago; already he knew that she was coated with curiosity, the way a peach is coated with bloom, or a mirror with mercury. It sat on her, contained her, integral as skin.

"Yes," he said easily. "My father's boat was moored at Kelkan: it's a small port in Turkey. How strange that you should know Daniel too. Were you friends at home? In England, I mean? I stayed once at his house."

"In Istanbul," Fran said. "We met there."

He said nothing.

She reached into her bag for new batteries and slotted them into her recorder. Looking up, she stared into his blue eyes. "You *did* know Daniel was dead, didn't you?"

"I heard," he said briefly. It had been Sutton who told him, plump Jeremy Sutton, hurrying up after a board meeting, the news giving his face the stiff fragility of eggshells. "From someone I knew at school."

"Do you have any idea why someone should want to kill him?"

Fran asked. She was thinking, *Something is wrong here.* Or, if not wrong, then odd.

Campion did not hesitate. "None whatever."

"Didn't you say you had a house near Lydd?"

"Yes."

"They found Daniel's body on Romney Marsh."

"I know that. In fact I even know the place where he was found: a little hut tucked down among the reeds near one of the dikes. Have you ever been there?"

"No."

"It's bleak countryside. Flat dank fields spreading to the sea; on a winter's evening with the sun going down and the mist rolling in, it can be very eerie. Dickens is good at re-creating the atmosphere of the place: you've read *Great Expectations?*"

"Naturally. It doesn't sound like a good place to die."

"Is any place? Unless you're ready to let go of life? And most of us are still clinging to it even as we tumble into the grave. You would be surprised at what a human body will do without, in order to go on living."

"What do you know about Gilles Laforêt?" she said.

He lifted his shoulders in a shrug. "What's there to tell? He's a good friend—treats me as though I were his son." He considered for a moment. "In spite of having my own home here, I seem to spend most of my time in his." He turned to face her. "Funnily enough, we lived opposite each other for years—my flat is directly across from his on the Ile St. Louis—before we actually met about eight years ago. He's seriously rich, of course: I'm never sure whether that's a curse or not."

Fran looked at her watch. "I'm afraid I must go," she said. "I have an interview to do tonight. And after that, the hospital . . ."

He saw her to her car, holding her arm; they walked like silent lovers among the evening crowds beginning to fill the streets.

"You are lucky to have a mother whom you love," he said suddenly.

"Didn't you say you adored yours?"

"I thought I did. It was only when I grew up that I realized how much I hated her."

"Why?"

"She turned away always from my love. I cannot think of anything more cruel than that."

"Loving someone places obligations on them that they can't always fulfill," Fran said slowly. "You should never expect to be loved back."

"How true. But a child should surely be able to assume he is loved."

"In a perfect world, yes."

"A child not loved will grow up scarred," he said. "Is it to blame for that?"

She laughed. "I often think that a person is only truly adult when he stops blaming his parents and takes responsibility for his own flaws." She inserted the keys into the lock of the car and turned them.

"You are wrong."

"Am I?"

"Some people are like bonsai trees," he said with passion. "They have been stunted with intent, deliberately not allowed to grow to their full height. Must the bonsai turn round to the oak tree and say: It is *my* fault that I am small and twisted? Of course not. It is the fault of those who so carefully snipped away at the tender shoots each time the deformed little branches put out a new growth."

You, with your safe English childhood, cannot possibly imagine what it was like to be me, he thought. Daniel had asked that once: "What must it be like to be you, Campion?" The question had burned him like ice: there was no answer he could make. He had wanted then to say what he wished to say now: You were allowed to grow up straight; there were no cold fires licking at your heart, no dark angel barring the way forward with her flaming sword.

"I have to go away for a couple of days," he said. "May I take you out to dinner when I return?"

"Ring me when you get back."

"And you must tell me all about the interview with the beautiful model. It's a way of life I know nothing about." Abruptly he put his hand over Fran's. "No one has ever talked to me as you have done," he said. "My mother . . . there is no one to whom I have ever admitted my feelings for her—except myself."

As she drove away he stood without moving on the pavement. *I did but see her passing by, and yet I love her till I die,* he thought. When he got back from the job in Sweden, he would do something about it. The thought was pleasant, assuaging some of the anxieties which swamped him; even the images of Leyla, never long absent, could not destroy its warmth.

▪ 19 ▪

SHE SAT VERY STILL IN THE WINDOW
seat, looking down at the street. Beyond the glass, the night was wild.
She could see in it a reflection of the bare white room behind her, so
startlingly clear that the letters on the spines of the books were legible.
Outside, pools of yellow light circled the stems of the streetlights. In
this unfashionable *quartier* beyond St. Denis, they were dim and far
apart. The plane trees on the opposite pavement jumped and twisted
in the wind. Rain spattered the windows and slicked the leaves so that
they shone like coins in the dingy light from the lamps. She always felt
safer at night. By day, she was visible, vulnerable, easy prey—darkness
protected her.

She often sat up here, watching the street, the patterns of light
and shadow, the moonlight across the roofs, the uncurtained windows
where sometimes lovers would embrace, women would reach their
arms above their heads to unpin their hair, a man would stare out into
the night. Sometimes it seemed to her that the world was divided into
those on the outside looking in and those, like her, who trembled on
the inside, longing to get out. She shivered, as though the cold air had
slid beneath her armpits. If only there were enough strength in the
wind to lift her, to carry her weightless, unwinged, above the roofs,
away from Paris and the necessities that tethered her there.

Long ago, Mikkele had read to her about a girl called Dorothy,
whose house blew away in a whirlwind. He was a poor reader, treating
the words on the page like so many stiles to be clambered over, mis-
pronouncing, substituting other words for those whose meaning he
was unable to grasp, so that the story wandered like a drunk, teetering
back and forth along the straight line of its narrative. Yet she had
never failed to be excited by the image of that prairie house filling
slowly with wind, plumping out like a shirt on a washing line, the
turbulent gusts setting the lamps swinging and the curtains swaying,

until it was so full of air that it had no choice except to float free into the sky.

She had had no idea then what a prairie was, just a vague image of blue-green distance. Nor could she fully imagine a house rooted so insubstantially to the ground that it could take off like a balloon. The tenements where they used to live covered the steep hills above the harbor like an army—and like an army would have stood against any tempest, however fierce. The impermanence of Dorothy's house had thrilled her.

In the street below, a shadow moved under the tossing trees. Leaves swirled away from the branches and darted up into the night sky above the lamplight like a flock of little birds, before dropping to the wet pavements to slide against the gutters. The shadow moved again, breaking away from the trunk of the tree which had hidden him, stepping out into the weak circle of light.

It was the man.

Terror filled her. How long had he been there? He must have taken the taxi behind hers, directed the driver to follow, then waited out there until the light came on. Or had he been out there before, without her noticing? She shrank back against the window frame. The loose coat he wore billowed as the wind caught at the hem and filled it like a sail. Anonymous in the dark, he stared up at the building. He was lit from above by the lamp, which cast shadows across his features like a black scarf wound around the upper part of his face; but she had no doubt that he looked directly at her window.

Did he know she could see him? She watched his black shoes and dark-trousered legs tread over the sodden leaves as he continued along the pavement, and was certain that he would make no sound as he walked. The wind was getting up. It scudded leaves along the pavements, lifted debris for a brief moment into the air, tossed branches. As darkness gathered, the streetlights shivered in the hammering air.

Pressing through the traffic toward the *quartier* near St. Denis where Sola lived, Fran reviewed the questions she wanted to ask. This ought to be a relatively simple interview: professional models like Sola were usually all too aware of the ephemeral nature of their news value, were usually eager to hand out the information necessary to promote themselves and their image while they were still hot items of interest.

Parking her car, Fran was surprised at the seediness of the surroundings: bleak streets, a few eczematic plane trees, windows inhospitably shuttered so that walking past them seemed like an intrusion. Whatever the area might once have been, it was now converted for the most part into multiple units. A scowling concierge tugged open the double front door of Sola's building and let Fran into a dingy hall with an old-fashioned iron-grilled lift built into the stairwell. Pulling its gates shut, she was slowly jolted up to the sixth floor, past grimy stairs and dim-lit corridors where, every now and then, a dirty window opened onto blank walls of dark gray brick.

When the lift stopped, she stepped out into a short, thin-carpeted passage. There was only one door. As she walked toward it she thought it seemed a curious place for such a beautiful creature to hide herself. Perhaps Sola found it a relief to slough off the smell of money and retreat here at the end of a working day; perhaps beauty was as much a burden as a disability, and required the redress such a place offered.

Inside her flat, Sola stiffened. She heard the wheeze and groan of the old-fashioned lift as it staggered upward. She heard it stop, the grating squeal as the gates were pushed open, then silence. Faintly, the bell rang.

It was him.

It had to be him. Ever since the first time she seen him waiting for her, she had known that sooner or later he would find her out. How had he gained access to the building? She heard the bell again. Slowly she put down her book and stood up. There was no need whatsoever for her to open the door and violate her privacy. In the half darkness of the passage she was aware of a fine buzz in her ears, the muted jangle as messages of fear and tension hummed along the wires of her nerves. Delicately she touched her fingers to the panels of the door as though the tips were sensitized enough to register the danger that awaited her on the other side. She had always known it would eventually come to this screaming quiet in the darkness, a confrontation, a letting go at last. If not with him, then with another.

She had felt for a while, several months at least, that things were starting to unravel. The center was no longer holding, but once it had whirled away into the darkness, there would at last be peace. So why did she stand here trembling, when she had only to open the door and get it over with at last? Was it because what she feared was not that it would be an end, but that it would not?

She peered through the spyhole.

Not him.

Not him at all.

Outside the door stood a woman, the English journalist she had agreed to talk to; she had completely forgotten that Nicole had arranged for the interview to take place here.

Taking a deep breath, she opened the door.

Fran blinked. For a moment the girl was almost invisible, standing there in the dim hallway. She gave an impression of having stood on that same spot for hours. She stared at Fran with her huge eyes: in this light they seemed much darker, almost aubergine, somewhere between purple and navy blue. For a moment neither woman moved. Then Sola gestured a greeting, holding out a hand, and Fran was reminded of a piece she had read somewhere, written by a German fashion editor: *To see Sola stalking down a catwalk is to hear the rustle of giant leaves, the stir and whisper of the jungle, the distant thump of the tom-tom, exhilarating yet dangerous.*

Involuntarily, Fran looked over her shoulder. There was no one about. The old building was quiet, the occupants of the flats on the lower floors were busy being at home behind closed doors. The street outside had been empty of humankind. And with the wind sweeping past shuttered windows, flinging itself through the trees, no one would hear if she were to yell for help.

What the hell *could* happen? She was being totally irrational. And thinking this, Fran became aware of another fear—Sola's.

What frightened the girl? Did she live here alone, terrified of rapists and mad axmen, trembling every time she heard a footstep outside in the hallway? Was that the price of being beyond beautiful? Or was there a more specific reason for her anxiety? Fran felt she ought to assure her that everything would be all right, the way she might soothe a child. She wanted to point out that the night was soon over and when the sun came, the fiends would disperse.

Instead she smiled warmly. "You do remember about the interview I set up with your PR department, don't you," she said.

Sola nodded without speaking.

"May I come in?" Fran asked.

The girl stood aside and Fran walked past her into the apartment. It consisted of one long, uncluttered room, painted white and almost empty. A single lamp of white porcelain stood on the floor, which had been sanded and sealed, and was bare except for two small oriental rugs of silk.

There were two squashy armchairs covered in burgundy velvet, with a low glass-topped table between. Against one wall was a stretch of low black bookcases. Along the wall opposite was a big bed covered in a black blanket. The window seat was cushioned in the same velvet as the chairs. Despite its wine-colored richness, the total effect of the room was severe, almost monastic. The walls were bare, contributing to the overall bleakness.

Except for one. Turning to take in the room as a whole, Fran gasped. Fixed to the wall behind her was an antique crucifix, close to life size. It must have come from a church or some religious foundation. The cross was of ebony; so was the realistically carved crown of thorns. The twisted body was made of brass, tarnished now and streaked with age. The sculptor had spared no detail: the muscles strained, the ribs heaved, the mouth was contorted.

Daniel, she thought piercingly. *Is this what they did to you? Is this what you became?*

She walked across to one of the armchairs and sat down. Sola watched her from the doorway. In the lamplight her eyes had reverted to their original color. Fran wondered whether the starkness of the room was merely a decorative ploy or a reflection of something more: of a soul stripped of comfort.

Sola cleared her throat. Speech fluttered in her mouth but remained stillborn, energizing Fran into a scrabble of activity in her big leather duffel bag as she brought out notebook, pen, and tape recorder.

"I'm doing a series on high-powered black women," she said. "You're at the very top of your profession so I'd like to talk to you informally, hear your views on the modeling world and the whole field of fashion generally. Also a bit about your personal life and your long-term aims. That sort of thing . . ."

Sola nodded. "Would you like something to drink?"

"What've you got?"

"Champagne. Or tea? I have some green tea."

"That would be lovely."

The kitchen hid behind louvered doors. As Sola went through them Fran caught a glimpse of eggs in a wire rack and a magnetic strip on which hung a set of graded knives. The rest of the tiny space was bare. While Sola filled a kettle and rattled cups, Fran looked at the books piled on the coffee table. Most of them seemed to be lavishly illustrated with glossy photographs of gardens. In the shelves there was a haphazard mixture. American paperback best sellers rubbed spines with Morton Prince's *The Dissociation of a Personality; Sybil;* Alvarez's *The Savage God; The Three Faces of Eve;* and R. D. Laing. Gardens, suicide, and schizophrenia: it seemed a curious blend.

"I'm sorry to disturb you at home like this," Fran said when Sola returned with a tray bearing a frail white teapot and two paper-thin porcelain cups.

"The arrangement was made," Sola said. "I should have remembered."

She spoke without rancor. Yet Fran realized at once that by coming here she had committed some fundamental act of baseness. She had no right to intrude into another life. Especially for something as ephemeral as an article that, while it might entertain or even instruct for a moment or two, was not going to have any profound effect on anything or anyone.

"Your PR person didn't seem to think you would mind," she said. At the back of her mind she was thinking, with surprise, *I spend my whole life intruding.*

"Nobody is entitled to speak for anyone else," Sola said gravely. Her soft voice robbed the words of any discourtesy. She wore a hooded robe of fine white wool, the soft folds piled high around her neck. "Please ask your questions."

Fran had never met someone so sparing, so economic, before. In all her actions, Sola seemed to use the smallest possible amount of energy necessary to complete them. And if they were unnecessary, like smiling, she simply omitted them.

Fran set her recorder on the floor by her chair and opened her notebook.

"You were actually discovered by Gallini, weren't you?"

"Yes."

"Sitting at a sidewalk café right here in Paris, I believe."

"Yes."

"You were a student, weren't you?"

"Not quite."

"What, then?"

"The friend of a student," Sola said.

Friend. Mistress. Lover. Once the money in the account which Kemal had opened for her was finished, there had been no other way to survive. Life modeling for student art classes paid very little, working in a café ruined the hands she needed to keep soft, and she did not have the right clothes for approaching the perfume counters of the *grands magasins*. And, she had told herself with self-loathing, what did a couple more men matter when her body had already known so many? The students had been kind; they told her so often she was beautiful that after a while, she even began to think they might be right.

It was like pulling teeth; Fran decided to abandon that particular line of questioning. Besides, the story of Sola's discovery was already well known—enthusiastically disseminated by Gallini himself. The café in the Place de l'Opéra, the girl in a huge beret of floppy purple velvet and a dress made of the kind of chamois leathers normally sold for washing cars, the talented young designer seeking inspiration or the New Woman—or both. Having found Sola, Gallini had begun to produce a series of leather clothes for her in the most startling of colors, and thereby made his own name, as well as hers.

"What gave you the idea of sewing together all those leathers?" Fran said.

"I liked the feel of them against my skin," said Sola.

Kemal had a jacket of gray suede that she had loved to rub against. Once, as she cried into the pillow after one of the pig-men had heaved himself off her and gone away, he had wrapped her up in the jacket and held her against his chest, murmuring soft love-words to her.

"Did you often make your own clothes?" Fran said.

"No. I knew an art student. The chamois dress was his idea."

"You're not originally from France, are you?"

"No."

"Where, then?"

"From Istanbul."

Fran looked up sharply from her notebook. Coincidence: it had to be. Nothing more than that. Not fate. Not destiny. She wanted to say, *I know Istanbul. Until the end, I was happy there.*

"And when did you come to Paris?" she said.

"When I was seventeen."

"Why Paris?"

"I was taught by nuns. One of them told me that Paris was the most civilized city in the world."

"Do you think she was right?"

"I don't like cities," Sola said.

"You'd prefer to live in the country, would you? I notice you have a big collection of books on gardens. Are you a gardener?"

"Only in my mind."

Yet that was not true. She looked, she did not touch. She had never, even in imagination, dug her fingers into soil, or felt the texture of a leaf. The gardens where she ran to hide were barren, without smell or sound. The plants in them—flowers, shrubs, fruiting trees— did not reach into the earth for sustenance or stretch upward to the sun. She had not realized it before.

Fran led her into a discussion of her work. "Modeling is always considered one of the 'glamor' jobs," she said, miming quotation marks around the phrase. "I'd like to examine the metaphorical dirt on the hems of those designer dresses. It must be a pretty tough way to earn a living, in spite of the glitzy image."

"That's right."

Sola did not smile, but Fran detected a softening in her posture. They went on to discuss the personalities of the business, the evolution of "style," the hardheaded manipulation of market forces.

Eventually Fran asked, "Do you enjoy your profession? You must travel a great deal."

"Yes. Though I don't see much. We're flown in and flown right out again as soon as the photo session is finished."

"What sort of places do you visit?"

"In the past couple of years I've been to the United States, to Spain, to Italy, to England, to the Bahamas," recited Sola. She was sitting up straight in the chair opposite Fran's, shoulders back, feet side by side on the floor.

"Which did you like best?"

"England."

"Why?"

"Gallini found a house in the country. We did some publicity shots there. You could see the sea far away across the fields," Sola said. "There was a garden . . ."

One night the wind had swept in across the marshes, driving the fog before it like clouds of sheep. There had been rabbits, too. From the windows of the house she had watched them in the grass, like earthbound birds.

"What part of England was that?"

"The south, somewhere. Marshland, very flat. Somewhere called Romney, I think."

Coldness clutched at Fran's bones. This was too much; this was unfair. The sense of being led relentlessly toward an end she had not known about, had not wanted to know, was overpowering.

She picked up her bag from the floor beside her chair and searched it for an unnecessary handkerchief, as though to emphasize normality.

"When was this?"

"About a year ago," Sola said.

Fran breathed deeply in, filling herself with air as though to drive out apprehension. She had intended to see what more she could find out about Daniel's last weeks; now it was as if she were helpless, overtaken by a force darker and stronger than herself. Inexorably, she was being shown the way to go. The fact that Sola might have been near at hand when Daniel died was something more than random chance, yet it would be lunacy to imagine that this fine-drawn creature could have been involved with his death.

She sipped the tea Sola had poured. On the wall, the grotesque crucifix hung in agony. Why that particular death? she thought. There were other ways, so why had Daniel died that symbolic, that resonant death?

She nodded at the crucifix. "Are you Catholic?"

"I was once. Now . . ." She shrugged.

"Do you believe in God?"

"There are many names for God," Sola said.

Fran stared at her. Was this another fingerpost leading her into the darkness? Wind thudded against the window. Rain spit at the glass panes, a small contemptuous sound. She reached her cup toward the coffee table. The action knocked her bag from the arm of the chair and spilled its contents over the floor. Keys, passport, wallet, a packet of tissues, lipstick. The papers received from Daniel and his mother slid quietly across the varnished wooden boards.

Sola gasped. She backed away from Fran. "Who are you?" she said. "Did he send you?"

"Did who send me?"

Sola pointed. "Where did you get that?" Her hand trembled. In the neck of her white robe, gold-set opals hung from a chain. Crouched to pick up the contents of her fallen bag, Fran could see the thin links vibrate against the girl's skin; she was surprised at the fear in her voice.

"Get what?" She held up the photograph of Daniel and the girl in the short white dress. "This?"

"Yes."

"It was sent to me recently. Why?"

"Because it's my photograph. Someone stole it from me."

Fran looked at it again. The separate components took on a different focus: the sea, the cypress, the white dress, the girl's dark face. She saw unmistakably what she had not seen before: The girl in the photograph was Sola, younger though no less unsure. She saw, too, how all the jigsaw pieces were gradually being slotted into place. Two days ago, looking at the photographs, she had recognized only Daniel. Now, she had met Philippe and Campion and Sola. The faces were no longer unknown.

The inevitability of Sola's involvement with Daniel, whatever it might have been, now scarcely surprised her.

"You knew him too?" she said. Unconsciously she brushed a finger tenderly over his half-hidden face.

"Who?"

"This man. Daniel Forrest."

Sola shook her head. "He was called Nicholas."

"He told you that?"

"It was his name."

Nicholas Marquend was dead. Daniel Forrest was too, of course. Fran wondered by which name he was known to those who had killed him. She wondered whether Sola knew of his death. In the end, she decided not to ask: the girl was already frightened enough of something.

She held out one of the other photographs. "What about this? It's also you, isn't it?"

Leaning forward to look more closely, Sola let out a cry. Snatching the photograph from Fran, she held it with both hands against her throat as though to protect it. She thought wildly, *Kemal and me, together there as though the years, the betrayals, had never been.* She saw herself again as she was then: Solange Bonami, the gawky, long-legged convent girl, ripe with love for the man who had corrupted her and whom she now tried without success to hate.

"Who's the man with you?" Fran said. Whatever his name, it would mean nothing to her, but she knew—she was being made to feel—that he must be another piece of the puzzle.

"Kemal," Sola said. "Kemal Effendi."

"Who is he?"

"He was . . ." She tried to decide the best way to define him. He had been so many things: landlord, lover, father substitute, seducer, and betrayer. ". . . a friend of my family in Istanbul."

"Did he know—uh—Nicholas Marquend?" *I think of him as Daniel now,* Fran thought.

"Yes."

"How do you know?"

"I saw him once, at Kemal's house. He asked me often about Kemal. He said they had been friends once but they hadn't met for a long while."

"What sorts of things did he ask?"

"About his business colleagues, mostly. The people who came to see him. Where he went on his trips abroad."

"And this man lives in Istanbul?"

"He did, but he has houses in other places; even one here in Paris."

"You left Istanbul about three years ago?"

"Yes."

"And you've not seen him since you left Turkey?"

"No."

Not seen, she wanted to say, though a thousand times I've run with panting heart after strangers, I've followed men along the *quais* and boulevards, thinking that this time it might be him, hoping, sick with excitement at the thought this time, at last, and yet, at the same time, angry beyond reason at the remembrance of what was done to me, so much so that I could imagine violence, could imagine tearing at the face I once kissed and still long to kiss again, could imagine sinking a knife into the body I need so much to feel within me once more.

Fran was excited. If Daniel had asked questions about this Kemal, he must have had a reason. "You must have been very young, still at school," she said.

"I was."

"Why should Nicholas imagine *you* knew anything about Kemal?"

"He came to Kemal's house once when I was visiting. He saw me there, I suppose." Sola tried not to remember the way Nicholas had glanced up at the bedroom door at the top of the curved banisters. "Then we met by chance in the city and he took me to a café to drink tea. I told him I was helping Kemal with some of his letters since I was taking a typing course at school."

"Is it possible he sought you out deliberately, in order to ask you about Kemal?"

"Very," said Sola.

"Did he ever say *why* he wanted to know?"

"No."

■■

When the English girl had gone, Sola put out the light and sat on the window seat. The street below seemed to heave with the motion of the wind. The trees beat at the wild air with their branches. Their trunks were wetly black against the gray of the houses on the opposite side of the street. As she watched, one of the trunks swelled, grew thicker, detached itself amoebically from its parent, became a separate entity. Became a man.

He was still there.

Before she could move, he was staring up at her window. She shrank back. With the light extinguished, he could not possibly see her, but somehow he sensed her there. His face was blank in the darkness, but she knew that it smiled. She knew, too, that if she flung open the window and fell through the streaming air, he would catch her in his wide black clothes and carry her off.

Where to?

Heaven? Or hell?

She groaned. She wanted peace. The cool earth of a garden. Leaves on her hands. Petals, cream and yellow, not roses but orange blossom, white lilac. Once, such images had been a comfort. Tonight, she found none, nor any peace.

• 20 •

FRAN'S SHOULDERS ACHED. FOR the past two hours she had been working on the remnants salvaged from Tom Brett's office, but although the kitchen table was littered with ash-grimed papers, she had so far found very little that seemed of any significance—beyond the fact that Tom's passport was not among the debris. It was the old-fashioned kind, thick and navy blue: the fire would not have had time to destroy it entirely. She picked up a newspaper cutting concerning the suicide of a French banker: as so often, the distraught widow was quoted as saying she could not understand it, he had everything going for him, there was no reason for him to kill himself. Fran put it on one side, thinking that Max might be interested in the item, and stretched, trying to ease the discomfort in her back.

Irritatingly, a pile of old newspapers which had been on the floor beside the filing cabinets had survived the fire almost intact. Like many journalists, Tom Brett's appetite for newsprint had been voracious: he must have been keeping these with the intention of going through them at leisure. She turned some of the dusty pages without much interest. Nothing was deader than old news—except old love. And nothing much changed. Tom had died a couple of years ago, yet the same concerns still hogged the front pages. She speculated on which items he might have wished to clip out and keep: terrorism had been making the headlines, so had some high-level financial shenanigans in London and the insider-trading scandals in the United States. In one of the French newspapers, she found a long article on Médecins sans Frontières and allied organizations. The Phoenix Foundation merited a couple of paragraphs; the saintly qualities of its young director another. Still turning pages, she heard a faint sound outside the window. Was it merely the wind which had been wandering around the garden, or was someone out there in the dark, watching her? She froze. For a moment, all she was aware of was the

sound of the slow blood moving around her body. Then her mind
clicked back into gear. She bent again over the table, as if she had
heard nothing. Coolly she decided that in a few minutes, for the
benefit of the watcher in the garden—if there was one—she would
get up without hurrying, fill the kettle, leave the room.

Despite her apparent calm, her ears roared as though they were
full of water. She breathed through her mouth, still pretending to sort
the papers, straining to hear further sounds. Was that a scrape of boot
on brick? A thump of body against sill? Trying to relax her rigid muscles, she thought her way around the weak points of the house. Everything was tightly bolted: short of breaking a window—which would
make a noise she could hear—the only possible access was via the
balcony outside her bedroom window.

If someone did burst in, how would she stop them? Suppose they
cut the telephone wires; how would she summon help?

The gun. She had to get the gun. With that, she would at least
have a chance.

Slowly, stretching again, she stood. She filled the kettle at the
tap, set it to boil, took down a cup and saucer from one of the wall
cupboards. She looked at her watch, then went out of the kitchen into
the dark passage leading toward the drawing room. She listened carefully.

No sound anywhere.

Silently she ran up the stairs. The gun was hidden in one of the
drawers in her bedroom. She dared not switch on a light for fear of
alerting any prowler who might be outside. In the dark, she pulled the
drawer open and felt among her sweaters. Adrenaline had heightened
her perceptions; as though they were eyes, the tips of her fingers
identified the softness of cashmere, feathery mohair, the stiff oiled
wool of her Guernsey.

The gun was cold. She lifted it out, shaped it into her hand.

She stepped over to the window and peered out at the dark
garden. The pear tree shivered ecstatically in the wind. Glimmering
white above the grass, the hammock threshed in a frenzy. Everything
danced: the whole world was in motion. She could see nothing that
should not be there. No alien shadow disturbed the night.

Nonetheless, she was reluctant to go back into the goldfish-bowl
kitchen. For a moment she considered opening the door and walking

right out into the tossing garden. However unwise it might be, confrontation was better than continuing fear. But if she left the shelter of the house, someone could slip in while her back was turned. No. Better to stay inside.

The gun lay under her sweater, against the soft flesh of her waist. She was thankful that Emilie was safe in the hospital. Visiting her earlier that evening, she had been worried by her mother's lethargy. Emilie had looked older, desolated. Bruises had shown under her skin.

Shoulder blades stiff and expectant—a knife under the ribs? a bullet through her heart?—Fran walked through the kitchen. Its colors seemed unnaturally bright. Steam dribbled from the kettle. A tap dripped. For the hidden watcher—if any—she feigned a yawn, turned off the gas, switched out the light as though too tired after all for the hot drink she had planned.

The house creaked about her as she went upstairs again, more slowly this time. If someone came up after her, who would hear if she screamed? She realized how isolated it was here. The house was set among fields surrounded by trees. The neighbors on one side were fifty yards away, separated by a small copse of hazel and birch; on the other was the village library, empty at this hour, and beyond it the *hôtel de ville,* its clerks and officials long since gone home.

Gilles Laforêt. The name sprang into her head. Bolder now, she switched on her bedside lamp, found his number, lifted the telephone. The tone purred; she dialed, not acknowledging to herself how much she had dreaded finding the line cut, the receiver dead.

The telephone rang ten times, fifteen, twenty. Was it the hollow sound of a phone ringing in an empty house, or the more fulfilled one of a telephone that was about to be answered? On the twenty-sixth burr, someone picked up the receiver.

"Hello?" she said. "Monsieur Laforêt?"

"He's not here." The voice was rough, uneducated. It was hard to determine whether it was male or female. "Who wants him?"

Gently she set the apparatus back on its cradle. The Laforêt housekeeper, probably; wakened from sleep, curlers in her hair, a dressing gown tied tightly to her indignant form. Or possibly some manservant.

She knew she would not be able to bring herself to undress. It was irrational, perhaps, but the jeans and sweater into which she had changed seemed to offer greater protection than a nightdress. Stretched on her bed with the gun lying against her thigh, she opened her bag and took out the brown envelope sent to her from Istanbul.

Daniel had wanted her to deduce something from its contents. She still had not worked out what it was. Even her guess that Tom Brett's investigations were involved could not be substantiated. She was working in the dark. She reread the letter then held up the photographs, one by one, waiting for the jolt of recognition, the rush of comprehension. Sola and Daniel. Sola and the unknown Kemal Effendi. Philippe, Campion, and Daniel. Nothing; she deduced nothing.

She laid them down on the counterpane.

No! . . .

No sound, yet the room was full of the unspoken word.

Look again!

She picked them up once more, stared at each one, felt herself into them. Sola and Daniel. He sat to one side of the picture, almost out of it. A terrace, a table, the sea beyond. Between the two was the bulging cypress; a line of stone coping, supported by squat balusters, bisected the scene. She strained over the details; there were almost none. Those there had been were faded now. On the table was the outline of a bottle, glasses—one full, one empty—and plates. There was a dish which might have contained salad. Something flat: a book, a wallet, a newspaper. Imagination washed the bleached black-and-white with color: turquoise sea, red wine, the dark green tree. No significance leaped out at her. She put it down.

The photographer had brought the man called Kemal farther into frame, otherwise the second photograph was almost identical to the first. Had it been taken before or after the one showing Sola with Daniel? She would have to ask. And find out why the girl had been in the same place with two different men. Was *that* what she was supposed to determine?

Picking up the last photograph, she felt the room relax around her.

Look, urged the soundless voice in her head. *Look!*

Masts leaned into the flat sky. Two young men laughed: the ones she now knew to be Campion and Philippe de Pierrey. To one side, secret, alone, Daniel stared from under the shadow of his hat. Whoever had taken the photograph must have stepped onto the shore: she could see the rounded top of a bollard, a rope stretching from out of the frame toward a cleat on the boat's bow, the name painted in black letters, too small to be read.

Read them

Cold now, the voice was insistent.

Read them Read them Read them . . . fading only as she swung her legs to the floor and stood up. In Emilie's bedroom there was a magnifying glass ("At my age, *chérie,* the eyes sometimes need a little extra help"), kept in the drawer of the bedside table. With the photograph in her hand, she walked across her own room and into her mother's.

The letters wavered in and out of focus, distorted by the curve of the boat's prow. She saw an *E*, an *I*, and *N*; more clearly, a small skull-and-crossbones. In front of them, an *O*—or was it a *D?* An *H*, or an *A?* She wrote down the letters she was sure of: *ENI.*

Before them came an *O* or a *D*: It must be a *D:* how many words were there with an *O* followed by an *E* ? Before that, an *A* or an *H*.

ADENI, she wrote. It sounded Greek. It could be anything. Boat owners stuck to no rules when naming their craft: the wilder, the better.

Around her, the air protested shrilly. *Fool Fool!*

She looked again at the final letter. The crossed bones could be an *X*, of course, with the tiny grinning skulls added as extra decoration. That would give her DENIX. Or, supposing the *D* was an *O*, OENIX. With an *H* in front of that . . .

It came to her then: This was what he wanted her to know, her insistent ghost. Inside her head, the resonances drummed. Slowly she replaced the magnifying glass in its drawer.

Phoenix: the fabulous bird, symbol of resurrection and regeneration, rising from flames fueled by the ashes of its own father. But more than that: Daniel had left her the clues but dared not use the word, presumably in case hostile eyes should see it and realize that he had unlocked the secret. But was it the name that was significant, or did it have more specific connotations? Was it, for instance, the sailing boat *Phoenix* she must home in on? Her mind ranged around the possibilities: could Campion's father be involved in drug smuggling, illegal immigrants, sexual orgies implicating high-ranking officials, money laundering? Had Daniel found out, and been killed to stop his talking? Did it mean that Campion's father was implicated somehow in Daniel's death? For a moment she stared across the room without seeing it. Coldly she thought, *If that is so I shall, if necessary, pursue him to the ends of the world.*

Or was Phoenix simply a name for something else? She remembered Carlos the Jackal: could Phoenix be the name of some other international hitman? If so, she'd never heard of him. Or was it a code name for some huge undercover operation which Daniel or Tom—or both—had somehow stumbled on?

She knew she was trying to avoid facing up to the one fact which screamed at her. The Phoenix Foundation. That was what Daniel had been trying to make her see. But what exactly was she supposed to understand? Was the Foundation a cover for something else? And if so, what?

There were so many questions she must ask, places she must go. Back in her own bedroom, burrowed into her pillows, she made mental lists. She would have to speak again with Alicia Forrest. Daniel's former commanding officer might know something. Philippe de Pierrey, Sola . . . Istanbul: she would have to go back to Istanbul.

Belatedly, the meaning of *Resurrection,* Hugo Campion's polished steel sculpture, became clear. The creative soul in torment, yearning toward a new beginning before the cold flames of sterility consumed it entirely. Did his subtle image of a phoenix have anything to do with the quest she was embarked on, or was it merely a serendipitous coincidence?

She wondered about Amy, his daughter, Campion's sister.

Glass cracked somewhere below her, a single sharp sound. She was instantly awake, only then realizing that she must have dozed off. Sleep blurred her grasp of reality. Had the noise been very loud or barely audible? Had it just occurred or taken place some seconds earlier? Upstairs or down? She sat tensely, staring alternately at the door and the long windows leading out onto her balcony.

Down on the kitchen table she had left the remains of Tom Brett's papers: was that what the intruder—if she had not just dreamed it—was after? And would it be enough for him merely to take them, or would he want more? Violence? A gratuitous rape? Her body stiffened in anticipation of pain. She clutched her father's gun. Her throat felt very dry.

Crack!

The same sound: this time there was no mistaking it. Someone was trying to get in below. Noiselessly she lifted the telephone beside her bed. Relief flooded through her as she heard the dial tone: she was not entirely cut off from the outside world. She pressed the REDIAL button; after a series of clicks the last number she had dialed—Gilles Laforêt's—began to ring. She held it to her ear, the peremptory sound pressing into the silence. Ten rings, twelve, fifteen . . . *come on, housekeeper, butler, whatever you are, hurry up and answer* . . . twenty. Brusquely the receiver was lifted.

"Help," she whispered. "This is Frances Brett. Call the police."

She heard the harsh sound of someone breathing, and at the same time realized that the ringing tones had continued.

Which could only mean one thing. Someone had picked up the extension in the hall downstairs. Someone was listening.

Nothing in her life hitherto had held half the terror that the quiet breathing of her enemy—standing below her in her own house —possessed. If Gilles now answered his still-ringing telephone, she doubted whether her lips would be able to form words enough to ask him for help.

It was not a test she had to take. Suddenly the connection was broken. The ringing stopped. For a few terrifying seconds the two of them confronted each other, unseen adversaries, separated by the thickness of carpets, beams, plaster, but joined by the cable. She was sure she could hear the beat of his heart. Her own emotion was fear; his, she knew, was malevolence. She sensed that he hated her, that he wished her dead. Why? She wanted to speak, to ask what he wanted, to plead for mercy. But it could not be as easy as that; feeling his power and ruthlessness flow toward her along the wires, she knew that like Daniel she would receive none.

She heard the clumsy sound of the receiver being laid on the table. No one could now call in; nor could she call out—unless she went downstairs and replaced it. It was as effective a way of snapping her line of communication as if he had cut the wires. And if he came upstairs to her, would her hands still retain the strength to fire the gun? She strained to hear against the wind outside: were those footsteps coming up the carpeted stairs, or just the wild pounding of her blood?

As there must come a point beyond pain, where pain no longer has meaning, so it is with fear. In the end, she reached a place where fear was so concentrated that it distilled into nonfear. She stood up, checked her gun, walked across the room and flung open her bedroom door. There was no point in stealth: he knew she was there.

Downstairs, everything was still. The hall was unlit; leaning over the banisters, she could see nothing. What was he doing? Was he simply waiting for her in the dark, knowing that eventually she would be drawn to him, sucked down into him as bathwater is forced by gravity down a plughole, helpless to go elsewhere?

The politics of terror—she refused to give in to them. She snapped on the light in the lower hall and started down the stairs. He would be in or near the kitchen, she decided. He could not know she had a gun, though he might guess that Tom Brett's daughter would have found some form of protection. He could not risk descending to the basement in case she came after him. He would be in or near the kitchen: filling his pockets, perhaps with the material she had spread on the table. He would know what he was looking for; if he saw it, he would take it.

She smelled him before she saw him. It was impossible to define the scent: pressed, she might have said it was the whiff of corruption, the odor of iniquity. Yet it was by no means unpleasant: the separate components included a spice she could not have named, something musky, the coolness of citrus fruit.

He was waiting for her by the door which led to the stone-walled larder. The kitchen light was on behind him; his head seemed unnaturally large until she realized that it was swathed in a black scarf, Arab fashion. All she could see of his face were his eyes; strongly blue, the iris was retracted to the size of a pinhole. As she had with Campion, she glimpsed something barbaric in him, something pagan, a sense of exhilarating speed as he rushed toward his fate across the burning plains of his life.

The image was brief, no more than a second's fancy.

She could not know that the man who watched her approach was feeling for the first time in many years a regret at what he had to do; a sense of waste. One embraced one's destiny: what else could one do? Yet there were times when destiny demanded more than was its rightful due.

He thought of the one he had been watching for so many nights, the one trapped by fate and circumstance in her own terrors. Soon he would make contact with *her* and put an end to them. Meanwhile, watching this one walk toward him, deciding how best to take her, he felt dispassionately that in other circumstances, they would have been friends—or perhaps not friends but colleagues, certainly, rather than enemies. She was strong, much stronger than most women. She would not be easily intimidated, however much she felt it.

He remembered another like her, in Beirut. That one had held out against him for so long that he had been roused to admiration before she finally told him what he had wanted to know.

When this one—Françoise Brett—came within kicking distance, he would dislodge the gun; it would be an easy matter to overpower her after that. And then . . . The bedroom would probably be easiest for what he had to do, and being upstairs, there was no risk of being seen through the windows. Undoubtedly she possessed more information than her mother. In addition, she was a different kind of woman and would respond in a different way; he was confident that he would obtain the facts he had come for. After that, there was the stuff on the kitchen table. Standing in the garden, he had watched through the window as she sorted the debris rescued from Tom Brett's office. She had been lying when she said it had been totally destroyed by the fire. He wished now that he had killed the mother: this one would have been easier to handle if she had been unnerved by a death.

He lounged, leaning easily against the wall, giving an impression of unconcern. Even though she had the gun, she would not know how to use it. More important, she would not possess the will needed to use it. Amateurs never did, unless roused by strong emotion, and then they usually made a botched job of it. That was what marked them off from the professional.

His muscles tensed. She was almost within striking distance.

Then, instead of coming nearer, she stopped, just out of his range. That irritated him. And with irritation came the slow stirrings of anger. Anger was good. He had been shown years ago that properly controlled, anger could be as effective as a weapon.

He hoped she would not speak.

Should she use the gun, Fran asked herself? Death was a heavy sentence to pass on a stranger. Even if he had assaulted Emilie—and there seemed little doubt that this was the same man—he had not killed her.

He carried no visible weapon but she knew how hands and feet could be turned into clubs; how legs became missiles, as lethal as any gun. She had no intention of getting within kicking reach of him. On the other hand, what was she to do with him? She doubted that he would be docile enough, even with the gun turned on him, to allow her to call the police.

For the moment, the gun gave her the upper hand. How was she best to exploit it?

"Who *are* you?" she said. She was astonished at the way her journalist's curiosity had taken over from her fear. Normal emotions seemed to have been suspended. With the gun trained on him, she was not even afraid. She saw why men found such a macho thrill in the possession of guns, why serial killers so often went in for an armory of weapons. Lonely, inadequate, a gun gave them a sense of identity because it conferred power.

He did not answer. She found she was tuning in to him as she did to a story. "Who are you?" she said again. "Why are you here?"

"It doesn't matter why." His voice was a whisper, impossible to separate into memorable elements. She would not recognize it again.

"What do you want?"

"Information."

"What makes you think I have it."

"Someone has it. You, your father . . . It is my job to get it back."

"Once you know something, you can't unknow it," she said.

"*You* do not know it."

"How can you be sure?" she said.

Behind the enveloping scarf the blue eyes did not waver. "If you knew, I would not be here," he said.

Did that mean that whatever he wanted was something physical: a piece of paper, a notebook, a photograph, rather than a name or a place?

A second thought followed on from the first: if that was so, Tom

Brett would have kept it separately. He would never have stored something so potentially lethal as this had already proven to be—if there was a connection with Daniel's murder—along with his other files, where Emilie might be at risk. In that case, where would it be? He had flown to Beirut direct from Heathrow: could he have hidden whatever it was in Notting Hill?

Apprehension spun a web around her. Emilie had mentioned that her attacker seemed to know about the London flat. She was possessed by urgency: it was vital that she get back to London and find it—if it was there to be found. Otherwise neither she nor Emilie could ever feel safe.

Meanwhile, there was the more urgent situation to deal with.

Kill him Kill him, urged the voice in her head.

He watched her eyes change. He was trained to notice such things. The slightest shift in the intensity of concentration could mean the difference between life and death. He had no illusions: life was cheap. There would be others to take over if he were killed. Yet he knew himself to be good, to be superlative, at what he did. If she killed him, their whole operation would be jeopardized. He tried to think of his own features in death: relaxed, smoothed out, would they perhaps hide his identity?

The woman in Beirut had said, "Thank you," when he had finished with her. That had infuriated him. Everything he did, every action he took, was governed by the needs of the job in hand: what had happened with her had been for himself alone. She was not meant to participate, yet battered as she had been by then, he could still remember the rise of her hips. It should not have been like that: it was for him, not for her. He still, years later, had not decided whether she had known that by thanking him, she had destroyed his pleasure.

He saw the determination in this one's eyes. He braced himself. She was going to shoot him: she clearly had little knowledge of guns and the shot would not kill him instantly. She would probably hit him in the stomach or the lungs; there would be pain, mess. It would not be the martyr's death he had envisaged for himself. He hoped he would not scream: he had seen too many deaths to be sure that he would not. Would she watch while he writhed in pain on the floor? Would she stand silent while the red blood burst from his mouth? He sensed she was capable of it. Already she had outsmarted him by not coming close enough for him to damage her.

He thought suddenly, I would like to have died in the place where I was born.

Kill him Kill him

But Fran could not do so. This blue-eyed whispering man had stamped her mother's hand with lighted cigarettes, had drawn back his foot and kicked her viciously in the ribs until the fragile bones broke. She ought to be able to kill him.

Kill him now Kill him now

If she did not do something soon, he would realize she was no threat to him. He would leap for her, like a dog. Easily she could imagine how he would rise from the ground, teeth bared, ready to seize her throat.

She lifted the gun, aiming at his chest. She had no choice.

I wish I could have died, he thought, in the place where I was happy, before I was sent for . . . before the woman corrupted me and set me along this pathway, so different from the one I had planned.

A car dashed the gravel outside the front door. Both of them, the anonymous man in the scarf and the girl with the gun, relaxed the intensity which for this short time had bound them together. Both of them knew that fate had saved them from a cataclysm.

A car door was violently slammed shut. Across the drive came footsteps, light and urgent. Someone banged the knocker, calling as they did so.

"Mademoiselle Brett! Mademoiselle, are you there?"

Slowly, Fran began to back away down the passage toward the door. Would she be able to turn the keys, loose the bolts, while keeping a watch on the intruder? In any case, he would not try to kill her now; he would be intent on escape.

With the lessening of danger, her fear returned. She knew that once she had opened the front door, once the man had gone, she would subside into shivering tears, she would tremble and feel faint.

What lucky piece of timing had brought Gilles Laforêt here? It did not matter; she was safe now. She reached one hand behind her, feeling for the key in the lock of the front door.

As soon as she did so, he moved. Swift as a shadow, he vanished.

One moment there, leaning gracefully against the wall, the next, gone. It would be pointless to go after him: the darkness would have swallowed him up.

Would he try again?

She knew that he would.

· 21 ·

SHE HAD BEEN AWAY FROM LONDON for three days; it might have been three months. She felt as though she was on a knife edge of emotion, ready to scream or burst into tears at the sound of a car horn or even a red traffic light. On the flight, hysterical laughter had afflicted her as she read the caption beneath a newspaper cartoon; minutes later she had looked at it again and seen nothing even faintly amusing in it. She told herself it was the natural aftermath of her encounter with the blue-eyed intruder. Knowing that did not make her seesawing emotions any easier to handle.

Stuck in the traffic jams between Heathrow and Kensington, she had dreaded what she might find when she got back to Notting Hill. If the flat had been ransacked, she was not sure how she would handle it.

But as far as she could see, the flat was intact. Undisturbed dust filmed the furniture. The locks had not been tampered with. She threw away the flowers that had died, and opened all the windows. Realizing that her hands were still shaking, she unpacked her briefcase, mentally listing the things she must do, in order of priority. For the moment, Daniel Forrest would have to take a backseat; she had a living to earn, deadlines to meet, a flat to search. In spite of this she found herself dialing Alicia Forrest's number before she had even taken the cover off her typewriter.

"Yes?" The voice might have come from another planet, so unapproachable did it sound.

"It's Frances Brett."

"Ah." Nothing so warm as emotion colored Mrs. Forrest's tones. It was hard to remember that this same woman had broken down in front of her, had spoken with passion of murder and retribution, had wept. "Have you found anything out?"

"A great many things, but nothing that really points anywhere in particular. I wanted to know the name of Daniel's commanding officer. I thought it might be constructive to talk to him."

"What about?"

"It occurred to me that whatever Daniel was ultimately involved in might have already started before he left the army."

"He's called Rupert Halliday," Mrs. Forrest said. "I think the regiment's in Germany at the moment. You could probably find out from the Ministry of Defense."

"I'll try them—"

"Is everything all right, Frances?"

Should she tell Alicia about the break-in? Would it frighten her too much? On the other hand, she had been the wife and mother of soldiers and she ought to be given the opportunity to take precautions for her own safety. "Someone broke into my mother's house in France," she said. "My mother was attacked—she's still in the hospital."

"My dear, I'm so sorry." The cool voice was suddenly full of concern. "Do you think this attack was connected in some way with my son?"

"I think your son was connected in some way with my father," Fran said. "I don't know why or how." She gave a small laugh, trying to keep any suggestion of hurt out of it. "As a matter of fact, I'm fairly sure that Daniel sought me out in the first place because I was Tom Brett's daughter—whatever may have happened between us after that."

Which was not much. Which was far too little to dream about for the rest of a lifetime. For a brief flash, she saw again the flower-painted bed in Istanbul with its silk hangings, and what might have happened between the two of them, if death had not intervened.

It was best to forget all that. "Do you know anything about Alexander Campion?" she continued.

"There's a name from the past." Mrs. Forrest paused. "What sort of thing do you mean? I haven't seen him for at least ten years. He was at school with Daniel—I remember he was going to be a doctor. Poor child: I believe there was a rather odd mother, though the last time I met him he was with his father." She laughed, reminiscently. "It was rather sweet. The two of them were so proud of each other, and so very alike. More like brothers than father and son. But since then . . ."

"What about something called the Phoenix Foundation? Did Daniel ever mention it?"

"Not that I recall."

"One last question, Mrs. Forrest. When I told you that Daniel was using the name Nicholas Marquend, you seemed taken aback."

"I was rather. That's the name he used when he was still in the army and working undercover."

■■

Fran telephoned the Ministry to ask about Rupert Halliday. Colonel Halliday was not available; they were reluctant to give out further information. Someone asked her in what connection she wished to speak to him, took her name and telephone number, and said they would call her back. In the interests of the article commissioned by the magazine in the States, she rang the House of Commons and was able to make an appointment to talk to the black woman MP on the following Monday. For a moment she contemplated Tom Brett's word processor, bought just before he was killed. It stood to one side of the broad steel desk, sheathed in a gray plastic cover. "The journalist's friend," he had called it. Although she had worked at a computer keyboard during her time on the national paper, she had not yet come to terms with this one. Deciding that she really must make an effort soon to learn its basic language, she settled down to type up her notes on Sola.

It was late in the evening by the time she had finished. She uncorked a bottle of wine and poured herself a glass, then walked through the flat, examining it for possible hiding places. Kitchen, bathroom, bedroom, sitting room: compact, convenient, intended as a pied-à-terre rather than a long-term home. The house in France had always provided the permanence in their lives. For the most part, Tom's possessions had been cleared away by her mother some time ago; she herself, still traveling light, had since added few personal belongings.

She thought herself into her father's skin: *I'm Tom Brett and I have something vital that must be hidden. I'm pretty sure that sooner or later, someone will come looking for it: they mustn't find it. I also know that at any time I could be killed on assignment: it must therefore be accessible to those who know how my mind works. Where shall I hide it?*

Her search was hampered by not knowing exactly what form the information might take. She looked at the rows of tapes beside the tape deck and wondered whether he could have recorded something onto a Beethoven quartet or a Mozart piano concerto. She decided not. He would have realized how easy it would be for anyone breaking in to simply sweep the lot into a bag and listen later at leisure.

She pulled furniture away from baseboards and scrutinized them. She examined the rear walls of kitchen cupboards and bedroom closets. She went over the carpets inch by inch, felt the seats and sides of the furniture, removed the mattress from the bed and the cushions from the armchairs, looked at the underside of every drawer in the flat. The exercise was painful. The disturbed air yielded up all too willingly the phantoms of her father's presence. His cheroots, his aftershave, the chalky smell of the ink he used to fill his fountain pen.

In the end, she was reasonably certain that he had hidden nothing in the flat.

■■

The bedroom curtains were cream cotton, unlined, patterned with meadow flowers. Lying in bed, she watched the early sunlight behind them, enjoying the way it enhanced the green of the leaves, the red of the poppies, filling the room with rich beige light. She thought about getting up, making tea, bringing it back to bed with a book. It had been well after two in the morning before she had finally gone to bed.

She focused once again on her father. Supposing she was right, and he did have some particular information, what form *could* it take? And if it was not here in his flat, where else might it be? He had moved around a lot; it could be almost anywhere. On the other hand, it had to be hidden where it could be found by the right person.

The doorbell rang. She looked at her watch: it was just after eight o'clock on a Saturday morning. The caller was probably someone who could not get any answer from the lesbian writer upstairs, a lady who wore red velvet waistcoats and looked like an unmade bed. Fran got up and eased the curtains apart so that she could see who was out there.

The caller was a man—definitely not for the writer upstairs. A dapper man, under a black umbrella. British Warm overcoat, dark worsted trousers, the sort of hat a racing commentator might wear. She frowned. Who was he, this unofficially official-looking person? And why was he ringing her bell so early on a weekend morning?

The man turned around. He did it very suddenly, as though he knew she was watching him. She had no time to duck out of sight. He stared at her, not blinking. Any normal man, faced with an early morning Fran, her long hair spilling down the front of a revealing nightdress—her special one of dark green satin edged in real lace— would have been unable to resist running his glance at least once down her body. This man managed it without any visible effort. He could have been taking a salute at the Trooping of the Color.

She moved away from the window. She thought about getting back into bed and ignoring him, and might have done so had she not been convinced that if she did, if she stayed in bed until midafternoon —or even next week—he would still be there when she eventually opened the door. She might as well get it over—but she took her time getting dressed. Normally on a Saturday morning she would have worn jeans. Instead, she chose a full skirt in oatmeal wool that showed off her slim waist, and a silk blouse of dramatic orange. It made her look feminine, and therefore vulnerable. And while she knew herself not to be particularly vulnerable, the man outside was not to know that, which might give her a slight edge in whatever they were about to discuss.

He did not ring again; knowing she was there, he simply waited. When she finally opened the door, he raised his hat. He was in his mid-forties, and smooth as a shark.

"Miss Frances Brett?"

She made no response. He knew perfectly well who she was.

"I'm Colonel Napier," he said. "From the Ministry of Defense. Might I come in?"

"What exactly do you want?" she said.

"I'd like to talk to you about Captain Forrest."

"What makes you think I'd know anything. I wasn't even in the country when he—"

"If I may . . ." Napier said patiently, making a shooing gesture at the door.

Fran did not move. "Since when did civil servants work on a Saturday?"

"The Army is a full-time occupation, Miss Brett."

There was no point refusing to talk to him. She already knew that she did not like him much; a man whose face registered nothing when it spoke to a fellow human being was a man who was cold at the core.

She ought to ask if she could see his credentials: no woman living alone in London should allow a strange male into her flat. But there was no point: whatever he chose to represent himself as, this man would have come equipped with the papers needed to back himself up. Although she would have preferred to shut the door in his face, she stood aside and motioned him past her.

He walked into her sitting room and sat down on the sofa, placing his briefcase on the coffee table in front of him. It was the old-fashioned expandable sort that stood on its base, rather than one of the modern molded kind which lay flat on its broad side. A small gold crown had been stamped into the leather above the lock.

"I'm going to make some coffee," she said. "Do you want some?"

"That's very kind."

She did not feel in the least kind. She felt like someone caught at a disadvantage. She did not need telling that producing this disadvantage was why Napier had called at such an early hour. She smoothed the collar of her blouse, twitched her skirt about, looked feminine. Napier's eyes did not leave hers.

"Black or white?" she said.

"Black, please."

When she came back with a tray, he had removed his coat and draped it carefully over the sofa. Without it, he seemed less hard. His briefcase stood open on the table with a couple of folders lying beside it, one red, one blue: the one in his hand was buff-colored. Was that a patriotic statement, or just chance? One or two papers had fallen onto the floor at his feet and his hand scraped along the carpet, picking them up.

Fran put the tray down between them, then sat down and poured coffee.

"Miss Brett," said Napier. He glanced quickly at his watch. His voice was highly bred, trained to deliver orders to underlings whose humanity he would recognize only where it was expedient to do so. "I understand that you have been in communication with Captain Forrest's mother." As he spoke his eyes flickered restlessly over the room, taking in its detail.

"What makes you think that?"

"I heard."

"My God," she said slowly. "The mills of Military Intelligence certainly grind exceeding fine. I suppose you were told that I'd tried to speak to Colonel Halliday and why. What did you do then, contact Mrs. Forrest?"

"Possibly." He was giving nothing away. "It also came to my ears that you intended to investigate the late Captain Forrest's death."

"Investigate? That's not quite true," she said.

"What are you doing then?" The voice of officialdom was frigid, and difficult to fob off.

"It would be truer to say I'm trying to reconstruct the last few months of his life."

"For any particular reason?"

Fran felt herself growing angry. "Several," she said shortly. "For one thing, my father is involved in some way—I haven't discovered quite how, yet. I think he had some information that Daniel—Captain Forrest wanted."

"What sort of information?"

"I don't know, but I'm convinced it has to do with why Daniel was killed." She looked at him defiantly. "Besides, Captain Forrest and I were in love." Saying it, she knew it was not true, though it could have been one day if things had been different. "When I discovered how he had died, and that the police hadn't found the murderers, naturally I wanted to look into it for myself."

"Don't." He sipped his coffee and put the cup down. He ran his fingers along the underside edge of the coffee table.

"What?"

"I said don't."

"Don't what?"

"Don't reconstruct, Miss Brett. Don't look any further."

"Why on earth not?" She stared at him in disbelief.

"Leave it alone," he said. He stared slowly around, his gaze resting on the stereo, on the word processor, on the television.

Fran slowly sipped her coffee, watching him over the rim of her cup. She had never seen such strange eyes. They were the sort of ice color that would guarantee an actor a lifetime's employment portraying senior Gestapo officers on the screen.

Daniel's eyes had held some of the same bleakness. She wondered if there was any passion in Colonel Napier: whether the nature of his work—whatever that might be—made it necessary for him to hide behind a mask of coldness. In spite of his well-pressed look, it was impossible to see such a man as part of a family, sharing the ordinary littlenesses with a wife, or fathering children who sat on his knee and made his face light up. He wore a tattersall checked shirt under a fawn wool sweater with suede patches on elbow and shoulder. She could imagine him in green Wellingtons and a quilted green jacket, taking careful aim with a gun, knocking live things out of the sky.

She laughed incredulously. "Is that an order?"

"I'm not ordering you to do anything, Miss Brett. I should be exceeding my brief if I tried to do that. I am merely advising you to stop."

"Would you care to tell me why?"

"Because you are likely to get yourself involved in something which could prove extremely dangerous." As he spoke Napier's hands probed the space between the cushions and the arms of the sofa.

"This is beginning to sound like some kind of spy thriller," Fran said.

"Very possibly," Napier said.

"And why should I take your advice?"

"Because frankly, Miss Brett, the last thing any of us needs is a lot of bloody amateurs stumbling about, confusing the issue and getting themselves killed." Once again his glance set off around the room, appraising the curtains, the sofa cushions, the carpet.

"Confusing which issue?"

He did not answer.

"Who's 'us'?"

Again there was no reply.

"Daniel was a professional," she said.

"Captain Forrest? Yes, he was."

"He still wound up dead."

"Not while he was in the Army."

"Then why are you bothering to try to discourage me from doing what I'm doing?"

"I am bothering, Miss Brett, because although he was no longer with us, there is always the possibility that whoever killed Captain Forrest wasn't aware of that."

"I wonder why." Fran had very little patience with Authority. She had learned from experience that when in doubt, Authority automatically took the negative line, simply because there were fewer comebacks when permission was denied than when it was granted.

"How do you mean?"

"It just occurred to me," Fran said slowly, "in my amateur sort of way, that Captain Forrest might possibly have been working undercover."

"Captain Forrest left the Army some time before his death."

"Officially."

"And as a matter of record."

"Of course it would be verifiable," Fran said angrily. "You'd have seen to that."

"It is also a matter of record that Captain Forrest was a reckless young man, as well as a very brave one. I can tell you, in confidence, we had no choice but to ask him to resign."

"He was kicked out?"

Napier folded one pale lip over the other and nodded. "Captain Forrest had access to some highly delicate and confidential information and chose to deal with it in an unprofessional manner." He blinked once. "Obviously we did not wish to ruin his reputation by bringing him before a court-martial. All we asked was that he go quietly. Because he came from a distinguished military family that had served this country well over several generations, we were content to let it go at that."

"You can't be serious."

"I'm always serious where serious matters are concerned."

"I feel as though any minute Richard Hannay's going to come bursting through the door."

"Fiction only works if it bears a strong relation to truth," Napier said. "And where security is concerned, matters probably haven't changed all that much since John Buchan's day."

"Security being the issue you don't want confused by bloody amateurs."

"Frankly, yes. We have no way of knowing who killed Captain Forrest. But if it is anything to do with the information to which he was privy, then I must strongly recommend that you leave well enough alone."

It is a recognized convention that, confronted with an insane sex killer, the heroine of a horror movie inevitably screams, "Why, you crazy dumbo, you're nothing but an insane sex killer," thereby provoking him into an attempted sex killing, when the clever thing to do would be to keep quiet and go along with his suggestions. Fran was very conscious of the fact that the best way to get Napier and his department off her back was to appear to agree with him.

"I see," she said slowly. "I hadn't quite realized the ramifications involved here."

"Please understand that I'm not saying there *are* ramifications," Napier said, sounding relieved at her apparent cooperation. "Merely that there might be. In which case, you would be better out of it."

"I suppose there's no chance that you'd tell me what these papers were about."

"None whatsoever." He smiled a shark's smile, full of teeth, and glanced again at his watch. "Perhaps I should emphasize that I have come along this morning for your safety's sake. In spite of what the newspapers hinted at the time, I don't really believe that Captain Forrest's death had anything to do with his former career in the Army, but while his murderer remains at large, that possibility can't be entirely ruled out. I hope that if you find anything that might be of interest to us, you will contact us immediately."

"What sort of thing?"

He stared once more around the room, then walked over to the windows and looked out. "I don't know—the information you say your father had, perhaps." Turning abruptly, he said, "This was your father's flat, wasn't it?"

"Yes."

"Let us know if you learn anything, Miss Brett. It goes without saying that we are concerned."

"I'm very grateful," Fran said. "Touched, might be nearer the mark. To think that the whole might of the Ministry of Defense has been put on alert just for me."

"You exaggerate," he said dryly. He was gathering his things together, bent over the coffee table. She wondered why he had bothered to remove the folders in the first place since he hadn't consulted them at any point.

"Not entirely."

"Thank you for the coffee," he said.

"Are you married, Colonel Napier?"

"No." He looked faintly surprised at the question.

"So it doesn't matter so much about giving up a Saturday morning to come into town."

"As a matter of fact, I was the one detailed to come talk to you only because my own flat isn't far from here," he said.

His smugness, his patronizing attitude, infuriated her. She took a deep breath. "I know about the Phoenix Foundation," she said. It was a shot fired at random.

He went quite still for a moment, then pressed shut the catch on his briefcase and stood up. He raised an unconcerned eyebrow. "Really? Some kind of charity, isn't it? What does it have to do with Forrest?"

She looked at him with increased dislike. By dispensing with Daniel's military rank, he had managed to make him sound like a wanted man, a criminal. "I don't know. I thought you might."

He stood in front of her, clearly not sure what to do. He was not as tall as she was; she guessed it bothered him. In the end, he said, "I can't tell you anything about it. Nothing at all. I will tell you this, however. Some very dangerous people are concerned."

■■

When he had gone, she sat still, going over the interview, for she saw quite clearly that was what it had been. Its purpose seemed less obvious. However, she had learned two things: one was that ostensibly Daniel Forrest had been forced to resign from the Army; the second was that mention of the Phoenix Foundation had caused a momentary rupture in Colonel Napier's composure.

There was a third piece of information in her possession, too. However much the Army might deny—via Napier—that Daniel had anything to do with them, they were lying. That was the only possible explanation for why they were still keeping tabs on his contacts, including Fran herself. It also explained Napier's twitchiness: he had been trawling her flat as they talked, looking for possible hiding places.

But hiding places for what?

The only explanation she could come up with was that both the French intruder and the Ministry of Defense were after the same thing.

She wished that made her feel more secure, but it did not. However much the government might bleat about democracy, the Army was state-controlled and as ruthless as any *jihad*-inspired terrorist group. She thought, *If they have not yet tapped my telephone, they will do so now.*

The flat seemed suddenly too small for her, and very lonely. She walked through a gray drizzle toward the Bayswater Road and turned into Kensington Palace Gardens. It was green and spacious there, uncrowded; the rain was keeping people away. She remembered with envy the long wide stretch of the land around Philippe de Pierrey's home—the soul requires a view if it is to thrive.

She had said to Emilie that the rich saw different views from the rest of the world: was the same true for men who dealt in violence? What had Daniel seen, looking out at that same sea of vine leaves? What had he seen in Istanbul? At the time, she had believed they were sharing a sense of its beauty and excitement. Now she realized she had been wrong. Clearly Daniel was looking for something beyond their joint present: he had been waiting for some event to occur. She had always envied her father his passionate commitment to his job: walking, head bent, through the rain, she realized that Daniel possessed a similar enviable engagement. Nothing had so far engaged her the same way; she wondered if such passion inevitably contained within itself the seeds of destruction.

■■

The telephone was ringing when she put her key into the lock of the flat. By the time she opened the door, it had stopped. She rang the hospital in France and checked that Emilie was still comfortable; she debated calling Gilles Laforêt and asking him to keep an eye on the house in Précy but decided against it. The police were already alerted to the fact that someone had broken in there for the second time.

Halfheartedly, she put some notes together for the in-flight magazine article and worked on some questions for the black woman MP.

By lunchtime, she had done all she could do in preparation. She considered whether to start working through the instruction manual for Tom's word processor, but felt too unsettled to concentrate. The sky above the roofs had lightened; faint shadows of chimney pots stretched palely along the still-wet slates. On impulse she decided to make a journey: to do something she should have done earlier and go on a pilgrimage.

■■

She had expected to feel something: nausea, revulsion, an echo of pain. She felt nothing. The land slid away toward the distant sea. Flat fields bisected by drainage ditches, reeds rustling in the faint onshore breeze, the cry of unseen waterfowl, a wide sky with a crimson sun preparing to roll toward earth's edge. A man had died here. She tried to feel a tremor of emotion, but could not. It was over now. Whatever of pain and degradation had taken place in the solitary hut on the marshes, it was finished and done with. She shivered; already the outline of the horizon was blurring, a cold mist creeping toward the land. By evening the whole landscape would be obliterated. As she had thought, it was not a good place to die.

She returned to her car. In the next village, she found a shop and asked to look at the local telephone directory. She did not expect to find a listing under "Campion," nor was there one. She checked under "Phoenix Foundation"; there was no mention of it. She drove slowly along back roads, following no particular route, but heading toward the little town of Lydd. Despite the fact that Campion's house was not listed, she felt sure she could find it. She had only to ask where the American film director was staying. The sun was low against the sea; the lanes were suffused with scarlet light.

Squinting against the brilliance, she pulled the sun visor down in front of her. Since the angle of the sun was farther around to her left, it did not help. She had always hated driving in such conditions: her father used to tease her about it, saying she ought to have roller-blinds fitted to the windows of her car. She reached across to pull at the visor in front of the passenger seat. It was stiff, not having been used since her father's death—she was the only one who had driven the VW, and then always alone. She drove awkwardly along, tugging until it suddenly came free and swung down to hide the worst of the sun. A rough edge where there was a tear in the plastic caught her finger; she sucked it, tasting blood.

The fifth inquiry she made told her what she wanted to know.

"American gentleman, is he?" the woman in the general store said.

"That's right."

"Fillums, or something?"

"Yes."

"You'll be wanting Priory House," said the woman.

"Where's that?"

"About three miles from here. Oh, they've had some wild sorts in there, I can tell you."

"Like what?"

"It always seems to be foreigners: film people or fashion people or television crews. We had Japs in there once. Blacks and all sorts, they've had. Still, you can't complain: they're good spenders, I'll give them that."

"What's the best way to get there?" asked Fran. She had absolutely no reason to go to Campion's house except simple curiosity.

■■

Priory House was a small manor in the Kentish style: flat-fronted red brick, peg-tile roof, a front door with two stained-glass panels. A brick wall surrounded three sides of the grounds; the front was open to the road, with a line of spiked chain hung between white-painted bollards protecting the lawn from careless drivers.

The windows were leaded, arched, and there were cruciform slits in the brickwork beneath the two gables. The front door, too, was vaulted, with flat stone pillars supporting a kind of tympanum of carved stone showing a risen Christ surrounded by the heads of saints. It had obviously come from some long-dissolved monastery. Fran decided it was from these pietistic details rather than from any connection with an actual religious community that the name of the house derived.

Had Daniel ever been here?

The question occupied her as she parked on a grass verge farther up the road and walked back. She thought she might feel some inner vibration from the imperious voice that sometimes seemed to take her over, but there was no sign. A curlicued gate of black-painted iron was set into a wing wall jutting out from the side of the house. She peered through into the garden beyond: she could see paths of red brick, box hedges, an apple tree. Michaelmas daisies were piled against the walls, tied together with garden twine. On the other side of the gate, two small bay trees sat in tubs. Lavender overhung the path.

Out of sight, someone was having a party. She could hear trans-atlantic voices, bursts of coarse laughter, Hollywood-type gossip:

"So I said: 'Listen, honey, you're a nice kid but we're looking for class here' . . ."

"By the time he's taken his ten percent . . ."

". . . tried to get Streep for the name part but she was tied up . . ."

"So *he* said: 'You wouldn't know class if it unzipped your pants and went down on you.' So I said . . ."

". . . Caine . . ."

". . . Redford . . ."

". . . hauled off and socked the little . . ."

Glasses clinked. From the open window above her head came the sound of two people engaged in strenuous sex.

It seemed a long way from the ideals of which Campion had spoken so burningly. She reminded herself that he probably did not know these people, did not share their values or their aims, that the only relationship between them was a business one.

Driving back to London, she tried to analyze him. Although she scarcely knew him, he drew her. At the Galerie Knabel and sitting in the café with him, she had been partly moved, partly repulsed by him; looking at him dispassionately, from this distance, she was surprised by the strength of her desire to see him again.

The red light was draining from the sky with the onset of evening. She flipped the sun visors back into position flat against the roof. The one on the passenger side did not shift easily against its plastic sockets, so she banged it into place. It needed lubrication of some kind

—did one put oil on plastic? She would try to remember when she got back to London.

For once there was parking space right outside the flat. Pulling the keys from the ignition, she saw the scratch on her finger from the torn plastic of the sun visor. Oil. There was lubricating oil in the small toolbox she kept behind the backseat of the car. Squeezing it onto the sockets, she worked the padded plastic of the sun visor back and forth until its movement lost stiffness. She had to search for the tear, not immediately visible, which ran along one molded seam: it was difficult to see how it could have happened.

She pulled down the visor in front of the driver's seat; there was a distinct difference in feel between the two. Her pulse began to race. She knew at once that she had found the information she had been seeking. Pretending to fumble around in the glove compartment, she glanced up and down the street and into the railed public garden opposite. A man with a small white dog on a lead had just passed. A young couple were walking toward her, arms around each other. Two or three anonymous people were getting into or out of cars parked farther around the curve of the crescent. As far as she could see, no one was specifically watching her.

Probing with thumb and finger the space between the two edges of plastic, she could feel that something had been tucked into the padding. She pulled it carefully out of its hiding place and recognized it immediately as a three-and-a-half-inch floppy disk, part of the software for Tom Brett's word processor.

Her stomach churned. Would the answers be there? The key to Daniel's death, the enigma of Phoenix, Tom's own involvement, the reason why Military Intelligence was interested? Would she find out now what exactly was going on?

She got out and locked the doors of the VW. It would not take long to teach herself the basic moves of the word processor: she only wished to read a single disk, not learn the whole language.

She ran down the basement steps and pushed her key into the Yale lock. The door opened before she had turned it. She realized immediately that something was wrong, even before she switched on the light and saw the way the flat had been demolished. There must have been a team of them, she decided: everything had systematically been taken apart. The television, the stereo, the furniture, the panel on the bath, the contents of the kitchen, everything.

Including the word processor. There was no way she could look at the disk tonight.

· 22 ·

ONE LOOK WAS ENOUGH TO TELL
her that it would be pointless to call in the cops. Whoever was responsible for the devastation had been completely professional: the police
would find no clues. Nonetheless Fran rang them, if only as a gesture
against the anarchy that seemed to be engulfing her. They came,
dusted the place for fingerprints, took down details. When they had
gone, she repacked her suitcase, pulled the door to behind her, and
climbed into her car.

"This has got to stop," she told her reflection in the rearview
mirror. There were patches of red color on her cheeks: the flush of
towering rage. There was little doubt in her mind as to who was
responsible. She had probably been under surveillance since Napier
left her flat that morning.

There were lights on in Max Blum's house. She was glad about
that. If the place had been dark and empty, she might well have
subsided into hysteria. She needed Max tonight; after too many
shocks, in too short a time, she was beginning to overload. When Max
opened the door, she stumbled against his chest.

"Hey, now," he said, drawing her into the hall. Stroking her hair
with one hand, he pushed the door to with the other. "What the hell
happened to you?"

She did not answer. She held on to him, breathing in his familiar
scent of Bull Durham pipe tobacco and two-day-old sweat, strangely
calmed by the rasp of his unshaven chin in her hair, then stepped
away, still holding on to his arm, and looked him over fondly. He wore
a sagging cardigan over a wrinkled shirt; under crumpled brown
corduroys his feet were bare. "Boy," she said. "I bet you get people
ringing up all the time for your fashion secrets."

He looked down at himself and brushed away a shred of tobacco.
"What's wrong with me?"

"You don't get any smarter, do you?"

"Only up here." He tapped the side of his head. "Have you come to stay with us?"

"Who's us?" Fran said warily. Although he was in his late sixties, Max still attracted women with the effortless ease of a kingfisher catching minnows. "I don't think I could face one of your Hampstead intellectuals tonight."

He spread his hands. "None on the premises."

"What about minor West End actresses?"

"Fresh out."

"So who's this 'us'?"

"A very dear friend of mine," he said.

"Have I met her before?"

"No." His smile teased.

She followed him into the untidy book-strewn drawing room. At once, she felt herself relax, the anxieties draining away from her. Shabby velvet curtains shut out the hostile world. A fire burned in the grate. The odor of whisky was strong. "This is Phyllis," Max said. "She shares the house with me."

Lying on one of the battered sofas, snout pink between mottled paws, a black patch covering one eye, was a young bullterrier. Fran laughed. "Funny how all your women look the same."

Max opened a cupboard. "What'll you have to drink?"

"Something strong and mind-numbing," Fran said.

"Whatever's up, it sounds bad."

"I think it is."

Phyllis got up and sniffed her carefully, then walked behind the sofa and fell asleep. Max poured a hefty drink, held it up, then added a couple of fingers and passed it to her.

"Are you going to tell me about it?"

She nodded. "In a moment. Just let me get my thoughts in gear."

She swallowed half the whisky in a single go, then sat nursing the glass, wondering where to start. Max settled himself into the rotting armchair on the other side of the hearth and stretched his long legs toward the flames. His kind eyes watched her; as always, the depth of his involvement with the problems of others, whatever they might be, seemed absolute. Fran smiled: that total commitment was what made women love him.

She began to talk about Istanbul. He listened, eyes closed; occasionally he leaned over to add whisky to his glass. She found herself playing down her feelings, as if Daniel was merely an acquaintance, someone she had gone out with a couple of times. She told him about her visit to Mrs. Forrest, passing quickly over her discovery of Daniel's murder, the attack on Emilie, the visit from the inscrutable Colonel Napier, the systematic dismantling of the London flat.

Max opened his eyes at that. "Taking a risk, weren't they?" he said. "Suppose you'd come back earlier?"

"They had to be keeping tabs on me," Fran said. "They'd have arranged some delaying tactic—a minor accident or an officious policeman booking me for speeding or something." She shook her head. "I can't see what the connection is with Daniel."

"Forrest," said Max. "I thought I recognized the name. Tortured, wasn't he?"

"Yes."

"Nasty case." He stirred in his chair, reaching again for the bottle beside him. "Mind you, there seemed to be a sort of poetic justice about it."

"Justice?"

"Considering that he probably caused a fair bit of pain in his time," Max said.

Fran felt suddenly cold. "What on earth do you mean?"

Max glanced at her sharply. "I thought everyone knew," he said.

"Knew *what*?"

He looked away from her. "It's one of those things about being a newspaperman," he said apologetically. "You hear some of the things that don't appear in print, and assume that everyone else in the business knows them too."

"What sort of things, Max?"

He raised his eyebrows at her tone, then said softly, "Oh, honey. I hadn't realized how you felt about this Forrest guy."

"Max," she said with urgency, "what is it you know about Daniel Forrest that I don't?"

"According to the rumors," Max said, "he was an Army interrogator."

The kind of rumors that circulate among newspaper people were generally founded on fact, even if they could not always be printed. Max's words were like a sudden blow to the stomach; Fran experienced the same mixture of pain, nausea, damage. An interrogator was a man who extracted information by any means he could—all too often that means was torture. She could have no illusions about the kind of work Daniel would have been involved in; despite the hypocritical mouthings of government, the British were no less skilled than any others in the use of calculated pain.

Images of time shared with Daniel crowded in on her: she saw again the dun-colored bird floating against the hills; the café boys carrying trays of tea glasses; his face between candle flames.

She shook her head. Surely it was not possible that the man she had known and almost loved could be what Max said he was. Yet she could not help remembering the bleakness of his gray eyes; the closed look he sometimes wore; Philippe's voice: *He was quite unable to accommodate those who strayed from his code.* And something else, a memory she had not even been there to share: a hare, sitting up against dark trees in the glow of a summer sunset, and the brutal crash of a gun. Unexpectedly, she also recalled Anna in Istanbul saying that a suspected arms dealer had been pulled out of the harbor. At the time it appeared to contain no significance; had she remembered it because in some way she connected it to Daniel?

She said, "Ever heard of the Phoenix Foundation?"

He drew in his long legs and sat up. "I sure wish I had your sources," he said slowly. "How in the *hell* do you know about that?"

He would not have believed it if she had told him her information came from a dead man. "I don't. Not really. But I think Daniel Forrest was involved."

"Figures."

"And maybe Tom, too."

"Where'd you pick that up? Tom told me he was keeping all his information well under cover."

"I figured it out," Fran said. "What do *you* know about it?"

"Not much." He reached again for the whisky bottle. "Remember the Swedish prime minister who was assassinated in the street?"

"Olof Palme. I thought they'd got someone for that."

"Except no one believes it's the right someone. You know that U.S. senator who was about to chair a committee investigating the illegal sale of arms to Africa: the one who was mugged and murdered on his way to his car?"

"Don Arlington," Fran said.

"Yeah. Him. And the English MP who was quote accidentally drowned unquote on holiday in the Lake District?"

"It wasn't an accident?"

"Not according to my information. As far as I can make out—and my source is being pretty cagey about it—there seems to be some kind of a hit squad in operation, knocking off anyone who gets too close to what's going on."

"Who's your source?"

He grinned at her. "You know better than to ask that, honey. But I'll tell you: he's fairly high up and works not a million miles from Whitehall."

"Okay. If this is all so tentative," said Fran, "how did they get onto it in the first place?"

"Pure random chance," Max said. "It's a beautiful thing, chance. All those facts, floating about in the ether, disconnected, solitary, lost pieces of jigsaw searching for something to slot into, and then someone like this Japanese guy comes along and wham! you've got a whole puzzle completed."

"Which Japanese guy?" Fran said.

"This student at Berkeley, doing a Ph.D. in criminology. He started feeding statistics on recent unsolved assassinations into a computer." The sleepy look had left Max's face. "He discovered what no one else had begun to suspect, that in just about every case he processed, there were similarities which made it virtually certain they'd been carried out by the same people. So he passed the stuff on to the CIA, who passed it on to their buddies in various other national intelligence bureaus. And guess what?"

"What?"

"When they added some of their own cases to the original work, they found the same thing. A distinctive modus operandi—my source called it a 'fingerprint'—pointing toward a single person, or possibly two. No more than that. Remember Carlos the Jackal?"

"Sure."

"It's someone like that, it's got to be. He's going to be in the pay of some organization—could be a government, could be a terrorist group, could even be—and this is the exciting bit—a corporation or cartel."

"Like the Colombian drug barons, you mean?"

"Since there are no obvious political links, they'd be the ones to go for. Except there are no obvious links to drug smuggling, either. Naturally the information went straight to the Drug Enforcement Agency, but they passed it right back—nothing to do with their department, they said."

"And what does this have to do with the Phoenix Foundation?"

"Absolutely nothing tangible, at the moment. On the surface, it's exactly what it appears to be: a well-funded medical charity doing a lot of good stuff where it's desperately needed."

"So why did you start pointing like a retriever when I mentioned it?"

Max tamped tobacco down into the bowl of his pipe with a grubby thumb. His expression was that of a dog who knows he is about to be handed a marrowbone. "Because nearly every time they feed names into the computer, this Phoenix thing comes up on the screen. Either the dead guy is associated with it, or someone in his family is, or he'd just made a massive donation to the charity funds or the guy that runs it just sent him a letter or *something*. It could just be coincidence, of course . . ."

"But you don't think so."

"You're a pretty smart girl, Fran. Would *you*?"

She shook her head. "I don't know."

"Tom thought it was money," Max said. "When he talked it over with me, he was convinced that money lay behind it. To keep an organization like that going, you'd need scads of the stuff coming in, all the time. Which means you'd have a hell of a lot of super-rich sponsors. He said it'd only take one individual to decide that he could make better use of all that dough than some kid with napalm burns or a woman who's just been blinded by chlorine gas, for the whole thing to start moving in a different direction."

"It'd have to be a clever individual."

"Clever, patient, and absolutely ruthless."

"I can't quite see the connection between diverting funds and knocking people off, even if they are super-rich."

"Exactly."

"How do you come into it?"

"Through the suicide angle. I found three, during my researches, all in the past five years, and all connected with this Phoenix thing. So naturally I wasn't going to let it drop when the name came up again in connection with something rather different. See, I was talking to Tom about it only a few weeks before he . . . uh. . . ."

For the first time that Fran could remember, Max looked uncomfortable.

"Died," she said firmly. "It's okay, Max. I've accepted the fact that he's dead. You don't have to pussyfoot around the subject."

"Right." Max splashed more whisky into his glass, then held the bottle up to the light. "Jesus. I'll swear Phyllis is on the booze, the way this stuff disappears. Anyway . . . Tom was convinced at first that it was drugs—he said narcotics was much the easiest way to get rich quick."

"But you just said that the DEA hadn't—"

"I know. Then he rang me up from someplace in South America, said he'd found something out that was really hair-raising, that we'd talk about it next time he came to England."

"And did he?"

"Honey, he never came to London before they got him in Beirut. What I think happened is, he was fairly close to identifying either the hit man himself or proof of whoever was behind him, though like all good newspapermen, he wasn't going to break the story until he'd got all the facts." Max gave her a long hard stare. "Want to see what I did last week?" He went over and picked up an atlas lying on his desk. He showed her a map of the world. "Look at this."

Fran did so. There were about a dozen black circles inked in with a felt-tip pen, mainly in the southern hemisphere. She looked up at Max, puzzled. "What's it supposed to mean?"

"Don't you see any connection between the places I've marked?"

"Not offhand." Though some of the names did ring a bell for her, she could not immediately link them to each other.

Max took the atlas away from her and shut it up. "Boy, for a clever gal you can be really dumb. In the past six or seven years, Tom was on assignment in all those countries."

"He was a foreign correspondent, Max. Naturally he'd have been there."

"Exactly. And guess who came in the same time he did, or even before. All the aid organizations, the medical teams, the voluntary groups who always follow in the wake of any disaster, whether natural or manmade."

Fran said slowly, "Including the Phoenix Foundation."

"Right. Which is why I never really bought that story about him getting caught in cross fire. . . ."

Fran got up from her seat and walked restlessly about the room. Finally she said, "Neither did I."

"Really?"

"I've gone over and over it in my mind and it just never sounded right. For one thing, Dad would never have been out in the middle of the street like that. He always cleared what he was doing with the locals. I don't know how many times I heard him say that you should never take unnecessary risks. Yet there he was, with François Vacherot, in a non-Christian sector notorious for kidnappings. And anyway, if for some reason he *was* there, so obviously western, why didn't they take him hostage? Why shoot him?"

"I agree." Max hesitated. "I didn't even know he was heading for Beirut. He told *me* he was going to Cyprus, said it was a jumping-off point."

"Do you think this Phoenix lot could have killed him?"

"I think it's more than possible."

"Because he knew too much about them?"

"Because he *guessed* too much."

"What was he guessing exactly?"

Max took his pipe apart and poked a cleaner into one end. "That's what I asked myself. Especially when I got the information back that as far as the DEA was concerned, the Phoenix lot were clean. If Tom was right, and money was the rationale behind whatever was going on, then drugs would have been the obvious way to handle it. So I took a closer look at all those countries."

"And found what, exactly?"

Max stretched his legs out again toward the fire and grinned. "All but two of them were poised on the brink of revolution, either via a military coup or a popular uprising. Some of them had guerrilla movements as powerful as the government that was supposed to be in control of the country. And they all boiled over at about the same time as the relief organizations came in." He reconstituted the pipe and patted himself in a search for matches. "And you know what everyone always needs in a revolution?"

"Arms."

"Right."

"There are always gunrunners, Max. It's practically one of the professions these days. People are always talking revolution, especially in the poorer countries."

"Yeah. But in these places I've circled, the revolution actually took off, or escalated out of control. But it's not just Third World politics we're talking here. Think about Northern Ireland. Or some of the more fanatical fringe groups, like pro-lifers in the States, or animal rights people over here. Someone's supplying them, or carrying out jobs for them, or teaching them how to do it themselves. And what better cover could you have than a volunteer organization, especially since they can bypass most of the hassle of getting through Customs."

It made sense. Fran had to admit that. "What's the motive, if it's not money?" she said.

"Sounds weird, but I'm thinking in terms of power. After all, whatever they say, some people *can* have enough money. Or they can get bored with having too much. So what else can you do?" He jetted blue clouds of smoke at the ceiling. "Think about it. Manipulating whole countries, altering economies: it's heady stuff. Like a James Bond movie—SMERSH strikes again and all that—only for real."

Somewhere at the pit of Fran's stomach was a sense of loss. She had been fired by Alexander Campion's apparent idealism and heartened by the fervor with which he had spoken of the sufferings of the people his organization was helping. That it should all have been a sham was the worst kind of betrayal.

Her face twisted with distaste, she said, "I don't want to believe what you're telling me."

"You don't have to. Put it down as one of Blum's wild theories. But I wouldn't mind betting Tom will have come up with something similar. Damn. I wish I knew what he did with the stuff he had."

"I do," Fran said. She found her bag and pulled out the floppy disk. "He put it on this, and then hid it where I would find it."

Max took it from her. "My God," he said. "You really are your father's daughter, aren't you? Where was it?"

She explained.

"And you haven't had a chance to look at it yet?"

"I hoped we could look at it on your processor."

Max shook his head. "Unfortunately not. Tom rushed in the minute these gizmos started coming onto the market. Mine's about third generation, not compatible with his. But don't worry: I'll have a scout round in the morning and see what I can come up with. If we can't find a machine, we'll find some computer whiz who can transfer the stuff for us."

"But this is strictly Your Eyes Only," Fran said firmly.

"I know that, hon."

"And the story is mine, okay?"

"I'm retired, remember?"

"I'll believe that when I see you in your coffin. Now, I'd better get to bed."

In one of Max's spare bedrooms, Fran found it difficult to sleep. The sheets were faintly damp and smelled of dog; the events of the day had disturbed her, dislodging anxieties that she had hoped were safely shelved. It was the first time she had voiced her suspicions about Tom Brett's death; now he came back to her as she searched for sleep, a big blond man, the anchor in her life, rudely torn from its moorings, leaving her to float adrift.

Someone had done the same to Philippe de Pierrey, she thought. She had not asked what traumatic event had occurred in his life; it came to her strongly that she should have.

There was something else she should have done. But what?

Only as she drifted finally toward sleep did she remember.

"Max!" She knocked on the door of his bedroom. "Are you awake?"

"Sure." He opened the door, still shrugging into a dressing gown of creased paisley silk. Even as she handed him the newspaper cutting she had brought for him from Paris about the banker's suicide, she was noting with a certain amount of amusement that Max slept naked.

"I found this in Tom's office: I thought you might find it interesting, for your suicide book," she explained.

He found glasses and put them on. When he had read the piece of newsprint, he frowned, thinking. She watched his journalist's brain ticking over, computing, working the possibilities. "We have a problem here," he said finally.

"What's that?"

"How do we know whether Tom kept this because he thought *I* could use it, or because he was interested in it himself?"

"If he kept it for you, then take it, and I'll go back to bed." Fran pushed past him into the cozy squalor of Max's room. A gas fire was popping under the Victorian mantelpiece, emphasizing the smell of good leather shoes and the feet which habitually wore them. She knelt by the fire and looked up at Max, conscious of rising excitement. "But just suppose . . . just suppose he kept it for his own information— why might he have done that?"

"You're right, honey. Absolutely right." Max, too, was aroused by the implications.

"The Phoenix Foundation again, I bet you," said Fran. "Rich people. The sort who sit on charitable boards."

Max drew in a long breath. "My God, could all this really be linked? If it is, we're onto the hottest story for years."

"*I'm* on to it," Fran said firmly. "*You're* retired."

"But you're going to need some help."

"Okay. As long as it's understood that it's my story."

"And what a story it could be," Max said, evasively. "Jesus: have you ever thought how fragile our safety is? I mean the safety of your average John Doe living in his suburban house on his suburban street?"

"Of course I have. What holds back the yobs: why they don't come crashing through the windows every night, why the violence is so contained? That's what you mean, isn't it?"

"More or less. And what holds them back is a mixture of fear of reprisal and a veneer—thin as cigarette paper, mind you—of civilization. But suppose you said the hell with all that. Suppose you genuinely didn't care about reprisals, about other people's lives. Think of it on a global scale." Max leaned forward. "I wonder who he is, the hit man they use. I bet when they eventually catch up with him, they'll find he's got no reason to live, so he doesn't give a damn about dying."

"Or else he's paid so much for each job that he can't refuse." She sighed. "Or perhaps he doesn't do it for money but for love."

"Or kicks. There are always the psychopaths who kill for the high it gives them."

"I'll go and see this Comtesse de Tresail when I get back to France," said Fran.

The two of them smiled at each other.

■■

When Fran was little, her father used sometimes to sing her to sleep. He had no voice at all, could not even carry a tune, yet he doggedly persevered, grabbing at notes here and there until he reached an uncertain finale. Those wavering interpretations of "Hush Little Baby" and "Golden Slumbers" were not to be superseded later by any fancy rendition; they still remained for her the definitive version. She had doubted, in the first rush of shock and outrage at the sight of the Notting Hill flat turned into debris, whether she would ever be able to use it again. She had felt herself to be on the run, hounded, shuttling between countries and homes, unable to find sanctuary. Now, lying between the Phyllis-scented sheets, remembering Tom, she knew that she would not give in so easily, she too would have to continue the song to the end.

When sleep finally came, the robed figure waited for Fran. She heard again the thud of nails driven home, felt the sweat of terror. When the figure came toward her she turned away, dreading the emptiness which lay beneath the hood. But it was still there, waiting, when she turned back. It had Daniel's face.

Fran slept badly and woke suddenly. There was a dead weight across her legs, making it difficult to move. In the faint light of dawn, she could just make out the piebald shape of Phyllis, twitching in dream.

She lay there facing the window, watching the room lighten with early morning, her mind busy with new information. Eventually Max would find a computer that would accept her father's disk—she hoped it would not be too long. There was a sense of urgency about the matter now; they could not afford to waste time. As she thought about her father's death, anguish pushed at her ribs. One day the pain would have lost its immediacy and Tom would be only a memory, but she had not yet reached that stage. As with Daniel, the raw sense of loss could still take her unawares.

Daniel: She did not want to think about him, did not want to contemplate the sort of man he must have been, if Max was right. It was odd how one single piece of information could alter all the perspectives from which she viewed him.

She tried to think, instead, about Philippe de Pierrey, and the making of wine, but other thoughts intruded. Melancholy filled her: she kept remembering Alexander Campion's arms around her and the solid feel of his body beneath his shirt. It seemed impossible to view him as some kind of international gangster; was he an innocent, manipulated by sinister forces within his own organization, or was he in fact the guiding force behind the trail of deaths Max had spoken of? Or was it simply a pattern, perfectly logical, that brought the Phoenix Foundation onto the computer screens? After all, the world of the super-rich—as Max had called them—was very small. It was natural that there would be some connection.

Later, she heard the morning papers being pushed through the letterbox and decided to get up. She knew she could not get back to sleep again: her brain whirred with the multitude of things to do, people to see, information to find. The allure of the facts still hidden like truffles in the rich loam of the unknown, waiting for her to unearth them, was almost overwhelming. Sitting at the kitchen table with the newspapers, she glanced at the front page. Britain was breaking off relations with Iran. House prices were picking up again after the winter slump. A police commissioner in Sweden had been gunned down outside his home. There were more floods in Bangladesh. Headlines, paragraphs full of news, articles she wanted to read: she could take none of it in. In her inability to concentrate, the events described seemed to be part of a wider world to which she temporarily did not have access.

∎∎

All evening Sola had watched him from her window. He was leaning against the tree below her in the street, staring up at her window. She recognized him now, and with recognition came an easing of tension. She thought: Now he has finally come I shall find peace again.

Her mind felt soft, the edges of thought blurred by the hash she had smoked earlier in the evening to relax herself. It occurred to her that once whatever was now to pass between them had taken place, she would be free to return again to the city where she was born. Tomorrow, she would book her ticket, by air this time, not by train. She could be there by evening . . .

The hatred she had once felt toward the man below had gone; instead a desert wind swept through her, igniting her. It was years since she had felt such fierce heat, such intense love. Images spilled across each other in her mind like a purseful of transparent coins: Kemal, Mikkele, her mother, Istanbul. That afternoon, during a fashion presentation for foreign buyers, she had looked into the darkness at the back of the room and seen him there, she was sure of it. For a moment his eyes had held hers, and she had tried to read the message they contained. At the end of the catwalk she had flounced and strutted, the yellow leather coat swinging from her shoulders. When she looked again, he had gone. She knew it could not have been a hallucination: where he had sat was an empty chair.

She leaned her head against the cool glass. It seemed too heavy for the slender bones of her neck to support. Her limbs, too, seemed weighted down; she wanted to open the window, lean out, let go. Despite her heaviness, she knew she would be able to soar across the roofs, to sweep and dip like a bird among the stars.

Below her, the watcher crossed the road and disappeared beneath the building's overhang. She waited for the upward groan of the lift, the faint pad of footsteps down the hall toward her flat. When he rang, she opened the door immediately and let him in.

■■

"How did you find me?"

"Chance," he murmured into her hair. "It was pure chance that you walked past me and someone told me who you were." He could not believe that it had happened as easily as this: that she should have walked into his arms without speaking, without surprise.

"I've looked for you always," she whispered back. The only light came from the streetlamp outside; the white walls of the living room picked up the dim radiance and threw it hesitantly into the middle of the darkness. It did not matter: she knew already what he looked like. She touched his smooth jaw, the dark hair on his head, the firm roundness of his shoulder. Her eyes were closed. She felt his hands on her body, slow at first, then faster, urgent, tearing at the clothes which lay between the two of them.

"Beloved one," he said, so softly she could scarcely hear him. He marveled at the beauty she offered him so unquestioningly, as though it was his by right. In the semi-dark, his head moved in ways which were piercingly familiar to her. Now that she herself was older, he seemed younger, as though the years which had hung between them were finally dissolving. Water welled up and spilled from her eyes. She wanted to say, "I weep because I am happy," but he was wiping her tears away with his soft mouth, kissing her with lips that were sweetly salt.

Naked herself, she slowly undid the buttons of his shirt and touched his chest. She had forgotten the slippery smoothness of his skin, unlike any she had touched since: her hands slid lightly across it and around to his back, holding him against her.

He touched her nipples with the flat of his palms. She slid his shirt down his arms and watched it fall silently into shadowed flatness on the floor. When he touched her breasts again, holding each in one of his hands, she felt herself grow damp with longing. His tongue touched her lips again, soft as ash falling in a fire, then pushed its way into her mouth. She took one of his hands and pushed it down between her legs; she felt his fingers solid inside her, not moving, taking possession of her. The soft deep tissues quivered inside her body; gently they leaped against his hand, again and again. She arched against him, impaled by the love which streamed from him like fire. "Ah," she said.

"Perhaps we should not," he said quietly. "After all, this is the first time we've—"

"We must," she said.

"Yes."

The two of them lay together on Sola's bed. Under her hand he seemed huge in the darkness; she brought him to the opening into her body and held him there, savoring the moment before consummation. Keeping her body in contact with his, he turned suddenly on the black blanket so that she was suspended above him. Her heat sucked him toward her. He did not enter her: she lay on top of him, smelling her sex on his hands, the spice of him in her nostrils. She thought: I will die of love if he waits much longer. With her head drooping against his face, she smiled and felt him smile in answer. She could smell something sweet and spicy on his breath and realized that he, too, was high. For some reason, this made her laugh.

"You are teasing me," she murmured, giggling a little.

"Not you—myself," he whispered back. He pulled her suddenly down, impaling her on himself, then pushed her up again, away from him.

She cried out. "Oh," she moaned. "Now. Please."

"Wait."

His face slid down her stomach and rested for a moment before moving farther down toward the waiting heat between her legs. He nudged her lips apart, nibbling, caressing her with long wet strokes of his tongue. She held his head against her thighs, shuddering, ecstatic. Each separate cell of her had taken on a throbbing fainting life of its own. It should always have been like this; from now on she knew it always would be. Finally, panting, he held her shoulders down against the mattress and drove into her. "Ah"—it sounded like a cry of pain. "Oh God," he said.

She rose to meet him, moving with him, murmuring against his chest, willing to die if it would bring him the same rapturous frenzied pleasure that she felt herself. Her body seemed to fill the universe as he dug himself into her, cramming her buttocks against his thighs, seeking the paradisal moment. When it came, he screamed, again and again, head thrown back.

It had never been like that before. Not for either of them. After a while, his tears fell onto her breasts.

■■

Waking as the iron-white dawn was just beginning to slide across the roofs opposite her window, Sola lay with her eyes closed. After last night, she felt that she had finally found her way back into the peaceful gardens to which she had feared she would never again have access. The effect of the drugs she had taken the night before still hazed the edges of her consciousness. She turned toward her lover. Her life had begun with him: now, because they need not part again, it would end with him. It was semi-dark in the room but she could see that he was awake, face sunk into the pillow, watching her. He put out his hand and gathered the chain around her neck into his hand. "Where did you get this?" he murmured.

She smiled, and put out a hand to touch his cheek. "You know as well as I do."

"Tell me."

"You gave it to me."

"Oh." He seemed vague. "I was never sure." Her answer seemed odd; he wished he had not turned on before he came here. His fingers hesitantly touched the three fire opals one by one. Surely there was some mistake. He raised himself up on an elbow. "I hardly dared believe it was you," he said gently. *"Mon aimée.* Beloved."

She started up. His voice: it was not the one she had expected, though gentle as his had always been. Terror piled up inside her, square and solid, bricks of it heaping themselves one on top of the other into a wall so high that she was afraid it would obscure her from the light, from the air, from life itself. She opened her mouth to scream. How had this happened? How could she have spent such hours of rapture with one man, believing him to be another? And with this man, of all men? Instead of giving in to the temptation of the hidden white powders, she should have stayed strong, as she had so many times before.

"What's wrong?" he asked.

Had he spoken aloud during their dreamlike lovemaking in the dark, would she still have mistaken him? His voice was his own; the likeness between him and the man she had supposed him to be, though distinct, was very far from complete. So far, in fact, that she must have been mad to think it was the same. Unless she had been bewitched. She remembered her mother's stories of *afrits,* of women possessed during sleep by incubi, of evil spirits inhabiting the upper regions of the air who could assume any human form they chose. Was that what had happened to her? How, otherwise, could she possibly not have realized before now that she was with the wrong man? How else explain the fact that she had given herself totally to someone she was not allowed to love? Was she always to be cursed like this?

"I thought you were Kemal," she said sadly.

He held her close against his side. Gently, he said, "Kemal is dead," and was horrified by the agonized cry of pain she gave. For a moment they lay together, two bodies, both beautiful, both lost.

She thought, *This is the last and most final of all the betrayals.*
She thought, *This must end.*

Without warning, she slipped away from between the covers. For a moment, she looked down at the man so like and yet not the one she had thought him to be. Beneath her shock sprouted the need for expiation, for justice. She had to prove to herself that she could control her own destiny. But to do that, she would have to act. He saw in her face what she intended and his own filled with alarm. When he tried to rise, she pushed him back down onto the mattress; his growing terror seemed only fair after the terrors she herself had been made to suffer.

Walking naked across the bare boards, she glanced up at the looming crucifix and thought sadly, *The past will not leave me alone.*

She went into the kitchen where the glittering knives on the wall waited for her like a smile.

The man saw in her eyes the madness of a shattered hope. As she lifted the knife he saw her intention and moved, swifter than a leopard, but too late. He was not to know, with death crowding in, that as the blade slashed and tore, Sola sought the refuge of her gardens. But the gates were locked, and when she peered in through the bars, desperate and afraid, she saw that winter had come, the flowers were gone, and in the barren beds were only blackened stalks and fallen leaves.

▪ 23 ▪

THE NUMBER FRAN HAD DIALED was answered by a voice which sounded half asleep. After two or three minutes of conversation, she realized that it was, in fact, drunk.

"Sir Hugo Campion?" she said. She had spent some time working on her approach. From what she had learned, any mention of Alexander was unlikely to provide an instant passport to Eastholme.

"Speaking."

"Hello. My name is Frances Brett."

He grunted.

"I've been talking to the features editor of *The Observer*," she said brightly. "They'd like to do a color spread of some of your work, and I'm to do the words to go with the pictures."

He gave another grunt, which sounded marginally less ungracious than the first one.

"Would it be possible for me to come down and talk to you, Sir Hugo?"

"I suppose so. When do you want to come?"

"As soon as possible, really. Your Paris exhibition is transferring to the Royal Academy shortly, isn't it?"

"Yes." He was silent for a moment, then unexpectedly said, "Come for lunch, why don't you?"

▪▪

Eastholme was a large early-Victorian pile, reached by a long drive through beech woods. Rain made them dismal; Fran tried to imagine it as a home for the unhappy child who had once been Alexander Campion. Uprooted from the cosmopolitan bustle of Paris, Istanbul, Rome, Vienna, what would he have made of these lonely woods, the long sweep of lawn toward fields and more woods, the quiet of the countryside?

Dogs scrambled damply toward her as she got out of her car.

Following them came a giant of a man in tweed kneebreeches and a clay-stained smock. He held out a huge hand and shook hers vigorously. His bearded face was unhealthily red; there were purple veins around the nose and across the cheeks. His eyes were bloodshot and very large, swimming about in loose-rimmed sockets.

Not falling-down drunk, Fran told herself, but well on the way. She held out her hand to him, smiled, said, "I'm Frances Brett."

"So glad you could come," he said. "Lunch will be in about half an hour. We've just got time for a sherry."

He led the way toward a side entrance, where he removed his smock and a pair of muddy walking boots. In his socks he padded down a red-and-black-tiled passage to a sitting room crammed with old magazines and dog baskets and plenty of comfortable shabby furniture arranged in front of a large hearth full of flickering logs. He poured sherry for Fran; for himself he half filled a cut-glass tumbler with Scotch and added no water.

"I saw your exhibition in Paris," Fran said.

"Did you indeed?"

"I have to admit that until then, I didn't know your work. I thought it was marvelous."

"They've staged it well." He sat heavily down in what was clearly an accustomed armchair and pushed thick fingers back through the tumult of his hair.

"It wasn't the staging so much," said Fran, "though obviously that adds enormously to the total effect—it was seeing the way you've developed over the years."

She knew she had to tread lightly. Though whatever she learned might eventually be the basis of a feature, she also had to remember that she had come here to find out more about Alexander. It would not be easy to probe into Hugo Campion's personal details without arousing suspicion—unless the whisky got to him fairly soon. It might be best to wait until after lunch to launch into the interview proper.

"I don't flatter myself you went to Paris just to see my work," Hugo said. "Why were you there?"

He was watching her under craggy eyebrows that could have been made of straw, so thick and coarse was each individual hair. She had the feeling that he was shrewder than he appeared. "My mother is French. She lives just outside Paris."

"Half French, are you?"

"Yes."

She waited for him to make the natural response, to say that his stepson also lived in France. Instead, he swallowed more whisky. After a while, he said, "Lived there myself for a while when I was younger. Had a studio up near Montmartre."

"Did you like France?"

"Very much. Very happy time. Met my wife there, as a matter of fact."

"The model for your *Leyla*?"

"How do you know that?" The thick eyelids blinked; beneath them the large eyes regarded her with moist suspicion. " 'S not in the catalogue."

Fran realized she had made an error. Alexander Campion had told her; she had assumed it was general knowledge. "I read it somewhere," she said evasively, "or perhaps someone told me."

But Hugo let the point go. Heaving himself out of his chair, he moved over to the decanters. "Strange woman, my wife," he said, pouring whisky into his glass and shaking his head. "Very strange."

"Will she be joining us for lunch? I should love to meet her."

"Not a joining sort of person," said Hugo. "Never was. Doesn't live here anymore, y'know."

"Oh. I'm very sorry. . . ."

"Don't be. I'm not altogether sorry m'self. Uncomfortable sort of woman, all in all."

"So you live here alone?"

Again he shot her a look from under his brows; she was beginning to find his compound of amusement and suspicion rather attractive. "From time to time," he said. She guessed that in spite of his alcoholic tendencies, he was still highly virile.

A housekeeper appeared to announce that lunch was ready. Although there were wineglasses on the table, Hugo carried the whisky decanter into the dining room.

It was a big room, with four long windows opening onto a prospect of wet lawns and two sweeping cedars bent under the weight of the rain. Beyond them was the mellow brick wall of a kitchen garden. Standing on a rug in front of the windows was a magnificent dapple-gray rocking horse.

"Isn't that beautiful?" Fran said. She touched the flowing mane of real horsehair, the saddle of thick red leather, the fiery red nostrils.

"Bought it for my girl," Hugo said. "Belonged to some Spanish grandee."

"Where does your daughter live?"

He wrested the prismed knob out of the whisky decanter and filled his tumbler to the top. "Don't want to talk about her," he said abruptly.

Addressing herself to the excellent lunch the housekeeper served them, Fran tried to think what the daughter—Amy, she remembered —might have done to deserve such a sternly Victorian veto. Illegitimate babies, running off with the chauffeur, smoking pot: for such sins, daughters might once have been sent out into the night, never to return, but in these enlightened days, parents had learned to tolerate almost all their children's peccadilloes.

■■

On their way back to the sitting room, where coffee was waiting, she could not resist running a hand over the rocking horse's rump. "It's gorgeous," she said.

"Used to be in the nursery, of course," Hugo said unexpectedly. He stood in the doorway. "Had him brought down here . . . afterward. Wanted to remember her as she was . . . she loved him. Called him after a horse of m'grandfather's." He pointed at a small oil which hung above the silver-laden sideboard and showed a row of stable doors and a small bow-legged man in a jockey cap holding the bridle of a gray horse in front of them. He turned away.

By the time she reached the sitting room, her host was slumped again in his armchair, staring into the fire. "Sit down, m'dear." He waved her toward the chair on the other side of the hearth.

"Shall I pour coffee?" she said. When he nodded, she did so, then got up and put a cup on the table beside him. When he ignored it, she added, as she might have done with Tom, "Drink it while it's still hot."

He laughed somewhere deep in his chest. "Talk to y'father like that, do you? Look after him, do you? Set him straight?"

"My father's dead," she said quietly.

He sat up a little. "I'm sorry, m'dear. Didn't mean to . . ."

"That's all right." Sensing that this might be the way in, she went on, "He was killed recently, in the Lebanon."

"Dreadful shock for you . . ."

"It was." She caught his eye and held it. "We loved him very much, my mother and I. He was much too young to die."

"Not as young as m'daughter."

"I'm sorry?"

The big swimming eyes did not blink. "Died when she was eleven. Car accident."

Appalled, Fran fiddled with the silver teaspoon in her saucer. "How terrible. I hadn't realized Amy was . . ." Underneath her more conventional feelings lay curiosity, though propriety and compassion stopped her from asking further questions. Why, when they were together in Paris, had Alexander Campion given her no indication that his sister was not still alive?

Hugo Campion's reddened eyes had grown suddenly sharp. "How do you know her name, anyway?"

This time she had an answer ready. "I did some research before I came," she said.

"But not enough."

"How do you mean?"

"Otherwise you would have known she was dead."

Their relationship—fragile and necessarily ephemeral—hung in the balance. Either he would order her out of the house, or he would tell her everything she had come here to learn. She could not decide where the key to unlocking him lay; with Alexander, perhaps, or by using her own bereavement? Or perhaps with neither. Perhaps it lay in pushing this battered man to talk about his daughter. Or in taking him into her confidence, telling him about her meeting with Alexander, asking him for his help. But to do so would involve so much explanation: she was not sure that in his present state she could hold his attention for long enough.

Before she could come to a decision, he looked down at his glass and said: "Murdered." The word exploded out of him in a kind of snort. *"Murdered."* He wiped his upper lip with the edge of his hand and she caught a glint of tears in his eyes.

"Your daughter was murdered?"

He nodded.

Instinctively she moved across to kneel beside him. "I saw the sculpture of her in Paris." She put her hand on his.

"Did it for her," he said. "First thing I'd done for years."

"And you only cast two versions of it." It no longer seemed to matter where she had obtained her information. If he asked, she would tell him.

"Yes. Don't own either of them. Can't even look at my own work anymore. My own daughter."

"Who does own them?" She vaguely recalled the name in the catalogue of the owner who had lent his version to the exhibition.

"M'stepson."

"Alexander?" Fran did not attempt to conceal either her acquaintance with Campion or her astonishment.

" 'S right. Bought them both, then came down here and smashed the mold so I couldn't make another."

Relieved that Alexander had become the subject of conversation, Fran wondered why he had lied to her about the sculpture and its owners.

Sir Hugo snuffled over his glass of whisky. "Loved her," he said. "Adored her."

"You did? Or—"

"Of course *I* did," he said, with the easy irritation of the drunk. "I was her father, dammit. Thing to do, love your own children. I meant Alexander. He adored her. As for that last business: knew there was something funny, Leyla accusing the boy of trying to rape his own sister. Ridiculous." He tried to rise, his gaze on the whisky decanter. She held his coffee in front of him and with a trembling hand he raised the cup to his mouth. "Shouldn't have banished the boy like that, not when he loved her so much. Never did understand why she hated him like that."

"His mother hated him?" Alexander had said the very same thing.

"Like poison." He handed her back the coffee cup. "Know him, do you?"

"I've met him."

"Then you can see what a mess she made of him. Shouldn't treat anyone the way she treated him."

Somewhere in the house dogs began barking loudly. She could hear the housekeeper shushing them. Rain pattered gently against the windows. "Why did she leave his father?" Fran asked. She refilled his cup with coffee.

"Far's I know, she found out he was carryin' on with some other woman. Found out that there was some little girl pregnant by him at the same time she was. Told me once that if her own baby had been a girl, would've left her there, but because it was a boy, she took it away with her, to spite the husband."

"Did you ever meet Alexander's father?" she asked.

"Why're you askin' me all these questions?" he said. "Wish you wouldn't, y'know."

"I'm sorry. I suppose I'm just naturally curious."

After a moment, he bent his head. She was horrified to see that he was weeping. Afraid of what he was going to say, she put a hand on his shoulder, telling herself that if she had any compassion, she would collect her things and leave. Lives, even the most ordinary, contained so much anguish. She had no right to wallow in someone else's pain. On the other hand, the desire to hear what Sir Hugo might say outweighed any scruples she might possess, and alcoholics cried easily, sometimes over nothing.

"Does he think I did it on purpose?" he said, his voice muffled. "Does he think I can forgive meself?" He looked up at her, tears shining in the contours of his rugged face. "Every minute of every hour, you're conscious of the enormity of what you've done. Know you could never put it right—know you're totally and absolutely to blame."

"What for?" Fran was feeling lost. Something terrible had happened, though she could not yet guess what.

"I loved her too," Hugo said. Tears fell through his beard to sit like pearls on the rough corduroy of his trousers. He put his hand on her arm and shook it violently. "She was my daughter, as well as his sister. I loved her as much as he did."

Fran wondered whether she should call the housekeeper, whether this kind of outburst was a normal part of the alcoholic cycle. She patted his shoulder, still unclear about the dramatis personae in what was evidently a long-endured wrong.

"I didn't mean to," he said violently. "God. Doesn't he think I'd undo it if I could?"

"Undo what?"

He was not going to answer, she could see. He was too caught up in his own self-excoriation; it sounded like familiar territory. "All I want's forgiveness, dammit," he mumbled, into his hands. "Surely, after all this time, fellow's entitled to some consideration of his feelings, some kind of . . . of appreciation that he's not the thick-skinned bugger some people think he is."

"Sir Hugo, I don't—"

"Look. Look at these." He picked up an album from the table beside him. "M'daughter. Amy."

She took it from him and leafed through the pages. The child Amy had been exceptionally pretty: big-eyed, dark-haired, lively. She saw cribs, tricycles, ponies, picnics, horses. Something about the span of photographs, from babyhood to preadolescence disturbed her: it took her a second or two to realize that Amy had had the same kind of looks as Sola.

There was a second album under the first. When Hugo did not offer it to her, she said: "Are those more photographs?"

"M'daughter's. Gave her a camera for her tenth birthday." Silently he handed her the imitation-leather album. Most of the pictures were of horses and dogs and a younger Hugo: thinner, less unkempt. Alexander, too, was a frequent subject, playing tennis, smiling, sitting on a wall. At the back there was a small square with the words, written in schoolgirl handwriting: *Alexander & his father.*

She turned it over. Dressed in school uniform, Alexander stood beside an older man whose arm was around his shoulders. Behind them were ancient creeper-covered buildings; the blurred images of other boys in boaters filled out the frame. Fran stared at them both, not believing what she saw. As Alicia Forrest had said, the two of them could have been brothers, so alike were they despite the years between them. Her spine felt cold. She felt as if she had made some momentous discovery that could lead to the places she wished to go, if only she could understand it.

The man with Alexander was the same one she had seen in another photograph, sitting with Sola on a terrace somewhere in Turkey.

She shut the book. There was a sound at the door. The housekeeper hovered, looking at her employer and shaking her head. Fran stood up. "I'll be back in a moment," she said. When Sir Hugo did not reply, she got her bag and went out into the passage.

"I'm sorry, Miss Brett." The housekeeper seemed resigned rather than regretful. "When he asked you down, I was afraid this might happen. He's drinking more and more these days."

"It doesn't matter," Fran said.

The two women stood together under the high-pillared portico of the house. In front of them, gray rain drove across sodden fields toward the low line of the Cotswolds.

"What exactly happened to Sir Hugo's daughter?" asked Fran.

"Miss Amy? It was terrible." The woman grimaced. "Just terrible. He was drunk as a lord; never should have been behind a wheel in that state. They were both killed: Miss Amy and the other gentleman."

"Oh no."

"Sir Hugo himself wasn't even scratched," said the housekeeper. "It might have been better if he had been."

"How did his stepson—Alexander—take it?"

"Very bad. It shattered him, poor lad. Came down for the funeral, went berserk in the middle of the service. Flew at Sir Hugo, sobbing and screaming. We all thought he was going to kill him. Had to call the police, in the end."

"What about Lady Campion?"

"Her? She couldn't even be bothered to turn up for her own daughter's funeral." The woman rubbed her hands up and down her forearms.

"Who was the other man?"

"Can't remember his name," she said. "Something foreign. Sir Hugo was driving him back to the station, and Miss Amy insisted on going along. He'd come down to see Lady Campion, but she refused to see him. Alex's father, he was, I think. It was dreadful."

"Poor Alexander," Fran said.

"It was sad times for everyone, Miss Brett."

But saddest, surely, for Alexander.

■■

As she drove, her brain tried to net together what pieces of information she had, but it proved impossible. For the moment, she did not know enough.

On the way back to London she kept a watch on the cars behind her, in case she was being followed. But it was difficult to be sure: so many cars, so many unremarkable colors and shapes. That cream-colored Cavalier—had she seen it before? Or that dark red Escort which had been behind her when she joined the A40 at Northleach: how long had it been on her tail? After a while, she tilted the mirror away from her. If she let it, paranoia would take over.

■■

On Monday, Fran interviewed the woman MP. Coming out of the Palace of Westminster, she looked up. The sky above Big Ben was blue, knotted with small clouds. A jet climbed, its wings catching the sun. Around her, monuments testified to the solidity of time and tradition, to man's tireless attempts to impose order on the chaos which constantly threatened to overwhelm him.

Instead of heading back to Hampstead, she rode the tube out to Heathrow. She called Max from there. He was still looking for a compatible computer. As soon as he found one, he would ring her: he had the numbers at Précy for both the telephone and the newly installed fax machine Tom had been so proud of.

"One other thing, Max," Fran said slowly. "It's just a long shot, really, but see what you can dig up about Sir Hugo Campion's wife, will you? Her name's Leyla."

"Lay what?"

She spelled the name out for him.

She was lucky: there were spare seats on the next flight to Paris. She ordered a drink from the flight attendant and let down the back of her seat; she leaned her head back and closed her eyes.

A long shot, she had said. After her years in journalism, she had learned that they were often the ones which most accurately hit the target. Belatedly, it had occurred to her to wonder why the man who had broken into her mother's house would wear a scarf around his face. Unless there was some compelling reason, it would obviously prove a hindrance. And what reason could be more obviously compelling than a desire—a *need*—to conceal his identity? But why would he bother to do that unless he knew that she—and Emilie—would recognize him? And how could she do that unless she already knew him or had met him somewhere?

Until then, she had not consciously admitted the possibility that

Alexander and the intruder might be one and the same. Having done so, however, it became all too easy to see him in other situations: stubbing out a lighted cigarette on the hands of a helpless woman, for instance, or even torturing to death the man who had finally caught up with him, despite the fact that the man and his family had once shown him kindness.

One by one, as she sorted through them, the facts seemed to support this theory. Indeed, there seemed almost too many pointers for it not to be true. And—yes!—it would explain what Daniel had attempted to convey through the title of a book: the saintly Alexander was in fact not a saint at all.

Did it fit in with what Max had told her? At first glance, she saw no reason why not. Alexander might even have set up the Phoenix Foundation out of idealism and a desire to give help to those who needed specialist care. And then gradually he had seen how easy it would be to pervert the Foundation's original intentions and found himself—perhaps without wishing it—embarked on the trail to deceit, extortion, and murder. It was not difficult to perceive how the child of a psychologically sadistic mother and a neglectful stepfather might have nursed a tremendous grudge against the kind of rich upper-middle-class society into which he had been flung—exactly the kind of people among whom he found himself when it came to setting up his organization. There was the additional fact that his aristocratic stepfather had caused the unnecessary deaths of the two people he seemed to have loved most. To someone of Alexander's background, revenge might even have seemed a matter of personal honor.

Through the window of the aircraft, Fran could see the Channel solid beneath her and seacraft dotted about on its choppy surface: freighters, a flurry of foam which must be a Hovercraft speeding toward Calais, a few white-sailed yachts.

She returned to Alexander. Given his brilliant mind, perverted by a lifetime of both deliberate and unintentional neglect—she remembered the passion in his voice as he spoke of the deformed bonsai tree —it was more than possible that he might conceive his revenge on a truly international scale. Not revenge on an individual, but on a whole class, on a whole type. Campion himself had told her that all the financial contributors to his organization were very rich: what could be more humiliating to the Establishment who sat on his various

boards—so he might reason—than to discover they had been supporting with their wealth a huge organization which underwrote terrorism, murder, or fraud on a grand scale, behind a philanthropic front?
Add to that a desire to control others, a love of manipulation—something she had so far seen only glimpses of, though aware that it lurked
at the core of his psyche—and you had a more than convincing sce-
nario.

The more she considered it, the more inevitable it seemed.

■■

By three o'clock she was unlocking the door of her car, parked at
Charles de Gaulle Airport. She turned toward the fashionable Paris
suburb of Neuilly and the house where the dead banker, Comte
Jacques de Tresail, had lived.

A maid let her in and led her toward the salon. From one of the
deep sofas a woman rose.

"I am Henriette de Tresail," she said. Her voice was husky; her
hair skillfully blonded, her person as immaculate and ultimately cold
as the coldly immaculate surroundings in which she sat. "Do please sit
down."

"It is good of you to see me," Fran said.

The woman shrugged. "I have little to occupy my time," she said.
She lit a cigarette and blew smoke into the air.

"You had no children?"

"No. Thank God."

"It was about your husband that I wished to ask," Fran said.

Henriette de Tresail arched inquiring eyebrows. "Yes?"

"He . . . er . . . killed himself, I believe."

"Yes."

"Could I ask—"

"Exactly as reported in the newspapers. With a revolver, in his
study." The Comtesse gave a wry smile. "Jacques always did the right
thing the right way."

Fran wondered if this woman ever showed emotion, or whether
her apparent coldness was a mask to cover real grief. She pushed
forward the newspaper cutting from her father's files. "You were
quoted at the time as saying that you could not understand why."

"He had absolutely no reason to do such a thing that I could find out. The police looked into it, too, and they could find nothing."

"It wasn't something like . . . well, another woman?"

"Certainly not. Jacques had a mistress, of course. I knew her well; we both agreed it was incomprehensible."

"What happened that day? What was he doing?"

"Tell me, mademoiselle, are you from the police?"

"No." Fran launched into the cover story she had dreamed up, part fact, part fudge. "My father—he was a journalist—also died in circumstances that were not entirely clear, and I wished to find out what he was investigating at the time. This newspaper cutting was in his office and I wondered if it could have had any bearing on his death. You must know yourself, madame, how one seeks for some kind of explanation . . ."

Madame de Tresail seemed to accept that. She nodded. "My husband went to the bank as usual in the morning. He lunched with a business colleague, then attended a board meeting. After it, he rang me to say he would be meeting a colleague for a drink but would be home for dinner at the usual time. We ate together. I had a bath and went to bed. When he did not come upstairs, I went down to his office and found him there." She looked fiercely at her cigarette as she stubbed it out in a crystal ashtray. She did not wish to remember Jacques with half his head gone, spattered on the wall beside him, nor the shape of the bloodstain on his desk, exactly like—she had thought at the time—the island of Crete, where they had planned to holiday later in the year.

"And his colleagues at the bank noticed nothing odd?"

"Nothing."

"Did he have any appointments that morning with anyone?"

"There was nothing in his book."

"Who was the business colleague he had lunch with?"

"The police talked to him—he too had seen nothing at all to suggest that Jacques might . . . do what he did."

"What about the person he had a drink with after the meeting?"

She frowned very slightly, then ran her fingers across her forehead to smooth out the lines that the frown had caused. "They don't know who it was. It was the only bit of his day unaccounted for.

There was a phone call from someone who did not give his name to Jacques's secretary, but nothing else."

"And he was all right when he got home?"

"Perfectly. We had our usual aperitif and then dined together."

"And he seemed no different from usual?"

Again she frowned. "Naturally, I've thought and thought about it. But I was excited about some stupid project of my own: I rattled on about it all through dinner; it's possible I simply didn't notice."

"Did he leave a note?"

"The police took it. He said he had got himself involved with something dreadful and that this was the only honorable way out."

"And you have no idea what the something was?"

"None whatever."

"There was no suggestion"—delicately Fran paused—"at the bank, I mean, of—"

"Embezzlement? Fraud?" Henriette de Tresail smiled ruefully. "Nothing whatsoever. Jacques was from a generation and a background that valued honor above everything: he would rather have died than be mixed up with something so sordid."

Which is exactly what he seems to have done, Fran thought. "What about the board meeting he attended? Was it something to do with the bank?"

"It is a charity. Jacques was a philanthropist—he often said that it was only chance that made him rich and that it was his duty to share what he had. I now sit on the board myself, in his place. A most respected institution."

"What is it called?"

"La Fondation Phénix. A friend of ours, Gilles Laforêt, originally suggested it to Jacques. It's a medical charity, raising funds for . . ."

The woman's deep voice went into explanations which Fran scarcely heard. Excitement thick as broth engulfed her. Was this it, the pointer she had been looking for—the first definite link between the Foundation and the possibility of worldwide financial chaos and murder?

Was it possible that the final meeting of Jacques de Tresail's final day had been with someone who told him that the whole Phoenix Foundation setup was in fact a front for something very different? It was the sort of information that such a man might find impossible to live with: death was better than dishonor.

Could that informant even have been Daniel? It was perfectly feasible. And had he subsequently been murdered in a frenzy of rage because, by informing Jacques de Tresail of the truth, he had endangered the whole dreadful setup?

She remembered Istanbul, and Daniel bending to tie his shoe outside a gate. Why had they been there? Had he taken her there deliberately, using her as cover in case anyone saw him? Was an untied shoelace the only pretext he could think of on the spur of the moment to conceal his identity when the man with the martyr's face had so unexpectedly emerged, and looked at her, and walked away? And was that face—could it have been—Alexander's? She could only remember a haunted look: nothing more.

■■

By day, the street where Sola lived was even more depressing. Last time Fran was here, darkness had protected the eye from the trash in the gutters, the rotting window frames, the peeling paintwork. The light of a coldish sun set among scudding clouds only intensified the squalor. Fran had already tried to ring the model at Gallini's but was told that she had not come to work that day. Trying her home again was a long shot, but necessary if Fran's plan was to succeed. She had not had time to analyze when exactly she became certain that Daniel Forrest and her father were victims of the same aggressor, but she was sure of one other thing: that she herself was alive only because he did not know where Tom Brett had hidden his information and thought she might. Once he got hold of it, there would be no reason for him not to kill her. Before that happened, she somehow had to flush him out.

At Sola's building, there was no sign of the concierge. Fran stepped into the rickety lift and was carried up to the attic floor. It smelled both fusty and, in some organic way, disgusting. Wrinkling her nose as she stepped out on the top floor, she was aware of silence absorbing her, as shrouding as cotton wool. The door of the model's flat faced her; like the Jaws of Death, it gaped at the end of the dimly lit passage.

Why was it half open like that? Fran frowned at the slice of dark space: what lay behind it? Something must have happened, something terrible, for Sola so to expose her privacy to the possible intrusion of strangers. As before, Fran was sharply aware of how lonely it was up here on the top floor, cut off from the rest of the building's inhabitants.

Unless she investigated, she would never know the truth, and she needed whatever information Sola could give her. There had been a connection between her and Daniel; now she knew that there was also some link between the girl and Alexander, via his father. Sola might well know something crucial.

Reluctantly Fran started toward the door again. The passage assumed the qualities of a nightmare: its proportions distorted, its length infinitely extended, so that she began to feel that however far and fast she walked, she would never reach its end. Since her last visit, there had been what looked like an unskillful attempt to brighten up the dingy cream walls. The illusion lasted only as long as it took her brain to register that these were not decorations but handprints. Like rust-red flowers they blossomed along the passage leading away from the flat toward the lift doors—some at waist level, others, ominously, down near the baseboard. At intervals along the dusty length of corridor, the floorboards were darkened with patches of something which had dried thickly into the wood.

Was it blood?

Keeping one eye on the half-open door, she knelt and dragged her forefinger through one of the stains. In the murky light it was difficult to tell whether the resulting smudge was due to dust or something worse. Not that it mattered; those spectral handprints said enough.

She felt inside her bag and brought out her father's gun. At least she had had the sense to stop at Précy and pick it up. Whatever had happened in Sola's flat, she had come too far to avoid it. She steeled herself for the very worst: blood and torn flesh; dead staring eyes, splintered bone. Slowly, she pushed open the door.

Despite the brightness of the afternoon outside, the apartment contained little of it. The short entrance hall was dark; instead of bouncing the occasional sunlight off its white walls, the big room was gray and subdued. At first glance, Fran could see nothing wrong beyond the fact that Sola had apparently left without tidying up. Clothes had been dropped here and there, and the black-blanketed bed had not been made. It was only after a long second look that she saw the pools of coagulated blood on the polished boards, the tattered state of the blanket, the rips in the mattress underneath. At bed level, the walls were splashed with brown; irregular liver-colored smears reached upward as though a bleeding hand had grabbed desperately for purchase on the wall's smooth skin. The smell of sex and something frantic hung in the blood-scented air.

Gun alert, Fran tiptoed toward the louvered kitchen doors and kicked them open. The little galley was untouched by whatever explosion had taken place in the main room. Nonetheless, Fran's sharp eye noted, with a curling in the stomach, that of the six knives which had hung on the magnetic holder last time she was here, one—the smallest and sharpest—was missing. Backing out, she looked up at the cruel crucifix, and shuddered to see a spatter of dried blood on its wounded feet.

The authorities had clearly not been alerted to the violence which had taken place, otherwise they would be keeping the flat under strict guard. Yet there had been two people here, very recently, and one of them had been badly hurt. Had Sola been the victim or the aggressor? Either way, where was she now? Fran turned to the clothes. As well as garments which were recognizably Sola's, there was male underwear, socks, a light jacket. When she picked it up, it gave off a faint spicy odor which immediately made her sweat. She prodded the jacket gingerly, feeling for the stiffness of a wallet or some means of identification. There was none.

There was another door, not quite shut. Slowly, avoiding the blood on the floor, Fran moved her feet toward it. Matte-black. A spherical brass handle, dulled now with dried blood. Dark handprints. Using the tip of her finger, Fran pushed it wider. Some object rattled along the floor, a flat cylinder, double-lidded. She bent and picked it up, twisting one of the lids: uncomprehendingly, she looked down at the tiny blue saucer of glass. Through the door she could smell soap and damp toweling—and something far worse: the results of the body's final relaxation before death. Mixed in with them was the ponderous smell she associated with a butcher's shop, and the iron stench of blood.

It was unnecessary for her to go in there. She could see from where she stood the black shape of an arm against the white gleam of the bathtub and the sprawl of long legs against tiles. Nonetheless, she reached for the cord that snapped on the bathroom light. She owed it to the dead body which lay beyond the door. Someone ought to recognize the pain which had led to this final ugly moment of despair.

She looked down at the face which rested against the edge of the bath. It was smooth, the brown skin unmarked by the wild streaks of blood which dribbled from the gashes tearing frenziedly across the chest and from the modest wound above the heart. On the cheeks shone tears; she touched one, feeling her own grief rise in her throat. Something which had once been beautiful was now no more than dead meat. Such waste, she thought; such intolerable sadness.

Lying on the floor was the knife missing from the kitchen.

■■

Going back down in the lift, she reached into her bag and brought out the photograph showing Philippe and Campion aboard the *Phoenix,* with Daniel standing to one side. It was possible that the concierge might have seen something. But dragged from her warm room, the woman pouted, shrugged, wagged her head from side to side. Yes, someone she did not know had come downstairs a couple of nights ago, though she had no way of telling from which *appartement.* No, certainly she had not seen blood on anyone, nor any wounded visitors, this was a respectable neighborhood, mademoiselle; such things might happen in other places, but not here. As for Mademoiselle Bonami, she had not seen her for a day or two, perhaps she was away, and the photographs meant nothing to her, mademoiselle, nothing at all. Not surprisingly, her eyes strayed continually toward the cobalt attractions of a television set which continued to whinny through some game show while she answered Fran's queries.

Fran told her to call the police.

· 24 ·

Having established with a phone call to the hospital that her mother was all right, Fran took the motorway to Reims. There was no point in procrastinating; it was time she took a closer look at the Fondation Phénix. Besides, after the horror of Sola's *appartement* she felt an urgent need for peace and order and the cleanliness of earth and sky. She wanted to see again the long, calm landscapes among which Philippe de Pierrey spent his life. She wanted, if the truth were told, to see Philippe himself. As she drove she kept a watch in the rearview mirror, but if anyone was following her, they were doing it unobtrusively.

She drove straight to the château, bypassing the Pierrey office in the town. The squat building seemed to welcome her, its old stone walls inviting. She desperately hoped Philippe would be there.

He was. The housekeeper pointed her toward the vines and, shading her eyes, she could see his tall figure among them. He seemed astonished to see her coming toward him through the leaves. "How did you get here so quickly?" he said.

"It wasn't that quick," said Fran, looking at him with pleasure. Although they had met only once before, his tousled dark hair and well-shaped mouth now seemed warmly familiar.

"But I only called the number you gave me a couple of hours ago. They said you were in England."

"I have been. Now I'm here."

"Good." Uncertainly, he smiled at her. She smiled back.

"Why did you ring me?" she said.

"Because there is something I wished to tell you." He knew he ought to say also that he wanted an excuse to see her again, but did not do so.

She smiled again, unexpectedly glad to be with him. "I'm listening."

"When I heard that Daniel had died, it was as though I had been kicked in the stomach," Philippe said. He walked up and down in front of her, frowning. "I kept trying to think why anyone would want to kill him—and in such a way. But now, I begin to wonder whether maybe he had not really resigned his commission. I think maybe he was still employed by the Army and that he was investigating something for them." He stopped in front of her. "Something, possibly, near here."

"Why did you think that?" asked Fran. He was echoing her own thoughts.

"Yesterday I was in the room where he stayed, looking through the books." His face reddened. He did not want to say that he had gone up to Daniel's room as a way of re-creating Fran's visit for himself, nor that he had stood looking up at the bookshelves, remembering the way her dark hair swept down toward her shoulders.

"Yes?"

"I took down the copy of *Great Expectations*—it was a favorite of Daniel's—and when I put it back, there was something hidden behind it. When I felt around, I found a gun."

He paused, waiting for her reaction.

Disappointment tugged at Fran's face. She had to force herself not to show it. Of *course* Daniel would have had a gun. Before she could say so, Philippe said, "I had to ask myself why he would wish to have a gun at Lavandière."

"An ex-Army man," she said flatly. "Or an Intelligence officer. It doesn't astonish me in the least."

"Oh." He seemed surprised at her reaction; almost hurt.

She followed him between the stunted bushes. Grapes hung in bunches among the leaves; the air was vinous and very clear. In spite of the sun, the coming winter lingered behind the breeze which came softly down from the hills.

"I love this place," Philippe said.

"It's beautiful."

"I love to watch the seasons change, and the way the cycles repeat themselves, year after year." He turned in a circle, taking in the land. "When I was at the Sorbonne, I joined a political group. We called ourselves anarchists, although we were really nothing more than bored kids—children of wealthy families seeing our last chance to rebel before we all settled down to do the things that were expected of us. Marrying someone suitable, taking over the family business. It was all very stupid and juvenile, at least eventually for most of us. But one of us took it very seriously. A boy called Jean-Luc Zulyan. He claimed to be a *pied-noir*—an Algerian—and he hated all authority, especially the cops. He had contacts with all sorts of people. He'd been in prison and met terrorists from groups all over Europe. Dreadful people like the Baader-Meinhofs and the Red Brigade. Once he brought someone to talk to us, someone very high up. It was horrible to sit there in the room with such a man, knowing that he had actually killed people."

Fran picked one of the creamy-green grapes and brushed at the bloom on the skin. She smiled at him again, filled with quiet. She felt no need to speak.

"I found this man quite appalling: so handsome, so young, not much older than I was. He could have been anything—a doctor, a teacher, a lawyer—and he had chosen to be a killer."

"Where does Daniel come into this?"

"Yes." Philippe smoothed a leaf across the back of his hand. "Another thing I should tell you is this: I saw Jean-Luc again last week, after you had been here. He was coming out of that monastery place over there—"

"La Fondation Phénix."

"Yes. Do you know about them?"

"A bit. Did this man see you?"

"No." He stopped, turning to face her. They were close enough for her to see in his irises the soft accumulation of flecks of green and brown and umber which together gave his eyes their particular shade of hazel. "Since your visit, Fran, I've thought much more about Daniel and his time here with us. Remember I told you he used to go out at night dressed in old clothes?"

"Go on."

"Why would a man do that? Surely not to see a woman."

"The English take women less seriously than the French do," she said gravely.

He laughed. "But they have brought spying to a fine art."

"You think that's what Daniel was doing—spying?"

"Why not?"

"On this Jean-Luc?"

"Perhaps that makes sense. Believe me, the man was a fanatic and I can't imagine that he has changed a lot since I knew him. I'm absolutely convinced that he was responsible for an explosion in Paris —" He broke off and turned his face to the wide sky, then added, "Someone I knew was killed."

"Someone you loved?" Fran asked. His pain was as pungent between them as pepper shaken into the air.

"She was an innocent. She should not have died. Jean-Luc murdered her." Anger throbbed. The murder of innocents was insupportable. "If such a person belongs to this Fondation Phénix, then even though they live in a religious house I do not believe they can be men of God."

All things come together. Chaos swirls constantly about us, but when the darkness lifts, there is sometimes Form.

As soon as Philippe sent the words swinging out above the fecund vines, Fran knew, absolutely, that he was right, as though the knowledge had been there since the first time she saw the arched gate in Istanbul, and the man with the martyr's face who had come through it into the street where she stood with Daniel kneeling at her feet.

All things come together. As memories, shifting like splintered glass, will come together and for a moment give the illusion of a perfect mirror.

She knew the man, had seen him again—recently. He had not been walking away, then, but facing her. His head had moved in the same way, like a bird watching for danger. And she was the danger.

She remembered the police commissioner she had read about only that morning, gunned down in a provincial Swedish street, in front of his red-painted, white-trimmed house: Alexander Campion had just flown to Sweden. She thought about Comte Jacques de Tresail: he had sat on the board of Campion's organization. And the man who had come so abruptly through that gate: it had not been Alexander Campion, but it might have been his brother.

All things come together, as they were doing here, in these flat fields.

"It's why he came here, I'm sure," Philippe was saying. He shrugged. "I can see that now. I thought it was true, what he said about wanting to go into winemaking. I even hoped he might one day go into partnership with me . . ."

Another betrayal, Fran thought. Daniel seemed to have been good at them. Can the end ever justify the means? And how often do the means which are used destroy far more than can be saved by the end that is reached?

"Do you think he knew who this Jean-Luc was?" she said.

"I'm certain of it."

She could not resist the urge to reach out to touch Philippe, connect herself with him in some way and give him comfort. She put her hand on his bare arm. Under her fingers the strong black hair felt as smooth as oil. It could be dangerous, she knew; nonetheless she wanted to stroke him.

■■

Later, she sat with the two widows, Philippe's mother and grandmother. They sat rigidly upright; ease and relaxation were not words they would comprehend. Opposite her, Philippe lounged uneasily on a rigidly upholstered sofa. She had not wished to stay for dinner, but he had insisted. She had told him that despite his conviction about Jean-Luc Zulyan, she did not think the real danger lay nearby, though it was worth taking a look around.

"Tonight?"

"Yes," she said. "After all, Daniel found something here that sent him straight to Istanbul."

"We might have to go there too," he said, and she had felt an anticipatory pleasure at the prospect of being with him in that turbulent city of towers and domes.

They ate in a big cold dining room, served by two maids. Across the table, the two widows watched her with eyes that judged. It was difficult to imagine that either of them had ever been young: somewhere along the way, all the juice had been pressed out of them.

The two of them spoke only of the business, addressing Philippe rather than his guest. He found himself growing angry at their rudeness, embarrassed even though he suspected it was due to singlemindedness rather than lack of courtesy.

Geneviève, his mother, said, "Philippe, there have been telephone calls. You will have to go to Spain."

"When?"

"As soon as you can."

"If I am here," he told her.

"Where else would you be?"

From the disbelief in her voice, he realized how far down the road toward nonentity he had traveled. "I may have to go abroad," he said firmly.

"When?"

"Very soon. Perhaps tomorrow." Fran nodded back at him supportively. She could not know, he thought, that part of the reason he intended to join her on her journey to Istanbul was so that he could lay to rest the gentle ghost of Mihri. Once that task was completed, there was so much that he hoped for from Fran herself; so very much. He looked at her with eyes that glowed, not caring if the widows noticed.

They were too preoccupied to do so. "But where do you intend to go?" his mother demanded.

"To Istanbul."

The bewilderment on her face might have been a cause for laughter if it had not emphasized the extent to which they had come to dominate his life. It had not always been like this; only since Mihri's death had he allowed himself to be so buffeted by the winds of indecision. Now, with Fran here, he saw them dying down at last.

"But you cannot do this," his grandmother interposed, her voice high and whistling. She was very old now, her grasp on life tenuous. He had not, he realized, expected her to last so far into his own life.

"Besides, you were in Istanbul not so long ago," said Geneviève.

"And you are expected in Spain."

"The two of you will take care of the matter, I don't doubt," he said. "As you always have."

"Why are you going to Istanbul? What is there in such a place for us, for the House?" Geneviève said. Her face had begun to screw itself into ugly lines.

"I'm not going for the House, I'm going for myself," said Philippe. "It is something I have to do."

"Is it to do with that girl you brought here once?" said Laure.

"No." He shook his head. He had never told either of them of

Mihri's death, nor did he intend to expose her to them now. He saw Fran grow still. "It is to do with Daniel."

The two widows exchanged glances. "Daniel is dead," Laure said patiently.

She speaks as though he is feebleminded, thought Fran. She wanted to say that the dead have as much right to justice, to vengeance, even to hope, as the living. Wanted to say, also, that the dead had few friends. The widows would not understand that, had anyone ever stood up to them in the past? *I would, if it was necessary. If it would help Philippe.* She wondered about the girl that he had brought to meet this formidable pair.

"I am going too," she said firmly. "We shall not be away long."

Geneviève ignored her. "There is business here that requires your attention tonight, Philippe," she said. She had not yet recognized mutiny, or that control was slipping from her hands.

"The business will have to wait," said Philippe. He stood up abruptly, the noise of his chair loud in the suddenly quiet room. "Frances and I are going out."

■■

They lay crouched between the vines in the field opposite the gateway to the complex of buildings which housed the Fondation Phénix. They had expected calm. Instead, through the wide-flung gates of the former monastery they could see a floodlit courtyard, the focus of intense activity. At least a dozen trucks were lined up side by side, their engines throbbing, while men in *bleu de travail* loaded them up with rapid efficiency. Hundreds of cartons labeled as sterilized dressings, disposable hypodermics, splints, and disinfectants were stacked beside each one, along with flat-packed kits of surgical instruments, plasma bags, collapsible stretchers, blankets, and sterilizing equipment. Every kind of emergency that might hit a devastated community had been catered for; generators, motorbikes, and inflatable dinghies were among the equipment being hoisted into the trucks. As the loading of each vehicle was completed, it nosed out through the gateway and roared off in the direction of the airport. Three white Volkswagen minibuses—the letters *FP* painted on the side in red—were also being prepared, and half a dozen Toyota four-wheel-drives with the same logo stood quivering, ready to head off after the trucks.

"There was an earthquake in Mexico last night," Fran whispered. "A bad one. I read about it on the plane this morning."

"Does that mean these people are who they say they are?" His voice was sour. "I don't believe it."

"Even if we get inside, what do you hope to find?" Fran's earlier certainty had given way to doubt: they had been watching the place for nearly two hours now and seen nothing in the least suspicious. Something else niggled at her: why exactly had Philippe been so insistent that they come here now?

"Something. There has to be something." Philippe was aware that he sounded less than rational. For so many months Mihri's death had fluttered before him, his memories of her torn and bloodied like the remnant of her white scarf. Running parallel had been his total but unprovable conviction that Jean-Luc Zulyan had been responsible. His recent encounter with the man had acted on him like a stimulant, enhanced by the emotion that Fran had stirred in him. He *needed* to prove that the Foundation was not what it seemed. Now, lying here among the vine roots with Fran's face close enough to kiss, he was afraid that his proof was slipping away from him. "I intend to find it."

"It may be in Istanbul," said Fran.

■■

It was another hour and a half before the last of the *FP*-marked trucks trundled out through the gateway, followed by the fleet of four-wheel-drives. The men loading the supplies had jumped into the back of the final truck; about twenty others, each carrying a black medical bag, had climbed aboard the minibuses, and the whole procession had turned in the direction of Reims. A final car stood waiting. Walking jauntily out of the shadows, a man appeared and stood for a moment beside it, checking something on a clipboard.

Philippe stiffened. "That's him," he whispered strenuously. "That's Zulyan." He felt as if his veins would burst with the effort he was making not to rush forward and kill the man with his bare hands. Instead, he waited beside Fran as the Algerian got into the car and drove away after the convoy. Within minutes, the courtyard lights had been switched off and the tall gates shut.

After the long throbbing of diesel engines, the shouts of the loaders, the glare of the floodlights, quiet descended with an almost audible thump. The ancient buildings returned to their normal state of calm. Gradually the ordinary noises of the night reasserted themselves: cicada chat, a night bird's croak, the distant rush of a train.

Philippe and Fran waited thirty cautious minutes longer before emerging from the vines. Keeping low and close in to the walls, they made their way to the rear of the complex.

"Can you get over?" Fran whispered.

Philippe looked up at the height of old brick. "Probably. There are plenty of footholds."

"Quite a drop on the other side."

"I'll have to go back to the car for something first. But I'll manage."

"I hope *I* will."

They separated. Fran followed the wall around until she came to the road, then walked toward the brass plaque and the bell set into the wall beside it. She pressed it and waited.

After a while, a metallic voice spoke in French from a hidden grille. "Yes?"

Using the same language, Fran said, "My car has broken down."

"What do you wish me to do?" The voice sounded surly, unwilling. It was not the voice of an educated man.

"I need to telephone a garage: I suppose the nearest one's in Reims," Fran said.

"One moment."

She heard the intercom cut off. She realized that even if she did succeed in getting inside, she would probably discover little. There would be no excuse for her to go farther than the porter's lodge, unless she could manufacture one.

There was more faint squawking. The voice said, "No one is here."

"You are," Fran said.

"Everyone has gone to give medical aid." The voice ignored her. "There have been bad floods, earthquakes."

"I'm not asking for medical aid," she said tartly. "Just the use of a telephone."

The intercom clicked. There was another long pause. She waited, tensed, as the bolts on the other side of the gate were dragged open. The man who poked his head out at her was small and dark, his underslung jaw giving him a simian aspect which the thick rough robe he wore did little to dispel. He glanced suspiciously up and down the road. "Where is your car?" he said. His accent was guttural, his French obviously poor.

Fran waved vaguely into the distance behind her. "Back there. I've walked quite a long way. This is the first place I've come to."

"Come in then." He stood aside to let her enter, then pointed her toward a door just inside the gate. Yellow light oozed from a small window: she could see pale walls, empty shelves, a table. "I'm only the gatekeeper, not a receptionist. You'll have to wait in here while I find a telephone directory." He shuffled away.

Once inside his lair, she realized he had spoken the literal truth. He was the keeper of the gate, nothing more, there for the sole purpose of opening and closing the heavy wooden doors which shielded the place from the outside. Any visitors would be directed farther in. In the center of it she could just make out the shape of one last minibus standing alone: none of the surrounding windows was lit. While he was gone, she pulled the drawer in the wooden table, and opened the cupboard set into the wall. One contained a poorly washed knife and fork; the other a pile of vaguely pornographic magazines. Entertainment for the long hours of idleness between opening and closing the gates, she guessed; it was obvious that this man was of low intellect and unlikely to be more than on the periphery of the Foundation's activities.

She looked around once more: there was absolutely nothing of significance—a dusty telephone, two chairs pulled up to an oilcloth-covered table, a tray containing a glass, a bottle of orange drink, and a mug, a single electric ring plugged into a socket on the wall.

Did she have the guts to slip out before the man returned and lose herself among the other buildings? If he was really alone here, she would surely find it easy to elude him. But before she could decide, he reappeared, carrying a directory.

By the light of the bulb above their heads, she saw that he was not old, as she had at first supposed, but about her own age, wiry and fit. When he slid the book around the table toward her, keeping a hand on its cover, she took it from him but he did not let it go. She edged round the table away from him. He followed. It gave her the opportunity she had been looking for. One more corner and she would have the open door right behind her.

She moved fast around the edge of the table and dashed for the door, hand outstretched for the latch so that she could slam it behind her. To her amazement, there was a key in the outer lock. She turned it. As she ran toward the central courtyard, she could hear his fists beating against the panels of the door.

There were no lights anywhere. She turned away from the modern building which ran along one side of the quadrangle: she had already marked it down as the residential quarters. Equally she rejected the chapel, which lay opposite. That left two other sides: the one in front of her, and the one behind, running from either side of the entrance gate to complete the square. She tried the first door of the two-story building directly facing her: it was locked. So were all the others along its front. She flashed her torch in at the windows: variously she saw gray metal filing cabinets, typewriters, computers, directories. Offices: they seemed an innocent and unlikely setting for the hatching of conspiracies.

She ran back toward the gate building: the doors along it were all shut tight. Peering in at a window, she found she was looking at what appeared to be a fully equipped and up-to-date laboratory. Farther along were stockrooms crammed with more medical supplies.

There was still the chapel. She made for it, keeping to the edge of the courtyard, her feet making almost no sound on the hard-packed yellow earth. The door was half open. She pushed it and smelled the chill odor she always associated with Catholicism: the wraiths of incense, damp stone, mustiness, slow dissolution. She beamed her torch around. The place was being used as a storehouse: the interior had been stripped of everything that once gave it meaning—font, pews, altar rails—and huge containers of supplies now occupied the entire central space. Narrow defiles between the crates and boxes permitted access. A couple of forklifts and a small derrick stood at the rear: high above them shone the guileless faces of stained-glass saints.

She thought, *My house shall be called the house of prayer, but ye have made it a den of* . . . what, exactly? Why did she feel that there was something anarchical about this accumulation of supplies heaped with such careless disregard on consecrated ground? Philippe's remark came back to her: *I do not believe they can be men of God.*

What could Daniel have found out from this place that had sent him to Istanbul under a false name? She sniffed, trying to distinguish something—oil, metal—that might prove the boxes stacked all around her contained not medical supplies but arms.

Something scraped behind her. She whirled around. Was that movement she saw, behind one of the vast towers of cartons? She switched off her torch and moved to the side in a crouching run so that she was no longer where she had just been. Stepping lightly, holding her breath, she made for the arched shape of lighter darkness which indicated the chapel door. But even as she moved, she stopped suddenly, her lungs tightening in her chest, her heart banging. Blood rushed brightly to her head: for a moment, fear darkened her vision.

When it cleared, the man was still there. Silhouetted like a crucifix, arms outspread against the doorposts, he stood with the night sky behind him, his outline in the long gown with the hood up over his head, irrationally menacing.

Fran waited, backed up against a wall of cardboard. Could he see her? Could he hear the pounding of her blood? She dared not even drop to the ground in case the rustle of her clothes gave away her position. She thought that the moment before death must also contain this same sudden knowledge of imminent infinity which blocks out all terror.

She forced herself to think rationally: he could not know where she was, nor could he advance farther into the chapel without the risk that she would escape. Perhaps the two of them would stand there for hours, until help came. But would it be help for him, or for her? She wondered where Philippe was, and with the thought of him came new strength.

Carefully she eased from her pocket a couple of coins. Slowly raising her arm, she flung one of them away from her, between the cartons. The noise it made was not convincing.

The man laughed, quietly. The backs of her knees began to tremble.

Suddenly he spoke, his voice a whisper that nonetheless echoed somewhere in the vaulted roof spaces. "Frances Brett," he said. "I recognized you at once from the porter's description."

She said nothing.

He spoke again. "Come out of hiding, Frances Brett. I shall wait for you, however long you stay there." He paused, as though expecting a reply. When none came, he went on, "And when the morning comes, we shall find you without difficulty." Another pause. "What happens after that is up to you."

Sweat ached in Fran's armpits; the soles of her feet prickled with fear. She wanted to cry out. She tried not to think of Daniel and how his final hours might have been.

Her opponent knew how to inspire terror: the whisper was part of the disorientation which always was the first stage in extracting information from his victims. The fact that she was here at all meant that there had been much more information in Brett's files than he anticipated—the fire had obviously not caused the damage he hoped.

Peering into the darkness of the chapel, he could not see where she was, though every nerve of him was alive to the danger she represented. If she was carrying a gun, as she had in Précy, he was in mortal danger: by now she would have realized how foolish she had been in not firing at him last time.

Once again he was aware of her fearlessness, and his own admiration for it. In the world he now inhabited, courage was perhaps all there was left to admire. Listening for the slightest sound of movement from the English girl, he thought suddenly, unexpectedly: *I am tired of all this.*

It had gone on for too long, this hiding in darkness, this stalking of innocents to protect guilt. But there was no way out for him now. He carefully raised his hand and adjusted the silk scarf which covered his face. The thing was a necessary encumbrance; if once he was seen, half recognized, by her, she would be able to snap the links in the chain one by one, and bring down the entire structure which had taken so long to build.

How much easier it would be if he could kill her outright without waiting to question her. But that was not possible: he had to establish how much she had found out and whom she had told. To do that, he had to catch her.

"Frances," he breathed into the dank air of the chapel. "Will you want it to be slow, Frances? Slow and painful, like Daniel Forrest? Or will you help us and make it easier on yourself? Make it faster?"

The whisper roared in her ears, filling the chapel with ugly sound. She wanted to ask, "Who is us?" even though he would be unlikely to reply. Instead, she bit down on her lower lip. These were the tactics of intimidation: they could work only if the victim allowed them to. Philippe was outside somewhere and the man who threatened her was alone—except for the porter. At least . . . Once again the doubts she had felt about Philippe burst into the open. Had she walked into a trap? It would be all too easy to dispose of her here, to stow her body among the piled cartons, for Philippe to return and say she had left for Paris, to shrug off further inquiries by saying he had no idea where she was.

She shivered. Yet underneath the fear she tried not to feel was the strange exultation of the journalist who has followed a hunch and seen it pan out into a full-fledged story. Because she now knew she finally had the incontrovertible proof she needed: the connection between the Phoenix Foundation and the death of Daniel. It should be only a tiny step from there to finding the evidence that would link them with her father.

This was the big one every journalist hoped for, the once-in-a-lifetime scoop that would put her up there with the legendary names like Max Blum, like Nicholas Tomalin, like James Cameron. Like, even, Tom Brett.

That was when she heard the sound behind her and realized that she was trapped.

· 25 ·

THERE WAS NO LONGER ANY point in concealment. "Who *are* you?" she said. Her voice felt dry and tense. "What do you want from me?"

He did not reply. She had not really expected him to. So she opened her mouth and began screaming. Noise helped to disconcert the would-be assailant, or so she had been told in her women's self-defense class. It might also bring Philippe to her aid.

The sides of the cardboard cliffs which towered around her were smooth, impossible to get a grip on; underfoot the floor was smooth, too, free of any loose object that could be picked up and used as protection. She was painfully aware of her lack of weapon; if either man caught up with her, she would not stand a chance. She cursed herself for stupidly leaving her father's gun in her car, back at the Château Pierrey.

A shadow moved behind the figure straddled across the doorway. Feet slipped on loose earth: there was the sound of a shot, and then another. The man at the entrance moved even before the first of them —but inward or out? She froze. Where was he? Who had fired the gun?

In the close darkness of the chapel she heard footsteps, a rapid breath, a flurry of air as though someone passed nearby. Shrinking against the cartons, she tried to still all movement within her body. If he realized how close she was, he would certainly try to grab her, if only to use as a hostage. As soon as she was sure he had passed her, she continued quietly toward the door. She dared not call out.

Then, as she waited, backed up in the shadows against one cold stone wall of the small porch, she heard Philippe call her name. When he called again, she ran into the courtyard toward his dim figure. She could see in his hand the long silhouette of a shotgun. "Yes," she whispered. "Let's get out of here."

Together they raced for the gateway. Philippe tugged at the small door cut into the larger. The door of the adjacent gatehouse stood wide. Out in the road, they made for Philippe's car. Adrenaline pumped into their bloodstreams and they ran like Olympic medalists.

Only when Philippe was gunning his car toward home did either of them relax. Then Fran began to shake as terror drained slowly out of her body, leaving it limp. "Oh, my God," she said. She buried her face in her hands, her wrists feeling almost too weak to support it.

Philippe put one arm around her trembling shoulders. "Don't think about it anymore."

"That man . . . his voice . . . the things he was saying."

"I heard some of it."

"It's that dreadful whisper." Fran turned to him. "Philippe, I thought I was going to die." Helplessly she began to cry.

Philippe drove without speaking, watching the road behind him in the mirror. No one came after them. He kept one hand firmly on Fran's thigh, realizing she needed the warmth of human contact. Thank God he had brought the gun with him. He was aware of bone-shaking anger; women, however strong they might appear, were creatures of emotion, prey to fears which men could only guess at. Fran had seemed so fearless; seeing her like this, self-control gone, brought a surge of tenderness for her. His hands tightened on the steering wheel until he thought he heard the leather-covered plastic circle crack.

In the courtyard behind Château Pierrey, he pulled to a halt. Around them, the outbuildings crouched in the night. Behind them, he could just make out the low bulk of the house itself. He hurried around to help Frances out of the car and held her tightly. In his arms, she trembled and fluttered, still reacting to her release from terror.

He wanted to kiss her, but thought it was probably too soon. There was nothing, he lied to himself, sexual in it, or in his desire to take her to bed with him, to undress her, to feel her long body next to his, to comfort and soothe her until she fell asleep in his arms.

He thought, *Perhaps these things will come.*

■■

Fran drove to the hospital. Although Emilie's ribs were still strapped up, the color was back in her cheeks. She wore an expensive bedjacket of yellow silk; it matched almost exactly the roses which stood in a vase beside her bed.

When Fran commented on them, Emilie smoothed the petals of one of the blooms. "Gilles Laforêt has been very kind."

"Mother," Fran said. "You know absolutely nothing about him."

"I told you before, Françoise, I know enough. Besides . . ." Emilie gave her daughter a long look. "Have I ever interfered with your life, *chérie*?"

"No, but—"

"Then do not interfere with mine."

"All right." Fran put a hand over her mother's. "Listen: I've got to go back to Istanbul."

"If it's to do with your father, Françoise, would it not be better to leave things as they are?"

"Not if there is a murderer running loose."

"His death was an accident. No one meant to kill him."

"Maybe." Fran made a pretense of studying the chart at the foot of Emilie's bed. Then she said casually, "Where did he say he was going, that last time?"

"He *said* he was going to Cyprus first."

"First?"

"Yes. Then on to Turkey." Emilie pulled her bedjacket closer, as though she was suddenly cold. "Which is why I never understood what he and François were doing in Beirut."

Grimly, Fran thought, *I'm beginning to think that I can.* If you had two people you want to get rid of, what better place to dispose of them than in a war zone like Beirut? Especially—her brain swelled with supposition—if, having picked them up in, say, Istanbul, you had access to a boat and could sail them along the coast, away from a country where their bodies might have aroused suspicion, might have pointed at someone or something, and to another country where an extra corpse or two would scarcely be noticed.

Blindfolds, she thought. Having arrived with your victims, alive but blindfolded, you put them into a car, drove them into an area where there would be few witnesses, untied the scarves around their eyes, and sent them stumbling off down the street. They would be blinded but ecstatic, blinking rapturously into the sunshine, thinking they had been set free, thinking they were safe. Before their vision fully returned, they would have been dead.

"Have you still got Tom's passport?" she said.

Emilie shook her head. "It wasn't among his possessions when they were sent back so it was probably stolen. Tom told me that there's a big black market in stolen passports out there."

She was probably right. It was pointless to speculate.

Emilie reached for Fran's hand. "I speak to you from a selfish point of view," she said. "There were only two people who ever mattered to me—you and your father. Now one of you is dead. Before you do whatever it is you have set your mind on, I ask you to consider what my life will be like if you, too, walk open-eyed into danger."

Fran kissed her. "I'll be careful, *maman.*"

"I shall pray that you are careful enough."

■■

The gates into Gilles Laforêt's carefully raked gravel drive were open. Fran turned in and drove fast to the foot of the stone staircase. A couple of cars waited there already: an old-fashioned Wolseley, carefully maintained in an admirable condition of waxed brightness, and a Peugeot Estate. Fran hurried up the steps and grabbed the iron bell-pull. She might have expected to feel nervous at what could turn out to be imminent confrontation. Instead, she felt exhilarated, nerves tuned taut as piano strings, ready to crash toward a crescendo.

But the servant who opened the door informed her that Monsieur Laforêt was in Paris, and not expected back here until the end of the week. She did not bother to ask him for the address: no well-trained manservant would give it to a stranger on the doorstep. Driving into Paris, she tried to decide whether it had been his voice which responded to her telephone call for help on the night that the whispering intruder had broken into her mother's house. She came to the conclusion it was not.

She had no trouble in finding Gilles Laforêt's *appartement.* The house was tall and narrow, its upper floors banded by small balconies. Several of the windows were already lighted, although the sun had not yet gone fully down behind the Parisian roofs. At the end of streets were occasional views of Notre Dame. She pressed one of the bells, and spoke into the intercom when his voice replied. As the buzzer sounded, she stepped into a severe flagged hallway with a stone stair-case rising upward, balustered in black-painted decorative ironwork, its shallow steps carpeted with green pile. At the top of the stairs Gilles Laforêt was waiting for her.

"Françoise, what a pleasure," he said, drawing her in. He kissed her lightly on both cheeks, pressing his softly stubbled face against hers.

"For me too," she said. She felt very light, as though she might take off into the air at any moment, as though half the blood in her veins had been replaced with foam.

"I feel greatly privileged," he said. "What brings you here?"

She smiled at him. "I was just walking past and wanted to thank you for your kindness to my mother."

"She is a delicious woman."

"Also, I hoped you might offer me an aperitif." It was an effort to sound as if she meant it.

The room was spaciously elegant: bottle-green furnishings, big lamps shedding cream-colored circles of light, a collection of *objets d'art*, from small equestrian bronzes to eggs made of pink quartz and rock crystal. A fire burned in an ornate grate of polished black steel picked out with brass. He opened a bottle of champagne and poured it into crystal *flûtes*.

Tipping her glass with his, he drank. "I hope this is the first of many visits."

She turned slightly so that she could see out of the long velvet-draped windows. Across the road, the windows of the opposite apart-ment were shuttered.

"You have seen your mother today?" he asked politely.

"I've just come from there. They're keeping her in hospital for the moment."

He shook his head. "A terrible thing to happen."

"At least we think we now know why," she said.

"You do?"

"Yes. A lot more of my father's papers survived the fire than I thought at first. And while I was in London, I was able to talk to the colleague he had been working with. In fact, I've just come back from visiting him." Her heart pounded suddenly. She hoped she had not put Max in any danger: if the Phoenix Foundation's personnel were as powerful and as organized as he thought, they would probably know about his working relationship with Tom and his close association with her.

"What did you discover?" He leaned back against his chair so that shadow from the lampshade beside him fell across his face.

"I came across some really important information that my father had stored on a computer disk. Not that I've read it yet, but his colleague is doing that right now, I hope." She leaned forward. "It's beginning to look as though he was deliberately murdered."

"Surely it was an accident. Wasn't he on an assignment in Beirut?"

"That's what we were all supposed to think. But I'm convinced my poor mother was attacked because someone wanted to learn just how much he had discovered about the people who subsequently killed him."

He seemed genuinely horrified. "Are you sure?"

She sighed. "To be honest, not really."

"Don't worry, Françoise," he said. Soothing as syrup, his voice caressed the syllables of her name. He smiled warmly: it was as though the doors to a stoked-up fire had suddenly been opened.

She jerked her head at the flat across the street. "Is Alexander away?"

"He's gone to London on urgent business," he said. "And then I believe he's flying to Istanbul."

"When?"

"As soon as he's dealt with whatever he had to do."

"How funny: I'm flying to Istanbul too." Smiling at her host, she wondered whose side he was on. Alexander's, she suspected, but whether united with him in innocence or in guilt, she had as yet no idea. Either way, she needed to use him if she was to achieve the results she desired. She did not say that if he had told her Alexander was headed for New York or Rome or Sydney, that was where she would have been going too.

He looked beyond her; his elegant hands clenched into a brief fist and a frown stood between his eyebrows. "Is this something to do with your father? Going to Istanbul, I mean."

"I hope so."

"This is a brutal thing to say, and certainly you can tell me that it is none of my business—but he *is* dead. Wouldn't it be wiser to leave it all to the police?"

She twisted her hands about. Did it look too obvious, too much the conventional gesture of confusion? "There isn't enough evidence for the police," she said. "Even with what my father's colleague was able to add, a lot of what I've told you is no more than guesswork. I've just got to find out the truth. I feel as if my life can't start up again until I have."

"Does anyone else know about this?"

"No."

"Not even this colleague of your father's?"

She gave a crooked little grin. "If you were a journalist, you'd understand how closely we guard our secrets. I suppose it's just become second nature to me not to tell people what I know."

He seemed to relax at that, the long fingers slowly uncurling to lie flat along his thighs. There was danger about; she could almost smell it, as intangible yet as distinct as the smoke of a fine cigar.

"Forgive me," he said, leaning forward so that his eyes came once again into the light. "But isn't it a little foolish of you to try to sort this out all on your own?"

"I don't think I have any choice. Until I've got some kind of evidence, I can't go to the police."

"And you really think there is evidence in Istanbul?"

"I'm certain of it. There is a strong lead I must follow up. After that . . . with any luck I can hand it over to the police."

In the grate, a coal flared up briefly, giving off small splashes of blue fire. He watched it, then leaned forward to take a brass poker from its place in the hearth.

She thought, *If he moved quickly enough, he could smash my brains out before I could even get out of this chair.*

"Listen," he said suddenly. He brought the poker down hard on the lump of coal and it split open, each piece catching sudden brilliant fire from the embers. "Without knowing too much about it, I can understand why you feel you must go to Istanbul. But as a friend of your mother's, I must say that I don't think it's a good idea for you to go alone."

She gave a helpless little shrug of her shoulders. "I don't know anyone I can ask to come with me."

He turned, the poker in his hand. "Why don't I give you Alexander's telephone number in Istanbul? He left it with me. I'm sure he wouldn't mind you contacting him."

Fran allowed a look of relief to flood across her face. "Really? Are you sure?"

"Absolutely. Or else I could tell him where you'll be staying when he rings me this evening."

It was far easier than she had expected. Gilles had responded almost exactly as she had anticipated; within a couple of hours Alexander would probably have the news that she was going to Istanbul to follow a definite lead. She gave Gilles the name of the Istanbul hotel she had booked into. It was not very far from the flat where she and Anna had once lived, where she had hoped for so much, where she had fallen in love with a man called Nicholas Marquend. Since then, time had tarnished his image. "It would certainly make everything so much easier if there was someone to call on if necessary," she said.

"I'm sure you can count on him."

In some cold part of her, she thought: Never. The only reason he has not yet disposed of me is because he is not absolutely sure how much I know, or how much I've passed on.

■■

Back in Précy, she phoned Max. She let the telephone ring for a long time before accepting that he was not going to answer. Calling Philippe, she found herself holding her mouth close to the receiver, as though afraid she might be overheard. "I did it," she said. "He'll tell Alexander I'm in Istanbul, and that I'm alone."

"That's good," he said doubtfully.

"You don't sound too sure. I thought we agreed this was the only way to lure him out into the open."

"*You* agreed. I simply went along with you. Do you really know what you're doing?"

"Of course I don't," she said. "I'm playing this whole thing by ear."

Without thinking about it, he said, "I don't know what I'd do if something happened to you."

"Nothing will," Fran said, after a pause.

Was she surprised? Angry? Embarrassed? Philippe could not

judge. He cleared his throat and was about to speak when she added softly, "Not now I've met you."

"Françoise," he said. Exultation washed over his heart.

"Yes," she said. He heard her cough nervously. "Listen, Philippe: I told Gilles Laforêt that I couldn't get started on my life again until I'd got my father's death sorted out. I hadn't realized just how true that is. It's not just Tom, though—it's Daniel as well."

"I understand. More than you can know. I loved him too."

"Well, once I've followed all this through . . ."

"Once you have?"

There was a long pause. He imagined its blankness resting like snow on the wavelengths which separated them, then thought, No, not snow, but icing, royal icing, thick and delicious, as though she were preparing for him a cake of such rich proportions that it would take the rest of his life to eat it. "Once I have, Philippe . . ."

"Yes?"

She laughed quietly. ". . . we'll see."

"The widows used to say that to me when I was little," he said. "It invariably meant that whatever I wanted wouldn't happen."

"My mother used to say it to me, too."

"And?"

"It always meant it *would* happen."

"What a lucky child you must have been."

Again the pause. "I think," she said quietly, "that maybe I'm going to be a lucky woman, too."

"Françoise," he said again.

"See you in Istanbul."

· 26 ·

FROM HEATHROW, SHE TOOK THE tube to Marble Arch and caught a taxi to her flat. Perhaps proximity to a goal tends to act as an opiate or a blindfold: certainly she had not noticed the passenger who sat four rows behind her on the flight from Charles de Gaulle and got into the adjoining car on the underground journey into London. Nor did she observe the taxi which followed hers to Notting Hill and continued along the crescent to drop the same passenger off two streets away, while she was still paying her own taxi driver. She took a long time over this, fumbling in her purse for money while she took note of the cars parked along the street. She knew she could not hope to remember them all; she tried to concentrate on the more unremarkable ones: the beige Ford, the maroon Vauxhall, the anonymous blue Fiat.

Putting the key into the lock, she prayed that Max had had time to ring one of the agencies specializing in cleaning up. He had: although not the comfortable place it had once been, the flat was at least halfway habitable again.

There were letters on the doormat, mostly bills, though one had been hand-delivered. It was from Max.

> *Think we're on to something. I checked out the Phoenix lot.*
> *All very high-class and respectable, and rolling in money. Not*
> *too keen on publicity, but I got some names for you—see*
> *enclosed sheet. Think I've tracked down a computer compati-*
> *ble with Tom's disk, at long last. Call me soonest.*

She telephoned him, but there was no answer. She checked her watch: eastern seaboard time was five hours behind London time. She dialed a Washington number, praying Anna would be home.

She was, and answered almost immediately. "Darling! How fantastic!" she exclaimed. "Are you coming over or something? Do you want to stay with us? We've got this simply amazing house, more like a palace than an ordinary home—even the guest bedrooms have Jacuzzis, can you imagine?"

Fran fielded the exclamations of surprise and delight. "Anna, you sound wonderful—"

"I am, darling. Absolutely marvelous!"

"—but right now I need some help from you."

"What? Anything."

"Remember that place we stayed in Istanbul?"

"As if I could forget."

"It belonged to a friend of Andrew Watson's cousin, didn't it?"

"That's right."

"How can I get in touch with him?"

"The cousin? Or the friend?"

"Either. The cousin first, I should think."

"I'd have to find Andrew's address, then. God knows what I've done with it, but it must be somewhere." Anna's good brain surfaced, cutting through the veneer of butterfly brightness. "Why, Fran? What's wrong?"

"A great many things, really."

"Is it to do with that Daniel person?"

"Yes. In a way."

"Did you ever catch up with him?"

"Sort of."

"How do you mean?"

In spite of the events of the past months, Fran still found it difficult to talk about Daniel. "The reason he didn't get in touch with me was that he seems to have been murdered," she said soberly.

"Fran! How utterly terrible." Anna dropped her voice. "Why? Or don't you know?"

"The police haven't found out much yet."

"Everyone in Istanbul thought he was a spy. It was obvious all that stuff about selling wine was just a front. But I guess you knew that."

"I didn't—not then. Why didn't you tell me?"

"Darling, I kept trying to warn you off him, but you wouldn't listen. You were absolutely besotted."

"Perhaps I was," Fran said. She did not add: Or I might have been, given half a chance.

"I'll have a look through my desk for you, all right?" Anna said. "See if I can find that telephone number for you, and call you back."

"Thanks."

"Fran, dear, I do wish I was there. You sound so . . . so forlorn."

"I'm not really. I've got over it now."

"Does one 'get over' something like a murder?"

"Other things intervene."

"Men?" Anna said, hopefully.

With a smile in her voice, Fran said, "We'll have to see," as she had to Philippe.

■■

She drove to Hampstead. Even if Max wasn't home, he might have left notes on his desk: something that could provide her with further clues before she took the flight to Istanbul in the morning.

There was no answer to her ringing. In the end she used her key to let herself into the narrow tiled hall. As soon as she had closed the door behind her, she could tell something was wrong. It was not just the smell of excrement which clung to the walls as thick as swarming bees; from the kitchen at the end of the passage, she could hear Phyllis whining and scratching at the door.

For a moment she stood fighting for self-control, dreading what she might find. Slowly, she pushed open the door of Max's sitting room.

The big room was insufferably hot. The two bars of the electric fire were on and lamps burned, one on the desk, two others near the hearth. Thick curtains were pulled across the windows into the garden. How long had they been like that?

She shouted for Max, standing at the foot of the stairs. There was no answer. It took all the discipline she possessed to make her feet carry her upward. Suppose she found him dead, strapped to a bed, tortured, bloodied?

He was not upstairs. Downstairs again, she realized that although there was no sign of a struggle, his desk had been rifled, the drawers pulled out and their contents dumped on the floor. What could have happened? She forced herself to think. Max had obviously been working at his desk when something interrupted him. Could he have been abducted—perhaps by the same person who had tortured Daniel to death?

Gilles said Alexander had come to England on urgent business: could this have been finding out what was on the disk? Or, at the very least, how much was known about the Phoenix Foundation? There was an urgency now that had been missing before. The Phoenix organization was obviously as aware of it as she was.

Phyllis was the next chore. Fran opened the kitchen door, grimacing with disgust as the stench hit her. The poor animal must have been shut up in here for at least two days.

She let the frantic dog out into the garden and set about cleaning up the mess. Looking for the broom and dustpan, she slipped the catch on the door of the walk-in larder and found Max himself.

"Jesus, am I glad to see you," he said, as soon as she had removed the gag that had been stuffed into his mouth.

"Oh, Max," she said. Tears came into her eyes.

"Get the whisky, will you, hon?" he said brusquely. "I've lost forty-eight hours drinking time." But his eyes too were moist, and when she had untied the flexible cord wound tightly around wrists and feet, he wrapped his arms around her and held her close.

Over more whisky, he told her what had happened. "I'm sitting there at my desk, right? And all of a sudden, Phyllis starts going crazy. I look up, and there's this guy standing right in the middle of the room, just staring at me. I guessed he was one of the neighborhood junkies, dropped in for a bit of quiet thieving—you know how their eyes go when they're doped up: dilated so you can hardly see what color they are."

"What color were they?" Fran said.

"Blue, if it makes any difference. Anyway, he comes over and picks Tom's disk off the desk and starts walking away with it, so I say, "Hey, bud, what the hell you think you're doing?" So he turns back, yanks the lamp out of the wall and lands me one on the head. All of it quicker than I could take a breath. When I come to, I'm lying where you found me—and let me tell you it was one of the most uncomfortable places I've been in my life." He grinned crookedly, not quite hiding his discomfort or the residue of fear. "First thing tomorrow,

I'm gonna call in the pest exterminator. Did you know there were cockroaches sharing the house with me?"

Fran smiled. "There are worse houseguests to have."

Max shook his head. "Christ knows how the guy got in without any noise—or alerting Phyllis. He must move like a mouse."

"Or a rat."

"Yeah." Swallowing noisily, Max moved stiffly to cover Fran's hand with his own. "Listen, kid. I'm really sorry about that disk."

"You can't imagine I'd blame you for losing it."

"I know you wouldn't." He sighed. "I don't suppose we'll ever know what it said."

"That won't stop me," Fran said. She stood up and stroked Max's hair. "Listen: Will you call in one of your lady friends to look after you? I've got to go to Istanbul."

"I'll be fine if you just promise to tell me all about it when you get back."

"Cross my heart and hope to die."

Driving back to Notting Hill, Fran wished she had chosen some other expression.

■■

As she sat making notes, Anna rang back from Washington.

"I found it, darling. Andrew Watson's phone number. Lucky I kept last year's Christmas cards. He's working for the British Council now, teaching English in Budapest or somewhere."

"What's the number?"

Anna read it out to her. "That's his office. He'll probably be there: Peter says they work fearfully hard in those eastern European countries."

"Thanks, Anna."

"My pleasure, darling. I'm fearfully curious."

■■

Fran explained to Andrew Watson who she was and what she wanted. He appeared bewildered, unwilling to hand out information to someone he did not know for considerations that appeared to be outside his daily round. Eventually he told her that his cousin was an accountant with a merchant banking firm in the City and reluctantly gave her his name.

■■

Fran finally caught up with Jeremy Sutton two calls later. His voice was moneyed, smug, pompous, everything she hated. She did not have to meet him to know that his upbringing and background had insulated him against those who differed in any particular from himself. For him, such people would be almost literally invisible; Shylock's cry *—If you prick us, do we not bleed?—literally unheard. She tried not to remember the end of that speech: if you wrong us, shall we not revenge?*

Jeremy Sutton was off to a squash game, his impatience with her inquiry unconcealed. "Andrew?" he said, when she had explained who she was. "What about him?"

"It's not him I'm interested in," she said coldly, matching his rudeness with her own. "It's you."

"What about me, then?"

"You have a friend who lives in Istanbul, I believe."

"I have lots of friends who live in Istanbul. Why do you ask?"

"One of them asked you to find a house-sitter for his flat about a year ago. Do you remember?"

"No."

"How can you have forgotten?"

He gave a huge impatient sigh. "Quite easily. My company has very close links with bankers in Istanbul. I'm often asked to find people who'll house-sit, to reduce the chance of burglaries while the owners are away."

"Anna Fairchild and I took this one. The owner was going abroad for six months."

"Who's Anna Fairchild?"

"She was up at Oxford . . . she was a friend of your cousin's."

"Look, I'm awfully sorry, but the name doesn't mean a thing . . . and I'm running late. I don't think I can help you."

"Please, Mr. Sutton, if you can't remember this particular arrangement, just tell me some names of contacts."

"For God's sake. This is ridiculous."

"Please."

"Oh, really . . ." She heard him click his tongue in exasperation.

"Um . . . Chelik, Niyazi . . . um, Idris, Medjit, Haluk. I can't think of any more, not that long ago."

"Thank you, Mr. Sutton," she said with exaggerated courtesy. "You've been most helpful."

"Good." He put down the phone.

■■

One of the names she had heard before. She took papers out of the flight bag she had been using as a briefcase for the past ten days. Among them was the catalogue for Hugo Campion's exhibition in Paris. She turned the glossily illustrated pages until she found the sentence she had been looking for—*lent by A. Idris*—*then put it down and leaned back, closing her eyes.*

The wheel had turned. Fate had brought her full circle to the point where it all started. Tomorrow she would be on the plane to Istanbul, back at the beginning.

■■

Before she left the flat, she put all the notes she had made into an envelope and addressed it to the man who had been in charge of the investigations into Daniel's murder. She dropped it into the postbox along the crescent before taking the tube back again to Heathrow.

Once again she failed to observe the man who had followed her to and from Max's flat, had sat tapping the steering wheel of an unremarkable beige car while she delivered Phyllis to the sitter, had driven behind her back to Notting Hill. Had she done so, she would have recognized at once the way his cold gray eyes flicked frequently to his watch, and the intent expression on his face as he walked some yards behind her to the airport booking hall.

·· PART · FOUR ··

ISTANBUL

· 27 ·

PHILIPPE DE PIERREY WAS AFRAID
he had made a mistake in choosing to stay at the same hotel where he
had stayed with Daniel on his previous visit. Apprehensively, he
waited for the memories of Mihri to rush in on him, to crowd and
trample him, but the streets where he had once walked with her in
ecstasy were peaceful, empty of her ghost, and the water in the harbor, ruffled by wind, no longer sighed her name but slapped briskly
against the jetties, saying nothing.

As a private act of expiation, he visited Mihri's parents. The
professor had shrunk, the plumpness sucked out of him by the loss of
his daughter; he still wore a suit of some palely perfect fabric, but it
had no life, hanging on shoulders from which the well-being had
vanished. His wife spoke not at all, her former shyness transmuted
now into silence. The photographs of Mihri had been put away; without them the leafy flat among the treetops had lost its central core.
The two of them smiled at him, even embraced him. The cling of
their despairing arms only increased his sense of culpability.

He hoped desperately that they did not blame him for their loss,
yet knew himself to be entirely guilty. If he had not fallen in love with
Mihri, if she had not come to Paris, she would still be alive, married to
the nice boy they had wanted for her; there might even have been the
grandchildren that now they would never know. However much he
told himself that she had planned to come to Paris anyway, he could
not shake off the knowledge that it was his fault they lived here alone,
bereft.

From her hotel room, Fran called his. It seemed strange to be
talking to her in this country to which neither of them belonged. He
disliked the razor edge of danger which underlay their conversation
and slashed whatever intimacy they might have otherwise achieved.

He could call to mind every detail of her dark, serious face as she
explained to him what she had found out since they last met. When

her voice cracked while speaking of Max Blum, he felt her anxiety as keenly as if it were his own.

"It'll be all right," he said firmly. "I know it will." He had nothing to base such confidence on, yet she seemed to be comforted by his words.

■■

Fran called the Istanbul number Gilles Laforêt had given her. There was no answer. Alexander, it appeared, had not yet arrived in the city of his birth.

■■

The next day, she walked through the Grand Bazaar. As always, the place was a kaleidoscope for the senses: throbbing with color, smells, sounds. Glitter and confusion filled the vaulted air.

Fran pressed through the crowds of shoppers and tourists, toward the little perfume boutique which she had named as their rendezvous.

Standing in front of its window, side by side, as though they were strangers met by chance, Philippe said, "Why have you come *here*?" He coughed, clearing emotion from his throat.

"Daniel came here once," Fran said.

"He brought me here too." Philippe wanted to add that this was where Mihri had first spoken to him, while Daniel bought perfume for his mother. Looking back, he remembered that Daniel had carried no packet when he emerged.

"I think the manager was some kind of contact," Fran said. "And when Daniel couldn't make some date we'd arranged, I've always been certain this was the man who used to ring me up to explain that Daniel had been called away—though when I confronted him later, he pretended not to speak any English."

The two of them separated again. They had agreed it was best not to be together in case Fran was being watched.

Inside the perfume shop, the manager came through the swinging brass chains smiling. It was the same man who had been there the last time, when she had been searching for some clue to Daniel's disappearance. Recognizing her immediately, he hesitated, the smile slipping momentarily from his face. He pushed it firmly back into place, but under the heavy lids his eyes were wary. "Yes," he said in French. "Can I help you?"

"I'm a friend of Daniel Forrest's," Fran said.

"Daniel Forrest? I am afraid . . ."

"Or Nicholas Marquend. I believe you were his friend too."

He opened his mouth to speak. Before he could deny it, she hurried on. "Perhaps you didn't know, but he is dead." She waited for a reaction: shock, surprise, sadness. There was nothing. "He was murdered," she said. The flat black eyes showed no change of expression, though there might have been a quiver of some emotion that she could not define.

She knew it was hopeless but pressed on. "Do you know anything that might help us find out who is responsible?" she said.

He shook his head.

"He must have told you something about what he was doing in Istanbul," she insisted.

He reached for one of the gold-topped bottles on his counter and gently pressed its plunger, sending a waft of Madame Rochas toward her. "You suggested to me once before that I have some connection with your friend, Monsieur Marquend," he said. "I said then, and I repeat it now: I do not know what you are talking about."

Fran knew now that she was not mistaken in the voice. It was this man who used to telephone to cancel her meetings with Nicholas Marquend. For some reason—perhaps of personal danger—he simply did not dare to acknowledge the connection. Perhaps she was exactly what Colonel Napier had accused her of being: a bloody amateur stumbling about, confusing the issue. Perhaps, by coming here today, she was endangering a delicate network which had taken years of work to establish.

Nonetheless, she persisted. "Do you know anything about the Phoenix Foundation?"

The sleepiness vanished; he licked his lips, started to speak, stopped, put both hands on the glass countertop in front of him, opened his mouth again, turned away to the dazzle of the shelves behind him.

Finally he came out into the center of the little shop and walked toward the door. He opened it, half bowing, his Asiatic face smoothly anonymous. Moving his shoulders, he motioned her out. As she passed him he murmured, so low that she scarcely heard him, "Someone is expected."

When she turned, the door had closed behind her and he was pulling down a blind to indicate that the shop was closed. He would not meet her eyes through the glass door.

She did not notice the man in the pulled-down hat who watched her through narrowed eyes and followed her back to her hotel.

■■

By arrangement, Philippe and Fran took separate taxis out into the hilly suburbs and met as if by chance. Sharing their memories of Daniel, they had discovered that he had taken both of them to a cream-colored villa. Fran thought that it might hold some clue.

"He obviously used us as cover," she said. "He must have needed cover all the time."

"I have a feeling," Philippe said, considering, "that Daniel must often have been afraid."

Fran looked at him with gratitude and took his arm. "He talked about that once, about serving in Northern Ireland and how exhausting it was to be frightened all the time."

They passed a great many cream-colored villas, but none was the one they wanted.

"I'm sure there was a mosque nearby," Philippe said. "We looked down on it from above."

"I remember a fountain—a stone basin in front of the house," said Fran.

They walked for most of the morning without success. After lunching in the rose-enclosed courtyard of a café, they started again, trudging through wide suburban streets, on and on until they felt they must be out of Istanbul altogether.

"Are we even in the right area?" asked Fran.

"That's the name he gave the taxi driver when we came here," said Philippe. He looked around at the anonymous houses set back in their gardens. "All of it looks vaguely familiar but I don't recognize anything."

It began to rain. Philippe opened an umbrella and they huddled beneath it. "Tell me about your stay in Istanbul," he said.

In the slippery rain, she did so. No one else was on the streets, though once, turning, she saw a black figure turn into a gateway: it was as though they had the city to themselves. She found herself talking without pain, almost without interest. Whatever had happened was over and past; the Nicholas she thought she knew was long overlaid with the Daniel she had learned about since.

It was late in the afternoon when they turned a corner and caught a view out across the Bosphorus. From here, the water looked gray and dirty, the shipping rusty. Behind it the land, shawled in low-lying cloud, seemed shopworn and faded. Immediately below them were the complicated geometrics of a roof: curves and squares and triangles, the roof of a mosque.

Philippe's grip tightened on Fran's arm. "That's it," he said. "I'm sure that's the mosque I remember."

Farther on they found the house itself, standing back behind stucco walls set with pale green metal rails. Beyond the railings lay the stone basin with the desultory fountain, the flat surface of its water scarred by the beating rain. They walked slowly past, noting the closed shutters, the weeds in the gravel, the general air of desertion.

"It doesn't look as if anyone's been here for years," Fran said.

"You're right. Let's go."

"Not until I've rung the bell." Fran pushed open the reluctant gate and walked up to the front door past overblown roses and shrubs that needed trimming. She pressed the bell and heard its peal at the back of the house, but nobody came to the door. The lower windows were all shuttered; she walked around the side of the villa, but there were no signs of anyone having been there recently.

"Whose house was it, I wonder?" she said to Philippe as they went on.

"Someone he called Kemal. He said he was into just about everything you could imagine, from drugs and prostitution to gunrunning and large-scale embezzlement."

"Gunrunning?"

"Yes. He said this Kemal—that's the only name he used—was one of the most charming men you could ever hope to meet."

At the next corner, Fran turned to look back. A figure in a wet black slicker was behind them; she watched it stop outside the gates of Kemal's villa, hesitate, then continue past before crossing the road and disappearing down a side street.

Philippe stopped. He took Fran's hand. She listened without talking as he told her of the memories still haunting him here, the love he had felt for Mihri, the first real love he had ever known. He found tears in his eyes. She held him quietly, her hands steadily gripping his arms. She warned herself that she hardly knew Philippe; she was nonetheless unbearably excited by the feel of his body. Earlier, he might have been ashamed, embarrassed to be weeping. Now he was aware of change within himself; like a snake, he had sloughed off his old rough skin and emerged sinuous, shining, stronger than he had been before.

Fran had feared that the city would be suffused for her with memories of Nicholas. She found that it was not. What she had tried to do in anger—heal the wound he had left—now occurred effortlessly. The growing strength of her feelings for Philippe warmed and at the same time surprised her: not ecstasy but ease; not frenzy but friendship. Like most women with a man recently met, she imagined herself in bed with him; making love with Philippe, she decided, would begin by being good. Whatever raptures followed would be the result of the contentment they already felt in each other's company. Six months ago, she might have scoffed at the idea of sleeping with a man with whom she felt comfortable. Love, she would have said, was not meant to be a comfortable emotion, not at the start. Now, she was not so sure.

Above their heads, rain drummed onto the curved umbrella silk. There was nobody about: the street was wet and empty. They looked at each other in silence, then Philippe leaned forward and kissed her. Fran kissed him back, closing her eyes, sharing his warmth, then slipped her arms around him, inside his coat, and laid her cheek against his chest. His heart beat strongly, steadily, under his ribs. She felt herself to be flowing onward at last, into the future.

■■

Later that evening, Fran walked across the Galata Bridge and searched for the arched door and the plaque set into the wall. It was still there: *The Phoenix Foundation.* She remembered the face of the man who had come out into the street. He had worn sunglasses; nonetheless, in retrospect, she recognized his face. She remembered Alexander saying he had forgotten that this branch of the organization existed. How was that possible?

" 'There are many names for God,' " she murmured. The phrase had been circling in her head for days, like a mantra.

She thought: Max is right. This place is a front, though it's also doing exactly what it's apparently set up to do: to send medical aid across the world. It's the perfect cover. We never saw inside those boxes at Reims; they could have held anything, from submachine guns to torpedoes.

All those rich, respectable patrons who think they are putting money into some kind of Christian-based charity—how could they know that they are funding the shipment of arms, financing terrorist training camps, supporting terrorist activities? If they found out the truth, how many of them would feel inclined to do as Jacques de Tresail had done?

The evening stretched ahead of her. For the moment there was nothing she could do. She decided to walk by the harbor; if anyone came looking for her, she would be safe as long as she kept among crowds.

Although the rain had stopped, the evening air was soaked and damp. Despite that, the streets were crowded. She kept with the biggest groups of people, conscious of no longer being an inhabitant, yet not isolated as once she might have been. Among them moved the tea boys, balancing their glasses of hot tea; shoeshiners called for clients, rubbing their brushes together at the sight of a likely customer; music drifted from the cafés, the same tinny outdated songs she had heard before when she was searching for Daniel. Now, they had no power to move her: she had changed, grown older, even grown a little wiser. If that meant that she was also tougher, then perhaps tough was not such a bad thing to be.

Down by the Galata Bridge, she leaned on the railings and stared down at the water. Even in the darkness, she could see the garbage knocking against the jetty with each movement of the oily surface. It seemed such a long time ago since she had first arrived, first met Daniel, first accepted that she would not see him again. She had spent too much time looking backward; she must clear things up and then start moving forward again. She was tired of marking time.

Thinking this, she looked up. There, coming across the bridge, his face briefly illuminated by each lamp in turn as he walked into and then out of the circle of its radiance, was Alexander.

Fate, she thought. Fate, chance, kismet. It had brought her here in the first place. Now it delivered her quarry into her hands. She knew she must not let this opportunity slip; it might be the last time she had the advantage of him. Almost without thinking, she moved casually toward the end of the bridge and waited for him to step off it. She was wearing jeans and a navy blue sweater over a white shirt: she tucked the collar inside the sweater to make herself less visible. When he set off up the hill away from the water, she followed.

■■

The man behind her shook his head, snorting quietly to himself with amusement. Unbelievably, she was actually following. The girl did not have a fearful bone in her body. He knew she would eventually have gone back to the apartment where she and the Fairchild woman had once lived; it might as well be now as later. His bones shivered inside their covering of flesh. He did not really want to see her killed; though he would do his best, he was not sure he would be able to save her. He pulled his shapeless hat farther down on his head and looked restlessly at his watch, wondering how long it would all take.

■■

Fran stood in the shadows across the street and looked up at the house. It had come as no surprise to her to discover where Alexander was headed; at some deep level she had known already. The place looked exactly as it had before: the familiarity of it reached out toward her. If she stood here long enough, she might even see the echo of herself—the self she used to be—come up the street and climb the wooden steps.

Lamplight shone on the cobbles; behind the drawn curtains of the upper floor there were also lights. The man she had been following had already gone upstairs and let himself in. Just before he closed the door he had looked back down into the street. She could not decide whether he knew she was there, or was simply taking a last look around before shutting himself in for the night.

What she had to decide now, was what to do. She realized it would be both foolish and dangerous to do anything except turn around and go back to her hotel, yet every journalistic instinct told her that now was the moment to find what she had been seeking—to confront, to attack. As a sop to safety, she walked swiftly away up the hill, found a telephone, and called Philippe. While she did not want him at her side, she needed him at her back. Ignoring his insistence that she wait for him to arrive, she gave him the address and put down the phone.

A few minutes later, she was knocking at the familiar door.

When he opened the door to her, the light from the room beyond cast a kind of halo around his head.

"We heard you were coming to Istanbul," he said. "I was expecting you. Come in."

Fran did so. She was confused. Something here was very wrong. His voice sounded strange to her. As she walked into the brilliant sitting room, into the light from the lamps of painted porcelain and pierced brass, she saw why.

Although he was very like him, particularly in his movements, this man was not Alexander. So how could he have known about her coming here? Unless Gilles Laforêt had told him.

Realizing the monumental—perhaps fatal—error she had made, she stopped dead. The silk carpets on the wall shimmered as they used to, their flowers spread like an orchard in spring across the uneven plaster. She drew in a deep breath, smelling again the spice and perfume which had grown so familiar during the six months when this place had temporarily come to mean home.

"Who are you?" she said.

"You keep asking me that, Frances," he said. His voice was soft yet chillingly clear. His blue eyes watched her steadily, without blinking, so that she wondered whether it was a facility he had deliberately taught himself. In the dangerous world of the professional assassin, perhaps even a blink could cost you your life.

"And you keep forgetting to answer," she retorted.

"You thought I was Alexander, didn't you?"

"Yes. You move like him, though you only look like him from a distance."

"My name is Mikkele. We share the same father," he said. "Perhaps that explains it."

"The man called Kemal?"

"Kemal Idris." He spat out the words. "He is a cheat, a fraud, a pervert."

"Alexander doesn't feel like that about him. Quite the opposite." She could not help her curiosity.

"Alexander saw a different side of him. That's because Alexander is a legitimate son, whereas I am not. I spent a week with him once, on our father's boat: he never knew who I was, although we are so alike. My own brother ordered me about as though I was a servant."

His rage makes him vulnerable, Fran told herself. Although she kept her eyes on his, she also took in the contents of the room around him, searching for something that could serve as a weapon. Real ones hung on the walls—curved daggers, a knife with a rock-crystal hilt and damascened blade, even a sword—but she doubted she could draw any of them from their sheaths in time to be of use. There were also any number of jugs and ewers of jewel-studded chalcedony or jade, brass pitchers, carved boxes; none of them would inflict enough damage to stop her opponent in his tracks.

The only object of any use was a carved alabaster dragon standing on a brass-topped table: she knew from experience how heavy it was. She stepped farther into the room, nearer to it. "You must have been the child who was the cause of Alexander's mother leaving Kemal," she said.

The blue eyes did not waver. "Who told you that?"

"I'm a nosy journalist," she said. "I know how to find things out. I was told that if Alexander had been a girl, his mother would have left him behind. You would have had a sister, then."

"I already have a sister," he said coldly.

"Kemal's daughter?" She was playing now for time. In some chilly place at the back of her mind, she charted Philippe's journey across the city to her side. Would he reach her in time?

"Certainly she is not." Mikkele's anger caused his concentration to waver momentarily. "Even he would keep his filthy hands off his own daughter."

It was the second time he had spoken of Kemal as if he were still alive. Somewhere there was a pattern to all this. Like iridescence on the shaken surface of a puddle, its colors swirled. What picture would they make when they were still at last?

"Are you going to tell me what this is all about?" she said boldly.

"So you still don't know?"

"Some of it. Not all. And not why."

He smiled. His teeth were very white in his brown face. "It is the why which is important," he said.

A voice called from another room. He turned toward it, then gestured to her to follow him. Her heart jumped with the unexpectedness of realizing that he was not alone here: what chance would she have against two? Even if she could manage to pick up the alabaster dragon undetected, it would only serve for one. Yet, even in such danger, she knew that nothing could stop her from seeing what awaited her in the little room across the passage. Even though he had his back to her, even though she could have made a run for it, opened the door, bolted down the rickety wooden staircase and away, curiosity not only impelled her forward but even gave her a spurious kind of courage.

Bloody nosy, Anna had called her once, in this very room. Bloody stupid was nearer the mark.

She followed him. Neither of them heard the careful turning of the handle of the outside door leading into the scented hall downstairs.

· 28 ·

AT FIRST GLANCE, SHE ASSUMED the figure confronting her was a boy. The cropped black hair, the waiflike body, something unsoft about the face, all increased the impression. He lay among embroidered cushions, smoking a cigarette, clicking a set of worry beads, the small sound brittle among the thick hangings on the walls.

The room was dimly lit, the light falling from a lamp set behind a carved screen of scented wood. In a corner of the room a square basin of black marble held two golden fish and a thin-stemmed waterplant. Joss sticks burned here and there, the scented blue smoke rising to join the more pungent smoke from the boy's cigarette. Fran sniffed. Marijuana? Or something stronger?

The figure raised lustrous black eyes toward her and she realized she was looking not at a boy but at a woman at least twice her own age. Although she was not oriental, her clothes—a high-necked jacket of black silk over rose-colored trousers—gave the impression of her being so. Around her neck were ropes of glass beads; more of them glittered around her wrists. Long diamond earrings hung from her ears.

"Who is this?" the woman said. Her voice was smoothly harsh, a mixture of oil and powdered glass.

"Frances Brett," said the man. He spoke with a kind of respect in his voice.

"Ah." The woman grimaced. "My one mistake."

"What do you mean?" asked Fran. She hoped she sounded more confident than she felt.

"When I forwarded the letter I found here to you in France, I knew I was taking a risk," said the woman. "Playing with fire, isn't that what you English say?"

"Sometimes." Fran made herself smile coolly. "If it's appropriate."

"I hope it is not." The woman's voice contained finality. She stared at Mikkele. "Nonetheless, she is the one who has given you so much trouble, is she not?"

Mikkele shrugged. "There has been no real trouble."

He did not add that although he recognized the inevitability of it, he had no real wish to see this English girl die. It would be wasteful, however necessary. Courage, tenacity, the ability to take advantage of circumstance; she had them all in abundance. They were characteristics that few men possessed, and fewer women. The same strength belonged to the one who now lounged in front of him, smoking her evil cigarettes.

When she had first approached him in Istanbul, he had been overwhelmed, dazzled, enthralled. He was fifteen then, lost and embittered. She had started by introducing him to the dissidents with whom he would later work, thus giving him a purpose in life: later she had opened up for him a hitherto undiscovered world of sexual delight. All these years later he could still recall the thrill of exploring her body, of reveling like a first-time tourist in its landscapes, its odors, its tastes. She had used him for her own purposes when he was still too young to understand what she was doing; though he now realized how he had been corrupted, he was still tied to her by the almost magical quality of the physical gratification she had given him. And the drugs—they had started soon after that first meeting, changing as he himself changed, growing more potent as his craving grew ever stronger until he realized that he was an addict, completely dependent on her. Now, although he had come to loathe her cruelty, and her obsession, he knew he could never leave her.

Through her, he had met people and gone to places he would never otherwise have known, a world of glamor and money that the poverty of his childhood had not fitted him for. Or perhaps had fitted him for too well, by making him too receptive to the comforts that riches could bring.

Fran saw how, when he addressed the woman on the cushions, all expression was smoothed away. Fear brings that blankness to a face; so also does hatred. He does not like her, she thought. Whoever she is, he dislikes and despises her. It was knowledge that might come in useful.

"Then why is she still alive?"

"Because, my love, she has not yet told us what she knows." He used the endearment mockingly, knowing how much she disliked even the pretense of affection.

"You must find out. I will not allow anything to get in my way." The woman looked up at him from her couch of pillows and put her head on one side. "Don't tell me that after all these years, you are reluctant," she said. The lids closed over her cold eyes and opened again slowly, like a toad's. "I thought you enjoyed the sight of blood."

He flushed at that, and turned his blue eyes away from her.

She is like a cobra, Fran thought. *She lies coiled there in the cushions, poised to strike. And her voice: it slides over her words like cold water, as though they were stones and had no life.*

Abruptly, she realized who the woman must be. Fascinating, fatal, probably even mad: it was easy to see how she had destroyed all the men she came into close contact with.

"I have nothing to tell you," she broke in. If her voice quavered, she hoped they did not notice.

"That's something we shall find out." Again the woman, tiny and jeweled on her multicolored bed of cushions, kept her eyes fixed on those of the man who though like Alexander, was not him.

Behind him, the thick hangings rippled as though a wind had passed over their bright silk blooms. A scent of sandalwood drifted lazily into the room, and was gone.

"Go on then," the woman said. She pushed derisive air down through her nose. "Get started." She settled back and let smoke dribble from her mouth. Though her eyes were half shut, Fran was sure she would miss nothing.

The man was powerless before her. He had tried for years to shake her off, to face up to his addiction and conquer it. But once near her, the memory of so much shared confronted and weakened him. The pictures slid across his mind: art galleries, sea journeys, the London tailor who made his first suit, the subway in New York, her face as she haggled over the price of his first gun. There had been many other boys since she had first taken him to the place in Istanbul where she used to live: a modern flat with stark black furniture and glass-topped tables. At first he had minded, until he realized that their time of favor was short-lived and why she kept him with her, even after he became a man, stubbled and coarse.

She laughed now, softly, as he had known she would. "Go on, then," she said again. She put out one of her tiny hands and lightly circled his ankle with her fingers. "My killing machine. My executioner."

His ankle burned where she had touched it. Wearily he moved toward Fran. There was deadness in his heart at so much unnecessary waste. He raised his hand to the front of Fran's shirt.

Fran lifted the alabaster dragon. Before she could bring it crashing down, he had chopped viciously at her arm. The dragon fell from her grasp, hitting the floor with a thud that gouged white splinters out of the wood. Fran shrieked: the pain was stupendous in the seconds before her arm went numb. It hung at her side, temporarily useless.

"Frances," he said. His blue eyes were wide. "Did you think I had not noticed it?"

She shook her head, tears cramming her eyes so that the brilliant room blurred. He fumbled with her buttons; there was a knife in his hand.

He was really going to do it. Really going to kill her. With that thought, Fran shoved hard with her left hand, connecting with his mouth so that he reeled back as his jaw snapped shut. For a moment he glared at her, then, before she could move, he had grabbed her arm and twisted it up behind her back so hard that she thought it would break.

The pain was horrific. "My God," Fran gasped disdainfully. "I've never seen a man so manipulated by a woman. She tells you what to do, who to kill, and you do it." She took a deep breath. She had one weapon: now was the time to use it. "I wonder what your father would think of the way you let her control you. It's just as well he's dead."

At that, he let go of her. "What did you say?" His voice trembled.

The crop-haired woman noticed it. "You are wasting time, Mikkele," she said sharply. Points of light from her earrings stabbed the air like daggers.

"Kemal is dead?" the man said. His voice was incredulous.

Stepping away from him, Fran said: "He was killed, in a car crash."

"When?"

The woman barked harshly at him. "She's lying. Can't you see that, you fool?"

"You can ask your brother Alexander. Or her second husband, Sir Hugo Campion," said Fran. "He was responsible for your father's death. She didn't bother to go to the funeral but she knows all about it."

He stared at the woman. He stepped toward her. "But you told me . . ." He sounded as if he was choking. "Everything was for Solange . . . you *told* me . . ." He moved closer to the jeweled creature on the pillows, then turned to look at Fran. His face was not entirely sane. "Kemal's money . . . she said we would bring him down . . . ruin him as he ruined Solange . . . and then we would . . ."

Fran saw the pupils of his eyes reduce in size as rage seized him. He still gripped the knife. The same kind of terror she had felt in the chapel near Reims paralyzed her: he was going to kill her now, for sure.

She faced death head-on—and death suddenly turned away, toward the piled pillows of many-colored silk and the woman with the boy's figure and the voice of a serpent.

She laughed when he stood over her, the knife in his hand. When he demanded, "How long have you known?" she laughed again.

"It's been years since he died," she said. "Years." Her contempt for him, for the creature she had made of him, was palpable.

"So why have you continued all this?" he asked. "What was the point?"

"Why not?" She lay back, relaxed yet wary. "I like to make things happen."

Seeing the indifference in her eyes, Fran thought with pity of Alexander. She had misjudged him: she wondered how he had managed to overcome his childhood with this evil creature. He had said, *She told me she hated children.* The seeds of what she had become must have begun to germinate even as Kemal's newborn son was laid in her arms.

"Besides," the woman said. "If I had told you the truth, you would never have stayed with me."

"You have taken my life from me for nothing, Leyla."

"It was nothing before you met me, Mikkele. If you leave, it will be nothing again."

He raised the knife.

The woman on the cushions stared at him, half smiling. "You would not dare to use it. Without me, what would you become?"

"Anything other than what you have made me," he said.

His arm tensed, the blade curving slowly through the air. Fran wanted to close her eyes, to turn away from the sound of its sharpness biting into its victim's body, from the sight of life weeping away through wounded flesh, vanishing. But she could not do so. No one of sensibility could watch such a scene; nonetheless she found her eyes fixed in fascination on the long slow sweep of the knife as it descended through a vacuum where every motion seemed to last for hours and time stretched toward eternity. The jeweled woman watched too, her face registering scorn, then disbelief, and finally fear. She scrabbled back among her pillows, pushing at them with her little hands, trying to escape the inexorability of extinction. The man stood above her, his face neutral, concentrating on the job that had to be done.

Strong passions bound these two: hatred, desire, obsession. Fran moved quietly toward the second door of the room. She felt safer here; she had an escape route, if the need arose. The sandalwood-scented draft stirred her hair again. Someone must have left a door open by the stairs leading down into the big square hall.

At the same time, her brain filed and assessed the new information. If Max's suppositions were correct, it was Leyla who had overdosed on power, on the manipulation of human beings as though they were simply pawns in some monstrous game of chess. If Fran escaped, then Leyla could be stopped and the game would be finished forever. But the woman would not easily let her go.

"Mikkele." Leyla's voice dropped into the room with the bite of acid. "You have work to do."

Sidetracked by his own absorptions, Mikkele had forgotten about Fran. Now his strange eyes moved across her face and in them she read that he no longer had heart for the business he was supposed to conduct.

He said, "No, Leyla. It's over. I want no more of the murders and the terror. Once I thought we had a God to serve and a good cause. I thought we were righting injustice. And that my sister . . ." His voice failed.

"Those injustices still exist. You've seen what the Israelis do in the refugee camps. You've seen how the rich nations drain dry the poor."

"I have. But that is not why you do what you do."

"None of that has changed." Leyla's voice rose.

"No," he said quietly. "But perhaps I have changed."

He thought of the sister he had thought lost to him forever, until he found her again in Paris. He had not told Leyla how he followed Solange in the street, and stood below her window in the windy night. He had planned to make himself known to her, but had hesitated. She had become something in the world; he was less than nothing— merely an anonymous killer in the shadows.

Leyla's smooth face remained still. Then with a movement quicker than the tongue-flick of a snake, she reached into the pillows around her and brought out a gun.

"Do as I say and find out what the English girl knows," she commanded. She shifted the gun so that it pointed at him.

He did not move.

"You know me well enough to know that I will kill you if I have to," she said. Her power over the man was on trial—all three of them knew i˙

"I've told you I don't know anything," said Fran hurriedly, as if to protect Mikkele. "All I've got are a few guesses about the Phoenix Foundation. You've infiltrated the boards of directors in various countries, so parts of the organization have become a front for shifting huge supplies of arms into unstable areas of the world." She paused. The faces of the other two stared back at her, blank and smooth as stone. "That's all, really. I presume the idea was to alter the balance of power."

"*Such* fun," drawled the glittering woman with the gun in her hand. "Alexander doesn't have the slightest idea of what was really going on. As for Kemal—"

"I wish Kemal were not dead," Mikkele said suddenly, as if dazed. Violence underlay the quiet words.

Fran was afraid of what was going to happen. As inevitably as a Greek tragedy, the events about to take place would do so. It was useless to pit oneself against the grander schemes of fate. As though she watched some silent picture on a colored screen, she saw Mikkele lift his knife once more, saw Leyla raise the gun and her finger tighten on the trigger, saw Mikkele stagger, bend, fall, saw his body wince as two more bullets hit him and blood leaped around the edges of the dark wells they made in his flesh.

The gun barked once more before she was out of the room and running along the gallery toward the central staircase. The hall below was dark; she fled down the stairs toward the safety of its shadows.

Before she could reach them, Leyla was above her, leaning against the gallery rail. "You won't escape me, Frances Brett," she said. She did not raise her voice.

Fran continued her hurtling flight toward the lower floor. She thought, *I am less afraid than I was in Reims.* Was that because then, death seemed more certain, more unavoidable? Or is it because after you have witnessed the killing of another, your own death assumes a certain insignificance? She wondered, heart pumping, whether Mikkele had died instantly.

Leyla leaned over the molded guard rail of the gallery, raised her gun again, took aim. Fran's flesh cringed in anticipation of the slamming pain the bullet would bring. She floundered through air grown suddenly thick; she stumbled, tottered, fell into the well of the hall, into the darkness. The front door stood open; through it she could see a glimpse of the road outside, the edge of light from an unseen street-lamp, the shine of wet cobbles. It was like looking at a painting of a make-believe world, distant and other, into which she would never manage to escape. She looked up at the woman's outline and the gleam of the hesitating gun as she took random aim into the darkness. Then, impossibly, another shadow leaped along the gallery.

A voice said, "No, Leyla. Enough is enough."

Crouched against a wooden chest of aromatic wood—sandal-wood: was that where the scent which filled the hall came from?—Fran watched in disbelief as a blade flashed twice at Leyla's back. Could it be Mikkele? Surely he lay mortally wounded in the room upstairs. Who, then, had saved her?

The woman leaning over the wooden balustrade gave a cry that seemed to fill the house. Languidly, as in a film-stunt sequence played in slow motion, she fell against the rail, then tumbled forward. Her small shape, bright as a hummingbird, flashed slowly, slowly, toward the marble floor below, glittering like a falling star as her necklaces swung out about her spread-eagled body, and the bracelets on her wrists blazed where they caught the light from above. As she came, drops of blood aureoled from her wounds; Fran felt them fall as gently as rose petals on her own upturned face.

The sound the body made when it hit the floor was one Fran knew she would wake in future nights and remember. Simultaneously she heard the smack of bone as the woman's head made contact with the paving. For a couple of moments, what was left alive in her made guttural animal sounds, the slender limbs jerking as though pulled by an invisible string. Her body arched, then drew in on itself and was still.

The man above looked down. The light from the room behind him outlined his broad shoulders. Dimly she could see the gray-blue gleam of his eyes, the somber outlines of his face. Her heart stumbled in her breast as she looked at his hands resting on the carved curve of the balustrade rail. "Fran," he said.

Without thought, she pushed herself upright. To think would be to solidify something that was better left half known, half feared. She blundered out through the open door and into the wet street. Behind her, she heard the echo of his voice again: "Fran."

Outside the air was fresh and cold. Some night-blooming shrub illuminated the darkness with perfume. She held her face toward the sky and stood there until the rain had washed her clean.

· 29 ·

IF SHE HAD NEVER GONE TO ISTANBUL, it would still have happened. The gods might have chosen another instrument to act as nemesis, but in the end the principal players in the tragedy would still have had to work out their individual destinies.

It would be months before Fran could view the events of that year dispassionately; years before her dreams were no longer studded by the image of a black-robed figure, and the sound of nails hammering into flesh.

We are not what we seem.

It was a thought which recurred in the days that followed that climactic night, after the police had removed the bodies, after she had answered their endless questions, after she had submitted to fingerprinting and allowed them to take away the clothes she had been wearing for forensic examination.

For a while they suspected that she herself had killed Leyla, pointing out that though the shots Leyla had fired at Mikkele might not immediately have been fatal, his injuries were such that it would have been almost impossible for him to have come after Leyla along the gallery, let alone find the strength to use his knife as Fran declared that he had.

She continued to insist on her version of events. It was easier that way, less disturbing, than speculating on an alternative. And after all, it *could* have happened the way she said. Just about. In the end, the police, without any proof, grudgingly let her go. She stayed on in the city with Philippe, trying to fill in more pieces of the puzzle.

After the inquest, he brought her back to France.

■■

She knew she would never again visit Istanbul. It was a part of her life that had gone forever, and with it the mosques and minarets, the reflecting pools of Topkapi, the soft ghosts which thronged the chill corridors of the Seraglio. With it, too, a lost love.

We are not what we seem.

Daniel had assumed for her now the aspect of a monster, as misled in his determinations as Leyla had been in hers.

Piecing it together afterward with Max, while Emilie stroked green buds into life with her paintbrushes, they realized that having judged Alexander guilty, Daniel had proceeded ruthlessly to hunt him down, giving no quarter, no thought for the results of destruction. Yet Alexander—in many ways more like his mother than he had ever suspected—was guilty of nothing more than self-indulgence. He enjoyed exercising his power, the exertion of charisma over people who might otherwise have barely noticed him—it was a small sin. For the rest, his idealism was genuine.

She had seen him once; he had telephoned to ask if they could meet before he set off for central Nicaragua. Events had altered Alexander: the effortless superiority over others on which he prided himself had been fractured by learning how easily his Foundation had been used for purposes quite opposite to those which were intended, how easily corruption had weakened—almost destroyed—the organization around which his work revolved. Luckily, the rot set in train by Leyla had been containable; those workers she had been able to buy were quietly dismissed, the loopholes in the organization were stopped up, scandal was avoided, the work of the Foundation continued, in the end, unhindered. Her ultimate aim had been to discredit Alexander, Kemal's son; in this she had not succeeded. The fact that Leyla was responsible meant little: the knowledge of her implacable hostility toward him was something he had long ago learned to accept.

As for Sola: "She obviously thought I was someone else," he kept saying. "She'd never seen me before, but she walked straight into my arms." Fran did not tell him he had been mistaken for his own father. Nor did she speak of Sola's involvement with Kemal, some of which she had found out by persevering questions while she waited for the inquest to take place. His image of himself had been doubly shattered: instead of trying to take the knife away from Sola as she plunged it into her own body, he had fled. It was a lapse Fran thought he would not easily forgive himself. She thought that out of his personal chaos might rise a stronger, if less confident, man. Walking with him across the Pont St. Michel, she had handed over the little box containing his blue contact lenses without comment. Flushing—"It was a childish trick"—he had tossed it into the Seine. Fran was not to know that the desire to change his appearance had been engendered years before, in a street in Bloomsbury, nor anything of the boy who had stared into a mirror and wondered, *Would she love me better if my eyes were blue?*

We are not what we seem. Kemal had seemed a wise and gentle father to Alexander—indeed, had been so. Yet to Sola he had been both seducer and betrayer, and to Mikkele, a ruthless pervert. Fran had not enlightened Alexander: he needed the sustenance of an illusion.

■■

"This Forrest guy had all the facts right," Max said, watching Emilie over the rim of his whisky tumbler. "He just fouled up on the interpretation."

"What about Tom?" Emilie glanced at him, then away.

"Him too. I guess. But we'll never know now." Max sighed. "Would've been a great story if that blue-eyed hashhead hadn't taken Tom's disk from me. Don't suppose we'll ever see it again."

"It's probably lying at the bottom of the Golden Horn," Fran said. If so, she was not altogether sorry. Had Tom's information survived, she would have been bound to write the story. As it was, it could safely be left in oblivion. She was acutely aware of the changes that had taken place in her. Different attitudes hung on her now, as solid as new clothes. Once she would have written the story anyway, patching it together from the scraps of information she still possessed. Now, she knew that to do so would cause Alicia Forrest immeasurable sadness. The woman had already survived the knowledge of her adored son's painful death. To learn what the son had really been might prove a mortal blow. Better to let her think him still a hero than suspect—as Fran sometimes sickeningly did—that he was responsible for the corpse left in the fowler's hut. Even if he were not, Fran no longer had any interest in the matter.

Sometimes she thought of the painted bouquets of flowers which had adorned the bed where she had hoped to lie in Daniel's arms. About Daniel himself, she dared not think. Nor of the house where she had spent six months of happiness.

Above all, it was the room in that house where two people had died that she could not forget.

■■

Time had passed, the wheels had turned. The same, yet not the same. The interconnectedness between the characters in the play in which she had briefly been center-stage might never have been completely unraveled. For a moment, lives had crossed and recrossed in a cat's cradle of interlocking synchronicity and then continued on the way the Fates had ordained.

Fran lay alone at night, knowing that some questions would never be answered. Perhaps it was best that way. Better still that they not be asked. She could rationalize the voice which pushed her toward a certain book in a bookshelf, or a closer look at a photograph. She could accept that her own instincts for survival had urged her toward killing the invader of her mother's house, whatever form she chose to give the voice which sounded in her brain.

What she could not make sense of, and never would, was the figure leaping out of nowhere along the dancing shadows of the gallery to plunge a knife between Leyla's thin shoulder blades.

Who was it?

Not knowing the answer, nor wishing to, she had gone slowly back to the house that night, soaked with cleansing rain. Not looking at the small body on the floor, she had gone slowly up the marble stairs and along the gallery, treading through blood to where the patterned light gleamed on flowered walls.

Mikkele lay there, a broken memento of what he had recently been. Despite the ruin of his face, he had been handsome even in death. He was dead when Fran saw him crumpled across the pillows where Leyla had reclined; his knife had fallen from his hand and lay just beyond the stretch of his reaching fingers. The blood on it was still bright; later tests would match it with Leyla's own.

■■

The knocker sounded on the front door of the house in Précy. Emilie lifted her head and smiled.

"That will be Philippe," she said.

"I know." Fran roused herself from her sitting position as though she were an old woman. Movement these days seemed to take so much effort; she walked as though surrounded by treacle.

"I like him."

"Me too, *maman.*"

"He seems a goo 1 man."

"I think he is."

Walking across the hall, Fran thought, *Yes, he is a good man.*

Opening the door to him, feeling his arms around her and the steady beat of his sound heart, she wondered in the most secret part of her whether he was good enough for her one day to tell him what she had done. How she had used her foot to move the knife closer to Mikkele's outspread fingers. How she had bent through the odor of blood and incense to clasp his fingers around its hilt.

Because otherwise, there was no possible way that the police could have been persuaded that in his last moments he had staggered along the wooden floor of the gallery with his knife in his hand and, dying himself, saved Fran from certain death.

■■

Perhaps one day, Fran thought, lifting her mouth to Philippe's, she too might come to believe that that was how it had happened, and that the eyes which had looked down at her from the balustrade, before she turned and ran blindly away into the normality of the wet street outside, had been blue and not bleakly, desolately gray.